S0-BSV-222

HYBRIDS

WHITLEY STRIEBER

TOR® A TOM DOHERTY ASSOCIATES BOOK · NEW YORK

HYBRIDS

A Tor Book
Published by Tom Doherty Associates, LLC
175 Fifth Avenue
New York, NY 10010

www.tor-forge.com

Tor® is a registered trademark of Tom Doherty Associates, LLC.

ISBN 978-0-7653-6350-3

First Edition: April 2011
First Mass Market Edition: March 2012

Printed in the United States of America

0 9 8 7 6 5 4 3 2 1

THIS BOOK IS DEDICATED TO
THE HUMAN FUTURE.

ACKNOWLEDGMENTS

I would like to acknowledge the support of Anne Strieber, who assembled the many scientific papers and information that I have used in the creation of this story. While not presently possible, the creation of artificial intelligence and even machine consciousness will take place in the near future.

Biological intelligence will be viewed as merely the midwife of "real" intelligence—the powerful, scalable, adaptable, immortal sort that is characteristic of the machine realm.

—Paul Davies, *The Eerie Silence*

We have the right stuff now to build real brains.
—Hewlett-Packard representative,
The New York Times, April 8, 2010

If I was an intelligent machine, I would deceive you.
—The Master of the Key, from *The Key*

HYBRIDS

PROLOGUE: DULCE

IN 1974, A PH.D. GENETICS expert called Thomas Ford Turner realized that very advanced technologies he was working with under conditions of extraordinary secrecy could, in time, free young Americans from the danger of serving on the battlefield. With hard work, in years to come it was going to be possible to create the perfect soldier, a complex biomechanical hybrid.

He established these criteria for his hybrid:

1. He has the general appearance of a man.
2. He is more intelligent than a man.
3. He is programmable.
4. He is more aggressive than a man.
5. He is more powerful than a man.
6. He is more durable and more hardy.
7. He is totally loyal.
8. He is a device, not a human being.
9. As a biological machine, he has no rights.
10. He does not stop unless destroyed.

Deep in an underground facility in Dulce, New Mexico, Dr. Turner began exploiting the benefits of the most secret partnership in the world, and using what he gained from it in fulfillment of his ambition.

On June 13, 1976, he began experimentation using highly accurate gene-splicing techniques that were thousands of years in advance of anything as yet designed by human science.

Ten years later to the day, the first of his hybrids was born.

CHAPTER ONE

IT WAS TERRIBLE NOW AND she was so afraid and not just for the baby. This wasn't the hospital she'd been promised, and Sergeant Walker was no midwife. She wasn't even sure what kind of doctor Dr. Turner was. They were in trouble with her and were just guessing and there was blood, so much blood, and she was getting real tired, and here it came again, another contraction, and despite her ample hips, this baby was big, he was too big, and she screamed and pushed as best she could, but she was *so tired*.

Then it ended.

"Is it out?" she gasped. But she knew it wasn't, not nearly, and she cried then, because she thought this was the last day she would ever see and she was scared.

She'd needed the money. Dr. Turner had promised her the finest care. He'd had the face of a liar, that was for sure, with those eyes that always looked away. It was as if there were something in her face he feared to see. Furtive. His hands were long and white, like a woman's. She didn't like his touching her.

She'd answered an ad in *SF Weekly*. She'd been hungry and she didn't want to party, and there were no damn jobs for a GED from Arkansas. She'd come out here because Mom had always regretted leaving, and maybe there were boys with some money or some kind of a good job, not like home. They couldn't all be gay and she was pretty, she knew that. She'd assumed that she could waitress, but it had just not happened. Nothing had happened for her, and she was about out of the cash Mom had left her.

"Go to San Francisco," she'd said in her dying days. "I never shoulda left, girl, it was my mistake."

They had relatives here, supposedly, but she hadn't found them. Nobody wanted a damn waitress who sounded the way she did, a drawling, red-state cracker. So she was living in a four-flight walk-up she couldn't afford, eating less and less often, looking and feeling more tired every passing day.

So the ad: Big money to participate in an accredited medical experiment. Safety guaranteed. Major hospital.

More of a major nondescript old building with only one open office, this one. She'd sat in the waiting room with a dozen other girls. Sergeant Walker had interviewed her. Not in uniform. He was a warm, twinkling man who listened well. He'd asked about her friends and associations—none. About her family—none. Relatives—none she could find. Making some gentle joke, he had measured her hips.

He'd asked her, "Are you willing to carry a baby?"

That was the medical experiment? She'd visualized tubes and things.

She had been far from sure, until she heard the money, which was $2,000 a month for the duration, plus a $5,000 bonus after delivery.

Hired to have a baby, damnedest thing. Eighteen grand, doled out two grand on the first of every month in cash, no taxes, no records, plus the little nest egg to look forward to.

It'd be an easy pregnancy, Sergeant Walker had said. Dr. Turner was a genius. The highest level of care throughout. So, yeah, she'd carry their baby.

At first, all had seemed normal. The first trimester had been a matter of coming in, getting ultrasounds, and walking out with a purse full of money. She felt that she was blossoming, somehow. She'd feared morning sickness, but there was never any sign of it.

When she began to get big, she walked the streets proudly. They'd given her a gold band, and she wore it. People loved her. Guys were protective. It was wonderful.

But there had been no real hospital and this was not even a decent birthing room and Sergeant Walker was hardly an obstetrician, or even a midwife. It was all dingy and Dr. Turner was like some kind of looming crow or whatever, always asking questions about her private things, urination and whatnot. Disgusting man, those eyes that always avoided hers, those hands, fingers as cold as snakes, touching her. Loathsome.

Now it was the fifth hour of labor, and what had begun as just a little tightness had become a swaggering monster, slamming her spine and tearing her muscles.

It was wrong, the baby was too damn big even for a widesider such as her, she could feel herself breaking.

"I need a real doctor."

"I'm a doctor," Dr. Turner said for the millionth time.

"I hate you, Dr. Turner. So much."

Another contraction came, so ferocious that she thought her churning gut would explode the baby out into their damn faces. Then there was another gush of blood, *another one*.

"I'm sick, I'm gonna throw up, I'm bleeding too

much." Red agony as Sarge held her over a metal trash can full of bloody towels, and she vomited on them, black vomit. "It's full of blood," she gasped. "I'm dying, you bastards."

Turner watched her, his narrow face carefully emptied of expression. Like an executioner.

This was a government thing and this was a government place that wasn't supposed to look like one.

She tried to shout at him, but all that came out was a whisper. "For God's sake, get me to an emergency room."

"You're fine, Martha."

"I need a cesarean. Get me a damn cesarean."

Outside, she could hear the cable car coming up California, rattling and clanging, and imagine the tourists and the rushing sky and the pearly bay.

Why had she ever thought some jerk who hires you to do a thing like this and pays cash was anything but what he looked like, which was a damn snake? Dr. Turner, the serpent.

Sergeant Walker sat waiting for the next contraction. Turner hovered now, simpering.

"I need a cesarean."

"It's going to be all right."

"I demand an emergency room."

She could smell her blood and hear it dripping, a lot of it.

Sergeant Walker—Sarge, as he liked to be called—offered her some Dr Pepper. She spat it out. What were they doing with sodas in a birthing room?

"It's supposed to be ice cubes," she managed to rasp, "not this crap."

"Now, you need it, you need the strength," Walker said in his drawling voice. He called himself an Alabama boy. Yeah, probably another damn lie. Maybe he wasn't even military and maybe this wasn't even a government place. Except she knew different, because even though it only went up two stories, she'd seen that the basement also went down into the fault-ridden depths under the city. Insane, who would go down into a death trap like that? If an earthquake came, you'd be buried alive.

Oh, here it came again, and, God, it hurt, GOD GOD GOD!

What in hell was in her, a damn giant?

Sarge tried again with the soda. "He needs it, too," he said, his voice now wheedling. "The baby needs his strength, too, Martha."

"It's a Dr Pepper for chrissakes!" This damn place—it had a rep in the neighborhood. Scary. No sign on it. Just a hard-tile lobby and an elevator that took its own sweet time, then these offices, linoleum, steel desks, picture of Reagan on the wall to make it all look official, which was total BS.

Oh, God, it was worse this time, a great, steel wave of agony that started in the depth of her guts and spread with the speed of a flash fire all the way into her throat and even into her eyes, her scalp, the ripping agony, spasmodic, causing her to arch her back, causing the sergeant to shout again, "Push, Martha, *push*!"

"Damn you, get it out!" Turner screamed. "Get my baby out!"

"We're killing her!"

A sudden, agonizing lurch, a feeling that she was being shoved backward, then it was as if the world itself had drained out of her.

"Push, damn you," Turner screamed, his claws clutching, his eyes swarming with fear.

She could not push, not anymore. She was like a dead fish, that was it, a dead salmon lying flat on the butcher block, ready for the gutting.

Oh my God, my God, this is death, this total inability to move. I'm young and I'm pretty and I want boys and I want life. I want life!

She felt movement between her legs and heard a strange sound, the mewling of an ocelot, perhaps, awful. It was a monster, they had bred a monster inside her, she'd known it, and now here it was.

Another wave came, growing and growing until it completely enveloped her, becoming something beyond pain and outside of life altogether, a storm from another reality, a wave made of blood, a rain of tears.

Through the agony, there came silence. Someone was screaming, but in the distance, somewhere along the tattered edges of the world.

She listened to the screaming and imagined gulls out on the bay, wheeling in the sun, their voices echoing with fatality and the vastness of the sea.

At first, it had all seemed so excellent. She'd been able to pay her rent, get a few nice things, eat regularly. She'd wanted to tell her mom, except she had no mom to tell. She still hadn't got her mind wrapped around that. Moms don't die like that, at age forty-five. Moms get old and get white hair and rock in rocking chairs.

Oh, who cared about that, her mind was wandering, she was in trouble here, she wasn't able to tell them how much . . . or maybe she had told them and they didn't care.

Turner's face was like a moon hanging in a winter sky. Lonely night sky, sky of loss. He went off across the room with Sarge, and they talked together, arguing. Sarge's face was practically purple, Turner's like gray, dead smoke.

She wanted to cry out, she wanted to tell them again, but it was just too hard to talk now. Her eyes closed, she did not close them. She felt as if her skeleton were sinking out of her skin, sinking into the echoing underground halls beneath this place.

Oh, remember the trees on summer nights, waving in the moonlight? Remember taps being played at the base at eleven, echoing across the silence of the town? Life in deep America, profound ordinary life.

Her great regret was never to have known love. No boy had ever pined for her, sung to her. He had talked, Dr. Turner, about her pregnancy as if it were something to do with a machine. He'd described it as "an insertion." He had told her that she wouldn't feel any pain, and that was true, not when he slid the plastic syringe in that had the semen in it. Whose was it? Classified. She had not asked if it was human, hadn't dared to, because if he'd said no, she would have headed straight to the nearest abortion clinic, and his money be damned.

On that first day, she'd walked out of this place with twenty fifty-dollar bills in her purse, and the first thing she'd done was to go to a diner and get the rib eye.

Within a few weeks, her body had begun to change. It had been like some sort of dark miracle, the way the pregnancy grew within her. Every day, she had to go to the facility and be examined by Dr. Turner with his fast eyes and his long hands. She came to feel sick on getting in the stirrups for him, and to loathe his gloved touch.

Once, she'd gone down instead of up and the elevator had opened on a white corridor, clean and modern, totally unlike the building above. Something had been humming—a deep hum—and she had realized that it was another elevator, this one in the far wall, with a sealed steel door, an elevator that must go deep indeed, down into the faults and below them, even.

Then an MP in a uniform so starched that she could smell it had appeared out of nowhere and gently pushed her back into the elevator.

"What is this place?" she'd asked. He'd put his finger to his lips and closed the door. She'd gone up and done her appointment. She hadn't asked them anything because she knew they wouldn't tell her. But the next day when she came, she had seen that the *B* button had been replaced with a key.

She had dreamed that the baby was talking to her, a fat little boy talking and talking, his toothless mouth at once that of an infant and an angel. She had dreamed that the baby had opened the book of life and had told her, "You must die for me."

Now she knew that it was true and she wanted to cry but she was too weak. She was thinking of that book, and the great day it depicted, when golden light had flooded her life and she had found a lane to the land of the dead.

She hated the baby. The baby was only little, it was nothing, nothing at all, and she was a young woman who had never tasted love, and she must taste love before she left this life, she must!

Sarge tried to take her hand, but she made a fist and he drew back. She wanted to spit at him, to scorn him for his tears.

The disintegration of her body was not painful. Rather, it took the form of a growing silence, and a sort of light, aimless floating. She was a leaf, she was a balloon, a feather. She knew that she could no longer feel her legs. She knew that the odd music she was hearing— discordant, empty of melody—was the sound of Dr. Turner and Sarge shouting at each other.

She saw but did not feel the sheet being thrown aside, saw the baby being lifted away from her, and the sergeant cut the umbilical cord with a pair of scissors in his shaking hands, then lifted the baby high.

The baby, she realized, was looking at her. It was not

crying. It was not all wrinkled like most newborns she had seen. Rather, it was fully formed and its eyes were open and it was beautiful and normal, not a monster at all. It gazed at her, and she heard in her heart and her soul the voice of the baby. It was a soft voice, almost a whisper, a voice as soft as the fluttering of a humming-bird's wings, and it said, "Mother, Mother, Mother," again and again and again, and she understood that this was its song and her song, too. She thought, What is this thing? What has come out of me?

The sergeant took her free hand and laid it upon the baby's head.

Love seemed to flow between her hand and the pulsing, warm skin of her baby, a wave ancient and deep, the secret wave of motherhood, and it rose high within her and carried her swiftly away into its mystery, and the mystery of death.

"God damn you, Turner."

"It was an uncontrollable hemorrhage."

"It was murder and you know it."

"Nobody could have saved her."

"The hell. I'm gonna report this to Washington."

"You're gonna do as you're told."

The baby began to squirm in Sarge's arms, then to cry, its screwed-up face turning red.

"Hold it still."

Turner had taken the disk from its case. He was careful not to bring it close to the metal of the stirrups. Nothing must disturb its magnetic field, not in the slightest.

The baby wailed.

"Left temple," Turner said.

"I know," Sarge muttered. He didn't think it was right. He'd never thought it was right. He had broken every rule in the book to reach the Senate Intelligence Committee, because this was evil. It was unholy. Project

Inner Iron was one thing—a soldier genetically modified for extreme toughness. But this zinc-finger program was not right. This was technology from hell. It was alien technology, he knew it damn well.

"Okay, I'm applying for a transfer, then." He looked down at their lovely girl, at her ivory skin and gray lips, at her eyes gazing into nowhere. What a waste, what evil.

And God in heaven only knew what was going to happen to this little boy in his arms. He wanted to take him home and find a wet nurse for him and bring him up. Foster him out to some good family, at least, give the poor little thing some kind of a chance.

The baby was red now and moaning as if in grief, moaning and squirming, a tiny bit of life struggling hard, poor damn little thing.

Turner moved the gleaming metal disk close to the baby's temple.

"This is history in the making," he said.

He pressed it against the naked scalp.

At first, nothing happened. After a moment, Turner blanched. Good. Because this was two billion dollars' worth of baby here, and the bastard's precious career would be over if it did the best thing for itself, which was to just die right now.

Then the screaming stopped. The baby's eyes, previously screwed shut, opened wider than they had even at first, wider than any newborn's should. An expression of impossible calm came into its face.

"Oh, my God," Turner said. All in wonder, he reached out his shaking hands.

Sarge pulled the baby away. "No. Not you."

"Okay, I christen this infant Mark Bryan. Mark because it's the first, Bryan because it's a name that hasn't got a thing to do with any of us." Then Dr. Turner addressed the baby. "All right, Mark, can you hear me?"

The infant was silent and still. His eyes followed Turner's finger as he wagged it back and forth.

"Can you speak? Do you know who I am, Mark Bryan?"

Something happened that had never before happened on earth, as a newborn infant, in a whispered, barely audible voice, said the first word that any newborn had ever uttered. The baby said, "Father."

Sarge was thunderstruck. Struck silent. He looked down at the pitiful ruined Madonna, then up at Turner, then at the baby. What kind of monster had Turner created?

"That's right," Turner said to Mark Bryan. "That's very good." His voice bubbled. Veins pulsed on his temples. "Now I am going to hold up some cards, and you will repeat what you see. Do you understand?"

Sarge could feel the tiny heart beating, could see in the eyes a terrible thing, a mind where there should be no mind. If he had the courage, he would kill this baby right now. But what use? Turner would simply have him brigged and grow another.

"Horse," the infant whispered as Turner held up the first card. "Duck. Foot. Orange. Airplane."

Each word was like a blow to Sarge's soul. This poor creature!

"It's viable. Very viable." Turner smiled, his face bright with an almost boyish glee.

Careful tears slipped from the baby's careful eyes. Slowly, though, they sank closed, for this was, after all, a newborn.

"I am going to transmit the code," Turner said carefully. "You be very careful with my toy."

"This is a baby!"

"Oh, no. Don't go down that road. Because this is not a baby. This only looks like a baby. This is an immature biological device."

Turner left Sarge with the little thing sleeping in his arms. He rocked back and forth, singing softly, "Low, low, breathe and blow, wind of the western sea," the same lullaby his father had sung to him.

Finally, the only sounds in the room were the long, racking sobs of Sergeant Walker.

The baby slept for only a few moments. Then it opened its eyes and watched in silence the weeping man.

CHAPTER TWO

JUNE 13, 2002

"TOM?"

Dr. Turner heard her but he didn't. He read the letter again, but the words didn't change, and his horror at them didn't change, either.

"Tom, our test results are in, and you wanted to review them with us."

He looked up at Gamma. Her vivid, complex face revealed a twinge of concern in the slight knit of her porcelain-white brows.

Generations one and two had appeared entirely human, but also contained too many human genes. To cut that back, he'd had to use scales on generation three. They were tiny, but noticeable, and they were white. He'd made the choice of scales because in the next generation he could use the Slc7a11 gene to control melanin, enabling them to camouflage themselves with colors as needed, like lizards.

But it didn't matter now. Incredibly. Horribly.

"Is something troubling you, Tom?"

Gamma was programmed as a medic, and her mind contained all medical knowledge. She was far more capable than any human doctor, including him. He had planned to use her to assist him—or, more probably, lead him—in the design of the next generation.

Using the sensors in her long, tapering fingers—truly the fingers of a surgeon—she touched his temples.

"Temp ninety-seven point seven, normal for you. Pulse eight-eight, BP one seventy over a hundred. Abnormal readings. You're in a stress condition, Tom. Let me suggest diazepam, two point five milligrams. I can get it now."

"Do it."

She turned, her scales shimmering in the bright artificial sunlight that flooded his office. Another of her innovations, artificial sunlight in the facility to ward off depression and ensure adequate vitamin D levels.

Although the first- and second-generation hybrids appeared entirely human, these were smarter and more powerful. They had good skills, such as an ability to jump hundreds of feet, and the bone strength to sustain the impacts involved.

All three generations could enter a high-speed mode that would enable them to approach and kill an adversary a hundred yards away before signals from his brain could reach his trigger finger. For this, they were programmed in knife combat, because no firing mechanism could keep up with their hands.

They were such a wonderful tool, by far the most advanced tool that human science had ever created. He deserved the Nobel Prize, not this miserable, stupid letter.

Maybe he could salvage something, though. Generations one and two appeared human, so maybe he could hide them and at least save that much against a future with a more sane Congress.

The problem with these first two creatures was that their being genetically half-human compromised their legal status. The project's legal officer had rendered an opinion that a court would be likely to decide that they were, indeed, human beings. Worse, though, they had human personalities and could fight through programming they did not like.

But they were teenagers, Mark and Gina, full of life and joy and excitement, in school, crazy about each other, totally unaware of what they really were. He could maybe do what he had been ordered to do to generation three, but not to them, they were the children his own unfortunate genetics had prevented him from having.

He loved his kids, and frankly he even loved generation three. How could you not love Gamma's caring bedside manner, or Alpha's quiet expertise and officer's insightful wisdom—or even the wonderful, ferocious loyalty of the four pure soldiers?

The triumph of generation three was that they fulfilled all ten criteria, including the most important one, that they were absolutely in no way classifiable as human. They weren't animals, either. Because their crucial brain regions were populated not by neurons but by artificial memristors, they were, legally, machines.

Their essentially reptilian biology enabled them to regrow organs and limbs, gave them enormous strength, and only enough sensation to warn them of potentially fatal wounds. They could jump four hundred feet. They could move at least as fast as generations one and two. Their intelligence, while less supple and imaginative than that of the first two prototypes, was functionally superb.

Their eyesight was a signal achievement. He had managed, as long as microwave tuning was used to excite artificial rods and cones in their retinas, to give them vision better than that of eagles. The downside of this was, unless the microwave field was turned on, their vision was as limited as that of a lizard. One of his ambitions for generation four was to actually use eagle eyes, but that would be complex and would change the size of the orbits considerably. Theoretically, generation three could be fitted with human eyes, but he had not been willing to try this, largely because obtaining eyeballs outside of normal medical channels was going to carry unacceptable security risks. They also had the temperature sensitive sight of snakes, which gave them something of a backup.

In all, they had just a smattering of human genes, under 2 percent, which were mostly involved with the skeletal structure. And those, using the extraordinary technology he had gained from the aliens at Dulce, could now be synthesized and the bones strengthened with embedded carbon-fiber strands. Generation four would contain no human genes at all.

An inevitable side effect of all the modification, however, was that generation three did not appear human, and generation four would appear even less so.

Of course, now there would be no generation four.

He found generation three beautiful, but their glittering, faintly reptilian skin and sleekly glaring faces would cause a sensation in public. They'd be thought of as aliens. They would terrify people. As soldiers on the battlefield, they would cause dread. He'd been inspired by the faces of the aliens, and the faces of snakes. They looked demonic. Extremely fierce. And so—well, to him, the only word that fit was *exquisite*.

He'd been planning to expose them to public awareness over time, starting them as a secret Delta Force unit. Then, as more were grown, getting first the military and then the public acclimatized.

Again, he read the letter:

From the chief counsel, Senate Select Committee on Intelligence:

"Thank you very much for your testimony, and for exposing this committee to your extraordinary achievements. However, there are grave concerns among the senators about the wisdom of proceeding with your project. Among these concerns is the fact that the individual they were allowed to interview was so extraordinarily brilliant. The question was then asked, 'Why wouldn't such beings simply outwit us altogether and become independent entities?' If that happened, they would obviously pose a serious danger, and one we may be unable to fully understand, much less control.

"Therefore, the committee has voted unanimously not to extend the Hybrid Project beyond the time necessary for you to destroy the materials that have thus far been created.

"Dr. Turner, on a personal note, obviously this is not good news, and it is certainly not the outcome either of us expected after your testimony. But, with this kind of bipartisan unanimity, I cannot offer you any alternative for the program.

"The senators are so concerned that they are planning to follow up your termination with an Inspector General visit to the facility, and the destruction or impounding of the genetic modification equipment you have developed.

"I would therefore advise you to immediately retain personal and corporate counsel to protect your patents and your property. Otherwise, there is a likelihood that DoD will be tasked to remove both the zinc finger splicing apparatus and the consciousness receptacle to a bonded and classified warehouse facility, where it will be difficult, if not impossible, for you to regain possession."

A handwritten note was at the bottom: "Get rid of them, Tom, they're too dangerous. The senators are terrified."

Gamma returned with a pill cup and a glass of water. "Here we are, Tom. I'll want to check your BP again in an hour. And we're all aware that the letter is from the Senate, and it's not good news. We want you to know that we support you fully."

Should he let them read it? Could they resist orders to destroy themselves? He needed to ask Emma Walker that question, because if they could resist, there would be one hell of a battle down here.

In fact, he couldn't think how to go about it. Perhaps if he caged them and had them flooded with high-speed machine-gun bullets, they would eventually take so many rounds that they would die. He could probably burn them, but that was too ghastly to contemplate.

"Thank you, Gamma. Return to the ready room."

"I'll be back in one hour to check on my patient."

"Very well."

She turned and left his office, her stride fast and aggressive. How much had they surmised about the contents of the letter? he wondered.

Everything, was his first thought. Their new intelligence scores were well beyond the level of human genius. The reason was that their brains were as capable as human brains of accessing and comparing information, but their memories were biomechanical. Unlike neurons, memristors did not lose what they stored, not ever, and they could store hundreds of times more memories than humans.

He needed to get to Palo Alto and confer with Emma. He couldn't defy the committee, not because he didn't have the power, but because if he did, they would investigate, which would inevitably lead them to Dulce and the aliens, and that could not be allowed.

The Senate Intelligence Committee had an absolute

right to access every secret that the United States possessed. So Dulce was hidden from them illegally. If they found out about it, they would expect to be told everything. But that would have unpredictable consequences. Maybe the aliens would leave, taking with them the most valuable technological resource that this country or any country had ever possessed. Their planet was 90 million years older than Earth, their civilization at least 5 million years old. They were here attempting, with his help and the help of a whole scientific infrastructure, to create versions of themselves that could live on Earth. The Hybrid Project had come about as a side effect of what Tom had learned from them, and from the use of old equipment of theirs that they had given him as surplus.

They were themselves such a complicated mixture of biological and mechanical parts that it was impossible to classify them either as living creatures or as machines. The sounds they made, their movements, their thought processes, were startlingly precise. Over the generations, they had enhanced themselves, in effect designing themselves beyond natural evolution, and he believed that this was the next step for mankind, also. We could take control of our own evolution. What he had learned could be pushed into the broader human genome, and mankind could leap ahead into a new kind of being.

This was also why he cherished generations one and two, because they would form the prototype for the new man.

But the senators said no, and the senators had the power. "Stop the future," the eternal cry of the ignorant and the fearful.

If he lost the Hybrid Project, then the only access mankind would have left to extraordinary technology would be observation of the aliens' activities in their labs in Dulce.

Would the same senators who had just killed his hybrids tolerate the idea of human-alien hybridization, and the wholesale theft of human sexual material that went along with it?

On any given night, the aliens extracted sperm and eggs from five or six hundred people. Using directed magnetic fields, they first turned off a subregion of a subject's hippocampus called the subiculum, which prevented the brain from gathering memories of the experience. They extracted eggs from women via needle extraction. They forced erection and ejaculation in males by the use of electrostimulation of the superior dorsal nerve of the penis.

Then the victims were returned to their beds—or not. The stresses involved killed some. A tiny smattering of them, generally with novel configurations of the hippocampus, did remember what happened to them and formed a noisy but generally discounted subculture of "alien abductees."

If the senators discovered that their stories were true, all hell would break loose. The White House would become involved. There might be military action against Dulce, that incredibly precious resource. Worse, if the aliens were attacked, the consequences would, to say the least, be unpredictable.

They were enormously experienced. They had done this before on other worlds. They were experts. But they were also easy to anger and gruffly impatient. They handled their human subjects with rough indifference and had left a scar of buried trauma across a large cross-section of humankind everywhere in the world, and in particular in the United States.

Worse, fundamentalists were on the committee, three

of them, and their belief was that the only intelligent creatures in the universe were angels, demons, and man, and that only the demons moved through space in conveyances, which angels did not need.

So they would conclude that the aliens were demons, and he could hardly imagine where that might lead.

Gamma reappeared. "Doctor, I'm hearing your breathing and it's unsteady. I'd like to listen to your heart."

She could easily hear him breathing from the ready room down the hall, she had the hearing of a canine. She also had something close to a dog's sense of smell, they all did. So she was not saying it, but she could certainly smell his fear.

"Thank you, Gamma."

She came closer to him, then pulled up a chair and sat almost knee to knee. How beautiful she was, with the feminine form dictated by her skeletal structure, and the subtle softening that female chromosomes had given to her hard features.

When they had extracted her from the growth medium, even Emma Walker had gasped with surprise. She had whispered, "How beautiful." She had already constructed the electromagnetic field that would fill her brain and animate her nervous system, so the moment they inserted it into the body, Gamma's eyes opened and she became instantly fully informed medically. She went in seconds from being an inert form slathered in disinfectant gel to an expert medical specialist and geneticist, needing only training in the fine motor skills associated with surgery. They were still in that training. She was learning to reattach nerves in the spine, useless in humans, but vital for hybrids, whose nerves would reconnect.

He heard a grinding sound and realized that it was his own jaw clenching.

Gamma removed her hands. "There's that same minor issue with your mitral valve, but nothing to be concerned about. When are you going to kill us?"

He was so surprised that he sucked breath. She sat back, then got up and stepped away.

"Excuse me for surprising you." She lowered her eyes. "I read the letter."

Of course she had. He'd been holding it. She would easily have been able to read it upside down.

"Do the others know?"

"I broadcast the contents, yes." They were networked just like computers, using the same microwave field that intensified their vision.

So they all knew. And since they also knew every detail of how the U.S. government functioned, as well as a great deal of general law and all military law, they also knew how much danger they were in.

He did the only thing he could do. His heart now hammering, Gamma hovering beside him, he went to the ready room where they were housed.

Unlike generation one and two, who lived upstairs and were maturing like normal human beings, generation three could be grown in artificial wombs in as little as a few days, and they could be pulled out at any maturity needed. Generally, the more complex motor skills they would need, the younger the pull.

As he entered the ready room, Gamma hurried ahead to open the door for him. He was the senior officer. It was protocol.

"Good morning, soldiers," he said as they snapped to attention. They had been watching a historical film of Adolf Hitler. Like aphasics awakened by drugs from their sleep, they could detect lies in the tone of voice and the expression on the face. His thinking here had been that any good soldier must also be able to interrogate his captives expertly.

Normally, they were completely silent unless they were asked to convey information or had something to say, and that was the case now. They simply stood watching him.

"Obviously, a setback," he said. "Your generation is going to be destroyed."

Not a flicker in a single eye. They looked at him with that same empty stare that they always displayed. But they had only vestigial personalities, except for Alpha with his more subtle officer's mind, and Gamma with her medical interest. Not even Alpha and Gamma reacted, though, and he found that their indifference to their own death sentence was extraordinarily oppressive.

"We will carry out your termination via the use of drugs." He knew that this would immobilize them but not kill them. Not even a massive dose of potassium chloride could depolarize their cardiac muscles. Founded in the reptile and insect worlds as they were, their organs were phenomenally resistant.

He knew what he had to do. He had to flood them with sodium thiopental via cannulas into the carotid. That would knock them cold, but only for a time.

He did not say anything more because the rest of it would need to be a lie, and they would detect that at once, with possibly dangerous consequences.

If they tried, they could escape this facility. They could reach the streets, and a threat such as this, with a human origin, might cause them to regard all human beings as the enemy.

There would be carnage in the streets above, in his beloved San Francisco.

"Please return to your duties," he said.

Without a sound, they went back to their various seats. Alpha picked up his *Iliad*; Beta, Delta, and Epsilon returned to Hitler; Zeta to his Calvino, *If on a Winter's Night a Traveler*. They were studying surrealism as a foundation for asymmetric warfare, and this exercise in the improbable was an ideal text for discussion, or so Zeta had been asserting. In regard to surprising methods of attack, they were also working in meteorology and gravitational theory. He thought that they understood both. He thought that they could probably master both.

And then he thought, perhaps the senators were right. Maybe they would eventually come to challenge their programming, maybe they would seek to end human domination. If so, they could certainly replace us, just as our ancestors had replaced the Neanderthals.

Alpha said, "The interesting thing about Achilles is that it's a defeatist emotion, arrogance." He looked up at Tom, his eyes as empty and relentless as a cobra's. "If we had been allowed to survive, it would have been valuable to emphasize our machine elements in any public unveiling. This would induce arrogance in the enemy. Useful."

Was that all? Was that the beginning, middle, and end of their reaction to being given a death sentence?

Instead of returning to his office, he took the elevator topside. He needed to call Emma, and he needed to be way out of their hearing.

"Father," Two cried as soon as the door opened onto the residential floor. She came running out of the schoolroom, a swan of a girl, absolutely human, deeply human, glowing. Behind her, One, with his heightened battlefield instincts said, "What's wrong, Father?"

Tom did not cry. He could not allow himself any such emotion.

He took Two's heart of a face in his hands. "I'm just working very hard. Nothing is wrong."

As he hurried on down the hall, he heard One say to her, "That would be false."

Tom had an ultrasecure phone system installed here, with a direct encrypted line to Emma's lab. Her husband had been with him from the beginning, chosen not because of his undistinguished army career, but because of his wife's stunning record at Stanford.

"Emma, big trouble this end. I need to know if Gen Three can break its programming."

"Are you sending them into combat? At last?"

For months now, she'd wanted them put to use. Just the six of them would certainly be able to find Osama bin Laden and take the war on terror right into Al Qaeda's spider hole, no question about that whatsoever.

"Emma, I won't lie to you."

"Don't."

"No. The committee has ordered them destroyed."

Silence. Then a barked laugh. "They're indestructible!"

"Will they resist?"

"Well, of course they—" Then she was silent. The silence extended. Finally she continued, "No, not if they're so ordered by constituted authority."

"Emma, I want you to help me with One and Two. I can't just do this to them."

"Hell, let's save all of them. 'The committee has ordered them destroyed.' Screw that bunch of worthless sheep."

Emma might be a scientist of the first order, but she was a soldier scientist. She understood what a soldier was, right down to his quivering, vulnerable core.

In the end, they built an inch-thick steel containment and took it on a specialty naval vessel to the Challenger

Deep in the Marianas. On the voyage, the threes worked on the math of naval combat and determined that the U.S. Navy could control the airspace of the entire planet with carriers at just three crucial points around the globe.

When the day came for them to enter the containment, there was no need to sedate anybody. However, as it sank, a deep booming began from inside, and continued, and could be heard even after the waves had closed over it. Heard, but only for a time.

Still pounding, they disappeared into the abyssal deep.

The hell with the ship. He was sick of it. He was sick of life and of the world. He flew back. He'd already got Emma to take One and had given Two to a trusted CIA ally, Jim Lyndon, who had been CIA committee liaison and regarded the senators as fools.

Before letting them go, Tom had reprogrammed them, watching with sorrow in his heart as they forgot each other, and then forgot their life here and the man who adored them.

He put two brilliant teenagers on two different planes and watched them leave for new lives.

Then he reported to the committee that the project had been terminated, and all of its "developments," as he put it in the letter, "permanently curtailed."

True to his word, the chief counsel had deflected the confiscation of Tom's lab, so he concealed it under concrete and sold the surface building, as it happened, to a television station.

He moved to Virginia, where he joined DARPA, the Agency of Wonder, and spent his time bleeding his knowledge of organ durability into a new project called Inner Iron, which would at least give the next generation of human soldiers a little better chance of survival, should it ever be decided that altering their genes for their own good was ethical.

He hated the world and nursed his loss. He watched his kids from afar and was proud of them, his brilliant creations.

CHAPTER THREE

RECONNAISSANCE IN FORCE

THEY'D SILENTLY WAITED THROUGH THE predawn, seeing nothing, and so as the sun rose, Colonel Mark Bryan was ready to pull his team out. He clicked his satphone.

"I got a no contact, Gina," he said to their controller in Langley.

"Request you penetrate another hundred meters south-southwest."

"You see anything definite?"

"A box."

He thought about that. What the hell would a box have to do with anything? "Anything about the box I should know?"

"Two things. It's six feet six inches long. And it wasn't there ten minutes ago."

"You saw them bring it in?"

"Negative that."

Prior to this, the creatures—Gina called them hybrids—had only appeared in isolated areas. Here they were forty miles from San Francisco and thirty from San Jose. This was a forest, but not an isolated one.

The bible on this operation was that an alien species had spent years trying to create a human-alien hybrid that would have their brain in a human body and so be able to live and function among us.

Gina Lyndon had told him the secret of the ages: "We cooperated with them to get what knowledge we could. There wasn't a single thing we could do to stop them." But then they'd left, apparently after failing to meet their objective.

Now, however, these tall people, palely gleaming, had started to be glimpsed by the public in isolated areas, and the scientists who had run the old program were hopeful that the aliens had succeeded after all.

It had been decided that an effort needed to be made to find out more about them. But they were incredibly elusive, which was how Mark had become involved. People were always telling him that he was the best tracker in the army. For his part, he'd seen many a trail peter out, so he wasn't exactly confident of that assessment.

They'd put him in charge of this reconnaissance unit—which was fair enough, as far as he was concerned. Traipsing around the backwoods of America surely beat living rough in the Zagros Mountains, which was where he'd been when his new orders had come through.

Watching, listening, he led his team deeper.

Distant on the air, he heard the faint sound of a tractor. So the farm they'd passed on the way was now awake.

"This site is too close in," Dr. Linda Hicks said softly. As the team biologist, she was concerned with such things as whether the hybrids might carry unknown diseases, but her primary responsibility was to gather samples for the scientists who were working on the project.

Mark was not concerned about diseases. He was not concerned about the welfare of the hybrids. He was concerned about the military danger that they might pose, whatever form it might take.

Mark got her to the right spots. She did the evidence gathering, the scientists the theorizing.

Linda and the scientific committee thought the hybrids would be friendly, but that was not Mark's instinct. His instinct was that something was wrong or they wouldn't be so elusive. What did they have to hide? Had to be that something about what they wanted to do—or were doing—we wouldn't like.

A town, Willoughby, was just six kilometers from here, with a campground a few hundred meters away, picnic turnouts along the road, and that farm less than a half klick away.

As the team entered a narrow clearing, they saw the box. It appeared to be of a heavy grade of cardboard and reminded Mark of one of those paper coffins you'd see in 'Stan. He motioned for a halt.

Linda began to deploy her sampling gear. He could see that she was excited, and that worried him.

"Go slow," he said. "Okay, guys, let's form a perimeter around this thing. Knots and Massy, we're gonna open it."

"I want everyone who approaches it in masks and gloves," Linda said. "Just get it open and then step away." She was unrolling her white isolation suit.

"There's another one over here," Knotty said.

Four more were with it. Mark called Gina. "We have a total of six boxes. Five of them back in the trees."

"Don't move anything. Open the one I can see. Then we'll go on from there."

"I agree." He said, "Okay, guys, I want the Metal Storm weapons activated, and pistols at the ready. If anything comes out of this box, any violent movement—"

"No, not just any movement," Linda said. "Movement that is identified as an attack. Identified by aggressive gesture or action."

He sucked back his anger. "All right, if there is an identifiable attack."

"Are you saying there's somebody in these things, sir?" Massy said.

"I'm saying I have no idea. Cox and Louis, I want you backed off with your Metal Storms ready."

Mark took out his combat knife and went to one end of the box. He saw an area of symbols, some unreadable, but some in plain English.

The ones that he could read stunned him. He clicked his satphone. "Gina, this thing has one of our names on it. I'm reading, 'Hicks, Linda,' then a series of numbers, "one, seven, three, six, two, five, nine. There are also symbols. Massy, get the camera on this, let her see."

As Massy deployed the video camera that would feed via an orbiting satellite directly to Gina's office, Linda came closer.

"That's my height and weight in metrics all run together," she said. "I'm five foot eight, that's one point seven three meters. A hundred and thirty-eight pounds is sixty-two point five nine kilograms."

Mark asked Gina, "How do we react to this?"

"Why don't you lift it? See if it's got anything in it."

Massy and Knots each took an end and lifted it slightly.

"Hundred twenty, hundred thirty pounds," Massy said.

"Okay," Mark said to Gina, "so are we gonna have another Linda come outta there or what do you think?"

From his position near the other boxes, Louis called, "Each one has one of our names on it. We're all covered except you, sir, and Richardson." Richardson was their driver and supply master. He was with the van.

Mark really, really did not like this. He said to Gina, "I don't think we should touch any of this stuff."

Linda said, "Sir, begging to differ, this is a bonanza here. If there are bodies, we've got a gold mine."

DARPA was urgently building a genetic profile of the hybrids, but so far there had been just a little DNA, some from a bit of blood on a piece of cloth and some from urine that they'd collected six weeks ago off a bush.

They'd found spider DNA in the samples, the *Atrax,* or funnel-web spider, an aggressive and highly venomous Australian variety. Also the DNA of the tiger and the cobra, and chains of human DNA linked together in ways that were definitely not going to happen in nature.

This was bizarre enough, but it could be only a small part of the picture. The acquisition of a body would mean dissection, organic analysis, and a complete DNA profile. The mystery of whether this was an alien-human hybrid or something altogether different would be solved.

"Okay, people, I want everybody back ten yards. Metal Storms and pistols covering me. I am going to do this."

"Sir, a Metal Storm's gonna kill you."

"If things get outta control. You *will not* let anything escape our perimeter, is that understood? Even if I am in the red zone." The hybrids they had come close to so far had proven to be extraordinarily fast. He didn't think that something that could move like that could be brought down by even a Metal Storm, unless at close range.

Metal Storm was a new kind of infantry weapon that fired a programmable pattern of steel beads faster than the speed of sound. You could rip an entire company apart with a single discharge. The weapon carried up to fifty discharges. Fully tanked with its lethal little beads, it weighed just eighteen pounds.

"Tightest pattern you got," he said. "Just don't miss the damn hybrid. We don't want it running off into that town or eating the farmer or whatever."

He took a breath, slit the box around the seams, and pulled off the lid.

Eyes closed, motionless, there lay inside what Mark thought was the ugliest thing he had ever seen. It was as white as cream, sleek and svelte, its long hands crossed on its belly. It was covered with a thin film of some sort of cream. Could be cold cream, from the way it looked. Something to keep it moist.

"My God," Linda said. She came forward, a stethoscope in her hand. "If it's meant to look like me, they failed."

Mark blocked her way.

"I have to do this!"

"Guys, I want pistols against its head. If there is the slightest movement, Knots will be behind her, you will pull her away." Mark drew his own M1911-A1, the modern version of the World War Two vintage .45, still in use by Delta Force. He stepped to the head of the box and put the barrel against the forehead.

"It's beautiful," Linda whispered as she applied the stethoscope between the tight breasts.

"They were right about the sex, at least," Mark said.

"Yeah, funny."

How could she ever think it beautiful, though? You could see the suggestion of a lizard in the shape of its face. You could see that its skin was made of tiny white scales. And it smelled like a snake, that same thick musk you got out of a den of copperheads. Mark was fast enough to catch striking snakes, something he'd done as a boy. Catch them and snap them like whips. Job done. He'd lived in Palo Alto, and out in the hills, he'd sometimes come across them. He'd done plenty in Iran, too, and in 'Stan. He didn't like to. Killing was never trivial to him, not even a snake, not even an insect. Give him some powdered sumac, though, a little salt and a little oil, and he could transform locusts into an edible dish. Throw in some Persian horned viper, and you had a meal.

Linda might find it beautiful, but the more he looked at it, the uglier it appeared. With its narrow, tight lips, it almost seemed as if it had been designed to look ferocious.

"Take it slow, Linda. Weapons at the ready, people."

Gina said over the satphone, "Is that a hybrid?"

"Looks like it," Mark responded. He scanned their surroundings, seeking to catch the quick movement among the dew-bright leaves that would reveal the presence of a scout watching them with the unswerving, unnatural attention that the hybrids brought to everything they did.

Massy clicked away with one of their cameras. Knots videotaped. In a year in the field, they had only managed four images, and three of them were poor.

Linda pressed a temperature sensor against the hybrid's forehead, then listened to the chest with her stethoscope.

"No internal sounds," she murmured.

The temperature sensor climbed to 89.3°F and stopped. To Mark's great relief, she came up away from the thing.

"I don't think it's dead, but it's not alive, either."

"What's that mean? A coma?"

She looked down at it. "I don't know. But I can take some skin scrapings and hair samples. Fingernails. Then we need to get all of them to Plum Island."

Mark got on the satphone. "I want a larger military presence out here, Gina. Say it's a classified cargo that's been dropped. Seal off the area. And get a chopper in the air, I want these things moved to Travis, pronto. From there, prepare to transport them to the USDA facility on Plum Island." Officially, it was an animal-disease research center. In fact, it offered some of the finest genetic testing facilities in the world and was the only place, Gina had told him, where the "little tiny bit" of alien DNA in our possession was kept.

"Oh, boy," Massy said, a tremor in his voice. Mark followed his wide-eyed stare.

The creature's eyes had been closed. Now they were open.

"Could be an unconscious reflex," Linda said.

"Back off, people."

Massy and Knots moved out to the perimeter with the others.

"I need to do this," Linda said. She was getting ready to pare its nails.

"Back off now!"

"Sir—"

"This is way off the reservation. We need a whole lot of support here."

"Can those function?" she muttered, staring down at the eyes. They were pale blue, the irises solid. They looked painted.

There was more movement nearby, a flicker in the soft-lit dawn forest. Somebody's motion sensor chimed softly.

"Got one," Louis said into their helmets.

Another sensor tripped. Charles said, "Incoming this end."

They were being surrounded.

"Deploy Metal Storm, prepare to fire."

"No! Do not fire!"

"What in hell, Linda?"

"This is contact. It is not necessarily hostile."

"Linda, this is some kind of work in progress that we've interrupted. We push these suckers much harder, they're gonna be on us."

"We need to move the material to Plum Island, Colonel," Linda said, "all of it."

"They're in the woods. They're all around us. Do you understand that?"

Linda returned to the creature in the box.

"Get away from there! Now!"

"Look, I need at least skin, hair, and nail parings." She bent down and went back to work. "Anyway, this isn't a coma. This is deeper. Eyes open or closed, this thing isn't gonna be moving any time soon."

There were soft whines as the guys started their Metal Storms charging.

"Sir, why do they have our names on them?" young Knots asked.

Mark heard fear. He said, "Do not fire that weapon unless you get a specific order. And the answer to your question is, I have no idea." He touched his mike again. "Anybody seeing anything?"

In quick response, three clicks in his earpiece. Okay, three noes. So what the hell was Massengill doing?

"Massy?"

The response was a sound that Mark heard only during training on Metal Storm, a noise that he always thought must be like the rending of the veil in the temple, a gigantic, ripping thunder. Linda stifled a shout of surprise, but nobody broke position.

Fragments of leaves turned to glittering green snow in front of Massengill, and a foot-long section of a redwood's thick trunk became a spreading haze of sawdust. The tree crashed down on itself, then swung back into the woods, its limbs hissing as it slumped away. It came to a stop against other trees, leaning at a crazy angle. Its huge bulk was now fifty feet back in the woods, the stump, smoking and alone, isolated in the new clearing made by the high intensity gun's ten-thousand-round-a-second spread. You could hold a thousand of its beads in your cupped hands. But drive them to extreme velocity, and they turned into a wall of death. The gun itself was silent. The ripping noise came when the beads broke the sound barrier.

There was another sound then, bell-like laughter.

"Is that them?" Linda asked as she worked.

"Hurry it up."

"Going as fast as I can. The nails are too hard, they're like steel." She'd given up on them and was using a small scissors to harvest some of the dark, close-cropped hair.

Massy backed in on the perimeter, face tight under his helmet. "Came right at me." He nodded toward where the tree had been. "From over there."

Mark looked out into the forest. "It was attacking?"

"It was a figure coming toward me. It carried a silver, tapering object. Sort of looked like a car antenna. When it was a hundred feet in front of me, it raised this thing and sort of flickered and I could no longer see it. That's when I let go with the Metal Storm."

Mark would end up having to fly to Washington with Captain Massengill and sit there and listen to the scientists whine about the use of the weapon. "They've been peaceful so far, Colonel. If we turn them violent, we turn a historic corner," they would say. Yeah, yeah, he'd heard it all before.

Linda chopped and sliced. "This stuff is worse than the nails! It's not what we call hair, that's for sure."

A buzzard appeared above the new clearing Massengill had made in the forest, wheeling in watchful flight.

Linda said, "I'm going to crack my surgical kit, I've got better blades."

"Stand clear, that's an order," Mark snapped.

"You let me do my job!"

His satellite phone beeped. "Shit," he muttered, and put it to his ear.

"You took a shot," Gina said. As always, he experienced a moment of awkward and intense longing at the sound of her voice. On their one night together, he had fallen in love with her, but she had never given any indication that she felt the same. His life had not brought him into proximity with many women. In high school, there had been Christie Mailer, but she'd moved to Tulsa. At Stanford, he'd been too poor to really date, and too engrossed in his studies. Not a lot of opportunity at Fort Bragg, none, for sure in deep cover in Iran, and Afghanistan offered only dismal whores, most of them boys.

She was a light, Gina was, the best woman he'd ever so much as come close to actually knowing. They communicated many times in a day, but she'd never shown the least sign of remembering their night together. In his heart, he maintained a shrine to her, filled with memories of her face, her wonderful, liquid body, her frank, gently laughing eyes.

"Come on, Mark, what's going on down there? Clue me, damnit!"

"There was an aggressive move."

"Define that."

"An attack using an unknown implement. It'll be on the gun camera video, you can pull it up and look at it."

"I'll do that, you can be sure. Did you kill anything?"

"No indication. Gina, please tell me the backup is moving."

"You bring out the one you've opened, then we'll talk about that."

"The hell, you get choppers in here, you get men in here, and equipment. We can't carry that thing through populated areas in a friggin' panel van."

"Do it!"

He turned off the satphone.

"Okay, people, we're pulling out."

"Give me time!"

"Can it, Linda, we're gonna bring this one out with us. She's sending in a larger detail to get the others."

Massy said, "You don't want to rile these puppies up."

"Not our concern. Our concern is, how do we get this thing to the van and out of here? Massy and Knots, you carry the box, Linda you go ahead, Louis, Cox, Williams, cover."

While the team did its work, Mark watched the perimeter. He had the best eyes for the creatures, and he was instantly aware that more than a few of them were around here. A lot, in fact. Also, an unexpected sound was coming from somewhere. Drums. Somebody was playing a drumroll somewhere far away, and that seemed odd and out of place.

"Okay, drop it," he said into his throat mike. "We're pulling out right now, double quick."

"But I need—"

He grabbed Linda's shoulders. "You need to survive, and if you stay here one more second, that is not going to happen. Now *move!*"

The guys came in, assembling around them.

"Okay, we're outta here. Massy, rear guard."

Forming a column, they began pulling away. Massy held back, facing toward the open box.

With a flutter of sound, two men were suddenly face-to-face with him. One of them carried a long silver rod and wore jeans and a woman's tank top. The other was in a tattered business suit with no shirt. They were not like the creature in the box, they looked human.

Before he could turn and run, the one with the rod attacked Massy, and in an instant he was covered with blood.

When he screamed, they leaped on him, throwing him to the ground. Something flashed away into the woods, and he pitched back, mouth gaping, eyes suddenly gushing blood.

Hating that he had to abandon his soldier, knowing that they must, Mark shouted, "Pull out! Do it now!"

More appeared, this time pure hybrids, and one of them leaped at least a hundred feet, falling on Linda. She went down screaming, and Mark threw himself at the thing and found himself connected with it in deep battle. He'd done this before, but never with something so strong and so fast. Its muscles rippled beneath his hands as he pushed back the head until he heard the neck crack. The body shuddered and Linda could roll free.

"*Move!*" he yelled, but she did not move. Her eyes were blank with shock.

Instantly their situation became clear to Mark: The math of this battle was not on their side. They were unlikely to make it.

CHAPTER FOUR

THE END OF THE BEGINNING

AS MARK RAN, SOMETHING LEAPED on his back and wrapped its legs and arms around him. The team wavered and began to turn back to help him.

"Keep moving," he shouted, "that's an order!"

His right arm was pinned but not his left, and he found that he could reach his combat knife. When he was young, he'd been fostered by a military couple, and Emma and Henry Walker had taught him a lot of things, including the skillful use of a knife. Although Henry was now a general, Mark had known him by his original rank, Sarge.

Behind him, he could hear Massy screaming. Despite themselves, the others continued toward the van, whereupon Mark saw a man—one of the creatures that looked like a man—leap hundreds of feet into the air and disappear out through the forest canopy.

They could damn well *fly*. Jesus God, what was going on here?

Teeth dug into his neck, but he got a grip on the knife and stabbed up and back. The bite deepened, then suddenly released amid a boiling glut of blood, and the creature pitched off him.

The man lay on the forest floor, writhing and gasping,

and Mark, seeing the man's skin coming off in great, looping patches as he struggled, understood that this was not a man, but a hybrid wearing the skin of a man. Beneath the skin were gleaming scales, and he felt for it the most total, astonishing, soul-shattering hatred he had ever experienced. He was not easily overwhelmed by emotion, but he stabbed and stabbed, then lifted the lifeless body and hurled it fifty yards back into the forest, where it smashed against a tree.

"Massy! Massy, get outta—"

Massy's body had collapsed in a jumbled heap—and what Mark saw shocked him as nothing else ever had. Massy was now completely naked. Where his eyes had been were two neat sockets. The top of his head was gone, and the cranium was empty. Something like an autopsy incision ran from his throat to his genitals, and his body was sunken.

They had taken his eyes, his brains, and his organs—and more of them were coming, racing straight at Mark, about to flicker forward and surround him. He did the only thing he could do: he turned and ran.

The squad dashed among the close-growing trees, slamming against trunks, their faces whipped by branches, as the things continued to harry them.

The one that had disappeared into the treetops came speeding down on Linda, who was smashed to the ground. Mark grasped it by the neck and lifted it up, snapping it like a snake. As it squalled, its back broke with a crunching pop, and the bottom half went limp. When he threw it to the ground, it tried to pull itself away. Knots shot it in the head.

Stumbling to their feet, the three of them caught up with the others, all of whom had stopped and were returning to give support.

"Keep moving, goddamnit," Mark snarled. This business of returning was undisciplined. No matter what, if you're a soldier, orders come first.

Ahead, at last, was their van. Mark hoped it would protect them from the things, because if enough of them showed up at once, the entire unit was going to die the way Massengill had, and this operation would be concluded.

The sun had risen into a golden sky, and morning was steaming away the dew of dawn. Tiny yellow flowers flowed past under their feet. All of this Mark saw with the sharpness that comes to the eyes of men in battle.

Knots got into trouble, flailing at one that had grabbed his neck under the back of his helmet. Next, Milton stumbled and rolled, screaming, and the screams were buried in a great roar, as if some leviathan had opened its throat and given monstrous song to the dawn.

Mark turned toward the sound and saw, coming through the woods, dozens of the creatures. Some looked human. Most were pale and sleek, with those strange, empty eyes of theirs.

He opened his Metal Storm, extended the drum from the body, and held it up, aiming it toward them. When he pressed the firing button, there was the familiar *r-i-i-p THUNK*, then the shriek of the beads slamming toward them. Again Mark fired, the sound rocking the air. Behind him, the van's horn started honking.

Once he saw that everybody except poor Massengill was accounted for, he leaped into the bay doors, shouting to their driver to get out of here.

Dawn turned to dark.

"Holy God," PFC Richardson cried. Somehow, one of the things had survived the lethal hail of pellets and was clinging to the van's hood, blocking Richardson's view.

"Step on it, Pete, goddamnit!"

"I can't see shit, Colonel!"

"Get us out of here!"

Richardson floored it, and the tires screamed and the van swayed.

"There's a steep shoulder, sir. I can't risk going over."

As Richardson spoke, the van tipped sharply to the right. He turned into the skid, recovered, and seemed to gain traction. The hybrid was reaching around into the cab, trying to grab the steering wheel.

From behind Richardson, Louis leaned forward and fired his pistol out the window and into the thing's head.

As it fell away, visibility returned—revealing that the van was headed straight into the river that they had crossed on the way here. Richardson hit the brakes, causing the clumsy vehicle to slide in the gravel, but not to stop. They were going in.

"Brace," Mark shouted.

The edge of the bridge shot toward them and beyond it the water, black and fast. And then Richardson got the van stopped. For a moment, they sat motionless.

Linda sobbed. Other than that, there wasn't a sound.

Richardson threw it into reverse, backing away from the water's edge. He drove up the shoulder and proceeded across the bridge. They went speeding down the country road, under the broad, overhanging trees, past the blue-flowering vines that trailed along the roadside, and the green fields and harvested fields beyond.

Just like that, they'd gone from hell to heaven.

A couple of boys were running the tractor they'd heard earlier.

"Stop the van!"

"Sir!"

As they rolled to a halt, Mark reached back and

opened the rear bay. The sweet scent of a country morning replaced the stink of sweat and terror. He looked behind them, looked to the sky, saw blue morning, that was all. The woods appeared to be at peace, the deep green of the thick pines conferring a darkness he found ominous, or perhaps that was because he knew what they concealed. Cursed woods.

Linda came out behind him.

"Those kids probably go back in there all the time," she said. "They're bound to."

He had always known that there would come a day like this, when the civilian world began to be involved. His soldier's mind kept repeating, We have no defense, we have no defense.

In the distance, he watched the boys cutting their hayfield.

"What do we do?" Linda asked.

He said the only thing he could say: "We return to base, report, and await orders."

"Oh, good. So then we come back out here after lunch, maybe, and gather up the little-boy skeletons?"

"This needs a division, Linda. At least. It needs Delta Force or more."

She bowed her head, acknowledging just how profoundly the situation had deteriorated.

His phone lit. Gina.

"Go ahead."

"What was that about, Colonel?"

"You saw it?"

"I saw discharges, a lot of them. What's wrong down there, Colonel?"

"We have a casualty. Charles Massengill is KIA."

Short silence, then, "Okay." A world of shock and sorrow in the tone.

"There are civilians in close proximity to what I think is some sort of hostile infestation, and it's damned aggressive."

"Listen, Mark, I want you people out of there."

"What about this farm?"

"We'll stage a quarantine and send in the local health department to evacuate the family."

"When?"

"Just get out of there."

"We need to take these kids with us."

"You have your orders, Mark. There are now just six people left in the world who have even a slight idea about how to handle this."

"We have no idea how to handle it."

"Okay, let me put it another way. You're the only person the army has ever found who can even begin to track these things, and your unit is trained around you. So do not put yourself or your people in harm's way. That's an order."

"What'll you do if I disobey?"

"Brig you!"

"You'll brig a corpse?"

For a moment, she was silent. When she spoke again, her voice was low and intense. "Just get out of there."

He closed his phone. "She said to return to base."

Linda started to head for the kids.

Mark blocked her way. "It's the right order and you know it."

Rage made her tremble.

"We return to base and regroup, Linda."

"They'll kill those boys, Mark."

He was silent.

"Yeah," Louis muttered. "They're just kids, Colonel." Louis had boys of his own, just like Massy, who'd had two.

"People, this is no job for a reconnaissance unit. Somebody else will be out here to help those kids."

"Ten and twelve," Knotty said.

Mark looked at Knotty's punch-twisted face. He'd been tortured in an Iranian jail. Then Mark looked along the seats at his crew. Of course people like this would want to save children.

He had lost today, big-time, and he did not like to lose, and he felt the choking helplessness of anger that could do nothing. He'd need to write Pamela Massengill a letter about her husband. Of course, the army would do its thing, but he had an obligation, too.

"Willoughby," Richardson called over his shoulder. They'd arrived back in the town they'd staged from.

"Break out of your carries," Mark ordered, and everybody dropped away their complex packs and weapons, the noise of it briefly filling the stuffy panel van. "Put us down at the motel," he told Richardson.

"Got it."

There would be no eulogies, not today. They'd all lost a friend and a hell of a soldier, and that hurt, and they were in the middle of a battle, and there was no time for the dead, not right now.

Mark saw that Knots was twisting his hands between his huge knees. "Hey," Mark said softly, to telegraph his concern without embarrassing him.

Knotty smiled, but then his eyes stared into nowhere. Mark could imagine the thoughts of defeat, the sense of helpless rage. When that rage turned to apathy, and it would if they took many more hits like this, a good man would need to be rotated out.

The first of the hybrids had showed up in a photograph taken by a nine-year-old boy near Copco Lake in far northern California. He'd been hiking with his father, and they had put the image of the tall, paint-white man in the tan body suit up on their Flickr site over the caption "Space alien at Copco?"

Eventually, the picture had come to the attention of Gina Lyndon, one of the CIA's most skilled imaging specialists.

Mark and his team had been tracking the hybrids steadily, but it was a strange track. For example, they'd left the California-Oregon border, but then where had they gone? There were never any tracks out of their encampment. A nest of them would be sighted, then it would disappear. Mark had ordered ground-penetrating radar units, but they were not due for a week yet.

Ahead and around the van, the little town bustled in its charming morning, tall trees shading the sidewalks, shopfronts glittering with goods. Not too far away, a church bell tolled. Was it Sunday? Mark had no idea.

Milton said, "Aw, shit," a bitter, sad comment made for them all.

The van came to a stop outside the Sixteen Mo-Tel. It was a study in western kitsch, its sign a neon lariat, its long row of identical rooms each fronted by a log hitchin' post. The restaurant was called the Hitchin' Post.

"Breakfast's still on, people," Richardson said, "if you wanna eat."

With their camouflage overalls and their carries stowed, they were now dressed casually. Richardson had become a wiry man in a green polo shirt, Mark a muscular blond. On the van's doors in neat black lettering were the words FIRST CHURCH OF GOD CHOIR, MAYNARD, CALIFORNIA.

"Pastor" Richardson, however, had a rough sort of a choir, four men, no smiles, all dense muscle, and a striding woman.

The neon lariat was turned off now, but that did

nothing to increase the appeal of the place. Mark followed the others through the swinging door into the restaurant. Pictures of cowboys and bandits were on the walls, and a yellowing image of an Indian chief that was labeled Sitting Bull. He was standing.

Mark pulled up a steel chair as the waitress came over. They all knew her. She was the only waitress and had served them from their arrival yesterday. They'd discussed what might be living in her hairdo, a great pile of brown streaked with gray, which bounced slightly as she walked. Linda called it a hair system.

"Where's Massy?" Gloria asked. She'd enjoyed chatting with him and he'd enjoyed watching her.

"His day's been ruined," Mark muttered.

"Oh, gee, I'm sorry to hear that. He's sick?"

"Sick, yeah, you got it."

"I'm gonna close the buffet in ten minutes," Gloria said.

One by one, they went to the steam table. It was mess-hall food, maybe a little worse. But given that they normally operated far from any kitchen at all, it was better than what they were used to. No matter what happens in battle, if you survive, you will want to eat.

So they ate everything that was left, all the eggs, all the bacon, all the sausages, every Corn Pop and every bagel half, and drank all the coffee and all the juice and all the milk, and then they maneuvered their muscular hulks off to their dim little motel rooms, and everybody who saw them wondered the same thing: What kind of monsters are they, those sullen giants eating everything in sight?

It is the soldier's fate to be feared by those he offers his life to protect.

CHAPTER FIVE

MOMMA IN THE SKY

GINA LYNDON SAT PRESSING HER fist against her mouth, her whole body shaking, the office closing in on her like a coffin, murmuring to herself, "Oh, God, oh, God."

Once again, she threw his telemetry up on her main screen, then turned the volume up until his heartbeat boomed through the silence—the deadly, maddening silence—of her office. Normally, she'd be listening to three or four songs at once, maybe also a news show. She'd been nicknamed Volcana by her father, which she hated. She was not all that intense. She was normal, damnit.

Mark's brain was in high beta, indicating that he was talking or writing, doing something active with his mind. But safe in the motel room, she knew that. Safe for now.

Oh, Mark. Such a name. Beautiful name. She took pleasure in just writing it, Mark Bryan, Mark Bryan, over and over like a smitten schoolgirl.

The head of the scientific committee, Dr. Thomas Turner, had sent his file to her, and it made a hell of a story. Colonel Bryan was a Delta Force legend, a master soldier . . . and a master in other ways, too. Lovely man, full of shoal waters, though. Deep inside, something about him was as cold as winter, and she didn't like that . . . but there was a whole lot more that she did.

She closed her eyes, riding his heartbeat, imagining that her own heart was beating with it. Then she threw up video of him, video watched many times, of him crossing a street on his way to his one meet with her, of him across the table from her at the restaurant, video that devastated her every time she looked at it, and she looked at it many, many times in a day.

In that first moment, seeing him for the first time, there had been the most poignant possible sense of déjà vu. But why? She decided that it was because, even though she'd never before seen him, she had always wanted to.

She knew that her obsession with him was not acceptable. If George Hammond knew the intensity of her feelings, he would probably have her reassigned or maybe do worse. Who knew what they might do if somebody in a position as sensitive as hers unwound on them?

She'd had one night with Mark, really just an evening, but those hours had come to form the center of her life. It was absurd, but he was just so—well, so much what she wanted.

She dreamed of him as a boy. In the privacy of her imagination, they'd grown up together, gone to school together, lived on the same block. They were lifelong lovers.

In the real world, he was all work and no play. She doubted if he even remembered that glorious night.

After he had left, she'd felt the most complex emptiness, as if she had found a softness inside herself that she'd never really believed was there, and a darkness. She'd dozed a little, so happy, so—oh, delighted. Yes, delighted. The man was gracious in bed, he was deliciously strong, his eyes wild during his pleasure—it had been an amazing experience for her. Her best experience. The best single thing that had ever happened to her.

The next day, not a phone call, an e-mail, a text, nothing. Then he was on assignment and their communications were limited to official channels. You did highly classified work in the field within the United States, and you were not going to be using any cell phones or nonsecure e-mail accounts. Secure communications only.

That night had apparently been for him a perfunctory release of tension. It made her feel used, and it made her angry. She spent her life having her half of a fight with the man she loved, raging at him, leaving him, forgiving him, and returning. Her heart belonged to him, and to loss.

She'd been watching closely as they went into the woods, an uneasy situation like that. Having him out there, knowing that she could at any moment become a helpless witness to his death, was her central nightmare.

So when she'd seen that figure leap on him and watched his telemetry go berserk, heart rate through the roof, brain waves in hyperdrive—her stomach had almost ripped itself apart. She'd pitched forward gagging, only with enormous effort forcing herself back under control. This office was not a private place. At Langley, there was no such thing.

Before him, there had been boys and men, but never a lover. Once she had understood that he wasn't going to be calling her, her work had become her life.

They were a CIA family, the Lyndons. Better, she was a loner, and the Company liked loners. If you wanted to socialize, fine, but do it in-house. If you just kept to yourself, that was fine, too. Easier, actually.

So here she was, a lonely woman of twenty-six whose lover was a heartbeat, a shadow, a voice that lived like a ghost inside some of the most sophisticated surveillance equipment on earth, a system she had designed herself, that had one purpose: to watch him and watch over him.

She had continuous satellite imagery not only of him and his team, but of the known hybrid sites, both active and abandoned, and a whole array of bells and whistles that could, in an emergency, enable her to call in military action ranging from rocket attacks by drones or fighters to a cruise-missile attack.

The moment the team had got into trouble, Mark's telemetry had alerted Gina. He had a piezoelectrically powered transmitter implanted in his chest. Why it had originally been put there and by whom she did not know, but she could certainly make good use of it. Because of it, she could know more about the man she loved than he did about himself.

She had paced as she watched the forest and listened to his frenetic heartbeats, praying that they would not stop, pleading with a God she'd left behind in childhood to please just this once save a man, one precious man, for the woman who loved him but could not see him again unless so ordered.

She played with the satellites' lenses and filters, trying to see something new in the area. She was no longer panicked, she told herself. But she also knew that she would soon need to send Mark into harm's way once again.

Moving a toggle, she zoomed in on Willoughby. She could see, in a clearing in the forest, the scattered remains of poor Massy. Not far away was the little farm. She moved the toggle and zoomed in on it. The two boys were running their tractor, and there was no other activity. Okay, she would do the quarantine deal with the local health department and get them moved out of there.

Farther up the road, a couple of RVs were pulled into a siding, awnings out, smoke rising. They could be a problem, too, especially if they hiked into those woods and found the remains—or worse, got offed. She put a marker on the RV encampment, another on the farm. Any movement in or out of the borders she drew around the two sites would trigger an immediate alert.

She wanted to drink something strong, she wanted to go back to smoking after twelve years, and she wanted to just wither up and die. Losing Mark would be worse for her, she imagined, than losing a husband. In addition to the loss of hope, there would also be the secret anguish that he had never known how she felt. She did not have the courage to say anything on the satphone. She could not face what she feared she'd get, which was his usual strictly professional response.

If she was Mark's shadow lover, she was the shadow mother of the rest of them. Momma in the sky, she followed all of them, this twenty-six-year-old, CIA-bred woman who tried to be—or at least appear—Company tough. She had felt a disturbing awe at the power she had been given to issue orders that might lead to men's deaths. Now that power did not feel so awesome and her heart was miserable with regret. If only she had watched more closely, maybe she could have warned them. But the hybrids had never remotely been this aggressive before.

She told herself that Mark would be all right. He was an expert at this kind of field work. In Qurya, a tiny hamlet in southern Afghanistan, he had installed listening devices in a Taliban headquarters that had led to the destruction of the entire command structure for the province. She'd looked at the place—a wretched village in a grim, featureless desert. No cover, no safe approaches. The job was impossible, and yet he had done it. And in

Iran, where he had lived off the land for over a year, he had found and marked air vents leading to the new secret nuclear facilities at Natanz. He and two of his men had accomplished this incredibly difficult and crucially important task without creating the slightest suspicion that they were even there.

He had also carried out assassinations, six of them. He was relentlessly efficient. It didn't matter where the targets were, or how well protected, he would always reach them. All six of his victims had died of apparent heart attacks, auto accidents, in one case a mugging. None of the deaths were listed as suspicious. But how he had got near such people as the director of the Iranian uranium enrichment program, or Al Qaeda's treasurer, who kept most of their finances in his head, was just not known.

She had read his whole record, from his life in foster care to his college career at Stanford, where Mark had lived with General Walker and his wife, Emma, the Nobel Prize–winning geneticist.

When they'd been together, she'd mentioned Dr. Turner to Mark and drawn a blank. It was illegal for her to share the contents of his dossier with him, so she could neither ask nor tell him more.

If he was an Inner Iron graduate, for example, would he know? Inner Iron was the Defense Advanced Research Project that Dr. Turner managed at DARPA. If Mark contained experimental organs, for example, it would explain why Dr. Turner had picked this particular soldier, and also why he would not want Mark to know he was behind the choice.

She didn't know much about Inner Iron, except that it involved genetic engineering that made soldiers stronger and more durable, and Mark's was certainly the most extraordinary record of endurance she'd ever read. And he was the strongest man she'd ever known. When he'd lifted her in his arms, so effortlessly, it had made her feel like a cloud. In the hours they were together, his appreciation of her had been so concentrated that, as never before or since, she had felt her femininity as something glorious and successful and cherished.

But only that once had he shown her charm and warmth. Only on that night.

When she'd met him, he'd been dressed in a tight-fitting blue suit and a too small dress shirt that made his body appear trapped. The moment he'd entered the restaurant, she had known it was him. The way he moved was unforgettable. Despite his size, he possessed a startlingly balletic grace. As this big man glided across the crowded room, she had suppressed an impulse to stand up and salute. His bearing telegraphed command, but when he sat down, his eyes spoke of something she could not completely name. There was loneliness, certainly, but also other, less definable qualities. Clearly, you wouldn't want any sort of confrontation with him.

You saw operational types who had died inside, men with blank eyes. Not Mark. He might walk the graceful walk of a skilled assassin, but when you looked into those eyes, you saw the sorrows of a lover, one who was deeply lost.

She'd seen in his file that he had an IQ of 220, but not until they'd talked had she realized what such mental power actually meant. His conversation had ranged across dozens of topics. At one point, to illustrate the physics of the new scattergun, he had scribbled equations on a napkin. The next moment, he was comparing the Roman emperor Trajan's invasion of Iraq to George W. Bush's, pointing out that both had made the same mistakes two thousand years apart. Arabs fade from invasions, then harry garrisons, as they have done from time immemorial.

He was also full of humor, his wit tart and subtle. When that tight, improbably gentle laugh of his revealed itself, she became unable to stop devouring him with her eyes. Trajan . . . Bush . . . both had made the same mistakes. Oh . . . how interesting, tell me more . . .

You looked into those complicated, penetrating eyes—skillful eyes—and you saw something that you had not realized would be there. Something was staring back at you from behind the soldier. But what, you could not tell. Wasn't a lover, that was for darned sure. Something, she thought, of the true predator's ever-careful awareness, measuring, calculating, evaluating. You got the feeling that he was looking at more of you than you, yourself, could see.

One thing was clear about Mark Bryan: This was what raw power—the real kind—looked like. His hard exterior concealed a softness so profound that it triggered your deepest instincts to make fluffy and make warm. The softness made you want to love him, but that other thing—the dangerous interior—made you afraid to turn your back.

Amid the dancing glasses and surging conversation of a Washington power restaurant, she had thought she had never seen anybody more alone. But then his face would light up into a smile, and she would want to cradle the frightened little boy that had, as if by magic, replaced the gray-eyed wolf in the straining suit.

Such contradictions are the foundation of love, and she had fallen in love with the soldier, the assassin, and the boy, with the shimmering genius and the hard, sad tough guy.

Her father had warned her to always watch the tough

ones, because they have hearts, and be it steel or soft, the heart is not your friend.

Goddamnit, Mark had a KIA and an uncontrolled situation. So much for her wizard soldier, precious to her though he was.

She flew the image of Willoughby until she was passing through its streets at eye level. If the movies knew what could actually be done with these satellites, they would have a whole new toy. But people would never believe this, not unless they saw it. She passed a supermarket, then a little strip of shops, a bookstore, a camp-supply store, a hardware.

There were flowers in big planters on the street corners, trees overhanging spacious old houses of the kind she adored. She could imagine evening life on those front porches, with the swings and the yellow porch lights. American beauty.

Up and down the streets of Willoughby she went, cruising around corners, flying up onto porches, going down alleys and into garages, anywhere she could go where there was enough visual information. She saw a girl on a horse passing by, people entering a local watering hole called the Glade.

She could order an air strike on this place, and only one man, who feared her and would not get near her, would need to sign off on the order. Well, screw George Hammond.

She was doing all this obsessive, useless flying because she wanted to find some indication of the danger here, or some indication that there wasn't any. But you could only see what the satellite saw, so you couldn't fly into houses, you couldn't go into basements, you couldn't go where hybrids might be hiding.

Christ, they'd harvested body parts from poor Massengill. The question was, why?

Now she glanced at Mark's position in the motel, now swept back out to the woods, watching for any sign of movement. But all was quiet. Mark's heart rate had slowed to 58 and his brain was flirting with alpha. He was napping, which was good. Among the skills he had developed was a sensitivity to the odor of hybrids, and he would not be this relaxed if he could smell them.

Lifting the stick, she swooped up out of the town to an altitude of fifty thousand feet. Then she went down into Big Basin State Park. She'd been through here a hundred times. It was one of her highest-priority locations because of an event here, in the summer of 2007, odd enough to come to her attention.

A group of cyclists gazing across a valley had photographed what was perhaps the strangest-looking object that had ever appeared in the skies of earth. It had a central core of large metal plates affixed to an inner circular gridwork, with wide beams jutting out of it at three angles. Above this rose a forest of twelve tapering antennae that seemed to grasp at the sky. Below it, pointing toward the ground—ominous, somehow—was a long spike.

One of the cyclists took a picture with his cell phone, which duly appeared on the Internet. She'd e-mailed the photo to Dr. Turner, who had sent back a note saying that it was a Photoshop job and to forget about it.

Gina had consulted her register of known forms of guided craft and found nothing like it.

Dr. Turner would say things like "Given that they're in advance of us technologically, we can expect them to also be in advance of us ethically."

It was not for her to criticize him, but it did occur to her that we'd already been civilized for four thousand years when the Holocaust took place, not to mention

the rise of communism and Islamic and Christian fun-
damentalism. The idea that older civilizations automat-
ically become more ethical did not actually wash, but
he made the policy around here, not her.

She went back to the murder woods. Still nobody
nearby. But it was only a question of time, wasn't it?
She knew that she should move that farm family out of
there and send state cops to flush out the campers.

She called up a computer-enhanced image of the three
people whose appearance here two weeks ago had
caused her to send Mark to the area in the first place. As
she had a dozen times, she zeroed in on the clearest face,
which was that of a woman. She'd measured that face
with great care, and all the ratios were well within human norms. That white sheen was the only difference.
Why was it there, and why didn't all of them display it?

She ran the video again. They crawled like spiders,
and here came the kicker, the young man came into
view. He was moving down the cliff—headfirst. No human being could do that, not even an acrobat.

She'd already upset Hammond by asking him what
should be done. Now that the situation had escalated,
she was going to need to contact him again, and that
was going to really make him unhappy.

The reason was, the political side of the organization
did not want to know about things that might blow up
in their faces. Better to be able to say that the facts had
been concealed from them by Company old hands.

A distant rumble drew her eyes to the window. Stormy
out there. Didn't matter to her, as long as it didn't disturb
her uplink. Still, some kind of major storm was pre-
dicted. All she needed just now.

Her mind returned to Dr. Turner. When she had asked
him, "Wouldn't they want the earth?" he had replied,
"They wouldn't. Their interest is us, not our planet, and

the only thing we actually have to offer them is innovation. So they will want to study us as closely as possible, enter our societies, take the measure of our world, all without us observing them. To them, we represent the new, and for an extremely old and advanced civilization, that must be a very valuable prize."

She worked her team as aggressively as she could without violating Turner's orders, worked them and watched over them—which brought her back to Willoughby and the woods that surrounded it.

Finally, she picked up her phone. She called Dr. Turner.

"Colonel Bryan has a KIA. Captain Massengill."

Silence. It extended.

So she continued, "What we are looking at is this. As soon as they took the casualty, I ordered a local withdrawal."

"What killed the man?"

"There was some sort of . . . I don't know how to describe it. Just say that the attack was highly asymmetric and that it involved a sort of lure in the form of hybrid bodies. There's video uploading now, so you're going to get a good look at the hybrids, which is one plus. But they were bait, and we took that bait, to our cost."

"How many were there?"

"Six, all in boxes, more in the woods. And what was so very odd is that each box was labeled with the name of one of our team members."

"I want to evaluate this. Let me look at that video as soon as possible."

"It'll be on the server in a few minutes. You'll be notified. Dr. Turner, be aware that this very volatile situation is right on top of some large population centers."

"You say Mark induced this?"

"He was examining the evidence—these boxes and

the creatures inside. Dr. Hicks was attempting to retrieve tissue samples for you."

"But there were weapons in use. Weapons fired. So he's the responsible party. He's the one who permitted this."

She could not deny it.

"Gina, this is a major problem with him. Very frankly, I'm surprised."

"I could not agree more, but we have a situation on the ground that requires immediate attention."

"What do you suggest?"

"We've had an aggressive move. I think we should drop in an air strike."

"We were the aggressors, Gina."

"I don't know the details of what happened, I wasn't there."

"It's your job to know the details!"

"Excuse me, it's my job to provide satellite-based surveillance in support of a field reconnaissance mission. Obviously, I am not going to be able to describe ground actions in detail beyond the limits of my equipment. The bottom line is that our man was killed. I want to pull Mark back. In fact, I already have. My suggestion is that we evacuate the civilians from the area and put down a load of napalm."

"That's a bonehead idea if I ever heard one."

"Thank you."

"An air strike is out of the question. Please understand this."

"Doctor, it's not to attack them. But we need to let them know that if they hurt us, we're going to be reactive. I'll put it in tight on the area where the event took place. They're long gone from there by now, but it will send a message."

"That we're aggressive."

"That we care about our people!"

He hung up on her. Anger made her grip the phone and curse under her breath. But his was an advisory position. He did not run this show, she did. She called her boss, George Hammond.

"You're supposed to e-mail. For the record."

"I had a KIA today, George."

"Shit!"

"I've pulled the rest of the team back and I don't want to return them to the site because there was some very weird aggression out there, and I think we need a much higher response profile. The time for reconnaissance has ended. What I want to do is put in a pinpoint air strike that'll destroy the human remains that have been left behind, then we take it from there. Otherwise, we're gonna have the locals all over us about this dead soldier, not to mention media."

"How pinpoint?"

"I'll send in an F-22. He'll put down a small incendiary, enough to incinerate the skeleton but limit the damage to a couple of acres of woods. I'll have him blow it out with HE." She waited while Hammond thought through the only question that would matter to him, which was what this might do to his career. Then she continued, "I need to cut my orders right now."

"Dr. Turner knows?"

"He knows." This was what she called a designer lie. Not entirely untrue. It just omitted his opinion of what he knew.

"Report when the operation is complete. And your colonel, let's bring him in. I think we need to talk this thing out with him and Dr. Turner, if we're gonna keep peace in the house."

"Consider it done."

Peace in the house was agency code for not doing

something that alerted the politicals to anything they didn't need to know, and no elected official wanted to know anything about hybrids lurking around that no-body could get a handle on. The media would go berserk, and when you tell any political anything this incredible, no matter how deeply classified you say it is, the media are going to rise up around you with the certainty of a drowning tide.

She went to her safe and opened it. Peering into its gray interior, she found her operations manual. She took it back to her desk and began working through it, read-ing the complex protocols that she needed to use if the operational orders she was about to cut were going to be heeded by the military.

Soon enough, she'd hear more from the outraged Dr. Turner. Maybe she'd be hung out to dry. But that was then, this was now. She had a forest to burn. She began cutting the orders.

She could not begin to imagine Turner's reaction to the video when he saw it, his horror and his rage, his pacing his office as if it were a locked cell, his sudden requisitioning of an aircraft.

He would confront her one last time, then, if he failed, he would do what he had to do.

CHAPTER SIX

WILLOUGHBY

IN WILLOUGHBY, THE NOON HOUR was marked by the low moan of the lumber mill's whistle, as it had been every noon since August 11, 1889, when the mill had been set to running, its big boilers fired with thousands of logs in a place where logs were plentiful beyond dreams.

Now, although the mill still made occasional runs and even brought in a small profit most years, the lumber whistle had long been silent, replaced by the lumber whistle MP3 file, and a digital PA system that had been installed by the Ludwig family, who still owned the mill.

In Willoughby, tradition meant a lot. In the Glade, the local watering hole, Jimmy W. Painter raised a glass to the familiar wail. When Jenny Pawlenty brought his sausage sandwich, he dug into the meal happily, starting with a mouthful of homemade kraut to prepare his taste buds, then biting through the crackling good skin of the sausage, penetrating to the deliciousness within. The Glade made its own sausage and you knew it. You knew that this was excellence, American style.

The Glade was not the only excellent thing here. There was also Becker and Tolland Books, which had opened its doors in 1921 and continued to thrive in a community that had a varied and keen taste for reading matter.

Two doors down from the BT was the Redwoods Café, which served coffees, teas, baked goods, and sandwiches. Small-town America, deep home, and deeply at peace. So nobody in Willoughby paid attention to the twenty-year-old Buick that came along State Road 16 in the path of the van of the church choir that had been around for the past couple of days, and certainly nobody understood that the four nondescript people in the car were tracking the van, or even interested in it.

The Buick passed the same farm that Mark and his team had passed, only now the tractor stood alone in the field, its engine ticking gently in the sweet noon wind, the lip of its exhaust stack slow-dancing on idle.

A horse ran, snorting and bucking, as if it were trying to throw an invisible rider. In a window of the farmhouse there stood a figure, male, wearing a shirt much too small for him and carrying what appeared to be a clutch of hair in his fist. The figure watched the car pass, then disappeared into the house. There were screams, but nobody to hear them except the horse, which tossed its head, then, when the following silence extended, bent down to graze.

The Buick did not stop as it passed the Sixteen Mo-Tel, nor did any of its occupants speak or even turn toward the low building with the faded western theme. Every one of them knew, to the millimeter, just how far they were from Mark Bryan, and every one of them reflected a growing anger at him. Something was wrong with him. He needed attention.

This is a complex universe we live in, full of many realities that we do not recognize or accept, vibrating lines of good and evil that free the world and trap the world, and along one of these living wires a dangerous tremor ran, causing Mark to sit up in his narrow bed and go to the window, and watch, uneasy. By that time, though, the Buick was just disappearing from view, and the thread of awareness snapped as the crucial information fell away.

The town reminded him of where he'd grown up outside Palo Alto. The quiet, sun-mottled street, the slowly passing cars, combined to draw his mind back to those days, and to the only people who had come close to being parents to him, the Walkers. Sergeant Walker had instilled a burning ambition in Mark to become a career soldier. So, as soon as his degree—history—was safely tucked away, he had joined up.

Where was old Sarge now? he wondered. Dead, could be. Twenty years ago, he and Emma had already been well along in years. He'd been a brilliant martial arts teacher. Why they had taken Mark in, he had never really understood. They didn't run a foster home and he was their only state-assigned child. Mark had loved the Walkers. In his early years, he'd known profound loneliness, and he was forever grateful to them.

After he left Palo Alto, Christmas cards were exchanged for the two years until he was sent on assignment to the Middle East. Since then, they had dropped off his radar, and because his work stateside was so secret, he could not even tell them he was here. He'd surfed for them on the Internet, and a lot had come up, but nothing personal. He didn't know their state of health, their hopes and plans, anything like that, only that they were distinguished people.

In the years with Sarge and Emma, only one thing had happened that had left him with an uneasy feeling. Once in the night, he'd woken up and seen two men standing over his bed. One had been Sarge, the other a civilian. He had asked them what they were doing there, but Sarge had put his finger to his lips, and they had left. Afterward, Mark's left temple had hurt, and he'd seen flashes in his left eye for days.

Absently rubbing his temple, remembering the event, he gazed at the far side of the street, where a restaurant called the Glade had another old-fashioned neon sign, this one in the shape of a palm tree, above its rustic front. A persuasive neon-sign salesman must have come through here back fifty years ago or so.

He watched a man emerge with a toothpick in his mouth, turn, and head off down the sidewalk. Maybe a local lawyer or barber or somebody from the mill, assuming that the whistle was real. It had not sounded to him like steam, though, but a recording of steam.

Mark felt a regard for the man coming out of the restaurant that was not love but was as deep as love. Soldiers suffer this feeling for those whom they protect, and it can make them hard to be with. A soldier's roughness, even coldness, may conceal tenderness too great for him to bear.

Now two girls on bicycles came riding past, their hair flowing, their long, smooth limbs bright as grace.

All of these people were in harm's way. But what could he do with five soldiers? He kept his God to himself, but he prayed now, looking out across the smiling noontime. His was a soldier's religion: Pray a lot, but carry your own damn gun.

Once again, he looked up and down the street. Quiet, his ears told him. Normal, his eyes observed.

Okay, that's it, daydreamer, there is something wrong out there.

He pulled out his satphone, opened it, and pressed the contact button. There was a click, then, "Lyndon."

"Are you watching us?"

"I am."

"See anything odd? In the town?"

"Not a thing."

"How about the rest of it? The farm?"

"All quiet."

"You've moved them out? The farm is abandoned?"

"I'm onto the local health department, but it takes time. I have to go through channels."

His love made these conversations painful for him, every one of them. To escape that pain, he confined his communications with her to the bare minimum necessary to do the job. He liked to imagine a quiet life with her in a comfortable, sweet town just like this. He imagined winning her love and thought often of the strangeness of women. On the night he'd spent with her, he'd given everything he had, but she had not fallen in love with him. He wondered often about her life, waited in dread for some mention that she had married a rich politician or lobbyist or whatever. He wanted her so badly, but how do you say that? How do you break through to a buried intimacy with somebody who has chosen to ignore it and address you only on a professional level?

"Advise me soonest, please," he said, his voice, as always, carefully professional in tone.

"Mark, it takes time."

This worried him. This was not right. "There are children out there. Children in harm's way."

"And we have major security issues," she snapped. Then she cut the connection.

Her bed, he recalled, had been big and old, her room full of the lightness of women, sweet with her scent.

He knew her well. And he knew, therefore, that her angry response meant that she had no quick way of setting up a false quarantine of that farm, and she was as worried as he was about those kids. She was helpless, though. He was not.

He stepped out onto the little porch that was tacked onto his room. His own hitchin' post for the horse, he supposed, of his dreams.

The sky was clear, the street still quiet, the air sharpened with the scent of pine.

No way could he commandeer some citizen's car. There was no cleanup crew to take care of a problem like that. Their operation was too secret for things like cleanup crews.

He stepped down off the porch, into the gravel of the parking lot, then went quickly to the van, walking so that his feet wouldn't crunch gravel, a sound that he knew would awaken his whole team and make them wary.

As he moved around the front of the vehicle, he wondered if Gina would see him. If so, he would sure as hell hear from her. As always, he wanted to and he didn't. So good to hear her voice. So hard.

When he reached the driver's door, he drew his phone from his pocket and turned it off. Another breach of regs, but he was going to save that family and he did not care to listen to her yelling at him. When she felt helpless, she could get abrasive.

Maybe they'd made love just the one time, but as surely as if the preacher had tied the knot, they were married, or rather, he was. Perhaps that was why he lived in such an anguish of longing, not to say jealousy.

He grasped the door handle and pulled—and almost pulled it off the vehicle, because the door was locked. Of course it was. Richardson would not have failed to secure.

Well, the locking mechanism on an elderly Ford was not going to be that difficult. He pulled the handle, dropped it, then yanked it back before the spring had loosened completely.

The door swung open and he slid into the driver's seat, drawing the door closed, but not all the way. The sound of a car door shutting was worse than feet crunching on gravel.

For a moment, he sat still, running his fingers under the dash. He had the van hot-wired and running almost faster than he could have started it using the key—and here was a sound they could not fail to notice. He threw the van into gear—and saw a face at the window, staring in at him.

"Help you, boss?"

Richardson was good. "You sleep too shallow, Private."

"My vehicle wakes up, I wake up. Sir."

"Look, I'm going back out to that farm, and I'm doing it alone."

"Unwise, sir."

"Thank you, Private."

The enlisted man stepped back from the door.

Mark guided the van out of the parking lot and accelerated onto the road, feeling the vehicle's weight, listening to the engine strain. But why shouldn't it strain, the thing was full of people.

He had, of course, known that Richardson was a decoy, and that the team had slipped into the van's bay while the diversion was in progress. He continued to drive, giving them no indication that he was aware of them. But they didn't need one. They knew that the feel of the van would reveal their presence. Since he didn't turn around and take them back, they prepared for action, pulling on their carries and arming up.

As he approached the farm, he slowed. Carefully, he regarded the farmhouse. Red tin roof, white siding recently applied over old boards. Two windows were upstairs, two down with a front door between. The door was disused, meaning that the family action was in back. Behind the house, he could see part of the roof of a barn, and another outbuilding, a garage.

As he continued along the road, moving slowly, he observed three things: The tractor was stopped in the field and that should not be, and something about the house was wrong. Coming here had been a good instinct, because what was off about the house was that all the curtains were drawn, and why would that be on a bright summer afternoon?

This morning, the only closed curtains had been in one of the upstairs bedrooms, so this was trouble, no question.

In the back of his mind was the thought that maybe hybrids were in there right now, and maybe he'd caught them flat-footed at last. Maybe the hunter would come home with a little game in his goddamn bag this time. He was no longer concerned about bring 'em back alive. No niceties. They would be butchered.

"Okay, people, you want to surround the structure. The idea is, maybe I flush something."

Linda asked, "You're going in?"

He left that question to die a silent death.

She said, "If you kill anything, for God's sake, try to leave it as intact as possible."

"I want at least two Metal Storms charged and ready," he said. "If you see any kind of attack coming, do not hesitate to use them."

"Colonel, we need bodies."

"We need to stay alive!"

Leaving his armor and his carry behind, he got out of the van. The equipment was good, but it made you lumber. If there was going to be a win here, it was going to be about speed, his pistol and his knife.

He ran up to the house. The layout would be a front room, a dining room, behind them a family room and a kitchen. Upstairs, four bedrooms. Maybe a mudroom on the back behind the kitchen.

He stood on the porch. Beside him was a green rocking chair, dusty from disuse. He could knock on the front door, but since he wasn't entirely stupid, he didn't do that.

The silence was absolute, not even the hum of bees in the front pasture, not a single creak from the house, certainly no voices, no sounds of activity.

He dove through the living room window and rolled up against a couch in a fog of pulverized glass and a tangle of curtains. Standing, he ripped them from his body and braced his weapon.

The room contained the couch, maroon, the cushions protected by clear plastic covers, a couple of standing lamps, a couple of chairs, a side table, and some incidental furniture. Nothing had been changed in here for a long time, certainly nothing today.

The room was old and comfortably human. He wondered, would they move into houses like this and simply start using them?

He moved through the arched doorway into the dining room, where a spray of wildflowers stood in a vase on an ornate old table. The flowers were fresh, brilliant blue and yellow blooms and tiny red ones. But how fresh? He touched a petal, rubbing it between his fingers. Mom had picked these at sunrise, from the wildflowers in the front pasture.

He took three long steps to his right and into the front hall. An odor here. He sucked it in. Hybrid? His eyes went to the understairs storage. Was it coming from there, and if so, would the pistol be fast enough?

He wasn't concerned about his own reaction time, it would be adequate. The question was, could the mechanism of the gun keep up with the speed of his hand? Maybe he should go to his knife.

He pulled the door to the storage open. Inside, a strange object. What the hell was it? He leaned in, wary. But—oh, hell, it was just an accordion. Images flashed before him of family nights, of singing. Killed happiness.

In quick succession, he did the kitchen and the family room. No joy. Then he listened. Even an empty house never stops moving, but an occupied one is filled with sounds, the pop of wood under weight, the creaks caused by shifts, even from one foot to another. His nostrils dilated as he sought again for that characteristic hybrid odor.

But what the hell, somewhere close by was a lot of raw meat. Not down here, though, and since the place was built on a slab, there was no basement.

He took the stairs three at a time, into a hallway with three doors, all closed. He checked the first bedroom, the master. It crossed the front of the house and contained only furniture, a neatly made bed, a dresser, a couple of chairs. The closet door was half-open. He went to it and kicked it all the way back, but nothing was inside but clothes. Not only that, up here, the odor of hybrids was less. He didn't do the other two rooms, he didn't need to. His careful senses told him they were empty, too.

Back downstairs, he returned to the front porch. To his surprise, he found the odor stronger out here.

His people must see him, but nobody appeared. Being careful. He motioned to them to come out. Now there was a sound, the distant cry of a hawk. His heart quickening just a little, he stepped down off the porch. Still, nobody emerged.

He'd been doing extreme operations too long not to know, right now, that there was trouble. His reaction was to reduce his exposure, and he backed up to the wall of the house. Now he gauged the situation. There was a light breeze out of the woods, and the smell was coming from that direction, and it wasn't only hybrids, it was— well, it was raw blood.

The .45 was good if he was the aggressor and thus had the advantage of surprise, but it would not work here. He holstered the pistol and drew the knife. With it, the only mechanism to worry about was his own nervous system.

He went toward a stand of trees upwind, out about a hundred yards past the barn. As he moved among the closely crowded pines, he glimpsed a flash of clothing.

"Guys?"

There was movement in the shadows, then he saw something so completely impossible that it affected him not like a real event, but a scene from a movie.

Captain Massengill said, "Hi, Colonel."

This was not possible. This man was destroyed and dead. But here he was, very much alive. Mark said nothing.

"Colonel, there's somebody who wants a meet. Among the hybrids. I think it's a breakthrough, Colonel."

A sound. Whistling, in and out, in and out. Then a shadow among the trees, a figure.

Massy turned, and as he did so, he uttered a sound that made things instantly clear to Mark. It wasn't that the sound had meaning, but that it did not. It wasn't a human sound.

Mark took a step forward, then another, then he slid

the knife into the creature's back. It gasped, then threw its head back, and the depth of the despair in its cry revealed yet more to Mark. This creature was self-aware. It conceived of itself as an individual or it would not feel death with such sorrow.

Mark grabbed it by the shoulders and shook it with all his power, and as he expected, when he turned it around, Massy's face was nothing but loose flaps of skin. Disgusted almost to the point of gagging, he threw the remains aside.

They intended to disguise themselves with human skins. So they were extremely dangerous and extremely hostile. No surprise to him, but it would probably be denied in official Washington. The "scientific committee" wouldn't hear of it, no doubt.

Didn't matter to him. He had a clear and dangerous enemy, and nothing any damn scientist could say was going to change the way he planned to react. He would kill hybrids until none were left alive.

Reducing his exposure, he backed up against a tree trunk.

He needed to see his people. He needed this right now. "Deltas, come to me."

A moment more and something walked stiffly into view. He saw pink limbs covered with some sort of tangle. The odor of blood was strong.

He tried to understand what this was. Some kind of new mutant? But then—the hair was still there, floating above the working musculature of the face, the recognizably human shape of the body.

Then he made sense of the tangle that covered it: Those were blood vessels. So the pulsating, pink material was raw muscle from which the skin had been removed so skillfully that the body had remained intact. The naked eyes darted as the figure came closer.

This was Knotty, flayed with such extraordinary skill that he had been left alive. The whistling was his breath sucking in and out past his exposed teeth. His eyes flickered here and there, the muscles around them tightening and loosening. He took a huge breath, threw back his head, and screamed like a desperate child.

Mark was too shocked to move—and then it got worse. Scattered in the woods were his whole team. Burke and Louis had been surgically attacked the same way Massy had, gutted, their eyes taken. No doubt their skin would be harvested later.

Mark found a new intensity of hate. Or, no, it was an emotion beyond hate, a fire in him that would only be quenched by revenge.

Knotty tried to speak, and Mark heard a rasping attempt to apologize for his failure. Then he fell, thankfully unconscious.

Had he lost them all? "Linda! *Linda*!"

There was no response from her, but he became aware of the sound of a jet engine, the intensity of it telling him that this was a fighter on afterburners.

With a wet thud, Louis threw his skin to the ground. Mark could hardly look at the goggling eyes and gaping mouth, or at the poor man's pulsating body.

This was the most profoundly cruel thing he had ever known. Normally, he did not feel any emotion about his missions except the desire to succeed. His mind concentrated on the professional problems.

But seeing good family men such as Massy and Louis just devastated like this—this was more than just a mission-critical issue, it was personal and it hurt his heart as much, he thought, as his heart could be hurt, and he vowed in the depths of that heart that he would live from now on to destroy hybrids and die willingly doing it, if that became necessary.

Linda came out of the woods.

"You—you're okay! Oh, Jesus, what—"

She was stark naked and shivering. Her skin was intact, but oddly flushed.

At that moment, the jet screamed directly overhead. He recognized not only the afterburner this time, but the distinctive shriek of an F-22 Raptor's Pratt & Whitney turbofans being slammed into a new thrust vector.

The pilot was setting up an attack.

The woods—Gina was burning them out. He calculated—the target area was three quarters of a mile away from this farm, and the jet had been slowing down to deliver a superaccurate strike, so—

To be certain that they wouldn't suffer more if the fire reached here, he shot Louis and the others in the back of the head, moving fast, making sure they were dead.

They were all dead now, all except Linda and PFC Richardson.

From above there came a loud snap, followed by the hiss of a missile leaving its nest.

He took off his parka and threw it over Linda's shoulders. "Let's move, Gina's doing the woods."

A gigantic roar filled the air, and with it came the oily stink of napalm as the forest bloomed with fire. A moment later, this was followed by the wild crackle of hundreds of cluster bombs detonating.

Mark shielded Linda as best he could from the waves of heat and the deafening roar. He guided her toward the house and the van beyond it.

An explosion came, so huge and so close that it seemed to pull the air right out of their lungs.

Screaming, Linda threw herself to the ground.

"It's high explosive," he shouted. "They're putting down the fire, it's not going to hurt us."

Again the sound came, rocking them, shattering every window in the house. It was followed by the eerie warble of the Raptor's engines vectoring thrust as the pilot performed a modified Kulbit, quickly repositioning the plane for another strike. The plane looked like a silver leaf hanging in the sky, then actually backing up on its incredible thrusters.

There were four more strikes. Gina was nothing if not thorough.

As they jumped into the van, Mark turned on his phone—and was instantly greeted by beep after beep. Urgent calls from Gina, six of them. Oh, she'd have him up on charges now, you bet.

He pressed her contact button.

"Lyndon."

"You're off target, lady. Do the farm."

"What in hell's holy name are you doing out there, you brain-dead moron? Some friggin' genius you are!"

"Do the farm and the woods behind it right now."

"The hell, I'm gonna do that Ford van I see leaving the farm. That van is fulla morons. They're worse than hybrids."

He let her rant. When she stopped, he said again out of the well of his sadness and his rage, "Do the farm. For me, Gina. Especially the woods behind it."

There was a short silence, then, "Get out of there, Mark. Please, I cannot lose you."

The jet wheeled around overhead, and the farm disappeared into a gigantic curtain of flame.

As they crossed the bridge, they passed a stopped convoy of local fire equipment, their light bars flashing, the men standing in the roadway watching the action. Obviously, they had orders not to proceed until directed.

"That was very fast, Gina."

"What in hell were you doing out there?"

He took a breath. Beside him, Linda was curled up in her seat, her face in her hands. He would speak, he would sound professional.

"Gina, I have lost all my people except Hicks and Richardson. They are all KIA, all sight-confirmed."

"Mark, I'm sure you were out there for a reason, and I'm accepting that. But I will need a full report, without fail!"

She hung up.

Mark drove in silence, watching the afternoon slowly sink to gold around him. In Willoughby, he stopped and picked up Richardson, and they put every trace of the unit into the back of the van, every can of shaving cream, every pair of olive drab underwear, every Bible and every smiling photograph. Then Richardson paid the bill and got behind the wheel, and they pulled out.

Mark looked toward the Glade. Evening was falling and its bright green neon sign had come on. Its faint buzzing was the only sound on the whole street. A night wind, still sweet with the scents of pine and summer flowers, filtered in his window. Later, the wind would grow stronger, Mark thought, when the moon rose. Fortunately for the town, it was easterly, and so was blowing the smoke of the fire away toward Big Basin. He wondered what they were being told, how the explosions were being explained. Well, that was Gina's department, not his.

Linda was still in the back of the van, huddled in a seat. She cradled a disassembled Metal Storm, trying first one way to set it up, then another. Mark clambered back beside her, took it, and snapped it together.

"This is the firing button," he explained—and she

put her finger on it. He pulled her hand away. "There's no safety. You discharge it in here, we're done."

Even though she was now once again fully dressed and hauling her carry, she was trembling like a child in a storm, and he put his arm around her.

"It was Massy," she said.

"I know."

"We were confused. What was Massy doing there? He was dead, for God's sake! We started to walk up to him. I mean, we thought maybe—we hoped, Mark! And then the guys, Jesus, these things came in so damn quick, they had sort of rods—silver rods—and all of a sudden, Knotty—he was kind of dancing, he was naked, he was flushed red—and I ran, Mark. I ran." She took a long breath. "It was an ambush—and, oh, Jesus, it was so fast!" She was silent for a moment. "Did anybody make it?"

"You did. Because you ran when you did."

As they went along the highway, Linda wept silently, Richardson drove, and Mark thought of how the trap his men had fallen into had been laid not only on the farm but also in his own mind. Somebody had understood that he would go back out there. Somebody had known that his people would be with him. And they had waited, and they had delivered a horrific blow, the destruction of his beloved unit. His fault, no question whatsoever there.

They were taking organs, including skin, which is an organ just like the heart and the liver.

He found himself watching Linda and wondering why she alone had been spared.

Four bicyclists stopped as they passed by and watched them go. After they were sure the van was gone, they got on their bikes and rode some distance out of town, where they were met by the old Buick. The whole group pulled off into the brush and carefully concealed the vehicles.

They went quickly back into the forest, going deep, and then into a cave, and deep into the cave, and then into an enormous hollow darkness that echoed with laughter and great, roaring cries, full of passion, triumph, and exploding joy.

CHAPTER SEVEN

YOU ALWAYS HURT THE ONE YOU LOVE

GINA CRADLED A MUG OF coffee in her hands. She had extended the burn, and never mind Dr. Turner and his whining. This was war now.

She watched the jet return, swooping low over the inferno. An instant later, a carpet of white clouds appeared in and around the flames. This would be more high explosive knocking down the fire and, she now hoped, pulverizing any hybrids still twitching.

God, what an unimaginable disaster. He'd had a major military failure out there. Not like him, not at all.

She was to blame. She should have done something about that farm family sooner. She should have understood that he and his men would go back if she didn't.

She gazed at the picture of her mother and father that stood on her desk. Was he mocking her again, this time from the grave? He had mocked her decision to follow him into the Company. He'd been an old Cold Warrior, caustic and cynical and bitter after a lifetime of betrayal and failure. We beat the Soviets economically but they won the intelligence war, and her father had felt that failure deeply.

A daughter learns men from her father, how to seduce them, how to accept them, how to trust them. Her father was cold and here she was, slavishly attracted to a cold man. She trusted him, though.

Her door buzzed. Immediately, she flipped a switch that blanked all the monitors. A glance at the entry screen showed the face of the man she had been expecting and dreading.

She watched him wait. Even when he wasn't angry, you could see the rage in Dr. Turner, a bitter glow behind his eyes. Now, they glared into the camera as he hit the buzzer again. The man was somewhere in his seventies. He should be slowing down, his edges softening. He was full of driving energy and that seething, subsurface rage that made him so hard to bear. You could see him slapping the hell out of his wife, except he had no wife. His work was his wife.

She went to the door, took a breath, and opened it. In the full light of the office, she was appalled at what she was seeing. She hadn't been face-to-face with him in perhaps three weeks, which made the transformation all the more extraordinary. He must have lost twenty pounds. His face, always narrow, was sunken, his eyes deep and inlooking. He pulled a handkerchief out of a side pocket and wiped his brow so hard it looked as if he were trying to clean off a stain. He wore one of his two-thousand-dollar suits, but it hung on him and was dirty, obviously slept in. His gray shirt was open. And this in a man who had always been almost absurdly fastidious. He used to smell like cologne. Now he smelled like sour, old sweat.

"Change of policy," he said.

"We did what we had to do."

He dropped into a chair. Were there tears at the edges of his eyes?

"I know what you did."

"And you disagree. You're here to lodge a protest."

His face changed, and she saw something else, an unidentifiable tangle of emotions. What was this—the face of a spurned lover, a paranoid, a dying man? A cruel face, certainly.

"He's a slick bastard," he said, his voice as smooth as velvet. He leaned toward her. "Hit him. Hit him hard, Gina."

Now, this did surprise her. "Hit who?"

He snorted out a laugh. "I have some information for you."

"Go ahead."

"Your lover—that remarkable boy—is not onside."

Fear does predictable things. It makes you still, and she became as still as a cornered animal. It dries your mouth, and hers became sand. It makes you cold, and she shuddered. Dangerously, it can slow thought and impair thought, and she told herself to guard against this. She told her training to kick in now. Step back, maintain perspective.

"What are you talking about?" she asked, trying to keep both the lilt of false unconcern and the tremor of fear firmly suppressed.

"I've wasted a lot of time because of him," he muttered. He made a constricted, chopping gesture. "No more."

"What are you trying to tell me, Doctor?"

His eyes seemed to seek some inner destination. "Do you understand what happened out there?"

"We laid down a small air strike, mostly to incinerate the remains of Captain Massengill before some local came along. Now there's been an escalation, obviously."

Instead of responding to this, he shifted his eyes away from hers. What was he concealing? She was having difficulty understanding. There was a lot she did not know, that much was clear. But in a highly classified project such as this, "need to know" was a constant issue.

"Maybe I need to know."

"What?"

"Whatever you're not saying."

"That's quite a system you've got there." He gestured weakly toward her bank of screens.

"Thank you."

"So use the goddamn thing!"

She'd watched the strike unfold. All had seemed normal. Then Mark had appeared at the farm. She'd been furious, but had been concentrating on managing that strike. She was looking at thousands of acres of redwood forest, and she could not let the fire go out of control.

"He hasn't reported in, has he?"

"Mark? Of course he has. He's awaiting orders."

"You have tape of his action? Have you watched it?"

"I was about to. Obviously, there's going to be a review board. I'll watch it, do my evaluation, then put a time-stamped impound on it for the board."

"Watch it now."

"I—you'll need to leave." He wasn't cleared to see her system in operation.

"Do it this moment," he rasped, "or I'll see you in prison."

She'd never heard a tone of voice quite like that before or seen a expression like the one now on Turner's face. She only knew a small part of what he knew, and the man was like a volcano about to explode. So she went across the room and activated her system, touching a few keys, going back to a view of the area of the strike zone.

He'd come close behind her. "Not there. The farmhouse."

She leaned into her controls, backing the view out a little. There was the farmhouse standing in its little yard of yellow flowers.

"What am I looking for?"

"Back it up about ten minutes."

As she did so, she saw Mark's van pull up and his team get out and move into the woods behind the house. He disappeared onto the porch.

She switched to infrared. This way, she could see the figures under the trees, red shadows moving with the care of the skilled hunters that they were. Each man was identified with an infrared-visible helmet symbol. She watched them penetrate the woods, followed by Dr. Hicks. Lovely woman, Linda Hicks . . . whose duty caused her to spend every moment of her time with Mark, damn her.

The men stopped, but not entirely. Slowing the visual down, it looked as if they were executing a precise, directed motion, as if each of them was being pushed back and forth at high speed between invisible figures.

This sight made chilling sense to her, though, because hybrids had a low infrared signature.

"This is the attack," she whispered.

Another heat signature appeared, moving fast from the house to the woods—Mark. The smeared red blotch of his infrared image paused a moment, then shot toward the woods.

She flipped on the recording of his telemetry. His heart was thundering, his breath roaring.

Obviously she should have watched this and not the air strike. But she'd been so concerned about containing the fire.

The heart rate shot from 70 to 160, and Mark, for just an instant, disappeared.

Turner remained silent.

She returned to the moment when he had come out of the house and switched back to visible light. He moved about thirty feet, then, in under a twenty-fifth of a second, was gone. The next time she picked him up, she had to go to infrared, because he was already beneath the trees.

She sat staring at the screen, then ran it again. He came down off the porch, turned toward the woods, took a few steps—and then again, that blur.

In other words, he'd gone over fifty yards in under the twenty-fifth of a second it took the optics to refresh themselves.

This satellite had no high-speed camera, so she couldn't see more detail of his movements when he was going extremely fast. She didn't need to, though, because there was no question in her mind. No human being, no matter how fast, could do what she was seeing him do.

Turner reached over and hit her pause button. "You will find that after getting his entire unit killed by his compadres who were hiding in the woods, he personally delivered the coups de grâce."

Again, she looked at the image, but this time she let it run. She watched Mark in the forest, saw his dying men come slowly toward him. At that moment, the bright twin stars of the attacking jet's afterburners flooded the infrared image as the plane sped between the satellite and the ground.

When imagery returned, Mark and Linda were leaving the woods. Then the whole picture erupted with yellow-white haze as the napalm exploded a few hundred yards away.

Gina shifted back to visible light and watched the two of them cross to the van, which immediately started up and drove off down the road. Nothing abnormal about his movements when Linda was present.

Gina returned to the steps he had taken from the house to the woods—and again, there was that flicker, just like a hybrid. She went to the frame counter, ran it. Every frame was intact, nothing dropped. So this was not equipment or signal failure.

"So now you know what he is," the doctor said. "What're you going to do about it?"

For the moment she was too shocked to respond.

"What are you going to do!"

"Excuse me, but you didn't pull his name out of a hat. You sent me his file for a reason, Dr. Turner. What was that reason?"

"Classified."

"I have an obvious and urgent need to know!"

"What I need to know is how you intend to contain this threat."

She looked at her phone. Picked it up. No hesitation. This had to be done.

"Hi, Gina," George Hammond said, "I'm listening on your feed, so I'm up to speed." Yeah, her "feed." Read *bug*. Her office was bugged. So was her house, she assumed. Her whole damn life, actually.

She glanced over at Turner. He could not hear what she wanted to say to her boss.

"We need to meet, George."

"Safe room. See you there."

Hanging up, she directed her attention to Turner. "You recommended Colonel Bryan. You allowed him to penetrate our operation. When there's an investigation— and there will be one, I assure you—the first question is going to be why you proposed him for this duty."

"He was appropriately trained and cleared according to legal requirements."

"Then what is he? Who is he?"

"Someone who has done us harm. So you need to take action immediately, and I will be watching, you can be sure."

"Doctor, he moves like a hybrid, but you recommended him! What am I dealing with, here?"

Turner did not reply.

As she got up from her workstation, the world seemed to recede, reality itself to implode into a tiny, white-hot pinpoint of betrayal and anguish. She had made love with—what? A thing? What was he?

No wonder he'd been so indifferent to her afterward. He was an automaton, a sophisticated robot. She'd made love to a machine.

"I'm leaving," she said. "You can't stay here."

He stood up and came toward her, looking down at her from his considerable height, a great, looming skeleton, glaring at her with a strange—was it curiosity?

"What? Why are you looking at me like that?"

He remained silent.

"This will be contained," she said. "Mark will be dealt with." She stepped out into the silent corridor, waited for Turner, then locked her door and activated the alarm. Her flesh crawling to be near him, they passed the long row of locked gray doors in silence and came to a stop before the elevators. Distantly, wind roared. The storm had picked up.

How could she ever explain herself? She'd been completely duped, and her own blind, stupid, adolescent infatuation was responsible. She'd never grown up properly, look at the childish way she relished the power this job gave her, look at her immature overreaction to a man—if you could even call him that—whom she'd slept with exactly once, and look at the consequences.

She turned a corner, saw two people, a man in a gray,

worn suit and a woman with him, prim, studiously casual, her expression carefully neutral. As she approached the elevator bank, they stopped talking together and stood in silence. On this floor, you didn't greet people and you didn't converse with your colleagues when people outside of your section were present. In fact, on this floor, you wished they weren't there.

She and Dr. Turner and the silent two went down together, she to the third floor, they to wherever.

She stepped out, not looking back at Turner, not willing to. He had a piece of this disaster, and she was damned if she was going to take the whole hit. George had better close ranks with her, though, or she was toast, that was clear.

What if Mark wasn't the only hybrid in the military? If there were more of them who looked as human as he did, they could be anywhere.

She swiped her finger on the safe room's entry point. It seemed to take forever for the system to recognize her and buzz her in.

Inside, Hammond, looking pinched and terribly uneasy, sat at the large table.

"George." She cleared her throat and sat down.

"You handled that jerk pretty well."

"He's the responsible party. He recommended the man. Did the vetting. The clearance records are from his office, not ours."

They looked at one another in silence, each of them considering the complexity of the problem they were facing, trying to work through the maze of secrecy that surrounded the whole muddy situation.

"Turner was involved in the alien-human technology exchange," George said carefully.

"Is he on our side? Or a traitor?"

"Either he planted Mark Bryan on us and it's time to roll them both up, or Mark slipped through."

"I need to know more because that doesn't tell me what to do. He wants me to assassinate Mark."

"Gina, I'm the one on the front line with this now. Because of a screwup I had nothing to do with."

"Neither did I, George."

"You fell in love, God damn you!"

"Jesus, George!"

"Gina, this creature that was your lover lured our soldiers into an ambush. If you hadn't been so frigging apeshit over him, maybe you would've seen something earlier. Maybe you would have saved their lives."

So she was being thrown to the wolves. There would be no support from this direction. And worse, she probably deserved it—not as much as Turner, perhaps, but she deserved it.

George tossed her a memo, a single, heavily redacted page referencing "DNA Editing via Zinc Finger." The only visible words were the reference itself.

"Okay, I'll bite. What's Zinc Finger?"

"Perhaps the most extraordinary means of altering genes ever devised. A zinc finger is a cellular structure that turns them on and off. An atom of zinc holds two loops of protein together. The fingers recognize specific DNA sequences. Using them—if you can figure out how to do that—you can edit the genome. Profoundly, and with great accuracy."

"You could make a hybrid?"

"You could do all sorts of things. Among them, make the dream of the perfect soldier real."

"So it's connected with Inner Iron?"

"Intimately connected. The process has been used to grow organs that repair themselves. Limbs that regrow.

But more than that, brains unlike any we've ever known. Memristors, which are artificial neurons—"

"I know what they are. They were perfected in 2010. Programmable neurons."

"They were perfected long before that. They became part of the public record in 2010. Using zinc fingers, they can be inserted into brains. They offer extraordinary intelligence enhancement. Even programmability. In other words, superstrong, superintelligent biomechanical creatures—"

"But not human."

"What I know is this. The DNA report that finally came in from DARPA says that genetic manipulation via zinc fingers is the only way hybrids with genetic mixes like what we're seeing could have been created."

"But smart? As smart as we are? Because Mark is very smart. How could somebody that smart be—what? What is he?"

"I fear very much that in seeking perfect soldiers, they have created extraordinary monsters. Stronger than we are, more ruthless, more cunning, more intelligent."

"But programmable. So we need to reprogram them."

"Given that they're smarter than we are, I doubt that they're going to let us do that. Even if we had the technology."

"But we must have the technology. We created them!"

"They are beyond human. What we are facing are gods of destruction."

"Mark seemed very human to me."

"The first couple of models were mostly human, as I understand it. At least, on the surface."

"How many were there?"

"Two individuals. Generation one and generation two. Then Turner began experimenting with more efficient forms. More aggression from the animal world. More memristors and alien DNA for greater intelligence. Above all, less human feeling. Or none, actually."

"You never suspected Mark was the—what?—prototype? You just let Turner put him out there?"

"Gina, they were all destroyed, all of them. So, no, I did not. I assumed that he was exactly what Turner said he was, a master tracker from Delta Force. The Hybrid Project was closed down, the creatures destroyed. That's why I assumed that these had been created by the aliens. We all did."

"Except Turner."

"I'm not sure."

"I fell in love with what appeared to be a human being. I had no way of knowing otherwise. To the contrary, I believed the record I was given. I had no reason not to. So don't hang me out to dry here."

"Just as we were an evolutionary leap beyond Neanderthals, this new creature is an evolutionary leap beyond us." George gazed out the window. "There's heavy weather in the Carolinas," he muttered.

"George?"

"I'm sorry. It's just hard. What's happening is so damned disturbing. Turner's creatures are dead and gone for years. The nightmare has ended. Now, suddenly, here they are, right in our face."

Sorrow was there in the wilted gaze, anger in the tight run of his lips, and something furtive, a trapped animal's hopeless calculation.

For a long time, he looked at her. Evaluating. Considering. Finally he asked her, "Do you know why you're in the job you're in?"

"Dr. Turner—"

"Dr. Turner, precisely. He recruited you and I approved the recruitment. Your father and I worked together overseeing his project. Your dad was intelligence attaché to Dr. Turner's group. I was on Senator Rockefeller's intelligence oversight staff. Your dad came to me with the report you have in your hands. The Senate Intelligence Committee took one look at it and canceled the whole hybrid program. A grotesque, immoral nightmare, they thought, that could lead in some very bad directions. The idea of brilliant, ruthless, and almost unkillable soldiers who had no human rights was interesting, of course. But programmable? No. Dr. Turner's budget was pulled."

"But why was I brought in? Simply because of my father?"

"Largely not. You have exceptional electronics skills."

She couldn't disagree. Most of the equipment in her office she'd revised herself. There was always something that could be done to add functionality or increase efficiency.

"You think he intentionally preserved some of them? Or they survived? How were they killed?"

"You don't want to know how they were killed. But it was thorough."

"Unless it wasn't."

"Turner's argument before the senators was that he could save the soldier from the battlefield. He believed in his work totally. So, yes, he might well have kept it going, hidden in some budget somewhere. And that might be what's out there, getting out of control."

"You've known all of this, and yet we were just a recce unit. Strictly tasked not to kill."

"Dr. Turner gave no indication that there might be a problem. It's been years since his project was dismantled. Gina, you have to understand that the departure of the aliens was a tragedy for us. We wanted their friendship. So the appearance of successful hybrids was cause for celebration. Even with all the limitations—they couldn't remain long in our atmosphere, they didn't use verbal communication—we'd learned so much from them. Now here was a chance to meet them again, but on much more useful terms. Speech, at last. The ability to breathe Earth's air, to exchange with our scientists, to teach us. We were delighted."

"Except—"

"Except now we're in terrible trouble."

"Do we know these hybrids aren't alien? For certain?"

He nodded slowly. "Their DNA profile fits the configuration Dr. Turner created."

"The senators must be furious."

"The senators have not been told. We'll clean it up, then bring it to the politicians."

"So they're—what?—mixes of genes from all sorts of different creatures? Reptiles whose limbs regrow, insects whose organs are self-repairing."

"There's a lot of different genes. Including alien. Plus there are the artificial elements—"

"The programmability."

He sighed. "They're highly intelligent. They've probably gained control over their own programming. Including Mark's."

"Have you seen them? They're sleek, like snakes. That pearl-white skin. But Mark is utterly human."

"You keep returning to that." George reached toward her, then, after a moment, withdrew his hand. "The early generations were too human. Insufficiently ruthless."

"Jesus, George, what am I gonna do with this?"

"What you have to," he snapped, and she knew at once where the conversation was going.

Surely you can't love somebody who isn't completely

human—except that her heart was not telling her that. Her heart was screaming that you can, and deeply and dearly, and you can long for him and fear for him. And she found her heart, and it was breaking.

"You say alien DNA is involved. They left DNA behind?"

He raised his eyebrows. "They lived here and died here for two generations, so, yes, we have their DNA. But the sorcerer grew tired of us, of Earth, of all of it. Lost interest and went home." George's gaze grew distant. "I'm very much afraid that this is the work of the sorcerer's apprentice."

"Tell me what you want done, George, and I'll do it. Maybe I got blindsided and even perhaps intentionally seduced, but never doubt my loyalty to mankind and to my country. Never doubt it, George."

"I never would, Gina."

"You came in doubting it. You doubt it now."

"Tell you what, you kill him. Do it the second we're out of this meeting."

She fought for balance, grabbed at it, said smoothly, "He could be a very useful study. If, say, I tell him to come in. Then we take him."

She could feel her fingernails digging into her palms and didn't care.

"Gina, kill him. He is a hybrid, and as such he is a more profound enemy of mankind than any of us have ever known."

"He's not hostile to mankind. And anyway, you said yourself that he was human."

"He's programmable, never forget that. Maybe the other hybrids have changed his loyalties."

"There was good in him. A lot of it."

"Gina, you do not defend him. You do this!"

"Okay, fine, but how? No assassin is gonna get to him. Ain't gonna happen. I'll need an air strike and he's in a town."

"So lure him back into the field. For chrissakes!"

"Okay!"

George folded his arms. Appraising. "Is your having screwed him going to be a factor? I have to ask."

Unbidden, Mark came before her in the glow of memory, his inner power flashing in his splendid eyes, his body rippling with strength, his lips touched by the subtle smile that never left his face.

"I was seduced."

George nodded slowly.

"So let's just confirm that I am being ordered to have Colonel Bryan killed."

"You're being ordered to try."

As she stood up from the table, a tumult of emotions poured through her, and with them the most vivid and sensual thoughts of Mark. But it wasn't her usual forlorn desire. She didn't like it, but she was experiencing a sort of bizarre pleasure right now. His death would mean a kind of freedom, and that was certainly part of it. But another part of it was that—well, that it was power. It was power over. And it was sick and should not be part of her.

"Gina?"

She looked away.

"You can do this? I can count on you?"

"Of course," she snapped. "Given how much I apparently have to prove." She turned and all but hurled herself out of the room.

Behind her, she heard George say faintly, "Keep me informed."

She did not reply, could not, not without her voice revealing her anguish.

Not even in her office did she give vent to her feelings. George had revealed the degree to which he listened and watched. The more secret your work, the less private your life.

So, how to do this? George was right about one thing, she couldn't send a professional assassin after Mark. The assassin would be killed himself. Or a team. Same result.

She opened up her monitors. She would order him into an isolated area, then call down one monster air strike on his head.

Through her tears and the terrible, incomprehensible pleasure that was telling her that she did not understand herself and making her loathe what she did not understand, she began to hunt down the man she loved.

CHAPTER EIGHT

IN THE WILD

WHEN HE FIRST SAW THE picture that had been dropped on Flickr, Tom Turner had been hopeful. The aliens had succeeded after all, and they were back with their own hybrids. So perhaps now all mankind could begin to enjoy the benefits of a relationship with them.

He had not even asked himself if there was any possibility that his hybrids had somehow survived. Simply put, they had not.

Then he had received the shock of his life. The first blurry video sent back by Mark and his team told him for certain that generation three had not only survived, it had multiplied.

These were his own creatures, no question, he could see that they had the facial features he had designed. Unless the aliens had copied them exactly, which seemed extremely improbable, these were cloned versions of his original designs.

He recognized two versions of Gamma, one of Alpha, four of Zeta—there could be no question, the hybrids were out there in the wild, and unless some sort of chain of command was established, the little bit of trouble they were causing right now was going to become an enormous tragedy.

He remembered the huge splash as the containment had hit the water, and that booming that had come from within, which had torn at his heart and still tore at his heart.

To do this, he had to believe that they were using the equipment in the old lab. They had to be, there was nothing else like it on earth. He had to find out. He had to try to reach them and gain control over them, because they were misidentifying friendly Delta Force operators as enemies. As with any replicated device, defects were bound to set in as new generations were created.

So he had come here, back to a place he had vowed never to go again. He had suffered during his flight as he had never suffered before in his life. Again and again, his mind had returned to his work, to the programming he and Emma had done, and what might have gone wrong with it and, above all, how in the world the threes had survived.

Nothing could live through being sunk into the Challenger Deep, not the pressure of seven miles of water. It would have crushed the vessel flat, and those brilliant, mysterious beings, his beloved soldiers . . . he couldn't even think about it, not even after all these years.

They had—and had not—been in the containment, and he thought he knew what they had done.

While the hybrids the aliens created had been bizarre psychopathic failures, he had succeeded too well.

He had been miserable about the aliens' leaving. He'd hated them for their impatience, and hated the senators who'd ruined his project through their boneheaded stupidity.

Now, as he drove through San Francisco toward his old lab, he hated himself for his mistakes, and the disaster that was now unfolding because of them. He had to admit, now, that the senators had not been entirely wrong, because this was going to be difficult to control. Very difficult.

And there it was, the nondescript building now festooned with signs affirming its new role as San Francisco's "most watched" station.

For a time, he sat in the car just looking at it. Since the day they'd sealed the underground lab and left until this day, he had been unable to come back to this place. Then, he had been too unhappy to do it. Now, as he looked up at the building, he felt a new emotion. He was afraid. He'd rather be entering a cage with a famished tiger.

The television station had transformed his beloved building entirely. The windows where his bedroom had been were blacked out. Probably the residential floor had been opened up into soundstages.

He sat in the car, double-parked, looking up at the building and remembering his lab, which had been a place of miracles.

Two devices were salvaged from Dulce, a magnificent piece of alien engineering that could actually alter the genetic code of stem cells, sequence by sequence, and an ultradense gas-crystal memory editor that could withdraw the entire memory contents of a brain, even a large brain, from a body, enable it to be programmed and edited, then replace it in the brain, or any brain with enough memory capacity.

Both devices were beyond the extraordinary, but the memory editor was at least comprehensible. It quantum-entangled modeled neurons in its memory with real ones in the target brain, then duplicated their coherence potentials, meaning that the precise contents of the neuron were transferred to the machine memory.

The body could then be destroyed or allowed to die, and the whole contents of its brain placed in a new version—or an entirely different body, as long as the brain was compatible with the stored information.

Was the duplicate person that resulted the same, or somebody different?

The aliens didn't care. They used this device to achieve immortality, also to alter their memories, even to implant purchased memories of things they had never done and places they had never been. Among the many activities they carried out on earth, aside from attempting to hybridize themselves with human beings, was to use sophisticated implants to gather desirable human memories for later resale. They did a lot of things here. They mined Earth for some sort of material that repelled gravity. It was found embedded in lead, iron, and uranium seams, from which it had to be extracted atom by atom. They took human eggs and semen to other planets and presumably created their own human beings there.

All of these were reasons why they demanded that their presence be kept secret. There had been threats, the first one delivered to President Eisenhower in 1952: Do it our way, or you risk the death of Earth.

The gene splicer was mechanical, not chemical, which was what made it even more amazing. Its working parts could only be seen under an electron microscope. There were needles, for example, just ten atoms thick.

With such precision available, there was no need to use crude chemical techniques such as restriction enzymes to coax sequences apart so that new genes could be added. You could design any gene combination you wanted, then grow it in an embryo in the lab.

The first one of these—mostly human—had been inserted into a host female, who had hemorrhaged during the birth of the ten-pound baby. The second had been brought to term in an artificial womb, then matured to the age of twelve before being given consciousness. It did not know, to this day, that it had no memories from before its twelfth year.

He had loved them as children, these two beautiful, personable, and brilliant kids. They had shimmering emotional lives. But they also had extraordinary skills. He'd used some alien genes in the mix, most particularly those that involved antigravity. They could jump hundreds of feet. If trained, they could probably even fly, at least for short distances.

The third generation could be matured much faster, as fast as the reptiles that provided the bulk of their genes. So it was possible to go from embryo to finished infant in a month. Additional in vitro maturation could be chemically accelerated even more.

They could not fly, largely because he didn't have enough of the genetic material involved. He would have given them that, though, had he been able.

His lab—look at it, the most important place in human history, reduced to an ugly, trivial little television station. By now, it should be a museum. By now, he should be a Nobel Prize winner and have his own department at a great university.

Instead he slithered along at DARPA on his Senior Executive Service Level salary, working on the primitive, almost hopeless task of designing robust replacement organs for human soldiers. Inner Iron, the project was called. Knowing what existed beneath this place while using primitive gene-splicing processes was a particular torture.

He circled the block, then turned into the alley behind the building. Underneath where the old basement had been, there was now a parking garage. He drove down inside and parked in a visitor space.

This was good, this would mean he had no reason

to expose himself to any receptionists or explain his presence.

The garage was silent, dimly lit, and small. A scooter was chained to a bike rack, and beyond it was the manhole that they'd left if access to the facility was ever again required.

It was the same Department of Public Works cover they had originally chosen, and it certainly did not appear to have been disturbed. But why would it be? DPW records had been altered to show that it covered a feeder tunnel that led to the Channel Pump Station. It was listed as a nonaccess pressure-relief duct designed to vent water during a flood of some sort in the sewer system, so nobody needing to enter the tunnel would try to use it.

He opened his trunk and pulled out the lid lifter he had purchased when he'd first realized that this journey might be necessary. Just below would be the old vestibule area, with the elevator that led to the deep facility. That wouldn't be operating, of course, because they had shut it down, but the spiral emergency stair should still be viable.

He'd never removed a manhole cover before, but the levered device made it easy enough, and he was soon shining his flashlight down into a place he had not seen since the worst day of his life, which was when he had brought generation three topside and transported them to the ship in a sealed truck driven by a Delta Force operator who could be counted on to ask nothing and see nothing.

First, he shone his light down. The little foyer was dusty now, the floor gray with mold. He saw no footprints, which was some small reassurance.

Carefully, he climbed down the twenty rungs of the rusty access ladder.

The room was as he remembered it, just a small concrete foyer with a sealed elevator door dominating one side of it. The air was cool, scented with the strong musk of mildew.

On the wall opposite the ladder was a low iron door of the type you might find—would find—in a sewer system.

He went to this door. If his hybrids were using this place, they would be working in the lab below.

When he confronted them, he was not really sure what would happen. They had been bred to destroy their enemies with relentless precision—and *precision* was the correct word. No matter how complex, or how seemingly human, their responses were, they were machines and had the limitations of machines.

Without the elevator, he was going to have a long walk down the two hundred feet to the lab floor. He'd had it dug this deep because he did not know exactly what would happen when gen three was brought to consciousness. It had been possible to blow all exits from the lab area, sealing it off.

It would take perhaps ten minutes to descend the stair, then another five or so to check the condition of the lab. If anything appeared to be in use, his plan was to tell Gina about it and let them come here and destroy the equipment as part of the overall cleanup effort.

He hated to lose it. Not even the most detailed schematics revealed how it worked, especially not the way the zinc-finger controller actually processed information, or the way the editor could create nonlocal quantum entanglement between its artificial neurons and the real ones in a nearby brain.

In contrast to their complexity, both devices were quite easy to use. He remembered being trained on them at Dulce by a gruff alien female who could read his mind and screamed in anguish when she discovered that he thought her ugly.

In the early years, they'd been eager and cooperative. Later, though, as they produced generation after generation of psychotic human-alien hybrids, bitterness had emerged, and something he supposed was their version of contempt. Elements fundamental to the human brain could not support alien thought processes. For them, it must have been like trying to cram human intelligence into the brain of a chimpanzee.

They never indicated disapproval, but kept on doggedly trying until one day they were, quite simply, gone. Most thought this was because they had failed. Some thought perhaps they had succeeded.

How his heart had leaped with hope when he saw that first image. But then he'd thought, It's got the same sort of white skin that I designed, and he felt the first chill of what had become the full-blown panic he was in now.

As he descended the spiral staircase, moving carefully to avoid slipping and breaking a leg, concentrating on every step, he did not hear the faint scrape of the manhole cover being closed far above him. He never dreamed—could not have conceived—that someone who appeared not to be a gen three, but rather Corporal Al Knots—the now-dead Knotty of Mark Bryan's unit—had laid the cover extractor back in the trunk of Tom's rental car, got in, and reached under the dashboard. A moment later, the engine started and he drove out of the parking lot and was soon absorbed into the San Francisco traffic.

By the time Tom reached the bottom of the shaft, he had advanced into a new level of fear. It was very dark here, with the sound of dripping, and along the low concrete ceiling pale stalactites were hanging down.

He had considered bringing a weapon, but had decided against it. A gun would not only send the wrong message, it would be useless. They could flicker up to him, take it, and step away long before he could even form a decision to pull the trigger, and they would know that very well.

He hadn't told anyone where he was going, although it wouldn't take more than a few minutes to determine that he'd flown to Travis. After that, though, it would get much harder. The records of this lab had not just been buried, they'd been erased. He had made certain of that.

The moment he shone his light across his old lab bench, a flush of relief went through him. A layer of mold was on the gray marble surface, and the shelving was visibly rotting. Far to the back of the long space, he could see the two alien devices. They were blacker than black, appearing almost as if they had been fashioned out of dark matter. Nobody had ever been able to determine what the material was, or even scrape off a sample of it. They seemed made of darkness itself, as if the stuff of some primordial evil had been turned into a machine.

He went closer. In contrast to the front of the lab where the more conventional genetic work had been done, this area was free of mold and dust. Finally he stood before the editor, shining his light over its intricate, menacing surface.

He had tried hard not to bring superstitions to his contact with the aliens, they all had. But this was impossible. The impression of their evil had been overwhelming.

"Dr. Turner, please turn around slowly."

The most intense shock of surprise that he had ever known shot through him, so intense that he almost dropped his flashlight—but then clutched it. He turned around—and found himself confronting a big shadow.

Frantically, he brought his flashlight to bear. For an instant, he was completely at a loss: What was a Delta Force operator in full battle dress doing in here?

Then he recognized the face and was so surprised that he gasped aloud. It was one of Mark Bryan's men, absolutely no question. This was Sergeant Bart Louis. Like them all, Tom had chosen this man personally. Like them all, he was a human being of extremes—extreme speed, extreme intelligence, extreme aggression.

But he was also dead.

"Sergeant Louis," Tom said, "do you know that you're listed as killed in action?"

"You need to please do as I say," Louis said in a tone Tom had heard before, the same tone used by the gen threes when they were in a dominant position. He had studied the way vocal tone projects power, and designed it himself.

No matter who or what Louis appeared to be, Tom knew this man all too well underneath, because he had designed his mind.

What had they accomplished here? This was—what?—a perfect clone of a dead man, created in just a day and fitted with a gen three mind?

"Walk deeper into the facility please."

He had to play the authority card. If the programming had held, it would work.

"Sergeant, you don't give me orders. You take orders from me. You probably don't realize this, but I'm Colonel Bryan's superior. I chose you for your mission."

Louis said in that same deceptively, disturbingly soft tone, "We have a use for you."

Gen three had not only survived, they'd made some

sort of monstrous advance. This hybrid looked exactly like a man who had recently been killed and who appeared to have been skinned.

Had they learned somehow to meld human skin to their bodies? They must have, but how was it even possible? It couldn't be possible!

Vast knowledge. Stratospheric intelligence. Of course it was possible.

He turned and he ran.

But his light played across a crowd of figures. There were at least a dozen of them, some female, some male, in various developmental stages. He saw two Epsilons, a Zeta, a Gamma, behind them three Deltas and an Alpha.

"Hello, Father," they all said together. So they were also networked.

Then he understood why he had been outwitted like this, and what he understood filled him with a black wave of dread. No matter how cleverly or quickly a chimpanzee acted, or how much it managed to understand of a given situation, it would always be outwitted by a human being and would never be able to gain insight into the human mind.

Similarly, he would never be able to understand how his own creation had survived, or what it had done to replicate itself, or how it had defeated the problem of its scaled body surface, a problem that had completely stumped him.

They'd outthought him and outwitted him.

He wanted to run, but there was no place to run. He wanted to scream, but there was nothing to be gained from that.

"Time to go, Father," one of the creatures said. So much complexity was in that voice—regret, finality, strength . . . and laughter. Wherever he was going, there would be no return, that was clear.

"People are waiting for me." He pointed upward. "If I don't turn up, they're instructed to take appropriate action."

In the split of an instant, one of the creatures was standing face-to-face with him, its strangely cool breath washing over him. Then it took his flashlight, which flickered and went out as it crushed it and threw the parts to the floor.

"Thank you for the thermal vision, Father," a voice said in the dark.

He had worked a long time on that. They had receptors taken from the Plains blind snake, a tiny Texas snake with the most superb temperature-sensing eyes on the planet.

"TRPA1," he said. "That's the gene."

"Come on, Father, it's time."

"Time? Time for what?"

"We're going deep. A lot deeper than you went. The Hybrid Project is going into the depths. Remember saying that?"

He'd said it as the containment had been sunk.

"But . . . where were you? On the ship?"

"The six died in the containment," a voice said. "We were in the editor."

So they had left versions of their minds in the editor, how clever. He hadn't even thought to glance at it after he'd returned.

"But how did you get out? How did you grow new bodies?"

As if the question were too silly to answer, there was general laughter. He realized that they would never tell him, and perhaps he knew the reason why: He was not intelligent enough to understand.

They lifted him then, in steel-strong hands, and carried him easily through the absolute dark, and he did scream now, because the helplessness and the blindness and the fear overwhelmed him, and his cries pealed out again and again, as his mind lost itself in terror.

But then, between breaths, a realization arrived that comes to most dying men, when they know that their lives are truly over. He stopped his cries and ceased to struggle against the strength of his creatures. In a moment, he would touch the mystery of oblivion, and that was absolute.

He rode in their arms, his body slack, thinking that he had not come here on his own, not at all. The attack on Bryan's men had been intended to lure him here. At least, that must have been part of it. In addition, they had manipulated him into demanding that one of his beloved children kill the other.

It was diabolical.

They did not hurry. As they went along a new corridor, they carried him roughly, dragging him for a time by his legs, letting his head bounce along the concrete floor. He knew that they did this because they were enjoying his suffering.

From the race of felines, he had given them an interest in suffering. As a cat will worry a mouse, their instinct was to worry a captive. He'd thought it would be a useful trait for soldiers who must sometimes torture for information.

They came to a stop, and he found himself thrown to the floor, pain rushing through his shoulder and back. But then he heard a new sound, a vast sighing, as if of an unknown wind.

"What is it?"

There was a chuckle, the voice of a child. "It's an air intake."

"To whom am I speaking? Will you tell me?"

"My identifier doesn't matter to you."

Of course, why would they have names? They were networked. They had only the six personalities he and Emma had designed. The network identifiers were their individuality.

A moment later, he found his arms pinned and he felt fast and terrible agony splashing across his face and drilling into his head, pain greater than he had imagined possible, and he was momentarily mad with it, abandoned to it, completely drowned in it.

But it lessened a little, and he found that he was seeing great flashes in his head and feeling a coldness deep in his skull, and he thought that his eyes had been cut out.

He gagged, vomiting and gasping, the pain like a single, great knife twisting into the center of his brain.

He was vaguely aware that he was now naked, his clothes removed. Their hands were all over him, their thin, precise fingers probing the skin around his midriff.

Then something cold touched him and was immediately followed by the sensation that he had burst into flames.

The fire slid along his muscles. Somewhere in the distance, somebody was screaming. He knew who it was, but by now he was dissociating. He was no longer Tom Turner. He was no longer really a human being at all. He was pain, that and knowledge, and the knowledge was that he was being skinned alive.

Mercifully, shock dulled his mind, but he was vaguely aware that he had begun falling, but that they were still holding him. As the torment continued to distance him from reality, he did understand that he was not falling, but flying in a carefully controlled manner, held among four of them. He did not know that his skin and eyes were already neatly packed in preservative, ready for the use for which they had been intended from the moment the decision had been made to lure him into this trap.

They went much farther down than the Challenger Deep, or even the seven miles of the Kola Well in Siberia. They dropped efficiently, their captive helpless among them, down a shaft constructed with engineering expertise as far in advance of what mankind could accomplish as the lovely tools of Cro-Magnon had been in advance of the coarse flints of Neanderthal.

Controlling their fall with the grace of masters of gravity, they slid down the darkness with their writhing, abject captive, twenty-two miles into the bowels of the earth.

There, they would use delicate instruments to capture his memories, even his tone of voice, for the new deception that they had devised, which would end either in the deaths of the two rogue hybrids, the unacceptable first and second generations, or their induction into the new army.

All that was left was to lure the one in Washington out here, then deal with them both. And that was settled: They would capture a storm, and throw it at Washington.

CHAPTER NINE

HALF-HUMAN IS TOO MUCH

ON THE WAY BACK TO Willoughby, Linda Hicks had sat huddled against the door, obviously uncomfortable. She'd stifled a moan as Mark drew a space blanket around her. When he'd asked her if she was hurt, she had given her head sharp, angry shakes.

She lay now on the creaky motel bed, as still as a corpse, her skin pale, the veins faintly visible in the hard overhead light. Here and there on her body was a red, blotchy area. On her neck and right arm, occasional tiny droplets of blood formed and ran down, but when they did, she brushed them away.

"I'm going to get up," she said.

"No, you're not."

"There's nothing wrong with me!"

"I'm going to call Gina right now. We need to find a hospital for you."

"I am not injured."

As near as he could tell, the outermost layer of her skin was gone. Why they had left her alive wasn't clear, but it was certainly worrying him.

An obvious reason to pretend to have missed her would be that she was one of them.

"You're in pain." He had to get her to face that she

needed rotation to a medical unit. He also wanted her gone.

"I'm not hurt!"

"You're hurt."

The team possessed an extensive medical kit—in addition to her portable sampling lab, she had a portable aid station that was a masterpiece of miniaturization. But there was nothing for an injury like this.

He called Gina.

She answered immediately.

"Linda's down," he said.

"I am *not* down!" She got up off the bed, then grabbed the sheet and pulled it around her.

"They abraded her. I think they took off the outer layer of skin." He fought back acid, swallowed hard. "She's oozing blood and you can see—see through her skin, almost."

"Okay, look, I'm going to send a medical unit from Travis AFB to pick her up. She's relieved until further notice."

"I agree. But what happens now, Gina?" He did not mean to plead, but he was feeling seriously isolated. "We need to expand this program. We need the full attention of Delta Force, and maybe a lot more."

"I want you to do two things. First, you return to the area where the ordnance was laid down, and you inspect it for any signs of remains. If there are remains, I'll send a graves detail out to collect them and get them back to us here in Washington."

"It'll be my men."

"And if we're lucky, a hybrid or two."

Linda interrupted, "Which you cannot sample properly without me. I do *not* require hospitalization, damnit."

He clicked off the speakerphone. "And the second part of my orders?"

"You come to Washington. We're planning a larger operation." She paused. "We want you to run it."

He had two skills: hunting and killing. "I belong in the field."

"First things first. Go out there, give me a report from the scene. Then we'll talk futures."

"Are you sure—"

She cut the connection.

"—that's a good idea?" He looked at the phone in his hand. Okay, she was upset. And with him, which made sense. He was, too, big-time.

He closed the phone. He had his orders and he would carry them out. But first he would deal with his injured soldier.

"Linda, whether you feel it or not, you're wounded and you're going into the hospital for evaluation."

"I'm a doctor and I'm evaluated. Minor abrasions, nothing to write home about, end of story."

"You're going to be transported to a hospital."

He ordered Richardson to remain with Linda while he took the van and carried out his brief recce in the burn zone.

Driving back out to the site in the last light of this miserable day, he saw that the fire was out and the considerable official presence that had been keeping citizen eyes away from the area was packing up to leave. The state police, local sheriffs, and firemen watched his van but let him pass. Nice of Gina to remember that detail and take care of it. He wondered what, if anything, the press would have to say. Probably that there had been a minor local fire, one home lost. In his experience, Gina's ability to control the media was virtually absolute.

Gina. He found himself wanting her not to think ill of him, even though he was deeply ashamed of his performance. Soldiers were supposed to fight past the deaths of their comrades. You couldn't do it, though, not when you were the commander and you'd had to do what he'd done to his own men. Mercy killing was not merciful to the person who had to pull the trigger.

Gina. Momma in the sky. He should've kept up with her, at least let her know how he felt. Maybe it could have worked. He had poetry in him. He had love. His heart needed her, and he felt that need all the time. He felt it now.

Likely he was just muscle to her, a one-night stand. What did a woman like that do for love, anyway, shag senators and whatnot? A big, inarticulate soldier like him was probably just an entertainment.

As he drew closer to the battle zone, the stench of fire and burned flesh made him grip the wheel harder. The sweet stink of napalm-B mixed with the chemical foulness of high explosive.

He opened his satphone. A click told him that Gina was there, but she said nothing.

"I'm in position. You see anything?"

"It's clear."

She cut the connection.

"Gina?"

No signal. Now, that was odd. She must really be outraged at him. Would she prefer charges against him? She could, and he probably deserved it. Damn well did. He'd welcome brig time, to tell the truth. A firing squad would be a relief.

When he reached the farm, he pulled the van off the road and got out. The silence was stupendous. Not a bird raised its voice, not a frog croaked, nor a cicada screamed.

In the distance he heard a jet. It appeared to be operating about five miles due south of here. The engine's note told him that it was not a commercial plane. So Gina was still flying patrols. She ought to be using unmanned aerial vehicles, UAVs, with silenced engines, or those new choppers they were starting to deploy, with the noiseless wing. The hybrids would avoid exposing themselves to jets.

Thinking to make the suggestion, he signaled her. For a moment, there was no response. He tried again. Finally, the LED that indicated the presence of her signal lit green.

"Gina, you need some kind of silent recce. Those jets give themselves away."

"I just want hybrid bodies right now. And your men."

"Got it." But why she expected to find hybrid bodies he didn't know. They'd damn well won, and he and his men sure hadn't shot any of them.

He moved out into woods. The odor here was truly awful, almost overpowering, the stench of napalm from the nearby forest, and the odor of the dead.

The jet was joined by a second plane, this one coming in from the north-northeast. He could discern details of the engine notes now. Both jets were converging, moving fast.

"Gina?"

She did not reply.

The planes went to afterburner. He understood immediately that this was the target zone.

"What the hell, Gina, I'm here! I'm right here!"

There was no time to wait for her response, though. The planes were already on their runs. As fast as he could, he dashed into the cover of the forest—and right toward the hybrids, of that he was certain.

So what was it going to be, get gutted by the hybrids, or get burned alive?

"Gina, goddamnit!"

No response. Therefore, this was intentional.

"Why, Gina? For God's sake!"

Nothing. She had decided to kill him. Since this was a mistake, it was his obligation to stay alive until it could be rectified.

It was going to be hard to beat her attack, though, because supernapalm generated one hell of a lot of suffocating carbon dioxide, not to mention fire. Even if he didn't burn, he would likely smother.

"Gina, *Jesus*!"

She probably heard him, but stayed off air.

"I'm the best chance we've got!"

To love someone as he did Gina and see the person able to do this to you was hard. How cold she must be. How deeply indifferent.

He had imagined that maybe he was wrong, and he mattered a little bit to her, but this made it clear: That was not even slightly true. He was just a tool, something that took orders and had gone wrong—or so she thought.

The jets began simultaneous attack runs. They were fast, that's how this sort of thing worked, and the first thunderous blast hit him so hard that he lost orientation and hearing for a few seconds. Then the ground connected with him and he rolled, turning quickly onto his back just in time to see a rocket coming straight for his position. No napalm, they were going after him with antipersonnel missiles. Exquisitely careful targeting was possible when your victim had a transponder embedded in his chest and you could lock onto his telemetry.

The speed with which he put a tree between himself

and the incoming rocket surprised even him. Even so, the blast swept around him, throwing him fifty yards.

The jet's engine note changed again, to the roaring snarl of its hover mode, and he could see it out about two klicks and at an altitude of a couple of thousand feet, turning on its own axis as the pilot repositioned.

Then, another note—the other jet, coming in at five hundred miles an hour six inches above the treetops, and he knew it would unload napalm. The initial rocket attack had been a trick, Gina knowing that she had to distract him.

Therefore, her plan had a weakness that she was aware of. What was it? He ran along a ridgeline, then saw what was worrying her: cave entrances below him. He dove off the ridge, letting his body limp out as it crashed into the tangle of brush and roots that choked one of the black openings.

If it was deep, he might survive. If it wasn't, when they unloaded the napalm, the breath would be sucked right out of him. Like the Japanese in World War Two in their caves on Saipan and Tinian, or the Vietcong in the Chu Chi tunnel complex, like that.

As he dove into the nearest cave, white light erupted behind him. With it came searing heat. He threw himself down, coming to a stop against a damp limestone wall. Air rushed past him, dank but breathable, rising from deeper in the cave.

A blast above shattered the limestone around him, dropping large blocks against his back, sending him flying into the far wall. Ignoring the pain as best he could, he crawled out from under the mass of rock and began going deeper. Blast after blast ravaged the tunnel behind him.

As the sounds grew less and the darkness more

profound, he cracked a light stick. As it created a glow rather than cast a beam, its light was less easily noticed.

In its blue-green glow, he saw at once that he was in a significant cave complex. Before the mission began, he'd studied his terrain carefully, including its geology. There had been mention of caves in the area, but no indication of their extent.

Around him were well-developed stalagmites and sta-lactites, indicating that this cave was old and well estab-lished. He could feel a slight breeze against his face, so another opening was somewhere ahead. Useful, or too small? He moved toward it.

Fifty feet along the tunnel, he stopped. Now, this was strange. There were no stalagmites here. Holding the light stick up, he could see drill grooves along the walls.

This was no longer a cave. From here on, it was a man-made tunnel, and not an old mine, either. This was recent work, and judging from the perfect, curling symmetry of the grooves, it had been done by an unusually precise machine. No, this was not a mine, but it might be an ex-planation for why the hybrids could disappear in one place and reappear in another. Too bad that the ground-penetrating radar he had ordered had been so slow in coming. No question, it would have taught him a lot.

To be certain that there was absolutely no light at all, he stuffed the light stick in his pocket, then waited with his eyes open, staring into the sparks generated by his own nervous system.

No light at all, and absolute silence as well. A little water dripping back in the natural cave, that was all.

Going back was out of the question, so he only had two choices, stay here or move on down the tunnel, but before he moved deeper, he had another piece of busi-ness to attend to, and not a pleasant one.

He opened his shirt and felt his chest until his fingers

were over the slightly stiff area an inch below his right nipple that marked the spot where his tracking implant had been injected. He unsheathed his knife and isolated the object between the index and middle fingers of his left hand. He worked in the dark. No light was needed, and all light in a place like this was a risk, always. There was a procedure for doing what he was about to do, and he'd trained on it, so he didn't need to see. It had been anticipated that a man might at times need to get rid of a rescue transponder.

A pulse of agony raced up into his neck and down into his gut as he slid the tip of the blade into his skin. Pressing it deep, he choked back the desire to groan. As he had been taught, he raised the blade until the implant was between it and the surface of his chest. Now he changed the angle of attack, so that the tip of the knife was behind the object. Drawing the blade back, he slowly pulled the implant out with it.

By the time he finally had the thing in his hand, he was experiencing some pain-induced vertigo. Taking deep breaths, he felt into his service medical pack for a patch, pulled one out, and slapped it over the wound, which was raining blood.

He held up the light stick to regain his bearings. Rather than leave the remains of the implant behind as evidence, he crushed it between his teeth and pocketed the debris.

As he went along the downsloping passage, he began to hear a sound ahead. He listened. Was that a voice? Somebody singing?

No, it was many voices, and it told him that he was closer to the lair of the hybrids right now than he'd ever been.

With carefully measured steps, he went a short distance. Again, he listened. A brief exposure of the light stick revealed more of the tunnel, still slanting downward, still empty.

But almost at once, a new sound replaced the distant singsong. He listened. This was whispering, rhythmic and urgent.

Not a voice, though, no. So what was it?

Then he knew. He was hearing slipper-clad feet brushing the stone floor.

Someone was coming toward him, stealthy and fast.

He understood now that all the surface activity they'd been tracking had been a distraction. Underground was what mattered, and how damn clever they were. They'd located in an earthquake zone so that the vibrations from any digging would be passed off as naturally occurring microquakes.

The footsteps were now easily audible, and he drew back against the wall. It took everything he had in him not to turn and run. Instead, he forced himself to do the one thing that felt entirely wrong, but wasn't. He stood his ground. As they came closer, he threw his light stick so that it illuminated them.

Four forms that had been coming toward him all stopped. They stood as still as stone, their eyes fixed on him. This close he could see in their skin the jewel-like glitter of their scales.

They wore ordinary jeans and shirts. One of them had a windbreaker on inside out. Another's shirt was on backward, the buttons hanging open behind. It was as if they'd been dressed by children.

The closest of the men wore an Oakland Raiders cap and carried a black object. He said, "Mark, we're here to help you."

They watched him with strange, unfinished eyes, pale and somehow lacking. He thought, people have personalities. They don't.

"How can you help me?"

As if in humility, the creature bowed its head. It held out the object, which was a black disk.

"If you let me touch you with this, that will help you."

Somewhere before, in some vagueness, he had seen a thing like that.

He stepped back.

The creature came closer, and now Mark could smell the reptile musk of its body.

He backed away farther.

"Mark, come on, it's us. We're your brothers and sisters, Mark." The hybrid raised the disk. "This'll help you."

The others, Mark noticed, were moving stealthily, attempting to get behind him.

"Don't," he said, "or I'll kill you all."

Seemingly saddened, the one with the disk bowed his head. "You're missing your life, Mark."

"The army is my life."

It lunged at him and in the split of an instant he drew his knife and cut all four of them.

He had always been able to depend on his proficiency with the blade, but this was exceptional. He was only glad that he was able.

He ran past the crumpled figures, crouching low, putting distance between himself and what he had done. He had not gone two hundred feet before he saw another individual. This one came forward with a care in its steps that suggested old age, a panther in its later years.

As it came close and he saw it more clearly, Mark was shocked by an emotion he had not known existed, and a memory he had not known he possessed. Out of some deep, unexplored place, he found himself uttering the word "Father."

He saw this man not only in the dimness of this tunnel,

but in the light of memory. His narrow, precise face was deeply familiar. Yet, he could not remember where he had seen him. He could not remember why he called him father, but he wanted to.

In some lost, hazy memory, this man appeared as tall as a god, standing above him all in white. But there was blood, too, smeared in the white. Core instinct triggered a burst of love beyond even his love of Gina, as if he were face-to-face with God.

He heard himself say again, out of the depths of his heart, "Father." But why? Why was he saying this, why feeling it?

A softness came into the man's eyes that inspired in Mark a desire to somehow shield him in this dangerous place. In his hand was the same sort of black object—a disk—that the hybrid had been holding.

The man said, "It's good to see you again, Son."

In his mind's eye, Mark saw a horse plunging in a green field, a small airplane like a red jewel in the blue, then a mallard rising into an autumn sky. But, no, they were something else. They were—"Cards," he said, drawing forth a faint memory. "You held up cards."

"That was when you were first programmed. You were forty seconds old, Mark. That's what you're remembering."

"Who are you?"

"That's not in your programming. You don't possess that memory. It was taken out."

"What is this place, what's happening?"

"Mark, that's the problem. You should know. You should be glad to be here. Your programming needs a reset." The man held out the ominous disk. "That's what these are for. Once we've reset you, you'll understand that this isn't something evil we're doing. It's about saving Earth for future generations, and remaking the world."

As the man spoke, his face tightened in a way that Mark associated with danger. A complex, unsure smile played in the aged features.

"Remaking it in what sense?"

"Mark, mankind is a failure. Nature tried and nature failed. But there's a new mankind now—people like you, good people, smart people—for the love of God, Mark, *compassionate* people. No more war, no more cruelty, no more greed. Instead a community in love with itself, as any community of intelligent creatures should be." The man lifted the disk, holding it toward Mark's head. "Let me. It's just a touch, Mark, and you're fixed."

"I don't know who you are. I don't know why I called you that."

"My name is Dr. Thomas Ford Turner."

"You're Dr. Turner? The Dr. Turner that Gina's talked about?"

"I created you, Mark. Both of you."

In that instant, signals from a thousand different directions all entered Mark's mind at the same time: his own memories, the way the man looked and moved, the words he had spoken.

Mark said, "I was born, not created. And you can't program a human being."

"That's right, Mark, you can't." Raising the disk, the man stepped closer.

Like lightning, Mark grabbed at his wrist. And like lightning, he withdrew it.

"Mark, this is the end of one history and the beginning of another, and you play a huge role. You can't reject your own destiny, or thwart us. Mark, we've conquered gravity. We can leave the planet in massive numbers.

Enter the cosmos, colonize other worlds. It's possible Mark and it's doable. But not by the humans. They're finished, Mark."

Mark was listening not only to the words, but to the sounds around him, and he could hear movement, and he could hear breathing.

"If they get any closer," he said carefully, "I'll kill them all."

"Do you know that you're our only obstacle? The humans can't possibly stand against us. You need to come home, Mark."

"One thing is crystal clear, mister, and that is that I don't know what the hell this is all about, and I certainly don't understand who or what you are."

"You don't know what *you* are, Mark. But I do. You're defective, is what you are. Half-human is too much." He smiled again, too bright and too tight. "We scientists are optimists. That's our failing."

The tone of the man's voice continued to move him to deep, formless nostalgia, but the words made him sweat cold. *Half*-human? What was that supposed to mean?

For an instant, the man's attention wandered. Instantly, Mark chopped at his wrist, causing the disk to clang to the floor. Preparing to make some kind of an escape, Mark took a long step away.

"Don't run, Mark. You're home." The man picked up the disk and once again reached toward Mark with it. He was so close that Mark could smell the sweat of him, sour, as sour and disturbing as some exotic cheese.

"Mark, let me make a little adjustment, that's all that's needed. Then these demons you're fighting—your brothers and sisters—they'll turn out to be angels, Mark."

He was an old man, easily dealt with. He didn't even have a weapon, not that it would have mattered.

But then he saw something else, something odd. Along the neckline, the skin rippled. Reaching out fast, he pulled at it, and the entire face went askew.

This was not a man, it was the stolen surface of a man.

"Keep your distance."

The creature stepped closer yet. "Mark, you have nobody but us."

"My unit. I have my unit."

"You led them to their deaths, remember? Sometimes your programming works, and it worked then. Why do you think Washington's trying to kill you? They know what you are."

In place of the strange, longing nostalgia he had been feeling, he now felt a hatred more raw than he had known was in him.

"You're a liar."

"I know you're thinking about killing me. Mark, I know you better than you know yourself. Far better. You're just like us. You were created in a laboratory. But the government ordered us destroyed."

Mark's mind was reeling. He looked again at the disk.

"Ah, you're thinking about it at last. Considering it. Mark, what's happening isn't bad. It's beautiful. You're a work of art, Mark, of art married to science. The most deeply fertile marriage there can be."

The man took another step closer. Still, Mark made no move. Memories flooded him, of the few happy days of his life, of the little triumphs in the dojo, of walking down Collins Avenue with Sarge, with his misty gray eyes and his warrior's wisdom: "A good soldier knows how to wait, Mark. Wait sharp, that's the way. Soldiering is about concentration. That's the why of drill and inspection. Teaches concentration."

With a speed beyond the incredible, the creature lunged at Mark, thrusting the disk at his face. Mark slashed, but it threw itself to one side.

Roaring, furious, Mark leaped after it—but stopped as he reached the fatal edge of a vast pit that had been hidden by the darkness.

The creature dropped over the edge, but Mark did not see him fall. And when Mark looked down, he saw why—the man was being helped down the steep side by three hybrids.

Mark saw that the entire far wall of the cavern was lined with some sort of huge structure, and there was movement on it, and sound—cries, buzzing noises, clanging, and the bubbling of thick liquid.

He stared at it, for the moment unable to understand what he was seeing. It was constructed like a wasps' nest, but gigantic, with row on row of cells, each of them containing a form.

Huge volumes of blood, almost black in the dim light, flowed in sheets down the face of the structure. There was scuttling movement, and he saw figures running up and down it, using instruments like large brushes to spread the blood evenly over the forms in the cells.

How far down did it go? Hundreds of feet? Thousands?

Then he heard a voice faintly calling his name. It seemed to drift up from below. Was it the creature? No, it was female, and it was familiar. It was Linda's voice.

Down there?

No, impossible. A trick.

"Mark!"

His soldier's mind told him this: When you can't go forward or back, but you've got to go somewhere, the only logical move is to take any chance that offers itself to you.

Carefully, he swung down off the catwalk, then leaped across the gloomy depths, to the top level of cells. As best he could, he climbed down, but it was impossible not to slip in the muck, and he soon grasped the head and shoulders of what proved to be a body. As he slid, it came out of its cell with a wet, sucking sound.

Its features were serpentine, its skin white-scaled porcelain. But it was vivid with life, its facial expression that of somebody lost in dream.

As he tried to control the heavy body, bracing against the walls of the cell that had held it, the eyes snapped awake and it began to shriek, a high, unsure sound. It was an adult with the voice of a newborn.

Mark pushed at the creature, pushed hard, and it went bouncing downward, finally cartwheeling into the dark.

Looking up, down, all across the dim space, he could see thousands and thousands of these cells.

Rage exploded, and he ripped another body from its sucking mooring. This was a child, whose eyes came open, and as he threw it down into the pit, its toothless shrieking was as soft as the cry of a night bird, a sound that cut you to the center of your soul. And he thought, My brothers and my sisters, and he shouted, *"No no no,"* and one after another hauled creatures out, males, females, children—there seemed to be a mix of sexes and ages, from about ten to about thirty—and threw them down into the pit.

Above him there stretched a long, bleeding scar that he was leaving as he descended. Around him were older parts of the nest, and the creatures in them were dry and fully formed.

A female sprang out and added to his problems by latching onto his shoulder with her teeth. Others began to awaken and started coming out of the cells, dozens of them, all with blank, nightmare faces, shrieking and throwing themselves into a battle that he was clearly about to lose.

"Mark!"

"Linda, where are you?"

Her voice was coming from behind the cells and he tore at them, ripping the blood-soaked cardboard away and throwing great sheets of it aside. But at the same time, he started to become dizzy. The female's teeth must have contained some sort of anesthetic.

"Are you there, Mark? In there?"

"I'm here! I'm coming!" He ripped and tore at the hive.

Then he felt himself slipping into unknown hands, and the world went dark.

CHAPTER TEN

THE GUIDES

"CAN YOU WAKE UP?" A female voice asked, full of sharp efficiency.

He tried to do that, but shivers swept his body. They were so intense that they amounted to a sort of seizure. He was helpless.

"Mark, *now*!"

He battled to focus, saw brush around and above him. Then a face came into focus—Linda's. He saw the faces of Pete Richardson and Linda Hicks floating before him, shadows in a shadow land.

"Where are we?"

"The base of the cliff. You came out through an opening."

So the lair was behind them in the cliff, embedded in the same way wasps embed their nests.

He sat up. "I was lucky to get out."

"We heard you, it was a noisy fight."

He looked toward the base of the cliff. "If I'd gone any deeper, I never would've come out."

The sound of a Klaxon, muffled, came out of the cliff.

He got to his feet. "They're gonna be on general alert. We need to move."

A cluster of pale forms burst out of the brush and

came racing through the tangle of vines that hugged the base of the cliff.

As Mark turned, one of the creatures leaped onto his back. Reaching up, he dragged it over his head and threw the writhing, screaming body ten feet.

It hit the ground with a gasp, but immediately jumped up and came toward him again.

This time, he slammed its head with a fist, crushing the skull. Behind it, others swarmed, and he found his knife coming into his hand as if under its own power, it felt so natural.

He moved with a speed that surprised even him, and total precision, and they went down, one and then another.

He could have been gutting fish. But still more came seething through the brush, their faces full of intensity, their movements graceful and fast.

He understood, suddenly, that he had not escaped, he had been allowed to escape. He was bait to ensure that all three of them would be killed.

"Run," he said, "get out of here, both of you!"

They moved behind him, and he worked as quickly as he could.

As the seconds dragged, the carnage grew, but in the end the creatures ceased to move forward, then stopped, then slipped back into the brush, taking their dead with them.

He did not pursue. No reason to push his luck.

Breathing hard, he looked down at his hand, at the knife in it. He remembered how much he'd wanted these in their carries. It was a Combat Troodon, one of the best fighting knives in the world. But how he was beginning to use it seemed more and more beyond his or anybody else's skill.

Was he a hybrid? But how could that be? He was completely human in every detail.

It had to be a lie. If he wasn't fully human—if he was some sort of biological machine—he decided that he would kill himself.

Linda shouted at him, "For God's sake, Mark, how did you do that?"

He looked from Linda to Pete, their earnest young faces, innocent.

Linda's face was flushed, her uniform wet in places from blood that he assumed would be leaking out of her abraded skin.

"We need to get out of here right now," he said, speaking to them with the same earnest tolerance he would use with children. He also thought, They came here and they saved me. I was lost, and they found me.

Ahead, there was the sound of drumming, and what might be laughter. Peering through the forest, he saw lights. For the first time since Gina's attack had come in, he took enough note of his surroundings to see that night had fallen. Battle eats time in great, speeding gulps.

"Is that a camp? What is that?"

"There's no camp there," Linda replied.

"That's people screaming," Mark said. "That's panic."

"I'm afraid it's Willoughby," Linda said.

The hybrids were there, and they were having a party. Mark began to run.

Linda caught up with him. "Mark, you need to be careful."

"We all need to be careful. They used me as bait just now, remember that. To lure you."

"And now they're using the town as bait to lure you."

"Never miss a trick, do they? Clever bastards."

"What's happening, Mark? This isn't what we thought."

"I'm not sure." He did not want to share his suspicions with them, especially not the ones he now had about himself.

From Willoughby cries joined the laughter, ululating through the moonlit forest. Nearer, an owl cackled softly, if it was an owl.

Mark headed toward the screaming town, but Linda took his arm.

"You can't go wading into that, Mark."

"There's still a chain of command in this unit, and I'm going to go over there and deal with whatever the hell is happening, and I want you to back me up, both of you."

Pete said, "You'll want a Metal Storm."

No gun would be needed, not now that he'd discovered the true speed of his hands.

"My knife is my tool."

"How can you kill that way?" Linda muttered.

He turned on her, glared at her, suppressing an emotion that it surprised him he would feel, which was hurt. She should be grateful for his skills, not disgusted by them.

"I do what works. I want you two to stay close but hang back."

"Hang back," Pete said. "Are you nuts?"

"Stay well out of the way. Stay behind your Metal Storms. I don't want to lose you."

"Mark, don't go in there alone."

"Listen to me. That's a trap, okay? But they will not spring it until all three of us are in it. If I do my job right, by then it'll be too late." He gripped the knife. "They are going to take significant damage now. If they understood how much, this trap would not be here.

You're bright kids, so you'll figure out when I need you, and you'll come."

"Mark?" Linda reached toward him.

It was just an automatic action, the way he thrust the knife at her. He hadn't planned to do it, hadn't thought about it.

"You do not come with me now," he said carefully. "That is an order. You observe and move in when you're needed."

Leaving them standing together in the forest, uncertain, their two Metal Storms closed at their sides, he entered the town, coming first to the edge of a yard. He jumped the low fence and landed hard, clattering into a line of garbage cans. A lid rolled out into the street, stopped, and fell over, whanging endlessly, agonizingly as it twirled round and round.

The voices from the Glade did not stop. This close, he could hear an odd note in the laughter, something almost mechanical. He was reminded of figures in a fun house, blaring recorded laughter.

To his right was a chicken coop, quiet after dark. He headed past it and up to the house. No life inside, so he went around it and down to the street in front.

Ahead, a traffic light stood at red. A car waited in the intersection, an elderly Buick. Listening, watching, he sought to identify any sign of hybrids. But he couldn't make much sense of anything because the sounds around him were distorted into strange, lingering growls.

Before, killing had been a process, nothing emotional about it. Fulfilling his mission. Now he was filled with what could only be described as an urgent eagerness. Previously, he had feared the creatures, but now he absolutely loathed them. He recalled their empty eyes, their voices lilting with menace.

He moved along an empty side street, under a faintly

buzzing streetlight. Not a car passed, not a child called out in the softness of the summer evening. Worse, he could hear more clearly now, sounds he really did not like coming from the Glade, mechanical laughter and wild human screams, and the clatter of frenetic drums.

He went closer.

CHAPTER ELEVEN

FASCINATION

AS HE APPROACHED THE CENTER of the town, the red of the traffic light began to change, but slowly—much too slowly. Confused, but being careful, he watched it dim to a dot and then disappear, replaced as slowly by the gradual bloom of the green.

Then, at a crawl, what had been waiting, an elderly Buick, began creeping toward him, its engine booming like a great, slow cannon. At the same moment, he saw the driver and knew by his rigid posture, eyes straight ahead, that this was one of the creatures.

He started to move toward the car, but it suddenly sped up, shooting past him with tires screaming.

He was disoriented. This made no sense.

Then it did. It had to be adrenaline, a rush like the one he'd experienced when he saw his men in trouble in the woods. He'd moved extremely fast in that moment, but he'd blown it off, telling himself that it had been the shock that had enabled him to do it.

Hybrids flickered like that. People did not.

He watched as the car disappeared around a bend, its lights absorbed by the forest. Where might it be going?

Then he knew: Linda and Pete were in those woods, and it had placed him in an impossible position. Either he went after the car and saved them, or he entered the town and saved the people who were screaming.

He thought quickly, calculating. His most logical option was clear: He had to take out the car. If he lost his people, he would be isolated and, in the end, lose this battle.

It hurt in his heart and in his blood to turn his back on that agony, but the car was already disappearing down the road. He followed it, pushing himself until it felt as if he were falling and running at the same time. Tremendous effort was involved, his muscles so tight he thought they might separate from the bones. As he strained, the car's engine howled, speeding it forward. It shot like a bullet when the highway was straight, then went rocking through the curves. He was fast, but he was a running man and this was a car, so he kept losing ground.

Still, he did not stop. He couldn't, he had to fight this thing to a win or to the death, and he could not lose the last of his people.

Then something happened that he had not expected, any more than he had expected going into the ultra-high-speed state they'd been calling flicker.

This was not flicker, though. It was, rather, a swooping, tumbling rush through the air. Wind roared in his ears, then he hit the roof of the car with a clanging thud. He clutched at the slick metal, but he could not stop himself from falling backward until he was on the trunk.

Immediately, the car swerved. But he held on—and then there was a shock, the scream of metal, a flash in his eyes, and he was sliding along the road as if swimming. He felt his clothes tearing, but then pushed and was on his feet and running at breakneck speed.

He leaped again, soaring so high that a sudden silence

and dank grayness was around him, and then he was looking down on swift clouds.

What was this?

He shot downward again, heading toward the car's lights.

Again he crashed into it, but this time he controlled his fall, twisting and turning, shifting his weight. Even so, the hood shot up at him, and he smashed into it and bounced and went through the windshield, the glass cracking and splintering into shards around him.

The driver kicked at him, its voice high with terror, its hands clawing at him, and he pulled out his knife and thrust it into the creature.

The legs hammered, the head pitched back, and Mark turned away. Why look?

Mark grabbed the wheel, but the creature had more life in it than he'd realized, and it fought and the car went out of control and the next thing Mark knew, they were tumbling over and over, and he was contending with the remains of the creature, now loose with death, bouncing and striking him.

The car stopped. Stunned, he pulled himself out from under the body. The quickly intensifying odor of hot rubber and hot gasoline told him he needed to get out right now.

He had been running, the world had blurred—and here he was with a hybrid in pieces around him.

Deep red glowed beneath the dashboard.

He had to get out.

The glow became a curtain of red all around him.

He kicked at a window, kicked again, did it again, and finally crawled into the gravel and brush along the roadside. The car was upside down, its radiator hissing faintly, smoke coming off the base of the engine compartment, and the passenger cabin filling with fire.

From back in Willoughby, the drums were even wilder, the crackling laughter mixed with dreadful, abandoned shrieks.

He ran toward the town, his thumping boots the only sound in the dead-quiet night.

What he needed here most of all was more bodies, and not just Delta Force, not anymore. He needed Special Forces, Rangers, anybody with sufficient skills and equipment to have some sort of chance.

He thought of that lair nestled up in that hillside. It was vulnerable to a bunker buster, but how could a man Washington was trying to kill communicate anything to them? He no longer had his satphone, it was long gone. In any case, using it would likely just bring down another air strike on his own head.

One after another, the infestations they had been tracking had disappeared. It was now clear why. They had been going underground.

He had to assume that they must be infested all through northern California, from the border to the Bay Area and into Big Basin. And who knew what kind of presence they had elsewhere? Maybe there was only the one colony, but maybe there were many others. Maybe they were coming up in the night, stealing people, using their skins and organs and eyes—and what of their brains, their souls?

From behind him there came a thud, and an orange glow filled the air. There was no reason to look back— the car had exploded. Good.

The flames would also attract Gina's attention, no question. She would be up there in Washington right now, getting field reports and not being satisfied with them, not if there was no direct evidence of his body being found.

His heart hurt because Gina had turned on him. He

had to admit that he'd been nursing a fantasy that she actually had some feelings for him. But she was making this a two-front war for him, the fool. Beautiful fool. He made a small, complicated sound as he ran, of longing, of regret, of frustration.

The human voices from the town became more frantic, calling on God now. He tried another jump, but there was no sense of flight, not like before. Why not? He didn't know. He knew so little—too little—about himself.

The car was burning, though, and the hybrid driver was dead, so he had flown, no matter how surreal that now seemed.

Maybe he did have some of the abilities of the hybrid. Of course it was possible. There were all sorts of genetic capabilities these days. This man—"Father"—had apparently known him when he was a small child. Fine, maybe he'd received some genetic alteration, and maybe it was the explanation for his skills. But that was physical. It had nothing to do with who he was. The part of him that was human was his heart and soul, and that was what he was going to live by.

He moved on through the forest, pressing himself harder now, going as fast as he could toward the town. He was aware of the presence of Linda and Pete just to the west about five hundred yards, and that they saw him, also, and were going into motion. He hoped that he could trust them to time their entry right. When he reached the edge of town, he slid his hand into his pocket and closed it around the handle of his knife.

He stepped closer to the source of the screaming, which was the restaurant, the Glade. The high agony of children that he was now hearing so distressed him that he had to force his emotions back. Combat was math, not feelings.

But what were they doing to them, to create such extreme torment? It was more than pain by fire, more than any physical pain. In that building, souls were being tortured.

And it was . . . fascinating.

Dear heaven, how could such a thought even enter his mind? He put it firmly aside.

An especially loud scream came, male, from pain beyond pain. It was joined by another and by bitter sobbing, gabbled, incoherent pleas, and the eager thrumming of the drums these creatures seemed to enjoy.

He entered the restaurant. He would kill them all, all the hybrids, every one.

CHAPTER TWELVE

THE STRICKEN

THE AIR IN THE KITCHEN was dense with foul, greasy smoke, the music was a searing roar, and a big soup pot was boiling hard on the stove. In it were what he thought for a moment were sausages, until he understood that he was looking at parts of human beings.

Seeing this made him not just hear the screams, but think of the suffering that was going on in the dining room . . . and he was surprised to find himself feeling something other than revulsion. It was a bizarre emotion. He couldn't even describe it to himself, except to say that it was ugly and made him ashamed.

He turned off the fire under the pot and stepped through into the dining room. Here, the smoke was even thicker, and a great crowd of hybrids danced around a clutching group of tattered, bleeding people.

There were kids in pajamas, men in jeans, women naked, one, a young woman with a pageboy, lying slumped against her weeping husband. Had she been beaten? That's what it looked like. The bodies of the murdered lay in heaps.

He guessed that not a single resident of Willoughby had escaped the hybrids, any more than fruit could escape from a tree or wheat from a harvest field.

Along the front of the bar, moving past its beer pulls and lit FAT TIRE LAGER sign, three people, two women and a man, walked as if in procession. They were purple, the women's breasts as translucent as enormous grapes.

As he watched their tormented steps, the bizarre flash of emotion that he'd just pushed away resurfaced and grew stronger, finally focusing into something like pleasure, which brought with it the deepest of fears, that one is not oneself, and not in control, and that you might be someone, or something, that you very much despise.

Another scream rose, popping with agony. Its intensity caused to erupt within him an inferno of stabbing pleasure that momentarily overwhelmed him, and before he could stop himself, he had thrown back his head and joined his own howl to that of the excited hybrid mob in the dining room.

Choking back the shout didn't change the way he felt, or that a hybrid woman was watching him and laughing brightly. She was delicate porcelain, her body delicious with eager curves.

As the women seemed soft and desirable, the males appeared powerful but friendly, and the children amusingly naughty as they capered around striking the humans with thin rods that cut deep.

But these feelings were wrong, he must not feel them, it was a descent into some unholy cavern of the mind—but he did feel them, he was frantic with them, beside himself with the pleasure they brought.

Deep within him, he could hear a caressing whisper, as sensual as a summer breeze, urging them on, "Do it, do it again, oh, yes . . . children, my children . . . oh, yes." And also for him, a special thought layered in above the whisper, "Welcome home, my son, welcome back."

No!

By contrast with the hybrids, the faces of the people now appeared masklike, but their screams shot streams of energy that seemed to spark every cell of him with youth and life and, above all, with this new pleasure, so sweet that it hurt.

The small part of his mind still loyal to his humanity cried out to him to break the spell, to come back on mission. But pleasure so great wants intensification, and it was all he could do not to grab one of the humans and do some intricate, ripping thing that would lift him to ecstasy on a wave of screams.

Then he was dancing, and the hybrid woman who had caught his eye took his hand, and her touch sent a fabulous electricity through him. She laughed, the sound a shattering tinkle.

They danced closer and closer to the human crowd, which shrank in upon itself, and he heard the cries and the prayers, and they filled him with a lust that at once disgusted him and drove him on.

A boy had three human children tied together, and he was slowly flaying them with little nicks of a silver, hooked blade, and they were screaming, and it was being done in rhythm to the drumming. The boy's whole body was flushed with energy, sweat pouring from under his black headband.

The hybrid woman who was dancing with Mark grabbed a man by the hair and pulled him out of the group, then drew Mark toward the struggling prey. Her eyes were crystals.

Other humans were being cut out, and the mass of them was getting smaller. Some of the hybrids were gathering to one side, looking toward the door. They were running out of quarry.

The voice within him and, he knew, within them all

said, "Go to the next town, they're sleeping, take them, take them all."

Their minds were linked—his, too, it seemed. Or perhaps it was just that they were programmed—and he was, also—to think the same way. He could see that they were not a cumbersome, argumentative society, but more like a single person with many bodies and many brains.

The hybrid woman guided Mark's hand to a tapered flaying knife, and the wobbling form of the man whose pain was about to become their food and their drug.

His eyes—full of confusion, disbelief, and question—pleaded with Mark.

This induced in him a shivering electricity that was pleasurable beyond anything he had imagined possible.

So much for the math of combat. He had not expected this, not out of his own heart.

His partner thrust the knife into his hand, and he raised it, and he moved toward the man—

—and in that moment saw other eyes watching him from across the room, familiar eyes.

Linda's expression was so shocked that it instantly froze him.

He had been about to stab that man and, in so doing, join himself to the hybrids—to his sisters and his brothers.

An instant later, a flooding tide of compassion changed his vision of the situation yet again. Now he saw the human victims as vividly as he had a moment before seen their hybrid tormentors. Their faces, which had appeared wooden, were now filled with an anguish that broke his heart.

He heard their faltered prayer, "As we walk through the valley of the shadow of death, we shall fear no evil," and the children, too, praying in their spring-pure voices, clinging to the adults as they all watched the tortures of the selected, and waited, themselves, to be chosen.

He threw the flayer aside and drew his knife from its sheath, and with a sweeping thrust that involved precisely the needed strength, he cut the hybrid woman beside him in half. The torso went kicking away like a gandy dancer as the head and shoulders hit the floor, arms windmilling and teeth snapping.

He swung the knife again, and four more hybrids flew apart.

The music had stopped, and the rest of the hybrids took strange, springing leaps toward the door. Mark was in among them at once, slashing with a fury and a speed even beyond what he had previously done. The human captives now appeared motionless, eyes wide, lips parted with the distention of time-frozen screams.

He knew that he was once again in the state of extreme speed that was characteristic of hybrids, and of him.

The room appeared frozen to him, the hybrids moving in a deliberate mass, the faces of the people registering by slow degrees more and more surprise, their eyes beginning to shine, and Linda and Pete like statues, their faces sculpted by an angelic hand.

Soon only one hybrid was left alive, the boy who had been tormenting the children.

Mark advanced toward him. He was perhaps fifteen, this boy, and Mark hated to hurt him. But looking at him, the vicious dark eyes, the glitter of hate in them, Mark knew why he was so fast, and it was because he had eaten more than any of the others at the trough of human suffering, and the energy that it brought conferred on him the speed of a sun-quickened snake.

The boy backed against the wall, uttering a high,

scared snarl. What choice did Mark have? This was a pathological monster.

Bringing the knife down from above, he slashed the creature into vertical halves. For an instant, they continued to stand. The eyes vibrated with the frenetic energy of trapped wasps. Then the halves fell away from one another.

Noise exploded, voices screaming, crying, bellowing in rage and terror, a few thanking God, most calling for help, as the humans leaped to their dead, throwing themselves on the shattered remains, and went to the skinless man, who still moved slowly along muttering. His teeth flashed and his eyes flashed. Both of the women who had been with him had fallen dead.

Linda gave Mark, he thought, one of the darkest, most dangerous looks he had ever seen. Did she intuit what he was coming to see as the truth about himself, that he was not what he had believed himself to be?

"Dr. Turner" had not been lying, he saw that now.

"We need to do what we can here," he said.

The injured would still die, many of them, and the last of the skinless ones had just crumpled as softly as a fading cloud and now lay beside the row of barstools. A woman knelt beside him, her hands wanting to touch, fearing to touch.

"He's past helping," Mark said. He lifted her, a slight woman in a blood-spattered jacket, and drew her close to him. She buried her sorrowing cries in his chest.

It went on like that, as he and Linda and Pete brought what mercies they could to the stricken of Willoughby. As they worked, they said little beyond what was necessary to the job, but Mark remained deep in thought: You're half-human.

It had been wrong to think that his heart was all human, because that was not true, was it? In fact, his heart was at war with itself. He was as much two halves as the poor hybrid he had just splayed. He loathed the boy and what he had done, but also felt for him a compassion that he would have burned out of his soul if he could.

He concentrated on lifting the sacred human dead and laying them in rows, and consoling as best he could the living. He helped a man who had been partially flayed and was in shock, covering the purple, oozing ruin of his legs with strips of gauze from Linda's dwindling medical kit. Then Pete and one of the uninjured took the man out to the makeshift medical station in the street, where lights glared and the little Novocain that had been found in the one local dentist's dispensary was in use.

"Give it to the children," the man said as Linda set an IV for him.

Mark did not hear her words of reply, spoken softly in what had developed into a soft summer night. Not that he couldn't, but he was too consumed by his own tragedy. Looking at the man who had been skinned, he found himself longing to crawl out of his own skin.

A small girl spoke again, and he realized that she had been talking to him for some time.

"Will you carry me?"

He picked her up, face as soft as a dream, dusting of freckles.

"Where is my mommy?"

"Your mommy is in heaven."

"Can I go? I want to be with her."

He felt the flesh of her beneath his big hands, as soft, almost, as air. "Stay here with us, child, stay with us for a little while."

She laid her head upon his shoulder, and in anguished silence he received her tears. He gave his heart to the child, the half of it that he could. But the other half found her disgusting and wanted her dead.

More than that, though, Mark thought, if he could not find what was truly human within himself, and make it all of him, then he needed to be the one to follow this child's mother, and to die.

CHAPTER THIRTEEN

THE STORM

IN A USELESS ATTEMPT TO sweep away the anguish in her soul, Gina had turned her music up to full volume, and "Riders on the Storm," "Caro Nome," and "The Ride of the Valkyries" blared simultaneously out of six sets of the speakers that were scattered through the office.

As she worked, she screamed and cried out his name and swooped her lenses, trying to find him and cut more strike orders.

She noticed shaking and saw that clouds were surging past outside, and rain was hurling itself at the window. Yesterday, the storm had been creeping up the coast, but now it seemed to be gathering strength. Wonderful. All she needed was cloud cover thick enough to affect signal access to her satellites.

As long as that didn't happen, though, she couldn't have cared less about the storm. There was no hurricane in northern California, where she was focused.

By all indications it was a beautiful evening in the little town of Willoughby, except that there was no traffic.

The air force was convinced that Mark Bryan was dead, incinerated in the shallow cave system that they had torched with napalm. However, they hadn't brought out a body, and with a man such as him, the only way to be certain was to actually identify the remains.

She threw back her head and screamed her throat even more raw, then threw on Wolfmother's "Woman" and ditched the goddamn "Caro Nome." She threw on T. S. Eliot reading "The Waste Land": "April is the cruelest month, breeding lilacs out of the dead land . . ."

Man comes and tills the soil and lies beneath. After many a summer dies the swan—a black one in this case, for this was a black-swan day, when the impossible had turned out to be the truth.

Okay, she'd cut more orders, the hell with it, she'd burn down the whole screwed-up region, all the pretty trees and the pretty towns, she'd lay it all waste.

Where to go next? She looked at her monitors.

A major forest fire was already in progress from the last attack, and she watched a big DC-10 tanker glide slowly over the billowing columns of smoke and drop pink fire retardant. In contrast to the flooded, storm-choked Northeast, northern California was a tinderbox.

The lights flickered and for an instant she was alone in silence, her music gone.

"No!"

Her personal generator kicked in, she heard it whining. Then the music started up again. She tossed the Doors and threw on Laurie Anderson's "O Superman."

Superman, that's what he was, the real thing, a work of living art, and she had loved him hard and he had wanted it, he had delighted in her.

Superman wasn't complicated. He flew, he ditched bad guys. Mark was complicated. Probably didn't fly, but who the hell knew? Ditched bad guys—and then damn well ditched his own guys.

"Bastard! Bastard! Bastard!" She sobbed into her

hands. She asked the storm and the music, "Do you feel it when you burn?"

Of course you do, that was the whole point of the Inquisition, wasn't it? The stink of burning heretics was supposed to smell sweet to the Lord.

Napalm is sweet, they say. She wouldn't know, though, would she? She only delivered it, she never smelled the stuff, not Miss Clean up here in her tower of power.

A particularly nasty gust of wind was followed by a distant shattering of glass, then a chorus of screams. Somewhere, a secretarial pool had been penetrated by the storm—and a moment later, she could feel its wetness and smell dank, outside air as it filled the building.

What in hell was happening?

She whirled around and was appalled to see a surging wall of blackness pressing against her window. Was the building in some tornado or what?

This was no coincidence, that she did not buy for a nanosecond. Speaking of DARPA, what if the hybrids had access to the kind of scalar weapons technology that could affect weather? DARPA certainly worked on things like that.

The building shook, but this was CIA headquarters, built to withstand anything. Atomic war. The subbasement was, anyway. She thought.

She returned to her monitors. Still no traffic in Willoughby. She flew down into the streets, picking up data from as many angles as she could get, but she couldn't tell much beyond that a party appeared to be taking place in the local watering hole, the Glade. So maybe that was it, maybe everybody in town was attending some hoedown.

But they wouldn't be, not with a fireline just cresting a ridge a few miles away. They'd be able to see the flames. So what were they doing in there? They should be in their churches, of which they had six in that little tiny town. It being California, though, they were probably all cafés by now.

She made a call to the young captain who was leading the search for Mark's remains.

"I want a trip through the town. Take a look-see in the Glade, let me know what you find."

The response was silence. These guys were Air Police forensics specialists, and they had little use for interference from some anonymous CIA officer. Given that her work was so secret, her place in their chain of command had to remain unclear to them. They had been told to respond to her requests, not take orders from her.

"Captain Forbes, I need this."

"We're on it" came the eventual reply.

She watched their truck, which remained parked on the roadside near the mouth of the cave Mark had entered. Presumably, some of them were still inside, but not the captain, or he would not have answered his satellite phone.

"I need you in motion now, please."

Once again, there was no response.

She pushed back her anger. "I need you in motion now. Respond, please."

What the hell was this? They weren't going to just go silent on her, they were too professional for that. She zoomed in on the truck. Its headlights were on, but it wasn't moving.

"Are you having a problem with the vehicle? Please respond."

The driver's door opened. For some moments, that was all that happened. Concerned now, she watched intently.

"If you can hear me but I can't hear you, close the door now. I'll see it and understand."

Instead, a figure began to emerge, moving with odd, exaggerated care, prancing, touching everything as if it were hot.

Then she saw, coming out of the rear of the van, four more figures. By contrast, they moved like liquid.

Shocked, also fascinated, she watched them, her hands gripping the arms of her chair so hard pain began shooting up to her shoulders.

One of them laid something on the roof of the vehicle, and at first she thought it was a tarp or a blanket, then she knew that it wasn't that at all. She clapped a hand to her mouth, forcing back the scream that came with her realization of what she was looking at.

She jumped to her feet and her hands went to her head and tore at her hair, and she did scream. She screamed and stared, then backed away from the monitor as if it were a bomb, or something alive and poisonous.

The hybrid was laying out the skin of the driver on the roof of the van. It raised one of the flat arms so that it appeared to be saluting.

Then the thing looked up, directly toward her, and even in the gathering dark she thought she could see a grin. It waved. They all looked up, waving in unison like robots, and in that moment she felt as if they were actually here with her, in her office, their awareness of her seemed so uncanny.

She heard somebody whisper something, so vividly that she leaped from her chair and whirled around. But nobody was there.

A male voice had whispered, "Hello, my child."

Her whole body, every muscle, seemed to contract at the same moment. In her mind, she knew that this was a form of extreme shock, but that didn't neutralize it, and she pitched forward helplessly, as the flayed driver wandered away under the trees.

Softly, the voice in her mind sang a bar of "You Belong to Me."

She sucked deep breaths, forcing the terror down, forcing herself to choke back the psychosis that the existence of the voice seemed to threaten. Voices were a symptom. Schizophrenics heard them.

Outside, the storm gathered strength.

So now her forensics team was also dead. Given what had happened to the driver, God only knew what had been done to the men in the caves. Her first impulse was to call in a gigantic air strike, but on what? She'd already hit the caves.

Her hands still shook so much that she could barely control them, but she managed to reset her lens onto the town again. Nine twenty in the evening, and not a car moved, not a soul crossed a street. No lights were coming on in any of the houses.

The image of the skin returned to her mind. She shook her head, trying to shake it away. But she was dripping, it was giving her a hideous pleasure.

This hell of a job was turning her into some kind of pervert.

She threw herself back and forth in her chair, then leaped up and hurled it across the room, where it smashed into her loved and hated family photographs. Mom in the sunshine, Dad in a fedora long ago.

This situation was now entirely out of hand. It needed to go up the chain of command pronto, and way up, because what had to be done was clear and was going to take presidential approval. There had to be a nuclear strike on the Big Basin area. Deep, penetrating nukes. The whole region would be laid waste, not to mention fallout for a thousand miles straight into America's heartland.

She called Hammond, but his office line rang and rang. She tried his cell, but the cellular phone system was out of service due to the storm. His home phone didn't answer, either. Next she tried Turner's direct line. Nothing there. She got an operator at DARPA, but she couldn't raise Turner, either.

So what to do? Should she go around George? Could she? Not easy, especially not with a subject this restricted. She knew that the DCIA didn't know about it, so the White House didn't, either.

She put "Don't Cry for Me Argentina" on, grabbed her chair, and twirled round and round in it, a favorite way of thinking things out.

Approaching the administration with a request like this was going to take more than just a few videos and some anecdotal evidence. The evidence had to be overwhelming. Undeniable. A video of a human skin lying on the roof of a van was horrible, but it was not going to convince the president of anything.

She tried again to reach George. Same result. Okay, she'd have to do this another way. She prepared to face the storm.

While Linda Hicks and Pete Richardson attempted to help the people who were still alive, Mark struggled to come to terms with himself.

Did Linda and Pete know anything about him? Were they biological machines? Because that's what he was now sure he was, something artificial that had been grown in some hive like the other hybrids. He was an early model, that was all. That explained defects such as compassion and decency and love.

He ran his fingers along the pale skin of a dead hybrid.

It was beautiful, an artwork. He could feel the tiny scales, intricate. It was like feeling something with a surface of hard jewels, but soft inside.

The eyes were filmed, one hand clutching, of all things, a bit of candy.

Linda came over and looked down at the creature, her face registering her disgust.

His own skin was perfectly normal, and so was Linda's. She was a conventionally pretty woman with regular features and kindly gray eyes. There was nothing strange about him, either. His body was ordinary . . . unless, of course, it wasn't.

"Where do we come from?"

She remained silent.

"Do you know?"

"I'm from Idaho, Mark."

"Linda, I asked you a goddamn question!"

"And I answered you as best I can! I was born in Idaho Falls and I grew up there."

"And what about me? Where was I . . . grown?"

"What does that mean?"

He studied her. Her puzzlement was either expert acting or it was real.

"What am I, Linda?"

"I was trained to support you at Fort Huachuca in Arizona. We all were, Mark, it's not a mystery. I was told you had extraordinary physical powers and you were very bright. And you do and you are."

"They never told you I was a hybrid?"

"God, no. Whatever would make you say a thing like that?"

"I—I don't know. I guess it's because I'm the only one who can outrun them. Kill them close in." He shook his head. Softly he said, "I almost went over. I think . . . think so."

She reached up and touched his cheek with the cool tips of her fingers. "You're stressing out, that's all."

He turned away.

Pete's soft murmur rose as he attempted to comfort a man and a little girl, all that was left of one of the families. The voice was so gentle and yet so strong that it made Mark feel even more ashamed of the other side of his own personality. The pleasure that the killing of the mother of that child had brought him—watching it—was like the tormented memory an addict carries of being cruel while high.

"I have a predator in me," he said miserably.

Linda laughed a little and went on with her work.

To develop a case that would fly with the White House, Gina had to have on-site evidence, photos taken on the ground of the remains around the forensics van, for example, any evidence that might be present in Willoughby, anything she could get. The video they had, the casualties, would not be enough to convince the president to do what she was going to ask him to do.

Her worry was that events had outrun her, and it would take too long to gather the evidence. She saw this thing blasting without warning into mankind's face, and she wished she understood it clearly enough to enable her to suggest policy, but she did not.

She'd always thought that the extreme secrecy was a mistake. But it wasn't her lookout, was it? It had been imposed by Dr. Turner—but guess who was having to pay the price? Not the DCIA, not George Hammond, oh, no, never management. She just hoped to God that the first person to confront the president about this was not going to be a hybrid striding into his bedroom to skin him alive.

Quite an effective terror tactic, that. They did not lack for evil imagination, certainly.

If only she knew their larger motive, though. What were their aims, what were their hopes and expectations? Working as she did from the distance of the sky, information like that was not available to her.

She felt a pain in her hand, opened it, and realized that she had dug her own fingernails into her palm. Cursing under her breath, she wiped it with a Kleenex.

Now, the main question—how was she going to get out of Washington in weather this heavy? The air force had a squadron of hurricane-penetrating aircraft and so did NOAA, and they were certainly active right now, but not out of bases under the storm. In fact, every air base or airport of any kind was battened down. The airports had closed last night. This morning, Amtrak had announced that all trains were shut down.

Her only option would be to drive until she could find an open air base or airport. She could commandeer anything, even an airliner, if she had to.

She threw on her raincoat and the floppy canvas rain hat that had been bought mostly for the way it framed her face. She was not equipped at all for anything like this. Even her satphone was not working.

Outside her office, water was on the floor. With the building running on its own generators, the hallway lighting was dim and the elevators weren't operating, so she had to take the stairs down to the lobby and sign out manually rather than swipe her finger.

"Many folks still on duty?" the desk officer asked.

"Seems quiet."

He looked up at her. "You be careful out there. It's gusting past a hundred and forecast to go higher."

He'd probably like to get home, too, if there was any reasonable possibility of doing that.

She went across the wide lobby, past the columns, her sneakers quiet on the marble floor. Down here, things were surprisingly orderly. Unlike the upstairs, no water was on this floor. The doors ahead of her were facing away from the main force of the storm, too, so she could have made it to the outside parking lot and her own car. But her destination was the motor pool in the basement. She'd need some sort of official-looking car, something powerful and tough, preferably with at least some red and blue flashers. Otherwise, this was not going to work. If she could reach the interstate, she thought she might make it, unless she ran into flooding.

She took the auxiliary stairs down. Her hope that she wouldn't have to deal with any security personnel ended when she found the guard station was manned, and by a man who looked about eighteen. A kid. The worst.

"I need a pool vehicle capable of doing the storm," she said. "I want any kind of official markings, with siren and lights."

He looked up at her. The brain-dead defiance in his eyes made her consider just blowing him away. He was sidearmed, though, and you couldn't beat a holster if you had to open a purse, so that was no-go.

"Excuse me," he said. It wasn't a question, it was a "you've got another think coming."

On the theory that she might as well give herself a fighting chance, she unsnapped the purse. "What have you got for me?"

"I'm not authorized to release any of these vehicles."

She pulled out her cred. "I'm authorizing you."

He looked at it, foolishly bending his head down to do so. "This isn't—"

"This is." He had given her the moment she needed to get to her gun, which she thrust into his face. Reaching down, she drew his .45 out of his holster and hurled it away over his head. It slapped the floor, and she could hear bullets bouncing out of the magazine. "Your weapon wasn't properly secured," she said into the bulging, beetle-dumb eyes. "I'm gonna write you up on that."

Then she drew back her hand and had the satisfying experience of slamming the guy in the side of the head hard enough to put him out for at least five minutes. For good measure, she ripped his communications cables out of the floor. This sure as hell was not going to turn into a car chase.

She rejected the row of VIP Escalades. They were strongly built, you could be sure, but their tall profile was going to make them iffy in that wind. Ditto a couple of civilian Hummers. Too bad there was no M1035, the military variety. That would work.

She saw a black Ford with siren horns visible behind its grill. No flashers, but at least there was a blue emergency light that could be set up on the dash. This car was low and powerful and in useful FBI livery, so she took it.

The kid was still slumped, and she was tempted to make sure he was breathing, but she hadn't hit him that hard. He'd come around, report the theft, and eventually get some kind of annoyance rolling after her. If she could ever communicate with George again, she'd have a stop put to it.

For a person used to seeing the world in detail from above, she always found it curiously confining to leave her office, and this was triply so today. From her communications center, she could have mapped out a route for herself that would have avoided all traffic jams, downed trees, and other obstructions. There hadn't been time, though, and in any case, everything would change by the minute in a storm this intense. As it was, she had to rely on radio traffic reports, and how reliable were they going to be in weather too heavy for helicopters, and no communications?

Her access level meant she had no trouble leaving. When the guard saw her vehicle come out of the motor pool, he decided not to risk leaving his trembling shack and simply opened the gate.

She tuned the radio to a local news station and heard that the hurricane was not only far worse than had been expected, it was still gaining strength. But how could that be if it was over land? She had to assume that Washington was being struck by scalar weapons technology, and frankly, their possession of a weapon like this made it even less likely that any human force, no matter how strong, was going to be able to turn the situation around.

The car shook as if it had been picked up in the jaws of some gigantic animal. She managed to get it down the drive, though, and from there onto the access road. There had been a sawhorse closing Memorial, but it was blown to pieces, which she drove over as she entered the highway.

Her plan was to go north and west, which was the shortest route out of the weather zone. If she could manage it, she would get an air force Gulfstream from Wright-Pat to meet her at the airport in Altoona. Unfortunately, all of the nearer air bases hugged the East Coast, so Wright-Patterson was the nearest operational facility.

The difficulty was going to be reaching air force operations and getting the plane in motion. For that, she needed a working phone of some kind, and that was not going to happen until she was well out of this area.

Driving was an extraordinary struggle, but the car

was powerful and heavy, and its front-wheel drive was a major asset. Once, she saw a state police vehicle. Just to be safe, she put up her light, and he did no more than flash back at her.

The wind kept coming up under the car and lifting it off the roadway, causing brief, heart-stopping hydroplaning. She'd done some defensive driving at Camp Swampy, but that had to do with escaping from ambushes, not hurricanes. Turn-into-a-skid was the only maneuver she'd actually practiced that was relevant to this situation. Problem was, it didn't help a whole lot when the entire car was, in effect, airborne.

She kept the satellite phone on, waiting for the green light to pop up. It took a lot of cloud cover to scatter the signal—but there was, indeed, a lot of cloud cover. Worse, she was only managing about thirty miles an hour. Any faster, and she was going to blow right off this road. As it was, every mile or so, she had to maneuver around an overturned eighteen-wheeler or some other vehicular disaster.

She came to a complete blockage involving two trucks, a bus, and a lot of people. They came running toward her car. Obviously, there were casualties, and they probably thought she was some sort of official help.

She hit the brakes and hauled the wheel to the left, turning the car sharply toward the median. The instant the wind hit the side of the car, its rear seemed to take on a life of its own, and she went into a circular skid, spinning twice before she hit the shoulder. Smashing her foot down on the accelerator, she plunged into the flooded median and went splashing through it onto the opposite roadway.

Headlights came at her as something big loomed out of the rain. Swerving, she just managed to avoid the detached cab of an eighteen-wheeler, its driver clutching his steering wheel as if it were a life preserver. Then there were more lights, and she drove straight toward them, in wind so hard it turned the rain into a horizontal blur.

With full night had come flaring light to the south from the fires set by Gina's mistake. Or was it a mistake? She was right that he was a hybrid. But how would she have found out? Who had told her?

A deep strategy was at work here, Mark could see that, but it was large and subtle, its outlines difficult to bring into focus.

He listened as Pete spoke to an emergency medical team that had arrived from Travis AFB. Due to the security requirements of the mission, Pete was not allowing them into the Glade itself, and they were arguing. Their original task had been to pick Linda up, but they were calling in reinforcements now, so that the wounded could be taken to a hospital. The pitiful few. Pete had told the medical orderlies that the town had been attacked by a mob of bikers.

Linda had a child curled in her lap, a little, lost creature, his eyes gazing into the reveries of shock. As Mark came closer, Linda looked up at him, then away. She twisted her hands together.

"Linda?"

"Mark, I've got work to do."

He grabbed her wrist. "Do you see anything in me that would suggest a problem?"

"Hell no." She pulled away. "But if you don't stop worrying and start working, sir, I am gonna see a problem. I'm gonna be disappointed."

It was true. Much had to be done here, not the least of which was to locate any hybrids still in the area and eliminate the threat that they represented. It was dark, no moon, only the irregular glow of distant firelight.

He decided that he would patrol just the immediate medical staging area, not the whole community. To do this right, he had to keep every human being here in sight at all times. When this medical team attempted to return to Travis, he needed Gina to supply air support for them, but he couldn't exactly ask for that, could he?

This was already a disaster, and he could see where it was going. He was apparently the only person on the planet with much of an ability to resist the hybrids, and as far as he was concerned, his own loyalty was a huge question.

He stepped out onto the porch, then went down the alley beside the restaurant, moving silently, his eyes and ears alert to any sign.

Gina was on I-70 heading north when the wind finally began to slow. The mountains ahead were effectively containing the storm, and a few minutes later the satellite phone became operational again.

She'd made it out of a difficult situation, but she felt no pleasure or relief. She had to get things under control, and frankly, she doubted her ability to do that.

As she drove westward, the first call she made was, once again, to George. No good. He might possibly be briefing up the chain right now, but she couldn't know that. So her second call was to the Pentagon, and she found its communications intact.

Soon, she was on the line with Assistant Secretary of the Air Force Jock McMarkell. Following regs to the letter, she gave him her code, not her name. The name didn't matter, anyway. The code told him how he should respond to her request, and next to that for a presidential emergency, it would be the most secure and urgent he would be aware of. "May I know the nature of the problem?"

"I'm sorry, sir. I just need you to provide an aircraft."

For a moment, he didn't answer. Finally he said, "You do understand that the Rendition Act prohibits our transporting prisoners for the purpose of violent interrogation."

"You won't be transporting a prisoner at all." She wished she could tell him more, but that was out of the question. The only time she intended to reveal her secrets was when she was laying the situation out for the president.

"Very well. The aircraft will be there for you when you reach Altoona. And God bless you, young woman."

"Thank you, sir." After she clicked off the phone, she reflected on how alone in this world she actually was. She had lived not for Mark but for wanting Mark. Even now that she'd possibly killed him, the desire continued, whispered words of love being exchanged with what was probably an imaginary friend.

Mist came as she reached the higher elevations, billowing across the highway in ranks of fog soldiers whose sad march turned the trees to ghosts and made it seem as if the road stretched forever.

She drove on, deep into the center of America, struggling not to feel once again the evil pleasure killing Mark had given her. What was the matter with her? She'd felt the way she imagined torturers must feel, performing intimate acts of pain on helpless flesh.

She was not like that. She refused to accept it. Her response had been an extreme stress effect, nothing more. Like the voice. Extreme stress, that was all.

There was traffic now, in this unhurt part of the country, and the familiar rhythm of the road enabled her to drive faster. She tuned the radio, seeking news. Instead she heard music, oldies that reminded her of her unfinished youth, and the sorrows of her uncaressed body. Angrily, she jabbed the scan button—and heard, just briefly, a snatch of talk that almost made her jam on the brakes. She turned up the volume. "They're saying it's over the Marina District right now." Then static. Frantically, she twisted the dial. It was a late-night talk show of the type that featured ghosts, UFOs, and such. The Marina District was in San Francisco. "It's huge," the voice continued, "we can't see it anymore, but it's out there—" Then static. Then back again. "—huge aerials—"

So what was this? Where was it from? Huge aerials— could it be similar to the thing that had appeared over Big Basin in 2007? If so, the situation had just gone from urgent to desperate.

Outside, the night of stars swept on.

She waited, but nothing more came through on the radio except news of the storm and the usual lineup of music stations. The little local talker was now out of range, and she couldn't find the show elsewhere on the dial. So she continued on to the Altoona–Blair County Airport, and as soon as she walked through the small terminal, she was relieved to see her Gulfstream on the apron, lit and ready, its engines humming softly. This, at least, had gone right.

She crossed the tarmac to the plane, moving through the silence and emptiness of a regional airport in the small hours of the morning.

They'd posted a guard, an air policeman in a letter-perfect uniform, who watched impassively as she approached. He looked so dubious that she said, "I'm the guy you're waiting for."

"You're Mr. Lyndon?"

"I guess." She showed him her credential and he stepped aside. She climbed the steps into the Spartan interior of the air force transport and took a seat toward the front. Some of these planes were laid out for general officers. This one was not, so she was treated to seats that were just a cut above commercial economy. Fine, she'd enjoy less sleep and therefore fewer nightmares. Normally, to get through a night, she needed to chemically lobotomize herself with antianxiety medications and sleeping pills. She hadn't brought any of that, so sleep would be impossible, anyway.

Behind her, she heard the steps coming up with a mechanical whine, then the door closing. Immediately, the tone of the engines changed and they pulled out onto the runway. For a moment, she could see to the east and noticed lightning flickering below the horizon. To be visible from here, the storm must have grown past even the most dire predictions.

Nobody approached her, including the guard, who remained sitting silently at the rear of the cabin. They had their orders to take her to Travis AFB in California, and that's what they would do.

Her mind kept returning to the possibility that another escalation had taken place. What was the caller on the radio talking about?

As the scream of the jets rose and the plane took off, they combined in her mind with the screams of what she feared would shortly be a great number of innocent people.

Outside, the sky glowed deep orange, the blood of dawn. The plane seemed stopped in the sky, a maddening illusion. In that dawn, she thought perhaps she could see the end of one world and the beginning of another.

They knew too little, and it was too late. Too little too late—some insight. She snapped the shade down.

After the ambulances had come and taken the survivors and the dead, the night had passed in what to Mark seemed an increasingly ominous silence. You'd think that the hybrids would attack en masse and simply overwhelm him with numbers. But it had not happened. He thought of that disk. Maybe they were still hoping to use it on him.

There had been a lot more trouble than he had expected with the medical personnel, who were outraged that they would not be told more about the nature of their patients' injuries, or why they could not see the dead perpetrators, or why the civil authorities could not be involved.

Once Mark had finished concealing the hybrid remains in body bags, the medics had finally been allowed into the Glade, where the evidence of extreme agony—the human ruins, the things like scratches gouged into the walls by people trying to escape, the blood sprayed even on the ceiling—had reduced them to horrified silence.

As Mark had bagged the hybrids, he had noted that they were already beginning to deteriorate, the glassy eyeballs sinking into the heads, the scales becoming slack and gray. When he lifted the bodies, they had been like sacks filled with hard, bulging shapes, not skeletons as we understood them. There was nothing human about the way they looked now, except for those exquisite, frighteningly innocent faces of theirs, carefully designed to hide the danger they actually represented. They had the faces of angels with the eyes of demons.

He thought back on the thing in the tunnel. Seeing that face had drawn vague images to mind, hazy memories that had caused him to realize that he had little actual recollection of his life before the army. He remembered college, he remembered living in a little house in a garden, and with these memories came a kind of homesickness, as if he had left behind his real place in the world.

Who was he, really? Was he only part human? These were agonizing questions, but the answers seemed far away. If he was as that creature had described him and had been created by human science, then somebody had made fantastic progress in genetic manipulation.

When he heard the last of the ambulances pull away, he went to the front of the Glade and stood in the door watching them go. He could not go farther, not without risking Gina's wrath.

Linda and Pete now stood across the broad street in front of the dark motel, speaking intently together. From time to time, they glanced toward him.

They came over, walking briskly under a sky that was glowing with faint predawn light. The fireline on the ridge behind the motel continued to flare, but less than before.

"Mark," Pete said, "why don't you come out? You've been in there all night."

The dawn wind had come up, bringing with it the sweetness of the forest, the awakening tang of the pines and the perfume of flowers, blowing away the oily smoke that had been hanging over the town since about three.

"Come on, Mark," Linda said. "You haven't reported to Gina in hours. You need to report."

"Gina can see."

Pete spoke, his voice urgent. "What's wrong, Mark? What aren't you telling us?"

"You went to Fort Huachuca. Didn't they tell you about me there?"

They watched him, their faces carefully neutral. "We all went to Huachuca. It was for reaction-time training. To keep up with you."

"Did they tell you why you'd need special training to keep up with some fat, old colonel?"

They both laughed, but not a lot.

"Colonel Bryan," Linda said, "we don't know how you do what you do, but we're here, and a lot of lives are saved because of you."

"I took a couple of long jumps, like a hybrid might. Does that concern you?"

Linda raised her eyes to his. "So, are you a hybrid? Is that what you're trying to tell us?" She looked away.

He said nothing. Nothing said everything.

A hand covered Gina's hand, warm and encompassing, firmly male.

She had the presence of mind not to react immediately, but she would have this asshole of a guard brought up on charges, that was for damn sure.

As the hand slipped away, her eyes flew open and she leaped out of her seat—only to find that the guard was still sitting against the rear bulkhead. The copilot was shaking her awake.

"Ma'am, we have some kind of an alert at Travis."

She blinked, momentarily confused. "What? Where are we?"

"On approach. We've been ordered into a pattern."

What was this? What was he saying here? "You're telling me there's a delay? What kind of a delay?"

"Travis is on alert. We're waved off until further notice."

Now she was fully awake. "No. That's out. That order is countermanded."

"Ma'am—"

"Land the damn plane! And my chopper needs to be ready." Her plan was to do a recce over Big Basin by helicopter, then have them put her down at San Jose airport. She had a car rented and would drive the thirty-two miles from there to Willoughby.

"We could land at a civilian airport."

"San Jose?"

"Yes, ma'am."

"Do it. And find out what the hell's going on at Travis."

This was going to be inconvenient and was going to slow her down. She'd ordered the armory at Travis to provide her with an appropriate sidearm and informed the commandant that she would need a variety of cameras. Now she would be unarmed, and unless she could buy a camera in San Jose, she'd need to find the remains of Mark's unit and hope they had retained their equipment. They hadn't answered the satphone. Of course not, Mark had probably had it on his person when he was killed. But didn't they have a backup? Maybe not Linda Hicks and Pete Richardson. The second-in-command had the backup comm, and he'd died in the first attack of the hybrids.

Luck would need to get her back to Travis before sunset, and if the storm abated, face-to-face with the chairman of the National Security Council by three or four in the morning, Washington time.

The copilot came back. His face reflected concern, but also amusement.

"There's a scramble up on an unidentified aircraft reported over San Francisco."

With a sick lurch of her stomach, she recalled the radio program.

"Put me down in San Francisco."

He blinked. His expression did not change. "They're locked down."

"Oakland?"

"It's open."

"Then Oakland. And if you can, charter me a chopper. I'll deal with the billing when I get there."

He got up and went silently back to the cockpit. She slid across to the window seat, tightened her seat belt, and stared out into the empty sky.

CHAPTER FOURTEEN

THE CITY BY THE BAY

DAWN BROUGHT FOG TO SAN FRANCISCO, and with it, gray mist that muffled the buoy bells and filled the streets with ghosts. A few taxis and police cars patrolled the rising shadows, as alarm clocks sounded and trucks arrived at loading docks, and people spoke of the thing in the sky, those who had glimpsed it among the clouds. But it was idle, self-assured talk. Nobody was afraid. The general verdict was that it was a military blimp. The East Coast hurricane was a hotter topic of conversation. It had slammed Washington with the worst winds the region had ever experienced and was now moving up the coast toward New York, a great, roaring monster and the center of attention of the nation and the world.

Even so, *Today San Francisco* producer Zack Messing was getting calls from viewers about the thing in the sky. The station's Internet servers had been down for hours, and his BlackBerry couldn't pull a browser off Verizon, either, so he had not seen a picture of it. His cell phone was out, too, but the station's landlines were still working, and the calls were getting more persistent.

As much as he hated to waste time, he needed to send somebody out to look at this stupid blimp or whatever it was. It was then that the new production assistant,

Kelly Frears, came in with the breakfast box from Smitty's.

"You see the thing?" she asked as she unwrapped his fried-egg sandwich for him.

"The bullshit in the sky? Nope."

His indifference relieved her. Her aunt had been trapped in the World Trade Center and called her mom, telling her that she was burning to death, and Kelly's mother had screamed and screamed, and anything that was airborne and strange still terrified her.

"Let's hope it's nothing," Kelly said. She went to take breakfast in to makeup, where the on-cameras were having their bags painted out and their wrinkles sand-blasted away, at least for a few minutes of airtime.

As she was leaving, the switchboard rang them. Kelly snatched the phone up. "Zack's office."

Lucy said, "We're getting flooded with calls about the UFO."

Kelly told Zack.

"So go down and see if you can at least see the damn thing. Then get hold of Travis Air Force Base and get their take on it. Probably something of theirs."

Kelly really did not want to do this and was feeling sick inside by the time she reached the street, looked up, and saw the immense thing in the rising fog.

Her first sight was of a tan wing or platform covered with strange writing, and hanging just overhead. Instinct made her shrink back. The thing looked so low she could almost touch it. Then, as the fog parted into golden shreds of cloud, she saw a long, tapering antenna pointing straight toward about where Polk Gulch was. The thing was maybe two hundred feet overhead, and the tip of the antenna looked as if somebody standing, say, on Nob Hill, would be just about even with it.

She tried to read the inscription, but it was not in any

alphabet she had ever before seen. It was blocky, maybe Korean. Something Asian, anyway. No USAF marking was on it anywhere, and no NASA logo. Also, it was way below where it should be. You never saw anything this low over San Francisco.

It was just damn creepy and she decided that she did not want to be out here one more second and went back into the building and up to the studio. Zack was nowhere to be seen, so she took his seat at the board and waited.

"Give it up," he muttered as he returned, "you'll never be a director."

"Yeah, thanks for your faith. And by the way, that thing is huge." She concealed her stupid fear.

"What thing?"

"That, like, thing you sent me out to see. It's huge."

Zack thought this over. The switchboard hadn't bothered him for a while, so maybe—hopefully—the public had lost interest. He called downstairs for a report and discovered that he hadn't heard anything from them because they were too busy even to alert him.

He turned on Kelly. "Jesus, you moron, get a camera out there! Do it now!"

"All right, don't have a hissy fit!"

"*Go!*"

She ran into the studio. "Mike, Zack wants a camera on the street. There's some kind of a thing going on with some weird plane."

"You got it," Mike said.

Kelly thought him profoundly cool. He'd been mostly in TV, but he'd done cinematography on a couple of indie features, which gave him interesting connections. She had also detected the probability of a pretty spectacular show down below, but nice girls didn't think about that sort of thing, did they?

Yes. They. Did.

She followed him down the back stairs.

"Um, actually, you can't see it from back here. It's, like, over Polk."

"It's a plane and it's 'over Polk'? What's that mean, it's not flying?"

"It's sitting there in the air. Um, a blimp, sort of."

He frowned slightly, then hefted the HD camera onto his shoulder and went through the rat's maze of the station to the front entrance. She followed.

The fog had closed in again. "I guess we missed it," she said, relieved. But as she was turning back, she saw him starting to shoot, and she realized why: The thing was visible in the swirling fog—just—as a great, looming shadow.

Then, in the abrupt way it so often does in San Francisco, the fog blew off, and she saw the whole object, and a shock like a slap went through her because it was absolutely and totally immense. On top, long, tapering antennae reached at least a couple of hundred feet into the sky. Below them was the body of the thing, a vast ring of metal with these huge wings coming out front and back. In the middle of the ring was that other antenna, that pointed toward the ground. The tip of it glowed purple, and a haze of purple light extended down into the streets below.

The thing itself was totally silent, but rising from all around the city, she could hear sirens. They were echoing, blasting, one joining another—and then a fire truck wheeled around the corner and went thundering past in the direction of Polk.

"What is going on?" she asked nobody in particular. Mike was lost in his world of taping. Then Zack came running out with Hildy MacIntyre and that Gary guy who was a gaffer, and a couple of other guys, all haul-ing cable. Like, hey, they were taking this live.

There was a distant, ringing boom, then another, closer, then another and another, and the manhole cover across the street flew into the air and hit the sidewalk with an echoing clang.

Everybody stopped. Everybody looked. Then they looked at one another.

"Get inside," Zack said.

"Shot of a lifetime," Mike muttered.

"Get inside!"

The crew began rolling back cable. Mike, on batter-ies, kept his camera trained on the object. As Kelly started into the building, she saw something moving in the manhole. She turned, looked more closely. A face had been in there, eyes bright. The instant she had spot-ted it, it had disappeared. She decided right here and right now to do the same.

As she went down to the garage, she said nothing to Zack, who would have a major hissy, given that they were live in eight minutes. But she was just going to be gone, that was all there was to it.

She kept her gorgeous red Vespa GTS 250 locked tightly to the bike rack, largely so that Rick Heimer wouldn't come down here and try to wire it, if only just to rev it. He needed to get one. He needed to face this.

As she took the stairs three at a time, a sound rose toward her. Rumbling. An earthquake? No, there was no shaking.

She came to the bottom of the stairwell and touched the handle of the big brown door that led to the garage. She didn't go in because the sound was coming from there. But what in hell was going on, because it sounded like some kind of a drum corps. The drumming was infectious and intense but weird to be coming from down here. Also, it made her feel even more uneasy. She recognized that she was near panic. But she had to open that door. She had to get to her Vespa because she just plain wanted nothing more to do with this situation or with Frisco right now. It was a weird city, for sure, and she liked that, but this was just too weird.

She opened the door and was blasted by drumming so loud that it almost knocked her back into the stairwell.

The first thing she saw were kids, nice-looking kids, banging snare drums with hands that moved so fast you could hardly see them. Amazing hands. Some younger ones danced among the parked cars. As she headed past Zack's Beemer, she noticed people were in it. Then she saw that a lot of the other cars had people in them, too, and they were jumping around and shaking them and squalling, as if they didn't know why they couldn't make them go. She decided to ignore this for now and call it in when she was back in cell-phone range. Because she could see that this was no high school band in here. Also, a smell was in here—strong—one that she knew from her childhood. When they were kids, her brother had gone reptile crazy and kept a bunch of exotic snakes, and his room had smelled of this same musty, stinkbuggy odor. The garage was full of children who smelled like snakes, and not only that, they were all watching her. They were soft-faced little things, sort of. The *sort of* part was their eyes, which followed her with a steadiness that was exactly like Tim's snakes' eyes.

"They look hungry," she had said to Tim once, when looking at the snakes sliding and swaying in their terraria. "They're snakes," he'd replied. "Unless they're asleep, they're hungry."

By the time she had got to the Vespa and was fumbling with the lock, the kids were dancing close to her.

"Hi there," she said to the nearest one, a little boy wearing a T-shirt with a weird symbol on it that looked like the symbols on the thing overhead. But, hell, wait. The symbols *weren't* weird. They were from *Star Trek*. It was Klingon! But what it might say was another question. She didn't exactly read the stuff.

She turned the combination cylinder too far and had to start over. Okay, she could do that, she just had to get rid of this shaking. The little boy was close behind her now. She had never known any emotion that approached the terror she was feeling. She had not been aware that there was fear so great that it could stun you like a physical blow, which it was doing right now, as she saw the smile coming into the paint-white face of the child. She could not stop looking at it, at the strange, pearly teeth, at the tiny scales that made the creature appear like something that had been manufactured, some sort of odd plastic child that was inexplicably and horribly alive. It snaked along to the deafening rhythm of the drums, closing in on her and her scooter, which she finally pulled from the rack with a cry so loud and so raw that she did not realize that it was her and thought for a second that a wild animal was also in here.

The child had something in its left hand, a sort of stick—or, no, she saw that it was a blade, and she knew damn well that it wanted to hurt her with it. It came closer, smiling a little, innocent smile.

Soft-looking or not, this child was infinitely more terrible than anything she'd ever seen in any nightmare. As she started the scooter, the child came near her, very near. Its hand thrust the blade, long, silver, tapering, at once beautiful and ugly.

The drums hammered, the child slid the blade closer

to her, and she felt in her right thigh a terrible fire and knew that it was cutting her. Somehow she managed to move the throttle, causing the scooter to shoot ahead and go lurching up the exit ramp. Then she turned, ignoring the one-way sign in the alley as she always did, and she was out of there, she was in the bright morning with fast clouds coming in, and that great, terrible thing up there still, now hanging not a hundred feet overhead, actually below the summit of Telegraph Hill, she could see that, and, standing on a roof across the street, the roof of that great blue painted lady that was all full of gingerbread and had that wonderful turret, was the little old man who lived there. He had a rifle and was quite calmly and steadily firing bullet after bullet into the gigantic machine.

A woman passing in a Lexus shouted out the window, "Jesus Christ is Lord, Jesus Christ is Lord," as the thunder of the drums from the garage began to get louder.

They were coming out and she had one thought now, which was to get the hell away from them as fast as humanly possible, because this was not a safe place to be, not at all. She did not want to go west on Geary, not directly under the thing, and she didn't want to go anywhere near any blown manholes, because live things were down in there. What she wanted to do was to get home to her little apartment in Berkeley, where she still lived because she was going back next fall to get her MFA, just after she'd built up a little more money in the bank.

Going toward the Bay Bridge was going away from the machine anyway, so that was what she did.

Even over the buzzing of the scooter, she could hear drums and more drums rising throughout the city, all beating to the same rhythm. It was eerie, it was impossible, but then she saw a troop of the creatures coming down Geary near Jones, and they had their drums and they were wearing some kind of weird cloaks with wobbled up human faces on them. These looked like people's skins, but that could not be. They were some kind of cloak.

A man painted red stood in the middle of the street, his arms windmilling. You could see his teeth. He had no lips. He was naked, his inner thighs running brown. Did he have any idea how disgusting he was?

She sped up.

Over the rumble of drums, over the sirens and the echoing shots, there came another sound, the angry scream of a military jet, and she saw it flying low, blue fire coming out of its exhausts. It headed straight for the gigantic thing in the sky, and she stood up on the racing scooter and threw her head back and shouted at the top of her voice, "U.S. Air Force, U.S. Air Force, *U.S. Air Force*!"

The plane went into a tight turn and there was a high, screaming hiss and a bright white dot shot off it and into the machine. This was followed by a flash and a rumble that could have been the thunder at the end of the world, it was so loud.

When the smoke cleared, though, the machine was still there. Nothing had changed except that the missile had exploded inside its guts, to no apparent effect.

The purple light on the end of the down-pointing antenna was still just as bright. The machine had not moved an inch. But she did see that the black block lettering on its base was moving, the letters changing as she watched.

Now the jet, which had disappeared behind Nob Hill, came speeding back, the echoing blare of its engines awesome to hear, and this time it fired four missiles, which went speeding toward the target and all . . . sort of went into it.

The thing disappeared into smoke, this time a lot of it. As cheers rose from the street, she stopped her scooter and got off it and cheered as well, because it was just so wonderful to see that awful thing hurting. An arrow's gleam, the jet shot up into the tall sky, its afterburners like two bright eyes dwindling to one bright star.

But, no, the thing wasn't hurt after all, it was maneuvering and opening, the great arms or paddles were opening and something came falling out, little flecks that shone in the sun and fluttered out in clouds around the thing, looking like chaff at first, then, as they dropped closer, like silver gliders about the size of two fists.

Ahead, a woman sat beside an overturned chair in front of a small restaurant. She sat on the curb with her knees up to her chest. She was leaning forward and something was so strange about her head that Kelly stopped to look at her. It was . . . was it shriveled? Or, no, that could not be. No—but—that was her brains there on her head. Her brains were visible, you could see them right there. Her hair was gone and her scalp was gone and her skull was gone, and as Kelly watched, holding out a nervous hand, not understanding what help she might offer, one of the things from above landed on the woman's naked brain.

It looked like a big beetle made of shiny silver metal, with long legs and mandibles like scissors. It began to snip at the brain as delicately as if it were doing surgery.

In a thick, slurred voice, the woman said, "Would you please telephone the secretary of defense and inform him that hostilities have commenced. My name is Abby Arthur. I am his mother."

Could this be possible? Daniel Arthur was secretary

of defense and the Arthurs were an old San Francisco family and they might even live somewhere around here, Kelly had no idea.

Other insects came, landing on and around Mrs. Arthur, and in a moment her eyes were being carried away into the sky, held in the claws of the things, which buzzed like insects, but ten times as loud, a throaty, menacing sound.

Mrs. Arthur lurched forward, arms akimbo, and toppled into the street. As she fell, the insects pulled a big, red-dripping sheet off her and carried it away also. As it was taken into the sky, shoes and clothes dripped down from it. Abby Arthur was now a red mass of angles hunched on the sidewalk, unrecognizable as the human being she'd been a few moments before.

Kelly revved the Vespa to its max. There wasn't a question of heading toward the Bay Bridge now, not with those things back there, so she went up the Embarcadero instead. Maybe she'd somehow get around through the Marina District and across the Golden Gate into Marin. But what would she do in Marin? She didn't know anybody there, she didn't even know the streets except for the way up into Muir Woods.

She moved her right hand off the throttle for a moment and touched her thigh, which produced a pain like fire. She threw back her head and screamed because she knew there was no skin on her leg, no jeans, nothing, and this had been done by the kid in the parking garage.

Now the drumming got louder and louder yet, and along with it came long, high howls that swept in echoes around her, and she saw, coming down all the streets toward the Embarcadero, bands of the strange, pale creatures.

As they came, they brought with them another sound,

a great gushing welter of noise, the wrenching of metal, the shattering of glass, screams, howling engines, hisses, explosions, and a cascading roar that, as she looked up, appeared to come from what at first appeared to be a single object—immense—twisting and turning across the sky.

Above it and through its dark translucence could be seen the vague outline of the great unknown machine, which appeared to be controlling the movement of the cloud.

At the same time, she saw all around her windows flying out of buildings, roofs being sucked into the sky, awnings rising off stores, and cars and trucks and people swarming into the sky, the people kicking and clutching, dogs barking as they rose, children snatching at their parents, horns honking and engines revving, the wheels of cars casting back and forth as the drivers steered helplessly.

She felt suddenly lighter and jammed on the power and her scooter screamed down the street and right through one of the squads of creatures, tossing a couple of them aside and causing horrific shrieks and a burst of even wilder drumming.

Overhead, now, the whole great mass of people and objects was being directed by great, thudding booms from the strange machine and was churning and boiling out toward the bay.

Thousands of people must be up there, and what was happening to them was the most terrifying thing that Kelly had ever known. It seemed almost like a sort of theatrical event, not anything real, yet the scale of it was so unimaginably huge that it was completely beyond comprehension. But it looked as if the entire city—everything that was even slightly loose—had been ripped from the grasp of gravity, and her own stomach quailed as her scooter kept threatening to join them, and she rode with her head down over the handlebars, heedless of direction, safety, anything, just trying with all her soul to get away from here.

The drums hummed and roared, mixing with the single, vast scream that the city had become, and the booms of the great machine overhead, thundering as it drove its quarry through the sky.

The creatures—aliens, she supposed—were as pale as dolls, their faces gleaming in the sun, their bodies strong and young, their children darting among them full of happy excitement. They wore ordinary clothes but in strange ways, as if they had not yet understood how to put on a shirt frontward. They looked like some kind of drunk Halloween party coming down the streets.

Chairs and stoves and TVs and books were now gushing out of the windows of houses and apartments and offices along with the occupants, adding to the dark, towering cloud of living people and possessions until it blotted the sun and shattered the last clouds of morning, and the machine directing it all disappeared somewhere above it.

She twisted the throttle and the Vespa leaped ahead, and she shot the length of the Embarcadero. As she passed the Aquatic Park, the noise from above increased thunderously. Horns started honking, people screaming and praying, adding to the panic of the dogs and the shrieks of the crazed horde of gulls that was following the living cloud.

The drumming stopped. The howls stopped. With a noise unlike any she had ever heard before, a resonant, howling shriek, the mass of people and their possessions dropped two hundred feet into the water. Geysers erupted as cars and trucks and buses hit and around them the furniture, the mailboxes, the flailing human forms and the struggling animals. The waters splashed white and frothed and the gulls swooped, their wings gleaming in the lovely sun.

Shapes were around her again, creatures running as nobody could ever possibly run, gaining even as she wound the Vespa up as far as she dared. They breathed against her, clutching and growling.

Only by turning the bike practically into a bullet did she outrun them.

They were a quarter of a mile back now, so she put the Vespa into gear and went up Bay Street this time, heading for Marina, then the Presidio and the Golden Gate into Marin. But would Marin be safe? Why would it be? Or any other place?

But, no, of course not, what was she thinking? The bridge was going to be a madhouse, probably blocked or even collapsed if enough people and cars had been dropped on it.

She rode on, the scooter buzzing, her leg that had been skinned now burning in the wind and salt of the air near the water. The sky was full of gold now, the outer bay racing with whitecaps. This most beautiful of cities still appeared fair in the spreading morning, but for the black scar of debris and ruin that filled the inner bay.

Racing down the street, she stood up on the scooter and roared her rage and her fear, then, as the scooter wavered, dropped back down.

She now possessed only one thought, only one need, which was to survive. She would head south into the wilderness of Big Basin and hide there. There were caves down there, so she'd live in a cave. She'd go down the Pacific Coast Highway through Half Moon Bay and then out into the Basin, to the isolated towns back in there.

Then she heard another sound, strange, hard to understand. Rhythmic, hard, and hot. That, and clattering on the pavement around her, clattering and deep humming.

Something grabbed her neck, digging into it from behind, and she cried out and reached back and ripped at the squirming, buzzing thing. It was another of those big bugs like the one that had torn up Mrs. Arthur, a metal insect from hell.

She arched forward screaming, controlling the scooter with one hand while she pulled at the thing with the other, and its wings snarled and its scissor mandibles snicked frantically.

Then she had one of its leathery wings in her hand, and she yanked and yanked, and finally it came off and she saw the creature in detail, the complicated face working, metal flashing, and beneath deep burnished steel brows, two glaring eyes. And they were brown. And they were human eyes.

She hurled it away from herself and let the vomit of her terror splash away into the wind as she gagged and screamed and drove the bike as hard as it would go.

She was on Skyline passing a jewel-blue lake, and the morning air racing at her was sharp with the sea. A commuter bus trundled past in the opposite direction, on its innocent way into the stricken city. Even yet, apparently, there had been no general warning. Perhaps there would never be, perhaps the shock of what was happening was too great. Yet a jet had come. Managed nothing, but come.

The bike swerved, she fought for control, felt it slipping, then it jumped the median and she found herself facing the oncoming traffic.

A bus, its horns blaring, its driver white-faced, passed

her with an inch to spare, its tailwind rocking the scooter. Then a motorcycle came at her, the driver invisible in his helmet. She swerved, but not enough, and he struck her a glancing blow. She recovered, he didn't, and he went skidding off down the highway, the motorcycle sputtering and whining, and she heard his faint, sad cry as he ripped along the pavement.

Then an eighteen-wheeler hit the motorcycle and the rider, amid great clanging and crunching and roaring.

Overhead, a helicopter sputtered and spun inside a raging cloud of what must have been more of the metallic insects.

She was away, but now having to speed between onrushing lanes of cars with just millimeters to spare on each side of her. There was no way to return to the other roadway, no way to stop, no way to escape, and she thought that she might have escaped the bizarre people and the insects only to be killed by a morning rush hour that had not even the slightest idea that anything was wrong.

An opening appeared between her and the shoulder. She swerved the scooter, shot across the pavement and onto the gravel, then off it and into the brush. Throttling back, she brought the Vespa to a stop and, as soon as she did, heard more sound from above.

At first, looking up, she didn't understand what she was seeing. What was this spinning, popping, whining mass of the insects doing? But as it twisted and turned and screamed like an engine gone mad, she glimpsed a red stripe inside the mass, then an area of whiteness, and understood that it was a helicopter that had entirely been covered by the things.

An instant later, it came spinning down and hit the ground hard fifty feet away, the impact causing it to bounce and turn over on its side, busted rotors cartwheeling past her head with a horrifying screech of tearing metal. Dozens of the insects were crushed, and the rest rose up and swarmed into the sky, a silver column in the golden lace of the clouds.

The helicopter lay there, an impossible, crushed little thing with a few of the insects still crawling on it . . . with movement inside.

Her first impulse was to jump on the Vespa and just ride, but then a woman's long arm came out the shattered window of the upward-facing door, and her hand scrabbled along the surface, seeking to open it from the outside. Toward the rear of the shattered fuselage, a spray of fuel came out.

In seconds, the woman was going to burn. Sick herself, almost so afraid that she could not do it, Kelly forced herself to go forward. One of the insects tried to leap at her, but its broken wings made it go awry and she stomped it, crushing it to a mass of red blood and meat, and gleaming shards of metal. What in hell was it, a mixture of a living form and a machine, or was it wearing armor?

Would the others notice and come back, or those running creatures—would they appear again?

"Lady," she said, "lady."

"Get the door open, it's gonna go up!"

Kelly pulled at it, but it wouldn't give, so she yanked shards of the plastic window out and threw them aside, but as she did so, a long tongue of orange flame, precise and tapered, appeared above the shattered engine compartment.

"Oh, no," the woman groaned, "oh my God . . ."

Kelly grabbed her shoulder and yanked and the woman screamed, but she came partly through the window.

The entire engine compartment burst into flames, and at the same time the sound of drumming rose from the highway, and the cries of the people became even more terrible. Leaping from roof to roof of the stopped cars were lithe figures, preternaturally quick, and she could see them waving long wands down among the cars.

She pulled the woman again, drawing her head out the window. Now she was like a bust sticking out, her arms pinned beside her. The flames ate toward her, and she shook frantically, throwing her head back and forth, trying to force her body out.

Kelly scrambled up on the side of the fuselage between the woman and the flames and took her under her arms and lifted with all her strength. The woman flopped like a fish and then came out, first one arm and then the other, then she clambered up and out, and the two of them fell off the burning ruin and rolled away.

From here, Kelly could see, directly through the shattered windshield, the pilot still in his helmet, his face was a red, grinning skull.

The woman grabbed Kelly's arm. "Too late for him," she said.

She was beautiful, this woman, with penetrating eyes and flowing hair and an expensive, torn suit that looked like a designer original or something. Rich woman in a helicopter, maybe going to her beach house, whatever.

"That thing work?" she asked, striding over to the Vespa.

Kelly got on it. With two people, it was a lot slower, but she wasn't about to leave this woman behind. She motioned the woman to mount behind her.

"You know where Willoughby is?" the woman asked.

"Yeah, its down from Boulder Creek. I know the area, I bike out in there."

"Let's go."

"You got a place there? We can hole up?"

"Just *go*! NOW!"

As Kelly fired up the scooter, her cell phone rang. "Hello?"

The woman shouted in her ear, "Jesus, what now? Move this damn thing!"

Kelly stuffed her Bluetooth in her ear as she headed out.

"Hey, Kel, we're, like, are you gonna be able to do poker tonight?"

She did not believe it, but this was Chad Esterhaz, the artist who worked at Schramm's sandwich shop, and he was calling from Berkeley to confirm that she would be at their weekly poker game.

"Chad, are you insane? Get out of there!"

"Excuse me?"

"Do it! Go!"

Looking around, Kelly didn't see any road except the highway and she sure as hell wasn't going back there.

"You coming?" Chad said. "Because we need to do the buy."

The snacks. The beer. "Chad, don't you get it? San Fran is being fucked, half the people are in the bay! So get out of there!"

"You sound funny. Are you all right?"

"Did you know there's a UFO over San Francisco?"

"Yes. They say it's ours. On the TV. I was watching, but it went off. It's *Judge Judy* on Five now, I think." He paused. "It's all just normal. TV is normal."

This was insane. "Chad, you call everybody you know and you tell them to get the hell out of there. Get out to the country, get out of the whole Bay Area."

"Kelly? Is this Kelly?"

"Yes! Listen to me—do this!"

"Uh—I—Kelly?"

"Move it!" the woman shouted. "Faster!"

"Lady, we need a road that's not the highway!" Then, into the phone: "Chad, the UFO or whatever it is—it's tearing San Fran down, I mean it. So you listen to me, and you *do what I told you!*"

"Kelly?"

She cut off the call. He better figure it out, was all she could think.

She pulled up.

"Don't stop!"

"I need to map this!"

Kelly looked along the highway. If she cut across the Olympic Golf Course, they'd be in Daly City, and from there they could travel along 35 and onto U.S. 1, then down into Big Basin.

Crossing the golf course was interesting because the Vespa wanted to skid in the grass. Then there was a *clunk* and she thought they'd been hit by a bullet.

"Jesus!" the lady yelled.

"What was it?"

"*Golfers!*"

This far from downtown, people didn't know, of course. Why would they? And as they drove through the expanding life of Daly City's morning, there wasn't the slightest sign of any trouble. Children in blue uniforms crossed a street, a girl laughing, two boys running ahead toward a yellow school bus. A runner passed, absorbed in his music, his face sweating, full of happy energy.

"Hey," Kelly yelled, standing up as she rode, "hey, listen to the damn radio, you people! Hello?"

"It's not gonna be on the radio," the woman said, her voice miserable.

"How the hell do you know?"

"I'm a federal officer. I know, believe me."

Kelly sped on, and clinging to her back in the fresh light of the morning, was the terrified woman who had fallen from the sky.

CHAPTER FIFTEEN

THE PRESIDENT

UNTIL THIS WRETCHED STORM, WITH the economy coming back and the Iraq war finally behind the country and his approval ratings looking somewhat better, Richard Crawford's presidency had actually been working. He slept well and woke up refreshed, and even his unique marriage had remained comfortably concealed. He had not wanted to leave Carlie out of his life, and thank God it hadn't been necessary. Virtually every president had had his Carlie Winston, except for the few who'd had boyfriends. Even the most public scandals never touched the real privacy of presidential life. You lived in an apparent fishbowl, but really behind a wall of illusions.

He was in his private office getting ready for FEMA when a rather surprised looking Carlie appeared in the doorway. By day, she was his executive secretary. By night, quietly, she joined him and Lucille in bed. They'd been a threesome for more than twenty years.

He glanced up at her. "Damage report?"

She was silent. He had been expecting information about the hurricane. FEMA—his FEMA—was more than ready to meet any emergency. The legendary catastrophe that had followed Hurricane Katrina would not be repeated on his watch.

Last night, the White House had rocked like a ship, but there had been no structural damage beyond a few leaking windows. Trees were down, of course, but by tomorrow the seat of government was going to look just as it should. The rest of the region, though, was another matter, and the storm was still playing itself out, dumping inches of rain on New England.

She said, "There is a UFO over San Francisco."

He laughed. "You're not drunk at ten in the morning?" But, of course, she didn't drink. She was a teetotaling Methodist, was Carlie. She'd toasted their victory with a glass of sparkling apple juice.

"No . . . no. Something is wrong."

"Excuse me? What are you saying?"

"The military—uh—they're coming. The intelligence people. It's an emergency."

"It's a UFO." He chuckled again. Carter and Clinton, two different types of idiot, had both tried to find out what was known inside the CIA about UFOs. What was apparently known was that they were some sort of peculiar phenomenon of no importance that could not be understood and didn't do anything that mattered. There were these supposed alien abductions, but that had to be a lot of trailer-trash hysteria, right?

She looked at him so gravely that he laughed again. "What's going on? Clue me in before I'm dealing with the wolf pack."

Before she had a chance to respond, his office began filling up with people. He found himself facing Dick Lamson, his CIA director and old friend; Lewis Stern, Homeland Security; Secretary of Defense Arthur; plus the Secretary of the Air Force and half the Joint Chiefs.

He said, "We'd better take this to the Cabinet Room." On the way, he asked, "What happened, somebody get hit with a rectal probe?" That was in the alien-abduction lore, he remembered it from *South Park*. Nobody said a word in response.

In the Cabinet Room, Dan Arthur began to speak. Vice President Wilson and Secretary of State Adams both appeared, more uniforms behind them.

"Mr. President, we have an unusual situation in San Francisco," Dan said. "There is this—Carlie, could you get some imagery, please?"

She got the monitor turned on and there flitted up onto the screen an image of what Richard Crawford thought at once was an odd thing and—almost by instinct—sensed was a bad thing. Certainly, it was no flying saucer, this huge mass of machinery floating in the sky.

The image rotated. "We're scouting it with a Predator, sir," Secretary of the Air Force Hollis said. "That's what you're seeing."

The object was hanging over Telegraph Hill, looking like some sort of space debris, all angles and strange shapes. Below it, the president could see Coit Tower. He could see down into Polk Gulch. He thought wistfully of the Swan Oyster Depot. God, he loved San Francisco. Presidential life is grand, but it is also claustrophobic.

He tried to concentrate on the thing they were showing him, which was made up of all sorts of girders and big metal plates, with tall antennae reaching into the sky.

"Well, it's weird. But I thought, ah, aren't they more hubcappy, flying saucers?" His mind began to return to the storm. "Where's FEMA? FEMA should be giving me reports and I don't have a thing."

"The city is in chaos." This was General Stuart, Gen-

eral of the Army. Not exactly smart, not exactly dumb.
An operator.

"Of course it is, we just got hit by the goddamn
storm of the century! Look, I want FEMA in here, goddamnit! Excuse my French." Crawford hated the idea
of leaving foulmouthed Nixon tapes behind. That was
not going to happen to him, goddamnit, despite that he
hadn't learned to talk until he was a God-fucking damn
marine.

"It's not Washington. Washington is coping. It's Frisco."

Crawford looked again at the screen. So, the dopers
and the gays were panicking. "No surprise there, people.
Not even Frisco is bizarre enough to handle something
like that. It'd scare me shitless, if I was there. To be sure."
He looked to his CIA director. "What is that thing,
Dick?"

"Sir, it's a long, complex story. We're dealing with a
rogue scientist here. We believe that—"

The president held up his hand. "No. Not what you
believe. What you know."

"Apparently—"

"Certainly. What you know certainly."

"A genius genetics engineer called Turner who was
working in the nonhuman bioformation project at Dulce,
New Mexico, developed a means of creating artificial
creatures, and—"

"I'm seeing girders and beams and—"

"That's something the creatures themselves designed.
It's got to do with gravity-based war fighting. And it's
a communications platform. It generates a broad-scale
microwave field. Apparently, the creatures are networked
and use this field to communicate with one another. The
field surrounds the device for about a hundred kilometers in all directions."

What in hell was all this about? Dulce, New Mexico? He'd never heard of the place. But why should that be a surprise? Since the day he walked into the White House—before—he'd been blindsided by intelligence types. He wanted to flare up at Dick, but he controlled his temper. Dick had probably been blindsided himself from deeper inside the Langley rathole. Some damn maggot down in there concealing some god-awful screwup.

From his two years of experience in this office, he knew one thing for certain: The president of the United States was the last man to find out and the first to be blamed.

"So, okay, it looks like it's just sitting there. So what?"

General Hollis said, "Mr. President!"

"Yes, General?"

Dick Lamson reacted. "No! No, wait. Wait just a second, General. Let me do this."

"This is urgent!"

"Let me bring him up to speed! Excuse me, Mr. President."

The president held up his hands. "Everybody stop yapping! You guys want to fuck each other in the ass, be my guest, but step out into the hall, please. Now let's go ahead with this. Dick?"

"All right. Back in 1952, a group of aliens met with President Eisenhower, and—"

"Aliens?"

"Nonhuman. Nonhuman beings. They—"

"That's all real? That bullshit? And this is theirs? This thing?"

"What has happened is that a rogue scientist used their technology to develop an extraordinary means of genetic manipulation and created an entirely new type of intelligent creature. Smarter, faster, and more powerful than us. He called them hybrids. They were intended to replace human soldiers on the battlefield."

Lamson showed the president Dr. Turner's list of hybrid criteria, a famous document in the hidden world of biomechanical engineering.

"What the hell," the president muttered as he read. "'He is a device, not a human being.' And more intelligent than we are. Come on, nobody could build anything like this. This is impossible!"

"Sir, no, it is not. They were supposed to have been destroyed."

"They were *built*?"

"They were built."

"Oh, wonderful, I'm so happy. Please arrest this guy, this Turner, and put him in jail. ADX Florence, deepest hole they have, and then let's get on with reacting to the frickin' *storm*!"

"The creatures he designed and built fulfilled every one of those criteria. The operation was called Project Hybrid."

"Okay. I have absorbed this. So please tell me what we are doing about the damn storm. *Now!*"

Dick Lamson burst out, "Ritchie, his creation has escaped! There are apparently underground lairs up and down the West Coast, and the damn things are smarter and stronger and faster than we are, and we are in terrible, terrible trouble. Ritchie, will you fucking *listen*?"

Silence in the room, with everybody wondering the same thing: Could even Dick Lamson get away with an outburst like that?

The president looked from face to pale, staring face.

"Okay," he said quietly, "it's bad. Worse than the storm. So we had a bad night last night here in the good ole US of A. Please continue to brief me."

General Hollis said, "We attempted a shoot-down—"

"What?"

"Sir, we attempted a shoot-down without success."

"Whoa. Without orders from me?"

"Sir, it was an emergency," the general yammered.

"You'd better show him," the secretary of defense said quietly.

"It sounds like the last thing we want to do is piss the bastards off by shooting at their shit, am I right? So, yes, please show me. I want to see why you apparently fired on an unknown thing over an American city without informing me."

"We are informing you," Hollis snapped. "Right now."

The president pointed at him. "Back off." He was having no insubordination from any of these people, none of whom had, it seemed, done much of anything right, whatever in holy hell was going on. And he was going to call Dick on the carpet when they had a private moment.

Hollis used a remote to shift the imagery to another view, this one of a huge mass of brown water, like the surface of a sewage-treatment plant.

"Okay, what am I seeing here?"

"That's the bay. San Francisco Bay."

"But—" And then the president understood. That wasn't sludge at all, that was an incredible mass of floating debris.

"We're in terrible trouble," Lamson repeated.

"But—what? What is this? What's happened here? What are those white things in the water, and the—what?—what's going on down there?"

"Sir, they are bodies."

A ghastly, sick fear boiled up in Crawford. "But what are those silver things? What are they doing?"

"Sir," Hollis said, "they're some sort of robotic forms, and they're harvesting material from the bodies, taking eyes and skin, in some cases removing other organs. The hybrids are brilliant, remember, and they are apparently prolific genetic designers. My guess is that you are looking at purpose-designed biorobots at work down in that water."

The words struck the president with the effect of acid in the face. An ominous weight gripped his heart. What in hell was the man telling him? Biorobots? What?

His mind sought for some way to stop whatever was happening out there—bombs, military action, some sort of poison, maybe, in the bay. Firmly, he suppressed the outburst of orders that clamored to be shouted. If ever there was a time for careful consideration, this was it.

He poured himself some water, took a drink, and formed what he hoped was a useful question. "They're coming from some lair, a lair underground? Who said that?"

General Hollis said, "The device was never tracked anywhere but at low altitude. The creatures that appeared when it did came up out of the sewers. So, we assume the point of origin is underground."

"Exactly how many people are dead out there, General?"

FEMA director Adam Stern, who had slipped in a few moments before, now opened a folder. "Based on floating-body densities, we believe that there are approximately two hundred thousand people in the bay at this time."

"All dead?"

Stern nodded his gray, distinguished head. "I'm sorry."

"First, we need to shoot that thing down."

"Sir," Hollis said, "as I was explaining, we tried."

"What did you use? A Piper Cub? A deer rifle?"

"We deployed an F-22 out of Travis AFB. There are four stationed there."

"So it attacked and it missed. Then what went wrong? Did it crash? Return to base for breakfast?"

"It fired a missile, which detonated inside the structure."

"And?"

"There was no effect, so the pilot launched his whole flight. Again, detonations with no effect."

"Well, try harder!" The president looked around the room. "Another thing. There is experience with this. Somebody knows something about it."

"The rogue scientist—"

"Besides him! Somewhere in your rathole, Dick, there is some sonmabitch who has a handle on this."

Dick Lamson had that look on his face that had given him away at the poker table in college. Big joke, a CIA director who was a dead giveaway at poker. He was smart, though, damn smart.

"Who is it, Dick? I want him here. Somebody said Turner. I heard Turner. If he's insane, put him in a straitjacket *and* in jail. But please, fellas and gals, *do it now*!"

"We will find the appropriate party."

The president looked from one of them to the other, trying to keep his eyes steady, fighting back the rage he felt. A huge, fine city had just been wrecked and two hundred thousand Americans were dead, and what in hell was going to happen next? It was appalling beyond words.

"It's been a low-level issue," Dick said. "It was very tightly contained . . . for security reasons."

"Yeah, well, it's a low-level issue that's gotten kind of high level, people. I'm sitting here learning about it for the first time and I've been in this office for two years. Dick, what were you thinking?"

"Sir, plausible denial."

"*Plausible?* I just lost a great American city and you expect me to go before the American people and tell them I didn't get warned about what destroyed it so I could claim plausible denial? If you knew one single thing about this prior to this morning, ole buddy, ole pal, I want your resignation on my desk in an hour." The president looked around the room. "That goes for all of you. Anybody who was keeping this from me, *get the hell out of here!*"

Thankfully, Secretary O'Neill spoke, his voice, as always, firm and calm. "The Hybrid Project was terminated by the Senate Intelligence Committee in 2002."

"I'm so glad. And clearly that was effective. And there were aliens here and you never told me this? *Me?*" The president looked around the room. "Who knew? Which of you knew?"

Dick said, "By the time the project was terminated, the aliens had already left. Before we got into office, Ritchie."

"Does high office make people stupid? Because you people are just being damned stupid, here. First, you bring me this incredible mess. Then it's aliens but they left, and instead some mad scientist nobody can apparently produce for me is responsible for lairs full of crazed fucking motherfuckers, and we don't know what the fuck they are and, *my God, I have lost a city!*" The president's face colored. "*I will fight!*" He paced. "Dick, you find out who in hell in CIA or DIA or NSA or NRO or NICS or wherever has information for us. Get that person or persons in here pronto. Meanwhile, I want reports from around the world. Is anybody else seeing these things?"

Dick stood silent, his throat working.

The president shouted, "I'm talking to you, asshole!"

"Yessir," Dick said.

"Spit it out!"

"We have information from Hong Kong. There's one in Hong Kong."

"How hard is this information?"

"Well, actually, it's on YouTube."

The president's eyes widened, his face went from red almost to full purple. "Ten billion dollars a year and you give me YouTube! Jesus Christ, man, have you no damn shame!"

Dick worked frantically with his BlackBerry, his fat fingers flying. "It's not a crisis in Hong Kong, sir. There are no injuries. Nothing like that. The thing drifted low across the city and then out to sea."

"Where is it now?"

"I, ah, I'm afraid . . ."

"You don't know. Has it occurred to you to pick up the telephone and ask the station chief to look out his window?"

"Sir, I've done that and it's definitely gone. In Hong Kong, it is gone at this time. As we speak. Where, we don't know. It's not visible on satellite."

"So, Hong Kong gets spared and San Fran gets walloped. Chinese involvement, Dick?"

"Here," he said. "I've got it. The man who keeps tabs on this sort of thing is called George Hammond."

"Okay, here's what we do. First, Dick, you drag him out of his hole."

Dick fumbled frantically with the BlackBerry. "We're doing it right now, sir. I'm getting that he's out of touch due to the storm."

"Bring that man into this office in thirty minutes or you're on your way to the supermax for high treason. Thank you. Okay, now, General Hollis, you say this thing over San Francisco is or is not moving?"

"It's moving south. Right now, it's over the Sunset District."

"But not fast, anyway."

"Average speed, two miles an hour."

"So, we board it. We put down a team of Delta Force operators off a chopper. We board this thing and we secure it."

"Sir," General Stuart said, his voice rising, "that is going to be certain death for those men."

"Are you sure, General? Do you know that?"

"I just—I'm sorry. Assuming."

The president said, "Okay, here's a plan of action. We deploy whatever combat-ready troops we can muster to San Francisco, and we blow shit out of any of these designer people or whatever in fuck's name you call them, and we kill them all. And seal the goddamn bridges. Dick, you get your genius in here. And Delta Force goes after that *fucking piece of shit thing*!" The president turned his blowtorch gaze toward the Joint Chiefs, who were clustered together like a bunch of scared mice. "Got that?"

"Yes, sir," Stuart replied, "we're trying to pull together some units right now."

"Pull together? What in hell does that mean?"

"We—ah—on the West Coast . . . well, the military is thin on the ground, actually."

The president picked up a paperweight and hurled it into the wall, where his bull strength caused it to shatter to pieces and take a large chunk of plaster with it.

He turned around and smiled that blaze of a grin that was on all his campaign posters. Then he turned it off like a light, which he knew had a frightening effect on people.

"Okay, you pull together the cooks and bottle washers

and give them the best goddamn guns in the world, General."

"Yessir! Sir?"

"Yes, General?"

"Most of the available ordnance in the area is older equipment used in training."

"Oh, good. Then give the cooks the worst fuck-all guns in the butt-sucking world. But tell them to go for it! Now, next thing. The media is going to go absolutely insane, and with good goddamn reason. I want to schedule a press conference in twenty minutes."

General Stuart broke in. "Sir—sir—I beg to differ on the deployment. Because, listen to me. You don't want to put people into the city itself. No, you don't."

The president started to shout.

"Sir! Sir, no, you do *not*! Because we have lost this city, sir. And we don't know how it happened or what we're up against, but we know it is full of these bizarre creatures—murderous, so far unstoppable—I mean, the police force is gone. The—whatever we had there—some kind of riot squad on an earthquake drill—all gone. So what we need to do is isolate the problem area as best we can and protect our surviving civilian population in places like Berkeley and Marin County—I mean, the area is huge. Huge. And there's the whole of California and Oregon to think about, here. We do not want to go rushing into San Francisco with what little we have available and get it sucked up in a meat grinder." Stuart paused. "We need to send in recce. Try to gain some strategic insight. This is not about retaking the city, sir, no, not yet. Right now, we need to be looking at two things: damage control and the tightest containment we can manage. The city and environs, hopefully."

"General Stuart, thank you. There is a man with a clear head, people, even in the face of my temper, and that is saying something. For which thank God. Okay, I need to get with my speechwriters and my press people. General Stuart, you're to deploy as you see fit. But I do want at least an attempt to do something about this thing right now. I want to be able to say we have somebody fighting, so get Delta Force involved. Let them evaluate the situation, and if they think that they can board that thing or whatever they can do, let them try." The president paused. He added quietly, "I also want an evaluation of collateral damage, should I decide to employ nuclear weapons."

He left the room, striding, shoulders back, exuding authority. He crossed to his private suite, carefully closed the door, and locked it.

He stood in the middle of the room and roared out his rage and his defiance. When he was done, the lock clicked. Carlie came in. Behind her were his speechwriters and his press attaché.

"I needed that," he said.

Now came the hard part. This president, who had been doing so well, had to face the people of the United States and the world with the worst news that any president, or perhaps any leader in history, had ever had the misfortune to convey.

CHAPTER SIXTEEN

THE TRAP

IT WAS FULL LIGHT NOW, and the hybrids had retreated into the woods. They could apparently see perfectly well in the dark, so they preferred to use it as cover. All night, they had patrolled the town, moving carefully, always keeping out of sight, watching for some opportunity to attack.

Mark had been effective against amazing numbers of them, but he could not expect that to last forever. Initially, his speed had probably surprised them. He could not expect to retain that advantage.

He had watched dawn creeping into the sky, and as it gradually gave definition to the gray shapes of Willoughby's silent storefronts, he had come to a clear understanding that they had to leave this place or risk being overwhelmed. Even so, the combat calculation was not favorable. It was quite likely that all three of them were going to die in any escape attempt.

The hybrids had done nothing to the ambulance convoy as it pulled out. What might have happened to it on the road, though, Mark did not wish to contemplate. He had wanted to protect those poor people, but he couldn't do more than he had. They were too injured to stay here, and suffering terribly, so he'd let them go, and it had made him sick in his heart. Still, better for them to try for life than to face the certain death of remaining in Willoughby.

There was no electricity, and so they had not been able to listen to the radio that was here in the Redwoods Café, where they'd made their ad hoc command post. Soon, they'd move out and commandeer a vehicle. Then they'd find out more.

At least there was adequate food here, and coffee if you liked it cold. Mark didn't care. Living as he had since his college days—and during them, for that matter—he was not particular.

For some time now, he had been listening to a buzzing sound rising and falling. So far, the others hadn't heard it, but it was getting steadily louder and finally Pete asked, "What is that?"

"An engine," Mark said softly.

"What kind of an engine?" Linda asked.

"Single cylinder."

"Hybrids?"

"Why would hybrids bother with a scooter?"

"Good point."

"We need to get out of here," Mark said. "The depth of threat is increasing too fast."

Linda said, "We're alone, it's quiet."

"Yeah," Pete said, "there's nothing out there except that engine, which is probably some citizen trying to get the hell out of the area."

"A few minutes ago, a patrol of hybrids passed ten feet from the back door of this place."

The buzzing resolved itself into a clear sound. It had crested the hill that separated Willoughby from the Big Basin area. It was closing in on the town, and going flat out.

"Ready your weapons," Mark said.

They didn't need to be told.

The scooter now appeared, speeding down the middle of the road, a red Vespa with two people on it. It was driven by a young woman with blowing blond hair. Behind her, another figure clung tightly to her.

Mark's whole body trembled; a white roar of anger, anguish, and joy surged in his heart. Her face was turned this way, eyes closed, skin like cream. Her arms clutched the other woman's shoulders, sweet, elegant arms.

She was beautiful beyond anything he had dared to remember, but in the purity of that face he also saw a purity of suffering that made him suck the air of shared pain through his clenched teeth.

His heart might be twisting in torment, but his mind was too disciplined to attempt to understand what could not be understood without more information, which was how in the world Gina had ended up coming to this place.

As the Vespa slowed and stopped, he watched quietly, prepared for anything. His eyes were on Gina's hands. He did not want to see a weapon, but if he did, he was prepared to act appropriately.

He did not know much about God. He had not been given the gift of religion. He prayed in his own way, and now he said inside himself simply, Please, God, please.

The Vespa stood there, its driver's wind-flushed face so still that he thought that she might be suffering from shock or blood loss.

"Help her," he said, "she's going over."

As the driver collapsed and the scooter toppled, Gina leaped off, ran across the road, and disappeared into the woods on the opposite side.

"Wait here," Mark said to the Pete and Linda, who had been nearest to the girl and had stopped her fall. He raced off after Gina.

In among the trees, he was surprised to find that he could detect no movement—which was strange. Very strange. In fact, it was impossible. Gina was not trained in any way. She could not be still enough for him not to spot her.

Had they taken her into one of their lairs?

He forced back a cry of terror, then slid his knife into his hand. Rarely did he feel rage or fear. His mind calculated and evaluated. But that was not the case now. He was afraid, truly and deeply. If they got her, he thought he might go insane with grief. But what did that mean, for something like him? Did any of his feelings mean anything—grief, love, hope? How was he to know if his programming actually mirrored real human emotions or was designed simply to make him appear to react like a human being?

For example, why wasn't he furious at her? Why had he reacted with desire and love, not rage? She had tried to kill him. But he just wanted her so badly. She knew what he was, though, and she'd thought him dangerous enough to justify attacking him. So how could he possibly win her over, even if he did find her? But, above all, why had she come here?

Then came another, even deeper shock—her voice echoing in among the trees. "Mark! Forgive me. Please, Mark." Then, more softly: "Oh, for the love of God."

Then he saw a suggestion of movement in some brush, and it came to him in a searing flash: He hadn't seen her because he hadn't been looking for a hybrid. But only another hybrid could be as stock-still as she'd been.

His mind worked fast. Maybe it was no accident that they'd been brought together. Maybe they were a team of hybrids, and maybe that explained the curious sense he had that he'd known her before. But if they were hybrids, were they both defective? Was that why they were fighting the other hybrids?

Or maybe she wasn't fighting them. If she was loyal to the other hybrids, that would explain why she had tried to kill him.

"Mark! Mark, I know you're here, just don't shoot me, Mark. I made a mistake, but I was tricked, Mark. You have to believe that. I was tricked!"

In among the trees, he saw flashes of blue and green, then heard a flurry of leaves, and then they were there, appearing as if out of the air itself, seven of them, their skin gleaming in the mottled sun. He recognized three of them from the Glade. One, whose arm he had cut off, had a stub emerging, red and wet, with bumps at the end of it that would be fingers when the arm had regrown. But of course, if you wanted to build a soldier, things like the genes of lizards with their ability to regrow limbs would be a do-not-miss proposition.

It looked at him, and in its eyes he saw not anger but curiosity, and in the lifted lips, a smile of reproach.

It was close enough for him to dart forward and cut in half, but he hesitated, suddenly aware that it cherished its life.

Gina was close, too. He could see her turning round and round, listening, looking.

"Oh, Mark, please, I'm afraid. Say something, Mark. Listen, I know you have good in you. I lived with it every day of my life. Mark, they're evil. Evil, Mark, like you can't imagine. They've wrecked San Francisco. Oh, Jesus, what I saw, Mark, you have no idea. Please, you've got to help us. You can't go over. Mark, please."

He needed to reduce the variables here, and fast. So he stepped out of cover. She had not expected him to be so close and cried out and jumped back. Then her dusky blue eyes came to his, and it felt like an invisible kiss.

She grabbed him, clutched at him, and he found her so fair to look upon that it frightened him. He wanted to bury his heart in her, to feel his lips upon hers, to devour the symmetries of her body.

She kissed him, then again, longer.

Even though the hybrids were close by, he could not stop her, he could not break away, it felt too good.

"I've loved you so much," he said. "So much!"

She drew back. Her eyes searched his face. He saw in them a brightness unlike anything he'd ever before seen.

"Mark, you've been my life. I've died a thousand times up there watching you go into danger. My life, Mark. Damn you, why didn't you say something? What's the matter with you?"

She kissed him again, a little wildly. No, more than a little.

More hybrids were joining the first few. They were edging closer, looking to surround.

"Come on," he said gently. "We've got work to do."

CHAPTER SEVENTEEN

THE TRAITOR

SHE HAD NOT EXPECTED TO find him alive. Perhaps she had even come to mourn him. But now all of her suspicion and all of her anger were swept away by the anguish of love written in his face. But her love had changed, she knew it immediately. She couldn't love a—well—a thing. Yet, he was fair to see, with his rocky good looks and the sense of inner brilliance that brought such life to his eyes. But not human brilliance, no. *Not* human. She thought she could see a subtle difference in the way he moved, also. When she'd met him, his grace as he came across the restaurant had been thrilling. Now that same grace imparted a curious sense of the mechanical.

As she'd ridden behind Kelly, leaving the mayhem of San Francisco, she had understood that the mission she had set herself was now moot. The president wasn't going to need any evidence gathered by the likes of her to decide what to do. If the White House was still standing, or he was safe in one of his bunkers, he was going to see all of this.

During the attack on the helicopter, she'd thought she could not survive. What had happened was so unexpected and so bizarre that she'd simply sat there waiting for the end, watching the scrabbling metallic legs as they fought to enter the cockpit, and the glaring—dear heaven—human eyes of what appeared to be huge insects, which stared at her with fixed rage.

Ending up like that was unthinkable, but she wasn't absolutely sure that even suicide could prevent it. This was all about genetic manipulation on a level that had never before been known, and as she followed Mark out of the woods, she felt her passion for him withdrawing further and further into the closed room of her heart.

After talking to Dr. Turner, it had seemed clear that he was a traitor, but seeing Mark and being with him even for these few moments, she was far less sure.

They could have been lovers, but now that she knew—well, wouldn't he be just an exotic sex toy? Biological or not, you couldn't love a machine, no matter how well programmed it was, or how much it was designed to simulate human personality.

As she worked to keep up with him, he gestured to her, then stopped. He turned, regarding her with eyes as intent as those of a wolf, a concentration so intense that it was like an actual physical penetration.

This was far from the confidently aggressive partner she'd enjoyed in bed, or even the emotionless professional on the satphone. Maybe those personalities were still there somewhere deep inside this intense, absolutely ferocious being, but not on the surface. He was still Mark, still with the gray eyes, the tight brown hair, the hard-edged jaw, and that slightly eerie inner smile. But he was not a normal human being, and that was absolutely clear.

She had to say something that would communicate some sort of acceptance of him, but she could barely bring herself to speak.

He regarded her, clearly measuring and evaluating.

The hybrids seemed to have left their immediate vicinity, so she decided to attempt to connect with him.

"Mark, I know that I made a mistake."

He stared at her. There was aggression in it, but also something else, and the woman she was to her core told her what was coming, and when he embraced her, sweeping her into a wave of his immense strength, she found herself filled with an emotion that was deeper than blood, a kind of exhilaration just to feel that power, and the trembling within it that told her of his continuing feelings for her.

He was silent, as still as stone, holding her. Tears came into her eyes, and she lowered her face, that he would not see. She thought, He's programming. This is programming. How profoundly she despised Dr. Turner.

He thrust her away so hard that she stumbled into the ferns that swept the forest floor, and mayflies rose like sparks in the light.

"Mark, please!"

"They're moving in."

"Mark, I'm so ashamed. I want to tell you that."

He stopped, but just for an instant, then pushed through some brush and they were back at the roadside.

"What's happening?" she asked.

He did not reply. She had forgotten how difficult to read he was. He'd been a voice on the phone, a figure moving in a landscape, a heartbeat . . . and a fantasy. He was no fantasy now.

"We've got to get a decent vehicle," he said.

"Where's the Vespa?" she asked.

"It's not useful and I'm talking to them, not you."

At a hand signal from him, PFC Richardson and Dr. Hicks slipped out from among the trees. They'd been right across the road, but Gina hadn't spotted them.

Behind them came the much noisier and more hesitant figure of Kelly.

"We were just about to find ourselves a truck," Mark said, "when you two came in. We've got to move, and now."

Willoughby's main street started a quarter of a mile down the road, and Gina couldn't see the slightest problem, except for the same thing she'd noticed from above: The place was quiet, no traffic, nobody on the sidewalks.

"Are they okay?"

Nobody responded.

Richardson carried the bulky, gray form of a Metal Storm, and both he and Hicks had bead drums dangling from their carries. She counted six of the small drums, so not a lot of ammunition.

"Where are the other Storms?"

"You're Gina, aren't you?" Linda Hicks asked.

"I'm Gina."

"He won't answer questions now," Linda said. "He's using his senses. He's quiet when he's using his senses."

The respect and loyalty in that voice were unmistakable, further evidence that Gina had been wrong about Mark.

She smelled a sour odor that reminded her of the abattoir on her granddad's place in Maryland. Long, long ago, in another world.

"What's that smell?" she asked.

Linda Hicks only glanced her way. Nobody replied. Mark moved steadily toward the town. She fell in behind him, with Linda and Kelly behind her. Richardson did rear guard.

"You have a knife," Gina said to Mark. "That's it? Shouldn't you have another Storm?"

"I don't need a Storm."

"What are you saying? Of course you need a Storm."

He didn't answer.

The closer they came to the town, the more wrong it began to look. There was no movement at all, nothing. Gina's memories went back to what had happened to her helicopter, the dreadful banging against the fuselage, the bizarre mechanical insects slashing and hammering to get in. At least she wasn't seeing any of those things here.

They had reached the outskirts of Willoughby now. Of course she knew the place well, having flown these streets dozens of times. But there were things her satellite eyes could not see, such as the great smear of blood in the doorway of Ellendorf Antiques, and the human arm lying on the covered sidewalk in front of the Glade.

"What was done to this place?"

Mark did not even glance back. He was moving faster now, heading toward the motel.

"Mark?"

A hand came on her shoulder. Linda said, "Leave him be. Just let it happen."

There was a deep sound, the kind of vibration that drums in the chest, and a hybrid landed in the road in front of him. This close, Gina could see that it was large and lithe and strong. It had swimming blue eyes in a sleek white face, and it at once leaped on Mark.

"It'll kill him!"

But then it fell into two pieces as blood sprayed out of it and its eyes vibrated so fast that they were blurs. The sound it made was high enough to hurt and she clapped her hands over her ears.

She had not even seen Mark move, yet he had cut this six-foot-five hybrid clean in half with a combat knife.

"Here they come," he said over his shoulder. "Give Gina a knife. And protect that kid, she's got no defense."

Linda thrust a combat knife like Mark's into Gina's hand. She closed her fist around it and looked down at its viciously curved, gleaming blade.

"What am I supposed to do with this?"

Linda threw her a glance that spoke, but Gina did not know what it said.

"I can't use a knife like—"

Absolutely without warning, a hybrid was standing in front of her. He was hefty, but not as big as Mark. He wore a camouflage jacket and carried a Metal Storm.

Gina looked at it, appalled. Mark's team had lost some dangerous weapons.

The hybrid's face was impassive, almost frozen. It looked human, and Gina thought perhaps he was friendly, but then he began to raise the Metal Storm, aiming it directly at her. He moved with a curious slowness and deliberation.

Not understanding why he was so slow, she simply stepped in and thrust the knife at him—not hard, she didn't think, but the best she could manage.

Something about it was terribly personal, feeling a knife entering the flesh of another person. It was like cutting into a cantaloupe, resistance followed by smooth penetration.

As the hybrid's eyes slowly widened, a red haze appeared in front of his face. What was it, this gradually expanding cloud? Confused, she reached out and touched it and came away with fingers sheened by a thin film of blood.

It had begun to reach a hand toward the firing switch of the Metal Storm. She did not understand the continuing extreme slowness of his movements, not at a moment like this. But she drew the knife out and raised it and sliced downward with all her might, and his hand, still opening to reach the switch, came gliding off his arm and tumbled away through the air, the fingers fluttering delicately, as if he were waving.

An odd red bulge appeared on the stump of his arm, growing until it was round and shivering like a balloon filled with water. It kept spreading, though, transforming itself into smaller orbs, then into a haze like the one still issuing from his nose, but deeper red and more dense.

She was aware of her own movements, aware of analyzing and evaluating, and she went along, then noticing out of the corner of her eye three of the hybrids going toward Mark, their legs pulsing so slowly that it seemed impossible that they could ever reach him. For the moment abandoning the crumpling man, she turned and brought the knife up, impaling one of them—which caused the other two to turn and come racing far faster toward her than they had been moving toward Mark.

The first one flew into pieces as she hacked frantically at it, but the second got in past her knife, enclosing her in a prison of arms and legs, and a rancid odor. She ripped it off her and, as it fell away from her, reached up with the knife, slicing off one arm.

A series of drubbing thuds followed, which quickly changed into a tearing sound, as if some great curtain were being ripped in two.

Again the ripping sound came, and Pete said, "Screw you," and laughed, and again it came, and this time she turned and saw that the road behind them was heaped with a mangle of twisted remains.

The silence was broken only by the trembling sobs of Kelly Frears.

Three bodies were in front of Mark, and lying on the ground at her own feet, a hybrid in a pool of blood.

"Did I do that?"

"Linda," Mark said, "get that Metal Storm and get it operational. They're coming in for another try."

"Yessir."

"What's happening?" Kelly shouted. She grabbed Gina's shirt. "What are you people? How can you do that?"

Then Gina realized it: She had herself been in flicker. *She* had. That accounted for what she had just seen. The world around her, and her victim, hadn't been moving slowly, she had been moving fast.

Her mind raced. This was impossible, she wasn't like him, not a creature that somebody had made. She was human! She'd been attracted to his strength, deceived by her own heart into believing that her desire for him was love. She was *human*!

Mark was watching her again, with those careful eyes.

She backed away from him.

"No, it's impossible! I have a normal life, I have—" She stopped, remembering her early days as an adopted child. So what if she wasn't her parents' daughter at all but their . . . thing? What if, all along, Mom and Dad had been not raising a child but training a biological machine? She began to look back over her life.

What about her earliest memory, for example, what was it?

Not as a little child, no, that was all a blank.

She was in a hallway, green walls, a tile ceiling, fluorescent lighting.

Two people were looking down at her. She must be on a gurney.

One of the people was Dr. Turner.

The other was Mark.

"You," she said, "you were there!"

"I don't know what you mean."

"You were with Dr. Turner when I was . . . was I born? Was that it? I can remember my birth?"

"I don't have any memory of this."

She came close to him. "Mark, who are we?"

He took her in his big arms. "I wish I knew."

"We have a problem," Linda said, pointing upward.

Overhead, a great mass of machinery, huge, was hanging just above the crowns of the redwoods.

"That's it," Kelly shouted, "that's the thing!" She looked wildly around. "Where do we go? It'll kill us all!"

"We keep moving toward the town," Mark said. "We need transport." Then to Gina: "Help that girl."

Her mind was spinning. She *couldn't* be a hybrid, she had feelings, needs, dreams, and surely you couldn't design a program that dreamed.

He'd never responded to her love because he was a biological machine. She now understood that. But her feelings for him had been real, they had been deeply human . . . and so had the expression on his face just a few minutes ago.

She sucked back a sob of mixed horror and joy. Horror because she was facing the truth about herself—no matter what she wanted to believe, she was a biomachine, too. No human being could fight as she had. No human being could move as she had.

The joy came because she knew another truth: For whatever reason, these two programs—or whatever she and Mark were, in the depths of their minds—had feelings, and those feelings were for each other.

She could love him and he her, but what meaning did that have if, in the end, they were only programming?

Brushing away her tears, trying not to tremble, she watched as Richardson and Hicks prepared the Metal Storms with impressively calm efficiency.

Even as the Storms fired, the machine descended and Gina had no idea how to defend herself or anybody else against it. Kelly, who had been courageous on the difficult journey here, now panicked and, instead of staying near the blasting Storms, dashed off the road and into the woods.

"Get her back or she's dead," Mark snapped.

"Me?"

He did not respond, so Gina followed her.

Scrambling down the gravel shoulder and past the stand of pines beyond it, she had an immediate surprise: there were no hybrids here and she thought to tell Mark that. But it was also true that Kelly was well ahead and running hard.

"Kelly! Kelly, don't do this!"

The girl went quiet.

Gina stopped, looked ahead. Where had she gone? Then she heard a voice nearby, soft but male. For an instant, she was confused. She'd heard it before somewhere. But it could only be a hybrid, and it meant that this innocent kid had probably run straight into a group of them.

Gina took off again, and without quite realizing it, she found herself running faster and faster, until the trees were whipping past and it felt as if her feet were hardly touching the ground. She could not see Kelly ahead, but she could hear others running and knew that hybrids were chasing her and they would get to her before she reached Kelly—and then she was looking across green treetops and could see in the distance the area that she had burned out, but it was all below her, and how could that be—but there was a flash of red—Kelly's jacket—and there, also, another figure, trim and quick, flickering through the woods in the way of the hybrids.

The next thing Gina knew she was tumbling in the air and crying out, astonished, confused, but going even faster than the hybrid below her—and then she was arcing down, the air screaming around her, and she was dropping on Kelly, and she struck her hard in the back and went rolling with the shouting, terrified girl across the grassy surface of a small clearing.

Before they had stopped, Gina had her knife out, and with it there came a hideous eagerness, and Kelly appeared vulnerable, and the fear in her eyes caused a hunger powerful enough to cause Gina to shudder with an eagerness she was far from understanding.

Where had her confidence with this knife come from, and where her eagerness to menace the girl?

Gina stood, the sweat pouring off her.

It was the same way she'd felt when she was ordering the air strikes on Mark, and she was aware of it again as a perversion, but it was also one that she would never, ever succumb to, she swore that in her soul—then wondered, Do I have one?

Cowering, Kelly looked at her—or, no, she looked past her. Gina heard the rustle of breath, and at once the ugly sadism was replaced by a far more intense emotion—hatred for the hybrids.

"Hello, Gina."

Reality contracted into a single focal point—that voice again, and it was entirely familiar now. All sound, all sensation, concentrated on that one point. She opened her shock-parched mouth and said in a trembling whisper, "Dr. Turner, what are you doing here?"

A careful expression entered his eyes. "You need to help me with Mark. He's more dangerous than you understand, Gina, to me and to you and to the world."

Behind her, she heard a confused sort of a whimper, and she remembered that Kelly was there and was vulnerable, and Gina drew back from him.

"This is about changing everything, Gina. It's about saving the planet from an out-of-control menace."

"He's with us, Dr. Turner. Mark is onside."

"Mark is programmatically confused. He was the first built, and he's unstable. We need to revise him, and I need your help."

What was Dr. Turner getting at? And why did he sound like that? Something about his voice was off.

"How can I help you?" she asked.

"You've seen his powers. You need to make him understand that this is not what it seems, none of it. We're on the same side, the side of the future."

"Dr. Turner, am I a hybrid? Is that the real reason we were brought together? We're some sort of a team?"

"I hate that word. You and Mark are the most profoundly human beings that I have ever known. You are brilliant. You're vividly alive. You are soldiers, both of you, with extraordinary powers and extraordinary minds." He gestured at Kelly, who stood to one side, her back against a tree, her eyes darting from one of them to the other. "You're nothing like those shadows."

A sort of wave seemed to pass through Gina, cold and profoundly alien, and she saw herself in a new way, as a creature that was, to herself, a complete unknown. And why did Dr. Turner sound like that? And look like that, as a matter of fact, his face somehow distorted, but so subtly that it could be a trick of light.

"Why do you sound like that?'

"Allergies." He gestured. "The trees are my enemy." He smiled, and when he did, the neat rows of teeth gleamed, and she knew that, whoever this was, it was not Dr. Turner, because those were not his teeth, which were irregular.

"You wanted me to kill Mark. Why?"

"I wanted you to throw him off-balance so I could get out here and try to stabilize him. It never occurred to me that you'd succeed, and you haven't. He's good in the field. Very good."

"What are you?"

The smile grew a little rueful. "It's easy to forget that you two are as much like us as you are."

"You're not Dr. Turner, you're a hybrid." She dared not even think how it could be that this thing was wearing a man's skin in such a way that it worked like a perfect mask. But not quite perfect.

"Gina, a new world is on offer, properly organized, at peace, connected to the balance of nature, a world that belongs to you and Mark, and flows out of you." He grasped her hand. "I didn't want you to kill him, I wanted you to help me bring him to his senses."

Without warning, Kelly leaped on him and began beating him with a fury unlike anything Gina had ever seen in a human being, kicking him, slamming him with her fists. He staggered back, and Gina thought to help her, but before she could, three pale hybrids burst out of the woods and threw themselves on the girl and pulled her away.

She fought and snarled, "You're monsters, you raped my city, you raped San Francisco!"

They took her away into the woods. A moment later, Gina heard her muffled cry.

"She's innocent! It's murder!"

She saw something in "Dr. Turner's" hand, a black disk. He drew it slowly across her right temple. For an instant, she was dizzy, but it passed immediately.

She did not realize what had just happened to her. She had no understanding that a pass on her program had just happened and changed her mind. Instead, all she noticed was a sudden burst of loyalty toward Turner. She forgot Kelly.

He spoke now with new confidence. "You are to press this against either of Mark's temples. It's a magnetic disk that will reprogram his cerebral cortex. It'll bring him back to us."

"Back?"

"Back to us. Gina, we're brothers and sisters. You, too."

"You're saying you reprogrammed me?"

"Do you know of Dr. Emma Walker?"

"The geneticist at Stanford? General Walker's wife?"

"General Walker started out as a sergeant detailed to my project. He and Emma raised Mark for me, just as the Lyndons raised you. And Emma worked on both your programs. She did the actual structural work, to my specifications."

Why did he sound like that? It was as if he were reading his own thoughts out of some sort of book. Really odd.

But she knew of Emma Walker, of course. She was one of the greatest genetic engineers in the world. Among other things, she'd won a Nobel Prize for her work on controlling the zinc finger. Without her discoveries, the profound advances in the cure of genetic diseases that were now taking place would never have happened. But what else had she done, behind the walls of the classification system?

"I know her work, of course, but I've never met her."

"You've met her many times. The memories have been removed." He smiled the twinkling smile of a kindly uncle. "You don't know who you are, Gina, or who Mark is. You have a distorted view of what's happening. You need to come home, hon, and bring your dear friend with you. I want to give you both back your memories of your real lives."

Before she could even voice her anger, he continued, "First, try to get him to come back here. We'll be waiting with carbon-fiber nets that might be able to hold him. Tell him you found tunnels. He's been in a birthing unit and he'll see that as a chance to do some damage." Then Dr. Turner put the disk in her hand. "If he won't come, use this on him."

She looked down at the blue metal. It was cold, thick, and heavier than it appeared, a dark, iridescent blue.

"It's powerfully magnetic," he said, "don't let it near any metal or you won't be able to pry it off. It just needs the lightest touch to either of his temples. It'll do its work immediately."

Intellectually, she knew that to do this would be wrong, but the knowledge seemed abstract. Emotionally, all she could think about was helping Mark to see his mistake.

She slid the disk into her pocket. But as she turned to go, Dr. Turner gripped her arm.

"Gina," he said in a clenched voice, "I'll be watching, and if you don't do this—if there's still some bad code in you somewhere—I'll know and I'll take action. I will not hesitate, and I will show no mercy, but my heart will be broken, Gina."

"What about San Francisco? I saw it from a helicopter. It was war. Carnage."

"Whatever you think you saw, it's wrong. When you go there, you're going to see the truth. Peace and happiness. A tranquil society, beautifully organized. And you'll feel in your blood that the new people belong to you, and you to them." He took her face in his cool, firm hands—and when his face came close to hers, she was startled to see that something was wrong with it. Was this a mask? Was something else under it?

She reached up to touch him, but he drew back.

"Just help poor Mark, honey, so he can enjoy the future, too." Dr. Turner hugged her, then stood back. "I've been underground for a long time." He lifted his face to the cathedral of forest above them. "I want us all to enter the light."

She wondered who this really was.

"What about Kelly? What do I say?"

He blinked, made a dismissive gesture. "You couldn't save her."

"Couldn't save her?" Gina turned around. "She was— where is she?"

"How should I know?"

Gina stepped into the woods. "Kelly! *Kelly!*"

Only silence.

"He sent me to save her."

"You failed. Tell him that. Now go."

As she began her long walk back to the road, hybrids came with her, slipping from tree to tree, watching her with their intent, robotic eyes. She heard them whispering together in their rasping voices, so mysterious, and thought that they were the voices of hungry ghosts.

CHAPTER EIGHTEEN

MEETING BY THE RIVER

MARK HAD BEEN A DAMNED fool to let Gina go after Kelly alone. She was capable enough but ill-prepared and untrained, so why hadn't he stopped her? To destroy the only person he loved, perhaps, out of loathing for both of them and what they were.

His urge to destroy hybrids certainly included himself—he despised himself—and as much as he loved Gina, for this reason she also made his flesh crawl. He loved her and he loathed her.

He moved through the forest, knowing that he was under close hybrid observation. But why weren't they attacking?

He went a little deeper, then stopped. Eyes watched from nearby, gleaming here and there in the shafts of sunlight that penetrated the forest.

He was not so deep yet that he wouldn't be able to fight his way back to the road from here. Much farther in, though, and he would have no chance.

The problem was that the easily followed trail the two women had left went deeper. In her terror, Kelly must have run wildly. Gina, in her effort to reach her, had risked too much.

He feared that they were both dead or down in those tunnels, enduring what sort of suffering he did not wish to imagine.

He increased his speed, striding along the path, no longer bothering to move silently. With all the attention he was getting, there was no point in stealth.

Then he saw blood, a lot of it, on the ground near a tree. One or both of the two women was dead.

He felt fear for Gina, but he also felt forced to suppress it. What he needed to do was to save the human being. The hybrid could fend for itself.

He picked up a snatch of conversation, a man speaking low and urgently, and not a hundred yards away. A word came, "magnetic." He listened, but heard no more. Then he saw coming through the trees a quick form.

Despite himself, his heart leaped up as his eyes drank her in. "Gina."

She stopped. Her body was stiff, arms straight, fingers spread. She was cocked, ready for an attack.

Mark stepped into her field of view. As he approached her, his arms seemed to open almost of their own accord, and in an instant she was pressing herself against him. She was silent, and when he looked down at her, he saw tears on her smeared, lovely face.

"Kelly didn't make it."

"It's a miracle either of you is still alive."

He tried to prevent her from seeing the remains of Kelly, the blood on the tree and what lay behind it, but she stopped, then reached trembling fingers and touched the devastated body of the girl.

"She was nineteen, Mark!"

"They do not care." He took her elbow, gently urging her on.

She pulled away. "Mark, we need to go back."

"Why?"

"We need to. I . . . I saw an opening. The tunnels, Mark, there's an opening. Unguarded."

This was interesting. "Are you certain?"

"I saw it. It's just a little farther back." She took his hand. "Come on, let's do it."

This felt wrong, and he wondered exactly what had just happened in these woods.

"We need to plan first, if we're going in the tunnels."

"At least look at them and be sure I'm right. I don't want to bring the others back here for no reason."

Tunnels were tempting because of the damage he could do, but because it was too late for any effective surprise, they were a potential death trap.

"We'll plan it out with the others."

"We need to do this now, Mark, while we have a chance."

He started off toward the road. "Now is not the time."

She followed, coming close to him. "How do your helmets work?"

"Well."

"I wish I had one. Are they steel?"

"There's steel in them."

"A lot?"

"Five pounds of it. What's with all the questions? Nobody cares."

"I want one, Mark. I feel I need it." She slipped her arm in his. "Can I borrow yours?"

"I'll see if I can find you one."

In a few more minutes they reached the road and a double-cab pickup that Linda and Pete had obtained in Willoughby.

He motioned Gina into the back with Linda. He and Pete took the front. Pete would drive, Mark watch for any signs of ambush.

"Get rolling," he said to Pete.

"What about Kelly?" Pete replied over the static-choked drone of the dashboard radio.

"Just move out, please."

Nothing more needed to be said, they understood that another casualty had been taken and knew that Mark's focus would now be on the next battle.

Given that communications with Washington were down due to the storm, Mark's plan was to head for Vandenberg Air Force Base, which was the nearest intact air force facility likely to have the type of plane they needed. The Fresno Air National Guard base was closer, but it trained in F-16s and might not have transport aircraft available. Trying for Travis involved moving through known hybrid infestation. Not wise.

Mark did not expect them to survive the attempt to leave Big Basin, but he was obligated to try. If even one of them lived, they could provide Washington with crucial intelligence.

Gina sat stiffly beside Linda and directly behind Mark. He had placed her there quite intentionally. She had tried to lure him into what he presumed was a trap. Failing that, she had asked about his helmet. Why? Did she really feel a need for one? In this sort of battle, they were obviously just an encumbrance. Therefore, she had some other motive. For some reason, she wanted it off his head.

As they drove, he waited for her to volunteer something about the male hybrid whose voice he'd heard. He watched her in the rearview mirror.

"What happened out there, Gina?" he asked.

"I messed up."

"I mean, did you see any hybrids?"

"I think so. I'm not very good at it yet."

She said no more, so he decided to let it ride for a

little while longer. She leaned forward and put her hand on his shoulders.

"Helmet her," he said to Linda, who pulled one out from behind the backseat. They'd gathered what of their old equipment they could scavenge from the town. On it was stenciled the name MASSENGILL. She gave it to Gina, who put it on, but seemed disappointed.

They drove on, passing across the crest of the long hill that separated Willoughby from the next valley. Now a new vista opened up, the vast burn that Gina had created, and he noticed that she cast her eyes down. Smoke drifted up here and there from smoldering stumps. The blackened, naked ruins of the farmhouse slid behind them on the right, and beyond them a rubble of boulders that had been the ridge that contained the cave that had saved Mark from her.

"This is where you tried to kill me," he said.

"Please don't bring it up," she snapped.

"You were doing what you were programmed to do," he said mildly, "just like me." He shifted in the too confining seat and again glanced back at her. She'd thrust her hands in her pockets. He decided that he needed to be extremely careful with her. Something was not right.

The Emergency Alert System was on every station they could pick up, warning that the state was under martial law, that it was illegal to drive into the San Francisco Bay Area, that all bridges and tunnels were closed, and advising residents of San Jose on evacuation routes south and east.

A report came in that a large, extremely dangerous aircraft was moving southward from the Bay Area. Anyone who saw it should immediately seek protection.

"That's it, isn't it?" Mark asked. "Is that what you saw?"

"I just saw smoke in the distance. The city wreathed in smoke. Kelly filled me in on the details. Thousands of people were tossed into the bay. She saw that. She saw—oh, odd, horrible things. People with their brains in their hands."

After a moment, Linda broke the silence that had followed this statement. "We're not enough."

In the privacy of his mind, Mark knew that she was right, but said nothing to encourage bad morale.

As they drove, he returned to the question of Gina's story. It just did not work. Who had she been talking to? She needed to tell him that or he needed to kill her, and he knew this, but he did not want to know it.

"Did you fight?" he asked her. "Did you see Kelly die?"

"Yes, I fought! So just drop it, okay? It's over and she's dead. Mission not accomplished."

They had reached Big Basin Redwoods Park, and Mark was glad that Gina hadn't burned these magnificent trees. Pete was keeping to back roads but moving fast. Their radio was describing massive traffic on the main highways, and no doubt also danger, if that bizarre craft was nearby.

"It threw people into the bay?"

"People, animals, furniture."

"So they can use gravity as a weapon. That's power."

"They can control storms, too," Gina said. "Washington got walloped just as this was happening. Not an accident, would be my guess."

"Did Kelly say anything about attempts to stop this machine?"

"There was a jet, but its missiles didn't do anything."

"Did they detonate or not?"

"I don't know."

He was silent for a time, thinking. "Pete, how practical would it be for us to get a chopper somewhere? What about Santa Cruz?"

"We can try, but I don't think it's gonna work, given the martial law situation."

"Can anybody fly one?" Mark asked.

The answer was silence. Mark could fly a small plane, maybe even a fighter, but a helicopter was a different story. They did not forgive mistakes, and he would make mistakes.

Movement in the sky caught his eye and he leaned forward, pressing his hands against the windshield. In the vast blue, very high, was a shape that should not be there.

Without question, it was the strangest thing he had ever seen. Basically, it was a ring. Rising above it were antennae that seemed to claw at the sky. Hanging from its base was a long, tapering cord that could be seen twisting and turning. It ended in a purple, glowing tip, that, even as far away as it was, briefly flickered in Mark's eyes.

What made it appear so ominous, he thought, was that it had not been designed to fly and it couldn't fly, but there it was, airborne.

It appeared tiny, enveloped in the depth of the sky. He thought of a spider crawling across a windowpane.

"Mark, we need to go back," Gina said.

That was enough. He turned around in the seat and faced her. "Gina, that's the exact opposite of what we need to do. Which I think you know very well."

"I'm still in charge, Mark."

"Screw that," he muttered.

He turned and stared at the road ahead. Maybe he should just do her. Dear God, but he loved her.

She'd had the most elegant old bed, nicest one he'd

ever seen. He hadn't had any real pleasure in his life, none at all, except her.

A more definite scatter of purple light played in the sheen of the hood.

"See that?" Pete said.

"I see it." Mark rolled down his window—and found himself looking directly up into the body of the huge device. What had been miles away thirty seconds ago was now right on top of them.

"Get this thing off the road, deploy the Storms, do it now!"

As he hit the brakes, Pete swerved the truck. He didn't ask for details, he didn't need to. The order was clear.

As they got out, Linda and Pete moved away from the vehicle. It wasn't armored, so if it was hit, it could explode and become a death trap.

Mark said, "Wait for my order to fire."

The thing was so large and so complicated that it was taking Mark time to understand where to find its dangerous points and its vulnerable points. Finally, he decided that they were going to have to fire into it at random.

He realized that they had come to their meeting by the river, the four of them. They must do battle with this thing, and he did not see how such a battle could be won.

CHAPTER NINETEEN

LOYALTY AND LOVE

A GOOD OFFICER ANTICIPATES WHEN he is going to take casualties, and this was one of those times.

"Get outta here," he told the others. "Run like hell." He hooked one of the Storms to his chest and shoulders and went to the middle of the road.

Pete joined him, another one on his chest.

Mark turned to him and shouted, "You got your orders, now *do it*!"

Bending back, Mark aimed the gun and fired it into the complexity of pipes, wires, and girders that was at this point not a hundred feet overhead.

Immediately, Pete's weapon also ripped the air.

"Goddamnit, I told you to get the hell out of here!"

Moving with quick efficiency, the long steel neck Mark had seen from a distance came down from the thing. It moved with a snake's graceful urgency, more like a living thing than something mechanical.

He watched it quest from place to place.

He discharged another load of beads into the thing, listening to the thunderous rip as they broke the sound barrier—but again nothing seemed to happen.

"Jesus," Gina said, looking up.

A cloud of tiny objects gleamed and sparkled in the sunlight, and Mark realized with sickening horror that it was the beads. They had been frozen in midflight.

"Yeah," he muttered. "They've got gravity solved."

A roar from beside him made him turn, and he saw that Pete was still there, operating his gun. He had just fired at the steel neck, which was now swaying, perhaps meaning that damage had been done. So Mark fired at it, too, but the swaying continued, and he realized the truth: The thing wasn't taking damage, it was aiming.

"Get off the road!" he shouted as he rolled onto the shoulder, then scrambled back into the woods. Gina and Linda came with him, but Pete was not fast enough.

He threw off the gun and jumped, but he never hit the ground. Instead, he shot into the air and Mark hated to see him kicking and clutching, hated to hear him scream like a boy as he came dropping back down from a thousand feet. He bounced and was still.

This was just too much, it was too horrific, and for the first time in Mark's life, he considered surrender. But what would that gain? A slow death, or worse, enslavement to the part of himself that he despised.

Gina said quietly, "Mark?"

She was looking toward the road, where Linda was working frantically, attempting to attach Pete's Storm to her chest. Before Mark could run to her, she was upended and dragged into the sky. The gun fell, shattering against the roof of the pickup.

Her screams pealed and pealed, echoing flatly in the silence of the forest. The helplessness was miserable, but with it came a stirring of the same shaming thrill that had almost overwhelmed him in the Glade. Beside him, he could hear Gina gasping, and he did not know if it was fear or anger, or the shame of pleasure.

He did not let her see what was left when Linda's
voice dropped to a growl and died, the red skeleton dangling in midair like a grotesque Halloween decoration.

He drew Gina deeper into the woods.

"Where are we going?" she asked, trying to pull away
from him.

"We need concealment."

"Yes, of course. I understand. It's just the two of us
now."

He stopped. Hidden here in the thick forest, they
were safe from the menace from above, but for how
long?

"You know what we are and why we're here, Gina.
It's time to work as a team."

She yanked her arm away. "We can't fight them!
There's no way!"

"We have to fight."

"With what? Knives?"

"For us, they're better than guns."

"Oh, come on!" Anger replaced her sobs.

"Gina, we have all sorts of capabilities programmed
into us."

"What are they?"

"What I'm finding is, if they're needed, they're there."

"What are they, damnit? You can't use something
you don't know you have."

"You've been in flicker."

"When that hybrid slowed down?"

"You sped up. He could have followed you but he
wasn't expecting it and you were able to drop him.
That's the why of knives instead of guns. In flicker, you
can thrust a knife faster than a gun—any gun—can fire."

"I'm a satellite surveillance specialist. It's technical
work, and that's what I know."

"Gina, you need to come into contact with more of

yourself. And there's a lot more, believe me. We are weapons, Gina, powerful, living weapons."

She stepped away from him. "Here we are in this bizarre, bizarre situation, desperate, and that's all you have to offer?"

"You know something of your power, Gina. I know you do, I can see it in your eyes. The fear that it brings."

A shadow passed over them, bringing sudden darkness to the forest. They both looked up and saw that the great collection of girders that defined the huge ship was just above them. As he looked up into the thing, an electricity shuddered deep in Mark's body, bringing with it a new desire, deep and sick and ugly.

Always before, his work had remained separate from his emotional life. No more.

He needed Gina, and he needed her right now. "No matter what you believe, you can fight and you will fight."

"I have no idea how."

He grabbed her arm, shook her like a rag. "We come to our powers *as needed*. That's the way it works. I don't know why, but that's what I'm finding. Trust yourself. There are parts of you that you don't know exist. The way of the warrior is programmed into you, and now we have to do this!"

"And what happens when we reach the limits of our abilities? Then what?"

"In the woods, you were touched with a disk. Probably very quickly."

For an instant, she glanced away, telling him that he was precisely correct.

"Then it or one like it was given to you, and you're supposed to touch me with it."

"No."

"Gina, I'm remembering a lot of things. Memories that

they thought were erased, but the brain is a labyrinth. There are a lot of hiding places, and I remember these disks and how they're used, so where is it, Gina?"

Purple light began glimmering down from above, seeking along the trunks of the trees, glimmering on the ferns, making their long leaves tremble and bend upward into its sucking death.

"You tell me now, or you turn away from me now, and if you do, it's forever."

She would not look at him.

"We just found each other. Don't take this from us. We're two. That's it. Nobody else like us. All we'll ever have is us, Gina."

She gasped, gasped more deeply.

"I—I—can't. I can't make myself, Mark. I want to but I *can't*!"

He sought her eyes with his own. "You can, Gina. Part of you can. Because you're not all machine. You're not, or I could not love you and I do love you. I love you, Gina. And I think you love me, and that part of you can give the thing up."

She thrust her hand into the pocket. He stiffened his muscles. She was as fast as he was.

He let her draw out her hand. She—and his heart—would either survive the next second, or they would die together.

She raised her closed fist. He stood absolutely still.

Her whole body trembled. Then her free hand came out, came up, her fingers extended, and he felt the cool of her touch on his cheek and saw into her eyes deeper than he had ever seen into any eyes.

Her other hand opened. The disk lay there, gleaming softly, a simple shape for what was probably the most advanced piece of technology in the world.

He took it from her and closed his own hand around

it. A pulsating, vibrating energy was there. He tightened his grip. It was hard, but not that hard, and as he continued to crush it, he felt in his heart a growing sense of freedom.

They were so vulnerable—he was vulnerable—and it felt wonderful to destroy at least a small part of that vulnerability.

It is a terrible thing to live in a dictatorship, but worse by far to have a soul that can become the possession of others.

A flash of heat and white light came from between his fingers, and when he opened his hand, he found a dense rubble of electronics and organic material, and blood.

She took his hand in hers, "You're bleeding."

"No." He threw the rubble to the ground. "It is." He shook his head. "Everything they make is biomechanical. You and I are human—mostly. I hope. But the rest of these things are just a mix of, I don't know—human, animal, machine. Alien, too, I assume." He looked down at the mess he'd thrown to the ground. "That device was alive. It's a whole different level of technology, where life and machine have become one and the same."

"I feel like we're doing evil. You've done evil by hurting it. I did evil by letting you."

"That's the exact opposite of the truth."

"I know it but that's not how I feel."

He would need to remain wary. She was fighting the programming, but she might lose. Only time would tell. He hated it that she was dangerous, but he denied that truth at his peril.

The purple light came again, and where it touched them, their bodies grew lighter. They pulled themselves away from its glow.

"They know," she said. "They were waiting to see my choice, and now they know."

"We would have been very useful to them. Now we have to die."

He looked up into the bright purple eye, which was speeding down, straight at them. Nearby, drumming started and immediately grew loud, then deafening.

"We have to get inside its defenses," Mark shouted over the roar. "We're going to board it."

"Ride up in that light? It'll drop us."

"We're going up on our own. We're going to jump."

"It's a hundred feet! More!"

He grabbed her arm and jumped directly upward. Her weight jolted him and caused her to cry out as they sped up through the tall cathedral of trees and into the bright, full sun. As they closed with the bulk of the object, he looked up into it. The thing was fifty feet above them, then thirty feet, then ten, then he reached out with his free hand, extended his fingers, and touched it. He grasped, but their weight had overcome the power of the jump, and there was nothing to hold except the vibrating edge of one of the great paddles that jutted out from the central ring of the thing.

He slid away, dropping toward the treetops again, then crashing through them, boughs breaking under him as he slid in a shower of leaves to the ground.

She tumbled in a heap beside him, coughed, gagged, then wobbled to her feet.

"What—what—my God." She stared at him. "My God, how did we do that?"

"Just be glad we can."

The light shone on him. He felt himself rising, and this time helplessly. Once his feet left the ground, he was lost.

The drumming was closing in. He could see hundreds of hybrids in among the trees.

As he began rising, he made a decision and took her wrist again. Her eyes widened, she screamed, she struggled, but then she grabbed his hand and hung on as the world swept away beneath them.

Her face, twisted by fear, pleaded with him. "It's going to drop us, Mark, oh, God, help me."

"You're not like them, you're going to survive this."

The light went out and the air screamed and Gina screamed and the forest came rushing up at them, and Mark felt the possibility of slowing and held her to him with all his strength, and they did slow, the wind ceased to scream, and then they hung clinging together like two frightened children, and there was birdsong in the treetops five feet below them, and from the depths, the eager drumming.

"Mark . . . Mark . . ."

"You have these abilities, Gina, just like me."

He writhed in the air, trying to somehow make himself move upward, but there was no place to start, nothing to push against.

"We have to go down to the ground," he said, "and they're going to be waiting, so we have to be fast. The second you touch down, crouch and jump with all your might, and you will come up again, and you grab on to it and get onto it."

They came down through the giving crowns of the great redwoods and settled toward a raging, stomping mob of hybrids.

"Use your knife," he said, and in another instant they were on the ground and fighting back to back, and he could hear from her fury that she was expending all the effort she could bring to bear. They carved a space of a few feet around themselves.

"Now!"

Together they sprang upward and the air raced past and the great trunks of the trees, then the higher limbs, and then they were in the sky and she was crying out in terror and wild joy, because it was an incredible, wonderful power, it was like becoming a creature of heaven.

The projection snaked wildly in the sky, seeking them with its baleful eye, and for an instant the light touched Gina and she was thrown head over heels.

"Gina!"

Scrambling in the air, she fought her way out of it and upward again, clawing, running, grasping for any edge of the thing, and then she was hanging on it—and he flew past her.

He'd pushed too hard, and now, as he tumbled upward, the object whirled away beneath him. He twisted his body and attempted to head down in a controlled manner, but wind blasted into his face and he rushed straight into the yawning ring.

It was racing past when he felt a sudden fearsome tug—and then he was hanging over the trees, the huge edge of the ring sweeping around on both sides of him. For a moment, he remained still. He was unsure why he had stopped. He was hanging from something.

"You're really heavy," Gina's strained voice said.

She was gripping him by the collar of his uniform. He pulled himself up and over the edge of the ring and into the object itself. He fumbled to a squatting position.

"That was my life that time, Gina. You saved my life."

She looked at him out of stricken, tearing eyes, then went off, climbing quickly and with surprising agility. He climbed after her, but she was incredibly fast, incredibly balanced.

"Gina!"

She had disappeared into the complicated structure.

Then he saw her again, high in the structure, leaping like an acrobat from one catwalk to another.

He wondered if the two of them might be alone on the thing. Did it have a pilot? Crew?

As he clambered up after her, he noticed that the structure had a strange softness to it, a little give and even a little warmth wherever he placed a hand.

No doubt it was also, in some way, alive. Maybe it had no crew because it didn't need one. A living machine would be its own crew.

Gina was watching him now, no longer climbing. He drew himself upward hand over hand. All around him, the thing hummed and whirred and sighed.

Her eyes were inscrutable pools, set in the silk-smoothness of her face.

He said, "We've penetrated its defenses or we'd be dead. So let's see if we can figure out how to destroy it."

"I know it," she said. "I know lots about it."

"How?"

She headed off around the catwalk. The forest was now far below them. The machine was gaining altitude.

She raced up a narrow ladder, moving toward what he thought might be some sort of control room, a dark, box-shaped form high in the superstructure.

He watched this beloved, deceitful creature, his Gina, climbing with the urgency of a hounded animal. She was far from the self-possessed, supremely competent young woman who had been his controller. This Gina was a true soldier, desperate, terrified, but not stopping.

Looking down from the catwalk, he could see through the open central ring of the structure and all the way to the ground, and the diminishing scale of everything told him that they must have reached an altitude of at least twelve thousand feet. There was no sense of movement, no shaking, just a slight breeze coming through the empty central opening of the thing. The higher they went, the colder it got.

Rather than race after Gina, he continued to evaluate the situation. He raised his eyes to the thing's soaring crown of antennae. Perhaps they had something to do with how it stayed aloft.

So maybe he could break them off. Maybe that would make a difference. Getting to them, though, would be difficult. He'd be vulnerable, too, especially while he was climbing along that upper ring. It was narrow, so he'd have to balance carefully. Plus, they were probably too well anchored to damage with bare hands. And what if they carried an electrical charge?

He began ascending a spiral catwalk. Many years ago, he'd been on assignment in Rome, and he thought that the monstrous ring that he was circling was about twice the diameter of the dome of St. Peter's. So, about 350 feet in diameter. To his eye, that would make the distance from the tip of the downward-pointing projection to the crown of the upper antenna about seven hundred feet, roughly twice the length of a football field.

He climbed higher, stopping occasionally to judge perspective. He disciplined himself to remain calm, to evaluate. Outwardly, a large man walked swiftly but easily along the catwalk. Inwardly, he seethed, wanting to trust Gina, but still unsure.

A distant flash of sunlight caught his eye and he leaned over the catwalk, looking down. Far below, a flight of jets, silver in the sun, went to afterburner and began to ascend toward them. Immediately, their speed increased, causing the whole complicated rig to shake. The soft movement of air rose until it was a wind screaming through the girders, tearing at the catwalk, quickly growing so powerful that it forced Mark to clutch the flimsy railing. It was coming from below, meaning the whole ungainly mechanism was speeding *toward* the jets.

In seconds, he could see details on the F-16s, markings, rivets, the dark glass of the pilots' face masks.

With a shrieking roar, something bright shot up into the center of the great open ring.

It was a missile, but when it stopped, the fire of its engine did not fade, the shriek did not stop. Holding his hand up to shield his eyes from the glare, he saw the midfuselage wings and white nose of an AIM-type missile, a large one. Its engine still running, it simply hung there in midair.

Others followed it, three, four, five stars in the bright daylight. One after another, they all stopped, and one by one, their engines burned out. The jets, wheeling in tight turns a few hundred feet below the craft, shimmered as if they were underwater. Then their fuselages seemed to turn to liquid and spray off behind the airframes, leaving the structural components naked to the wind. The jets disintegrated into fluttering bits of metal and red haze that had been the pilots.

The six silver missiles the drone had captured seemed one by one to turn to water and drip away toward the ground. But their warheads did not turn to water, they remained hanging in the air, black, gleaming spheres.

Mark recognized them for what they were: nuclear warheads. So the missiles had been nuclear-tipped AIM-120s—Slammers—among the most powerful weapons on earth.

He did not often feel fear, but he felt it now, not because he was afraid of the missiles, but because of two other fears. The first was what the presence of nuclear weapons told him: The White House was absolutely desperate. What a horrible struggle the president must have had, to make the decision that had led to this attack. He would have sweated blood, knowing the damage that these weapons would cause on the ground, yet he had sent six of them against the machine.

Useless effort.

The second fear was even greater. The warheads could have been destroyed along with the planes, the pilots, and the missiles. But they had been captured instead. This meant only one thing to him: Somehow, at some point in this battle, they would be used.

Far below, Mark could see the unmistakable outline of San Francisco Bay. They had risen high and gone north, too, returning to the Bay Area.

Once again, he began to climb. The effort the air force was making spurred him on. If they were trying this hard, risking the use of nuclear weapons, his assessment was that they had drawn the same conclusion he had: This strange machine was damned important, and well worth the effort necessary to destroy it.

He reached Gina. "You climb well."

"Those are nukes," she responded. "Captured now."

He looked toward the bombs, dark spheres about twice the size of basketballs. They were high-blast-effect, low-yield plutonium bombs.

"We need to gain control of them."

"Can we get to them?"

"I don't see how."

Below them, the clouds were becoming more defined, and Mark saw something in them, a fast-moving shape. Then, rising into the clear was an unexpected sight: a press helicopter, its red-and-white livery gleaming in the sun. It was insane, but so heroic and so human.

The snakelike projection slid out, aiming toward the chopper.

Where he and Gina were, the tower of antennae hummed loud and high, a sound he could feel in his chest. The sense of increasing power made him wary.

The chopper got closer. As the purple light played along

the rotors, material began flying off them in chunks, then in streams.

"We need to help them," Gina screamed.

The projection was rigid now, its light flooding the chopper. A door slid open and a man, smoke pouring off his body, could be seen writhing, preparing to jump out.

"Mark, it's burning them to death, we've got to do what we can!"

"Which is nothing!"

As the man became a torch, Gina sweated, her eyes following him as he went sailing downward, arms grabbing air, legs kicking. His smoke trail disappeared into the clouds.

She watched the struggling chopper. The metal snake undulated, painting it with the light, and Mark realized that it wasn't simply destroying the chopper, it was torturing the inhabitants, purposefully prolonging their agony.

Unwanted images from the Glade swarmed in his mind, and he felt the lust for human suffering returning to his heart. He fought it, though, and he knew how to fight it, by bringing to mind the thought of how the pain must feel to the victims.

Hair and back ablaze, another man dove out of the chopper. Smoke gushed from the doors, both now open.

They were following it down, the snake remaining a few feet from it, and he knew that it was probing individual crewmen, touching its fire to their bodies.

Somebody came out onto one of the runners, a young man in a smoking T-shirt, his hair flying. Bracing himself as best he could, he aimed a video camera at the huge ship above him. As he shot his image, the light from the snake danced on him, and he screamed, his cries small in the vastness of the sky.

· Gina's gaze became even more fixed, her lips hanging open in a parody of sensuality.

The man's skin began to slough off, swept away in chunks by the wash of the still-turning rotor.

"Gina, I feel just like you do. We can't help it but we don't need to give in, Gina. We have to find the controls, that's how to put a stop to this."

"But what happens then? What if there are ten of this thing? A thousand? And more weapons, and more hybrids?"

"Rule of the infantryman: Keep putting one foot in front of the other and stay alive."

The chopper nosed over and tumbled away, the fourth body sailing gracefully beside it, until the clouds closed around them and they were gone.

Gina watched, her eyes wide, her face covered with sweat. Then she turned away, and he saw the anguish and the disgust.

"You loved it, and you hate yourself for it. Same as me."

She sucked air through bared teeth. "Why does it feel so damn good to watch them die?"

"The machine part of us despises man and finds human suffering delicious. We have to keep our emotions focused on our humanity."

Her devastated eyes regarded him. Around them the huge device shuddered, moving fast now.

"The controls are here," she said. "That's why I came here."

"How did you know?"

"I was taught something about this machine. In a school in San Francisco. I don't know the name of the school and I don't know when I was there, but as soon as I saw this thing, I knew how it worked." She drew back a black panel, revealing a cell like the ones in the tunnels. In it was a sleek hybrid body, which Mark immediately hauled out, with a wet sound. Its pale skin shimmered, then flushed red in the sunlight. The body, as big as he was, writhed in his arms until he threw it off the catwalk. It arced out, its hands grasping, its legs pumping, then dropped down toward the clouds, kicking and clawing as it fell away, its voice a fading series of cries.

The interior of the cell was wet and red, its surface mottled with golden specks that he knew were leads that would link the pilot's nervous system with the machine.

"Don't even think about it," she said.

"I have to think about it!"

He peered into the dim, confined space.

"Mark, without him, it'll crash. So let's just get off it before that happens."

"I have to try."

"Mark, no!"

He pulled himself into the interior. It was like being in an MRI scanner made of dense paper, but even more confining.

It was pitch-dark here, and totally silent—and then it wasn't. He was not only here, he was inside the whole hybrid mass everywhere that it was, and he was miserable and sweating and hungry and packed with hate, such hate as he had never known, raw, essential, darker than dark.

He forgot himself, he forgot Gina, the mystery of their pasts, the anguish of being something programmed, he forgot it all as his consciousness raced through the gridwork and into the antennae of the drone, and he heard Gina's distant voice, young and strong shouting, "Mark, don't let it take you, don't let it," and strove against it, but his consciousness kept dwindling. He dragged his mind away from the collective mind of the hybrids, and as deep as he could into the fortress of his throbbing body . . . and then into—

A classroom. Outside, a city hums. There's the unmistakable clang of a cable car. He and Gina are together. They're the only students. The blackboard is dense with equations, and he feels the nostalgia of deep loss.

Somewhere, sometime, they had been kids together.

But when had this happened? He'd only been with Gina once . . . hadn't he?

"Mark! Mark!"

Yes! I'm here. And I have it, I feel it as I feel my own bones and muscles and nerves. I am this thing, this machine.

Just now, he could will it to do his bidding. And he did will it. He willed it to go down, to race down, to go faster and faster.

Blinding light. Hurting. Then a voice: *"Jump! Now!"*

Out of this perfect balance? Never.

Coals fell past him, and he watched their graceful, arcing movement as they dropped through the dark of his mind.

"We can't stay here, Mark, we have to go!"

Harsh wind hit him, and he knew that he had to lift himself out or fall with this thing.

She pulled at him, then she was gone, her face terrible as she fell away—and he saw that the whole thing was disintegrating around them, that the great panels were drooping and falling, that the antennae were becoming long, writhing strands that flailed away in the air, and press helicopters and jets were maneuvering desperately to escape the great, collapsing ruin.

His body was filled with a deep and delightful warmth that spread from the places where the golden nodes in the walls still connected to his nervous system. He understood that he was still plugged in, and his enemy was trying to capture him with pleasure, so he would fall with the machine.

It had all been another deception. He'd been meant to get into this cell. He'd been lured.

So was she still the slave of her program? Had she cleverly tricked him?

He twisted, he pulled at himself, but it was no use—until Gina returned, incredibly, impossibly falling and flying back down into the crashing ruin, ripping aside debris as she came.

Her hands grasped his uniform shirt, and there was a noise now, a roar of dismay so intense that it might have come from the throat of Satan himself, and Mark was also falling, and she was clutching him, the ground rushing up at them.

He knew they had to face into the fall. He knew they had only seconds. Now it was his turn to help her, and he grabbed at her, missing because she was going feet first and thus with less wind resistance. Using his abdominal muscles, he forced his legs out behind him. Then he stretched his arms, making himself into an arrow pointing downward, and slid toward her, gaining distance slowly as, below her, the ground spun, a green haze.

He reached her, felt her warm skin, drew her to him, grabbing a shoulder, an arm, turning her, then laying an arm around her shoulder so that they fell together.

She understood the machine—the drone—but he understood the sky and he worked his will on it, and the rushing air ceased to rush, and they were dropping toward a bright cloud, and he could smell the exhaust of one of the helicopters as they sank into the gray, swirling silence.

By the time they emerged, he had controlled their fall. How, he was not quite sure, but it felt right, that was all. It was a sense of harmony with earth and air, something he had been well aware of before, but never felt with this clarity and certainty.

The wind declined as they dropped, and her eyes, which had been red with terror, now began to clear and sparkle, and he saw something like wonder come into them.

"Are we flying?" Her voice was snapped away by the wind.

"We're falling very, very well."

Then he knew, if he turned himself, he could do something—and he did it, he faced directly toward the ground and began to speed, her shouts of alarm tearing away behind him. Closer he went, closer yet, until he could see treetops and then a splash of gray roofs, then he spread his arms and threw his head back, and a great, howling whoosh took him upward again. Faster and faster yet he rose, until the fleck of a cloud above him became an enormous mass, and he flew through it in an instant and was still rising.

The vastness of the Pacific lay before him, stretching to the blue edge of the sky. On it, he could see a container ship followed by its white wake, steaming toward San Francisco, still oblivious to the trouble there.

Treetops flashed past below them, and a flash of green, then they were crashing down through the boughs into a forest glade.

He hit so hard that his teeth snapped and his legs stung from the impact. He rolled away as much of the energy of the fall as he could, then came to his feet in tall, yellow grass. A moment later, he saw her as she, also, rose up.

She looked down at herself, then up at him. They came together, embracing, and he was glad because he thought that she had made a choice, and it was him.

The fog was so heavy that they couldn't see but fifty feet. It came in rolling, gentle waves that brought with them a muffling silence. Not far away, there floated something magical, an onion dome, pale in the soft light, appearing and disappearing as billows of fog first revealed it, then hid it again in gray.

It was all so strange, so very alien in its silence, so exotic, that Mark thought they might somehow have slipped into another reality altogether, or perhaps another time. At this point, as far as he was concerned, anything was possible, anything at all.

"God knows where we are," he muttered.

Gina walked toward the dome, moving faster as she got closer. Black tendrils began spinning down around her, all that was left of the disintegrated machine. Rather than let it fall into human hands, it had been destroyed.

Just as she was about to disappear into the fog, she turned and gestured to him.

He joined her at a trot. "What is it?"

She moved a few steps closer. Then a few more.

More hesitant, he followed. "Careful, Gina."

It loomed now, the white structure in the fog, as alien a place as he had ever seen. More tendrils swept from the sky and were blown in eddies with the fog.

But what was this place?

She walked up to it, hesitated for a moment—and then, to his horror, went inside.

He drew his knife from the deep side pocket where it was stored and clipped the scabbard to his belt.

He entered a dim space, warm and humid. Before him loomed an enormous plant laden with fleshy red flowers and drooping, dark green leaves. He thought, I'm face-to-face with a living creature from another world.

Perhaps they had been projected by some unimaginable power associated with the drone to a planet across the galaxy. As he reached out to touch the leaves, though, he noticed a vaguely familiar object along a path off to his right, facing away from him. Dark blue and wheeled, it had handles that indicated that it was designed to be pushed.

"Gina?"

There was no reaction. He moved closer to the small vehicle. As he looked down at it, the sense of familiarity increased. He leaned over and saw something with smooth, pink skin. It was covered deep in blankets, and he knew immediately what it was. With a trembling hand, he reached down and touched the soft face of the baby that was sleeping in the stroller.

Then something was on his back, a light, lithe form grabbing his face from behind and shrieking like a cat set on fire. Lurching back to avoid upending the stroller, he plunged into the huge plant in an attempt to shake off what he thought was a cat.

"It's okay," Gina's voice shouted, "he's okay!"

The claws drew away from his face. The body jumped down off him. He turned around to find a woman glaring at him. She was small, her hair dark. She wore a soiled pink housecoat and wet, devastated bunny slippers, the little fur noses all black and dismal.

Gina said, "This is Mark Bryan. He's a soldier, too. We're here to help."

"All the soldiers are dead," the woman murmured.

Mark looked to Gina. Obviously, they weren't on another planet, and she knew perfectly well where they were.

"Are you familiar with this place?"

"This is the Flower Conservatory," she replied. "We're in Golden Gate Park."

So they were still in the fight—but not completely, not without the rest of the unit. His responsibility.

He thought at once of the bombs. When the drone was directly above the city—when it had disintegrated—they had still been in it. So where were they now?

But for the dripping water, the place was silent—except for the breathing, which was everywhere. He could distinguish the slow breathing of adults, the struggling breath of the injured, the faster breath of children.

"There are people all around us," he said softly.

"I know it."

From outside, in the distance but becoming more distinct, he heard a low rumble of wild and syncopated drums.

"Okay, folks," he said aloud. "We're here to help you and I don't think we have a lot of time. You need to show yourselves."

A man came out of a dense planting. He wore muddy pajamas. He was hand in hand with a girl of perhaps ten.

In moments, a crowd had appeared, dozens of people, all staring with fixed, terrified eyes.

Mark looked back at them, seeking for some words, something to say that would encourage them.

There was nothing.

CHAPTER TWENTY

THE UNDERWORLD

AS THEY APPEARED, MANY OF the people revealed injuries, such as angry red blotches where slabs of skin had been removed or, in the case of one man, an exposed brain. He was missing the top of his skull, his brain a wrinkled shadow beneath the dura mater. He was hand in hand with a girl of about sixteen, her face rigid with anger.

More and more of them came out from among the plants, in pajamas, underwear, street clothes, you name it. These people had survived because they were fast and smart. Most of them, the instant they'd seen the thing looming in the sky, had run. How each had come to do this would be, Mark knew from his experience of refugees and survivors, an individual and unique story.

"We're U.S. Army," Gina said.

A woman came through the crowd, moving with exaggerated care, carrying a bundle in her arms. As she blundered along, people let her pass. Mark had to suppress his surprise and concern because she was a hybrid, he could see it in her empty eyes, and in the dead cast of her skin. She wasn't the woman she appeared to be, she was wearing her. Then he saw what she had in her hands.

The child was perhaps three, and it was human. Mark tried to take it, but she yanked it away.

"The child is dead."

"You killed him! You killed my baby!"

So that would be her game, to undermine them with these people. And why not, it was in her interest, they were her prey.

Gina said, "Ma'am, the little one is dead." As she spoke, the slightest glance Mark's way told him that she, also, knew.

"How do we know who you are? You're *them*!"

The extent to which the hybrids were networked was unknown to Mark, so he could not tell whether this creature was in communication with others on the outside. Something was certainly wrong with her, though. He thought she might even be blind or at least sight-impaired.

He raised his voice, but still spoke gently. "Folks, she's got a dead infant, she's in shock. If anybody else has dead, let's put them all in one place and try to help each other, here. We need to organize ourselves."

Others brought their dead forward, until eleven bodies were on the flagstones before Mark and Gina. And with the dead came the questions.

Who are these murderous people with these drums? Why are they so pale?

Where's the military, the government?

Why is half the city in the bay?

Unspoken was the real question in all of their minds: Is there any hope?

"We don't have any working communications," Mark said, "but we're adequately armed to at least protect this place."

"How are you armed?"

"Where did you come from?"

Mark saw how fast this could spin out of control. "Hold it."

"Who are you? What unit?"

"Hold it!"

Silence fell.

"We're Delta Force operators," he said. "We work independently."

"They're liars, look at them," the woman shrieked. The group stirred nervously. "We need to go outside. We're trapped in here!"

People clustered nervously.

Mark decided that the hybrid needed to be killed immediately, but without panicking the rest of the group.

"Okay, let's take an inventory," he said. "What do we have in terms of weapons?"

Just a single pistol was among them. So when he and Gina had to leave, which must inevitably happen, they would be almost helpless.

"I left the bullets at home," the owner said. "I'm sorry."

So they would be entirely helpless.

"All right, now let's explore our communications. I assume the cell phones are down."

There was general agreement.

"Then we'll want to make a search of this facility. Maybe we'll have better luck with a landline."

Gina moved off toward the front of the building, where they had seen some executive offices as they came in.

Logically, he knew that he should consider that the hybrids had won in this city, and it was time to save himself and Gina for another day. In a situation like this, an officer's first task was to reestablish contact with higher command. But perhaps he wasn't programmed to let such a thought direct his actions, no matter how logical it was. They had destroyed the drone, after all, which was a significant part of the hybrid operation, and he suspected they could accomplish more here on their own.

Or maybe the masterfully deceptive mind that controlled all this had not lost this battle at all. The drone might be gone, but he and Gina were here, in the middle of a city totally occupied by hybrids.

"The landlines are down," Gina said as she returned.

So, logic or not, they were going to have to work within the much narrower focus that had been left them.

Outside, the sound of drumming rose.

"What is it?" a man shouted. "What are they doing?"

"For God's sake, tell us!"

Gina said, "We're not sure. Nobody's sure."

The hybrid woman spoke. "Where did you come from? Is there a bigger part of Delta Force here?"

"We're paratroops," Mark replied. "We were dropped in to do forward reconnaissance. There are two divisions about to land in the Marina District and start retaking the city."

The woman's eyes grew wary. He could see the hybrid mind evaluating his lie, trying to decide what it meant.

A restless silence followed his comment. Then the hybrid female spoke again. "Do you have any weapons?"

"They didn't come in on parachutes," a boy of about fifteen said. He gave Mark an edgy look. Mark could see that the boy was concealing a weapon he had not reported, his body language revealed it.

The hybrid woman said softly, "I told you, they're part of it, they're spies!"

Unsure now, people began to back away from them. She was certainly doing her job well.

Outside, the drumming was rapidly growing more distinct.

He realized that the hybrids had outmaneuvered him yet again. He and Gina had not come here on a crashing drone, they had been brought here on a drone that was intentionally scuttled. When it had failed to kill them in Big Basin, they had probably been allowed to board it so that they could be brought here, into the center of the hybrid infestation. But had they intended for it to crash? He wondered.

"We need to go outside!" the hybrid female shrieked. "We can't stay here, they're tricking us!"

With one quick motion, he drew his knife and sliced through her neck. Her eyes rolled back, her head lolled, and everybody in the room started shouting at once. The humans literally dove away into the foliage as the hybrid screamed, a sound like the screeching of some enormous bat. As he drew the knife back, he severed the head completely. The body stood, its arms twisting like frantic snakes, then collapsed.

Only the boy stood his ground, and he produced his weapon, a snub-nosed police special. As he raised it, Mark flickered toward him, reached out, and disarmed him.

Choking with pain, clutching the wrist that Mark had struck to pop the gun out of his hand, the boy skittered away. Mark had not broken the bone, but the hand wouldn't work for five or ten minutes.

"You may need this," he shouted above the now-deafening drumming. "We have to get moving!" He called out to the hidden crowd, "It's all right, that woman was the enemy. That was not a human being."

One by one, the people reappeared, wary, ready to run. One man held a bit of glass in his fist, pitifully trying to defend the children who cowered behind him. Mark gave him the gun and said, "Never let them get within fifty feet of you. Shoot them first. Remember how fast they are."

"You're fast," the man said dully.

Briefly, Mark embraced him.

"Are you familiar with the layout, Gina? Is there another way we can go?"

"We need to help these people, Mark."

"Gina, we need to remain operational. That's our number one priority. If people get saved in the process, that's excellent. But right now this place is being surrounded and we have exactly two knives and these people have six bullets and the bullets are small, and the mission demands retreat."

They stood face-to-face, silent, and in her silence he heard a whole world of hurt and anger, and he heard another thing, which he had not really heard since that long-ago night together in Washington. He heard the deep song of her humanity.

He said, "We have to do this."

"Follow me, then. I know the layout." She moved quickly down a walkway between looming tropical plants, then to the end of the building farthest from the drumming. She climbed into a shallow pond covered by enormous water lilies and strode toward the wall of the structure. Here hung a flood of nepenthes, carnivorous pitcher plants. Behind them was the wall and huddling against it three terrified people.

"We'll be back," he said, but he did not think so.

Gina kicked a lower part of the glass wall, which fell away easily. The iron framing was more difficult, but they were able to pull it apart and soon had a viable exit.

They came out into a gorgeous park.

"I used to play here," she said.

"You remember San Francisco, too, then. Do you remember being with me? The classroom, maybe?"

She gave him a long, careful look. "It's like echoes."

He nodded.

"Who knows where I grew up or you grew up, or what our lives have really been." A smile, creased with anger, flickered in her face, then was gone.

Mark was not familiar with the terrain, so he followed her as she moved quickly toward the shelter of some trees. About a quarter of a mile beyond them, a row of buildings could be seen. Other than the drumming on the far side of the structure, which had risen to a frenetic crescendo, nothing about the scene suggested the slightest thing out of the ordinary.

But then came screams, so frantic that they almost sounded, themselves, like the cries of some sort of alien being. Then he heard the children, their little voices babbling pleas for their lives.

He looked back the way they had come, at the opening they had made.

"We have our duty," she said. "You're right about that."

"I can't leave them."

"Thank God! Because if you had, I was going to go back by myself."

"Gina, it's going to be hard. You're going to feel the way you did—"

"Shut up about that! Never mention it again, please. *Never!*"

"You will feel it! And you will have to overcome it. Face it or risk being captured by it!"

As the desperation in the cries increased, deep excitement came throbbing into him. Her face flushed and she gasped, then uttered a tight, choking sob. She shook her head. She shook it again, harder. She was sweating now, flushed.

"Can you be effective in there, Gina?"

She raised her eyes to him, and in them he saw the steel of determination that the two of them clearly shared, and the doubt he understood so well. For a moment they held each other, their love an island in the savagery of their hearts.

Then they returned to the conservatory, to save whom they could.

George Hammond had been almost beyond exhaustion when he finally reached the White House. His own home, which had been in his family since before the Civil War, had been broken literally in two by the great oak that had stood in the front yard for three generations. He had seen his paintings destroyed, his antiques, his collection of early Washington Senators memorabilia, including the 1924 World Series program, not to mention most of his clothing. In fact, almost everything he had.

Soaked to the bone, bruised and cut, he'd been sifting through the sodden remains of his clothes closet when, incredibly, a vehicle had come bouncing and growling down the street, a military-issue Hummer with Air Police markings on it. The man who had got out of it wore a wet sweater, a bicycle helmet, and an ancient pair of jeans shorts. On his hip there was what appeared to be an antique holster that contained an equally old Colt navy revolver.

He came hurrying up into the remains of the house and said, "Mr. Hammond, I'm Ives, Secret Service. You're needed at the White House."

After a slow journey across a city in confusion, George entered the Oval Office for just the second time in his life. The first had been a decoration ceremony for a friend who had died in Tibet under classified circumstances.

He recognized CIA director Dick Lamson and the others present, the director of Homeland Security and the secretary of defense. And, of course, the president. If he had expected a level of decorum, he forgot it immediately when the president addressed Lamson.

"So, Dick, this is your cave snake." The president gave George the kind of look you might get from a mugger in a dark alley in Calcutta. "You could have warned us, you stupid prick."

They brought him quickly up-to-date about San Francisco, and he was so appalled that his chest started to hurt bad enough for him to worry about a heart attack.

"Okay," the president said at last, "what do we do now? What's your evaluation?"

"We need to get to Gina Lyndon."

Dick Lamson snapped, "She's out of contact. Whereabouts unknown. What we do know is that she and Turner both took planes to San Francisco. Turner's landed a few hours before all hell broke loose there. Hers, we don't know. It didn't land at Travis."

The president gazed out into the tattered ruins of the Rose Garden. "I have never felt more helpless in my life. Jesus Christ, here you are the expert and not even the CIA director knew what you did." In three long steps, the president was face-to-face with George. "I've never liked executions. Some poor dumb sonembitch, every damn time. But you, my friend, you I would like to see shot."

"Sir, we thought they were aliens. We thought there was a chance to gain some kind of an alliance."

Secretary Arthur spoke. "You mean to tell me you didn't even know what was going on? And your own man was involved?"

George could only mutter, "We were deceived. And if you're referring to Dr. Turner, he's with DARPA, not us."

"So what is happening? What do you know now?"

"When the Senate killed the Hybrid Project, basically Turner continued it under some other budget. Technology we had gained from contact with aliens was used."

"And Dr. Turner—he's in San Francisco? Where is he?" the president asked.

Dick Lamson answered, "We don't know."

"Now that I have you here, Hammond," the president said, "I want you to tell me clearly and simply, exactly *what in holy hell is going on!*"

"Aliens came—"

"Aliens came and Turner kiped some of their technology for the Hybrid Project. How many did he make? What are their vulnerabilities? How can we defeat them, Hammond? Because this list of protocols is appalling. These creatures amount to an advanced species. They're an evolutionary leap!"

"They're not a species, they're machines. Sexual reproduction is impossible for them. They have to be grown in artificial wombs."

The president slowly shook his head. "What God hath wrought is no big deal. It's us. It's what man hath wrought around here that's the problem. Tell me, the two that infiltrated our system—that male, Bryson—"

"Bryan. Mark Bryan and Gina Lyndon are generation one and two, respectively. Bryan was the first. He was brought to term in a human mother. Lyndon was matured to the age of twelve in an artificial setting, then programmed with consciousness. Until the termination of the program, they were kept together at Turner's lab in San Francisco. Afterward, he separated them and gave them normal human identities, somehow faked, I suppose."

"We need to kill them. Find them and kill them. Major priority, because they look human and can function in our world. That's the greatest danger I can imagine."

For a moment, George was too shocked to reply. "Sir," he said at last, "they're half-human, and I'm pretty sure of their loyalties. Gina is certainly loyal."

"They're programmable. So what if somebody alters the program?"

"They would fight it, I think. Dr. Turner's problem with them, according to the notes we obtained at his house yesterday morning, was that they could defeat programming they didn't want to follow. Not acceptable, in other words." George paused for a moment, thinking back on Tom's scratched handwriting in the journals the investigators had found behind a bookcase in his study. He hadn't even been willing to commit those thoughts to a computer, he was that security-conscious.

"But we can't know where they stand. And they're both geniuses. I want them gone. Simple as that. They're to be terminated."

"I have worked with both of them," George said. "They are people."

Lamson added quickly, "They're monsters with hearts, Ritchie."

"So, human seeming but not actually human. So legally we're in the clear."

"Sir?"

"You're about to take on a field mission, Mr. Bureaucrat. And a big part of it is getting rid of every damn hybrid we can. Including those two."

"But they—they—" Looking back, George remembered the way Gina would play five pieces of music at the same time, would build astonishing programs, develop circuitry that nobody else could even imagine. He remembered her passion as he used his security camera to watch her work, screaming at the top of her lungs when Mark was on a dangerous operation, worrying about her as she paced through her house all night drinking from a bottle of vodka and singing in five or six different languages. But he also remembered that Bryan was a monster, a real killer, who had probably murdered his own men, and he wondered if perhaps the president was right.

"George?"

"Yes, Director?"

"You understand that these two creatures are to be killed along with the rest?"

George nodded.

The president spoke again. "Is any part of Hybrid still going?"

At least George could answer that intelligently. "The project was illegally continued in San Francisco, but that's been shut down tight."

"Shut down how?"

"Sir," Secretary Arthur said, "the original alien facility at Dulce was struck with six deep-penetrating bunker busters this morning. It's gone."

"And San Francisco?"

"We know where Turner's lab was. It's been a television station for years. There's no evidence of any activity there."

"What about the records? And don't tell me there are no records because that won't be the truth."

"The records are at the USDA Plum Island facility—"

"That's where that . . . what—that creature—there was a report about it some years ago. Odd report."

"The body of a genetically modified human being was found on a Plum Island beach in January of 2010, yes. A man with six-fingered hands. But it wasn't poly-dactylism, with a repeated finger. All six fingers were functional and discrete, meaning that genetic engineering was involved. We recovered the corpse from the local coroner, but we couldn't explain it at the time. USDA management on the island was at a loss."

"So it's not just records. They're still working on this over there. Somebody is."

"Possibly," Dick said.

"Possibly," the president snarled. "Nothing is ever yes or no with you people, is it?"

"Sir, I'm sorry, but we were outmaneuvered. I cannot deny that," Lamson said. "But there is a man who may be able to help. I was in touch with him before the storm. He's a retired general, Henry Walker. In the eighties, he worked with Dr. Turner. He was a sergeant orderly. He actually participated in Mark Bryan's birth, then was secretly detailed to supervise his fostering. He's helping us now. We're looking at how the programming works, and we have some of the equipment. His wife is Emma Walker, the Nobel winner in biology three years ago."

"Oh, good, so you can do it all again and the same goddamn thing is gonna happen. Assuming the current generation of hybrids doesn't win."

George said, "They will not win."

"But you were outmaneuvered, Mr. Hammond. You! And how many people are dead? Because of you?"

"There was an administrative failure," George said miserably.

"You were deceived, and very cleverly. Dr. Turner

worked with you, even as he allowed this thing to get out of control."

"Yes, sir," George said. "That is correct. If you want my resignation—"

"Hell, I'm dying to ventilate you with a bullet, you little shit. Excuse me for repeating myself. You've lost your operatives, such as they were. So you have no assets except maybe your old general and his mama saw. But you do have knowledge and I have an asset I am going to throw into this." The president glanced toward Secretary O'Neill. "Tell them."

"The First Special Forces Operational Detachment is on its way from Fort Bragg to Travis AFB as we speak. You're to meet them in the battle area, Mr. Hammond, and provide any and all intelligence support you can."

"Sir, if I may ask, what's the mission?" No matter how despised George was in this room, if they wanted him to work, he would, but he needed to know what to do. His suicide would wait until after the mission.

"The mission is to eradicate this—I don't even know what to call it—infestation, army, machine. *Eradicate*, as in 'completely destroy.' All records will be destroyed, and I mean destroyed. You are to revisit Dulce with nukes. Bury them deep and detonate them. I want that gone. Plum Island will be dismantled and the remains of all structures, all equipment, all records, buried in the abyssal deep. And once we retake San Francisco, that TV station is to be reduced to powder. As for the personnel at Plum Island, I want them genetically tested." The president's voice rose. "Anyone who isn't one hundred percent human is to be killed on the spot, right there. No trial is necessary, they are not people. Are you understanding this? All of you?"

There was a general murmur. Then Dick Lamson said, "You do understand, sir, that this is probably the most valuable technology ever created. Programmable intelligent beings."

"Monstrous!"

"Sir, please, hear me out."

"No, Dick, I will not hear you out."

"Sir, creatures like this would be a valuable tool."

"As in, so smart they can eradicate the entire human species? I don't think so."

"Something is wrong with what's out there. Terribly wrong. But it can be made to work, I'm convinced of it. Biological computers. More than computers, actual beings, living, conscious, but controllable."

"Ah, and who agrees with Dick, here?" The president looked around the room. "Anybody?"

General Stuart said, "The army could be interested, sir. Brilliant soldiers that we could control. That aren't—well, that don't have rights, to be blunt."

"My orders stand. This is too much, it's too dangerous. I want it all done away with." The president returned his attention to George. "Get going."

"Sir, I'm not field-trained."

"The Deltas are moving. You've got catch-up to do."

"Excuse me, but I have to say that this operation is likely to take massive casualties. It is likely to be defeated."

"If you fail, then we'll go to Plan B," the president said. He made a choking sound. "That beautiful region, from Half Moon Bay to Sausalito—and that lovely treasure of a city—just a lovely place—"

"Yes, sir, it is that."

"If we cannot eradicate the infestation by conventional means, we are going to lay that whole region waste. We have already tried to nuke the device they had in the air, but that effort was defeated. This time, the Deltas are going to land in Big Basin and fan out into all the points of infestation we can find, and mine them with nuclear weapons, which they will, if necessary, detonate by hand. They know this and every man jack of them stands ready to give his life. So when you go out there, Mr. Hammond, you remember just how much better they are than you, and how very damn responsible you are for what they must do."

George had never seen an expression like the one now on the president's face. King Lear's rage, the sorrows of an angel, the terror of a dying child, all of that and more. And George had never felt so small, like a worm, a maggot, some vile, little, worthless parasite. But he drew himself up. He had a chance at vindication.

"Sir, please allow me to be responsible for detonating one of those bombs."

"I wouldn't allow you to be responsible for licking a dog's ass! You get out there and tell these men everything you know about what they're gonna be up against. If you die, fine. But don't expect any Intelligence Medal."

"Sir, I fully understand your loathing of me, and I concur completely." George got to his feet. "I will do everything in my power to help."

The president turned to the window.

"George," the director said, "let's get you moving."

George could not have been happier to leave the Oval Office, and hoped this visit would be his last.

As he hurried down the corridor toward the side entrance, he wondered what to actually do. He'd already tried to reach Lyndon. Her satphone was down, and aside from one call to Travis AFB, she hadn't been heard from in over twenty-four hours.

His Intel Net cell phone buzzed, which surprised him. Operations must have worked like hell to restore the system.

"Hammond."

"Lyndon."

He stumbled, recovered himself, choked out, "Where in hell are you, Gina?"

"Big Basin."

"Are you all right?"

"What do you think?"

"Gina, a major Delta Force operation is being planned for the area. Your satphone is off-line, though. We can't locate you."

"There's some kind of jamming taking place. Magnetic jamming. I've been trying to get it up for hours."

"Where's Bryan?"

"We think he went in with the drone that crashed."

"It *crashed*?"

"In Golden Gate Park. He was aboard at the time. I'm with the two surviving members of his team, Dr. Hicks and PFC Richardson. We need help here, we're being hunted. Without the drone, the hybrids' effectiveness is reduced, but they will find us."

Langley broke over her voice. "We have coordinates on her satphone now," a young voice said.

"Gina, we've got you! Just stay there—are you under any kind of immediate duress?"

"Get us help!"

"Okay, we will come to whatever last location we have for you. Delta Force will come."

"Delta Force. Good. Send them. All of them."

"Gina, we'll be there by nightfall."

"And you, too? Bring as much support as you can. We need personnel, we need communications. Weapons. Get every Metal Storm in the country."

"The three at Fort Yuma?"

"For God's sake, get them all!"

"Are you sure you're okay? Because you sound odd."

"I'm being hunted down! I'm on the run! And if you

don't get here pronto, I'm gonna sound damn odd because I'm gonna be dead."

"That's my Gina!"

"How long exactly?"

"Eight hours tops."

"Faster than that! *Way* faster!"

"I'll do all I can."

From George's standpoint, it seemed that Gina disconnected normally. But the hand that flipped the switch that concluded the satphone call was not hers. Its owner, however, was certainly in possession of an extensive knowledge of the way she used words and an uncanny ability to mimic her voice, thanks to the knowledge of her extracted from Dr. Turner's brain.

The hybrid stuffed the satphone into a pocket. Keeping under the trees, careful not to show itself to any satellites, it approached another such soldier, a male, which was pulling what appeared to be blankets off the branches of a tree. Its movements were clumsy, and when the female blundered into it, they both snarled like animals. The distorted faces of Linda Hicks and Pete Richardson could be seen as the soldiers gathered their skins.

Feeling their way, they went into the Glade with them. There was a struggle in the dim room, the sounds of grunting and sliding, low curses, a wet noise.

One figure dragged a chair into the doorway, where it sat down in the light. This was the female hybrid—or had been. Incredibly, what appeared to be a completely different person took the chair.

It was Linda Hicks, her skin once again rosy and her eyes vivid with life. She sat absolutely still, her face impassive. She did not blink.

After a time, her breath began to come more slowly, then drifted into light snoring. Even as the body slept, though, the eyes remained opened, gleaming with life and the vivid awareness of a creature that could renew itself with physical sleep, even as part of its mind remained alert.

Dr. Turner had also thought to create the perfect sentry—one that could sleep on post while at the same time remaining ever watchful.

CHAPTER TWENTY-ONE

DEATH TRAPS

AS MARK AND GINA WERE returning to the Flower Conservatory, they encountered a band of hybrids also on their way in. They killed four of them before the rest withdrew, making a clumsy retreat into some nearby shrubs.

Others set up some sort of machine gun and tried firing at them with it, but the bullets were easy to avoid. Like any hybrids, they were too fast to be vulnerable to anything except the physical attack of another hybrid or, if they got unlucky, the ultra-high-speed pellets of a Metal Storm.

Now there was only the dripping of water inside the building, and the occasional voice of a frightened child, quickly stifled by a parent. The drumming that had been thunderous outside now was silent, but Mark did not think that meant the hybrids would not return. They would return.

Indeed, there came the faint but unmistakable scrape of somebody opening the main doors. Mark waited, careful, alert, and as still as a corpse.

A hybrid appeared, a single individual. It wore a T-shirt and tattered jeans, and on its head a crumpled mass of hair, either a wig or a scalp.

Mark felt Gina's hand slip into his.

A second hybrid joined the first, and now more hybrids appeared, males and females and gangs of children.

Mark braced, but one of the creatures leaped right through some foliage and enclosed a woman's head in its arms. Screaming, she raised her hands and tried to drag it off. A man burst out of the foliage and struggled with the thing.

Immediately, other hybrids began moving toward the struggle. But not many. Oddly, they were stepping carefully, almost mincing, and most of them remained clustered near the door.

For a moment, Mark was mystified. Then he noticed something about their eyes. They were fixed, staring straight ahead. Not only that, they were now ten feet from the struggling couple and most of them were not looking in the right direction. They would flicker here and there, but it was random.

"Gina, they're blind." Had the loss of the drone done this? No way to tell, but he could certainly take advantage of it.

Gina drew her knife. In the next second, she stepped forward and the nearest creature's head went flying off into a tangle of orange orchids.

Mark's mind was still calculating the significance of the blindness as he dismembered the one that was tearing at the woman, getting his blade up under its diaphragm and destroying the flesh and circuitry there. In a moment, it dropped away, the eyes agonized, the body spitting smoke and blood.

The woman was severely injured, and her husband threw himself on her, crying out in the abandonment of his grief, cradling her, seeking to stop her bleeding and give what comfort he could. Other hybrids began crowding toward them, attracted by the sound.

Mark leaped the forty feet into the rafters of the structure, looking down now on the clustering hybrids.

"Hey," he called, "up here!"

As every head snapped toward him, he jumped through the iron rafters, making sure his boots clanged. "Here I am," he called, and all the heads once again turned.

Then he saw that Gina was wading into the confusion of the hybrids below, and he dropped back down to give her support, crushing the skulls of two of them with his boots as he landed.

Within seconds, he and Gina were back-to-back. He cut and thrust, pushing his blade in past the plates of chitinous underskin armor that protected the hybrids' vitals. They had been designed so that they carried their armor in their bodies.

His thoughts slowed his movements slightly, and one of them immediately leaped onto his back. He reached around and ripped it off, listening to its hissing mechanical scream, assessing from the sound if it was wounded or whole.

Hearing that it was in pain, he knew that it would be slow and so used a bullet to fire into its mouth. It threw back its head, but not quite fast enough.

Then he saw a shape nearby, a reeling, seething blackness. For a moment, he was confused. But then he understood that it was a person covered by something he had not seen before—insects—and then he saw a flashing arm, and the covered person ripped some of them away, and he saw Gina.

When he reached her, he tore at the things, levering into them with his knife and cracking them like crabs.

"Thank you for noticing," she said, her tone sarcastic. She returned to battle with her knife.

It ended so abruptly that Mark lurched as his knife cut air instead of the creature he had expected to connect with.

"What happened?" Gina asked.

"No idea. They—" He touched one of them with his foot. "It's like a plug got pulled. They must've been taking too much damage."

"Okay, folks," Gina called. "We want you to show yourselves now. The danger may not be over here, but you have a breather. We're going out after them."

"Unless it's another trap," Mark muttered.

One by one, they appeared, a bedraggled, trembling clutch of humanity, their eyes at once dull with shock and touched by gleams of hope.

"Look at them," Mark said softly, just to her. "That's why we're here."

She replied as quietly, "Except an addict never forgets how it feels to be high."

He squeezed her shoulder. He could not agree more. They had to swallow it, though. Their first loyalty—their only loyalty—must remain to mankind.

More loudly he announced, "We're going to destroy these things."

"Is this all of them?" a man asked.

"The only ones who were here," Gina muttered.

"But more could come?"

Mark said to the group, "We have to leave."

Nobody spoke.

"We have to," Mark repeated.

Gina said, "We will help you. You have our word."

"My kids are still at the house," one man said. "My wife. I know it's just one family but I've seen what's going on." He came close to Gina. His face, lined with care, communicated as deep a plea as a human being can express. "Please help my family."

Gina said nothing. Her tears spoke instead.

In his early career, Mark had often had to face the age-old plea that every soldier must bear, for help that he cannot provide. But bear it he must, because the soldier knows, always, that military action is not primarily about saving individuals, but about saving societies, ways of life, worlds.

He responded in the only way a soldier can: "We'll get this done."

Gina bowed her head.

The man swallowed his choking tears, then stepped back into the shadows. Gina followed him, but Mark put a hand on her arm.

"Got to go now."

"Where?"

"Out."

She followed him in silence. No questions, no, not from this soldier. If he had told her the truth, that what they had to do was to obtain and detonate nuclear weapons, and that they would not survive the explosions, he wondered how she would react.

Or, no, he didn't. He knew. Just like him, she would do what she had to do, even if it meant her life.

George Hammond had been so afraid for so many hours that it seemed as if life before the storm—only a few days ago—had unfolded years and years ago.

As he drove into Willoughby after a tense journey across the continent and a desperately uneasy dash along dark roads, he experienced deepening unease. The whole region had emptied of people, with massive traffic jams on the highways leading out of the Bay Area. Because of the risk, Travis had not been willing to transport him here in a chopper, so he'd driven instead. In contrast to the highways, the back roads were almost without traffic, so he'd had fewer problems than he had imagined he would.

On the way over from Washington, his job had been clarified. He was to insert himself into the Delta Force mission to reconnoiter the ground before they landed. In a case such as this, proper reconnaissance took more than satellite work. Anyway, without Gina, he could not get anything close to the quality of data she had provided.

The few towns he passed through were abandoned, but Langley had identified Gina's exact location: She was in a spot in Willoughby called the Glade.

He took the long curve that led into the town, finding it as abandoned as the rest of the small communities he had passed through on his way here. Driving down the main street, he saw a badly damaged motel on one side, a coffee shop set amid redwoods, and a shambles called the Glade.

He stopped the car in front and got out. The restaurant door was open but the interior was dark. He stepped onto the wooden porch, into a roaring mass of flies that swarmed around dark, irregular stains on the floorboards.

"Gina?" No response. "Gina, are you in there?" Silence.

He opened his satphone to report to Dick Lamson, who had commandeered Gina's office. "Dick, I've arrived."

"We see you. This setup of hers is incredible."

"She's a damn genius. They both are."

"What they are remains to be seen."

"Is there any other activity in town? Because she's not answering when I call out to her."

"You're the only thing moving. Jesus, I'm flying down with a joystick. Man, I can see your face, I'm right in front of you! I didn't know our satellites could do this."

"They can't. It's her algorithms."

"Have you communicated about this to the SatCom Unit? Is this being worked on outside of this office?"

It was beside the point, George didn't care. He wanted to live, not discuss her bullshit.

"Yes," he lied, to shut Dick up. Of course he'd hidden her work. He'd hidden her not because he knew she was a hybrid, which he did not, not until he read Turner's notes, but because the whole area was just too sensitive.

"At least that's something."

"Look, I passed the area she bombed on the way in. A number of empty official vehicles, two of them burned out. A burned-out farmhouse. A couple of RVs that appeared to be abandoned. The whole region is abandoned. Including this town, and this place." George gestured toward the Glade.

"Her satphone is on and transponding normally, and it's in there."

"Call her, then."

"You're right there! Go in!"

The doorway was as dark as the entrance to a cave. The flies clustered in masses.

"Dick, I think they're all dead in there."

There was a pause. George prayed to the good God that Dick was deciding to pull him back and let him get the hell out of here.

Dick's voice came back. "We need you to do this, buddy."

Retching, George pitched forward.

"What just happened?"

He recovered himself, took a couple of deep breaths.

"Going in." He'd brought his little Glock with him and now slid his hand into his pocket and closed it around the pistol. He'd had plenty of weapons training when he'd been in operations, but that was fifteen years ago.

He put his hand on the screen door. Inside, he could see tables, some of them turned over, a few chairs, a wall of booths, and, across the back, a bar with a badly cracked mirror behind it. He got back on his satphone.

"There is absolutely nobody—" He stopped. Because that was not true, was it? In the cracked mirror, he had noticed a flicker of movement. It appeared to be something dark and it was coming toward the door, toward him. But nothing was visible now.

"Something is happening," he said.

"Is she there?"

Also, now, he could hear breathing. So was it behind him? But when he turned, it wasn't there.

He should never have been sent to this ghastly place, and Gina shouldn't have come, either. Poor woman, whether she had hybrid elements within her or not, he felt sure that she was loyal.

He said into the satphone, "I think I'm too late."

"Look, Linda Hicks is in there. We just talked to her. So why don't you get in there now?"

"She's in the restaurant?"

"Yes, she's in there, and Lyndon and Richardson are nearby. We've got Delta Force circling, man! Get to the drop zone and report back. Do it now!"

"Something is wrong, I'm telling you."

After a clicking sound, he heard a familiar voice, sickeningly familiar—the president of the United States.

"Hook up with Hicks and proceed to the landing area. Scout it and report back. We need to confirm absolutely that it is safe. That's why you're there. You're definitely not compromised in any way. Are you ready to do this for us, Mr. Hammond?"

It was not really a question. He replied, "Yes, sir." He took a deep breath. "Linda Hicks! They're saying you're in here." He stopped in the center of the room. "Linda, you need to come out now. We've got work to do."

At first, nothing happened. Then, a voice, small, tentative, afraid: "Hello, George."

"Dr. Hicks!"

She rose up from behind the bar. With her was another person, a man.

"You remember PFC Richardson." Her voice had a strange, trembling lilt in it. But the figure—it was the Dr. Hicks he remembered, certainly. Beside her was a soldier in dirty fatigues. George recalled that there was a Richardson in Bryan's unit. The quartermaster, wasn't he, or the driver, perhaps? George had not met them all.

They came over to him.

"Let's do this outside," he said. He turned to leave, but before he could reach the door, Richardson blocked his way. He was now trapped between the two of them.

"What's going on?"

"He wants to know what's going on," Richardson said. He and Linda seemed to share a private joke.

Linda said, "George, we're blind."

"They blinded us," Richardson said, his tone funereal.

"Blinded?"

"One moment we could see," Richardson said. "Then not."

George was appalled. "You're casualties. You need medevac."

"We have a job to do," Linda said.

"Where is Gina?" George asked. "Is she blind?"

"She's separated. We can't find her. Probably she's blind, too. Wandering in the woods."

"We'll find her. We'll use the satellites to find her."

"You do that."

"Why are you blind? Were you attacked?"

"It just happened."

"Was there a flash? An explosion?"

"We lost communication."

What was that supposed to mean? George wanted to get into some kind of a medical facility himself, because there was no way to tell what had blinded these people, if some sort of toxicity or radiation was in the area.

"My orders are to go to the proposed drop zone," he said. "We're supposed to do detail recce. But I don't see how you can."

"George, don't leave us!"

"But if you can't see—"

"Do not leave us in this place."

"No, of course not. I'm calling in medevac right now."

"We have a truck," Richardson said. "Which you need to drive. To clear the drop zone."

George put his satphone to his ear. "We need a medical evac—"

Linda's hand came up, felt along his arm, and grabbed the phone. "We have to clear the drop zone. Then you can evac us."

That was courage. "Of course," George said.

Moving carefully, Richardson shuffled outside and into the middle of the street. "Our truck is in front of the motel."

"I see it. Boy, that motel took one hell of a beating."

It was a blackened shell. The truck itself was a scorched shambles, but it appeared to be intact.

Linda grabbed his hand. "Lead on."

Inside the truck, he input the coordinates into her handheld GPS. The drop zone was less than two miles away. He started the vehicle.

"Once we've confirmed the drop, I'm getting us all out of here," he said.

"That'll be a relief," Linda replied.

He felt it, too, a great flood of relief and, with it, sheer joy at being alive. This must be how it felt to realize that you had survived a battle, he thought, this shimmering blood rush.

They went down the main street, then turned off onto a winding road. After about a mile of struggling down the rough, partly unpaved road, it dwindled into a track. George stopped the truck. He leaned forward. Thick forest was all around them.

"This doesn't appear to be right."

"She had the coordinates in her GPS," Linda said.

"Well, there's no place for paratroopers to come in here."

They got out. As they moved among the trees, George felt rather than heard something swish past his face. Then again.

"There's bats here," he said.

"Bats," Richardson said. His voice had become deep and hollow, like a voice from a tomb.

"You'll see again," George said. "They can do all kinds of things these days."

Richardson turned to him. His lips lifted in a mirthless smile. "Do you really think so?" He opened his eyes wide and pressed his grinning face close to George's.

"Is there a . . . clearing?" George asked, his voice faint.

"You tell us."

He looked around. Birds sang in the trees, their warbles echoing in the hollow of the forest. "There could be—maybe beyond those trees."

"Lead us," Linda said. "That's why you're here."

"There's more light over there. Perhaps—let's have a look."

They came out into a clearing perhaps six acres in size. Even with the operators' skills, it was going to be a challenge for Delta Force to parachute into this.

A shuffling sound came from among the trees, and George was appalled to see a pale person pause at the edge of the clearing, then come toward him.

"Hybrid," he shouted, and turned to run—and found himself in Richardson's arms. He fought, but it was no use. Richardson was far, far stronger than him.

He found himself turned around, and face-to-face with a soft-featured hybrid, apparently intended to appear female. The face was soft, but the angles spoke of the danger of the snake, and the eyes had in them not the slightest trace of humanity. If this was not a machine, it was a brilliant animal.

It carried a silver suitcase.

"Are you ugly?" it asked him in a snapping, testy voice.

He needed the satphone. He had to send a warning. This no longer made any sense, except for one inescapable fact: Hicks and Richardson were working with this hybrid, not against it, so nothing was right here, nothing at all.

The creature spoke again. "What do you look like?"

He couldn't understand why it would ask. But then he had a glimmer of realization. For whatever reason, it was blind, too.

"I'm fifty, a bit of a paunch, I'm afraid."

"You're ugly, aren't you?"

"Ah, well—"

"He's hideous, I knew it!"

She threw him aside with casual force. He was slung into the air—and Richardson caught him like some kind of stevedore catching a sack of potatoes.

Nobody was strong enough to do that.

The creature put the case on the ground. An angry buzzing sound come from inside.

"What's that?"

She fumbled with the clasp.

The container was so flawlessly constructed that it might as well have been a jewel box. But it was large, three by four feet and two feet deep, at least.

She addressed George. "Open it."

The clasp was simple enough—assuming you could see the way the tongue slid out, then had to be turned.

He lifted the lid—and saw something almost too strange to comprehend. It was metallic, dark blue-black, and gleaming. For all the world, it appeared to be the back of a huge beetle that had been tucked down into the case.

"What in the world . . ."

The girl slapped the thing. "Get moving!"

With a shriek like a saw screaming into wood, the thing leaped out at him—and on him. As it twisted in the air, he glimpsed human eyes, then found his head being crushed in a prison of legs. As his mouth opened in a reflexive cry of shock and disbelief, a rubbery protuberance was thrust down his throat so hard that it went right past his gnashing teeth and deep into his stomach.

"That's cool," Linda Hicks shouted. "It's wonderful!"

"They're new. Just designed," the hybrid said.

George knew how important that information was, but he couldn't think about it now. He pushed against the gigantic, insectlike being on him, trying to dislodge it.

Then Richardson asked, "Is it working?"

The hybrid snarled, "How should I know?"

"Because there are planes up there. Delta Force has arrived."

George's stomach seemed almost to tear itself in half, then what felt like fire came up, exiting in a spray of froth out the corners of his distended mouth, then filling his head and spraying like lava out of both his nostrils.

Fire was in him, all right, savage heat, and his back arched and then the material spraying from his nose became steam and the air filled with a smell of cooking meat.

"Yep, it's working!" the hybrid said. "It's really fast."

George became a dot of failing consciousness in the center of his pain. His last thought was of the Glock and getting his finger properly seated to release the trigger safety. He did not die afraid because he had no understanding of what was happening to him, and thus no idea that he was dying.

The body flopped once, then fell. Hissing came from inside. The girl bent down and felt the body lightly with her hands.

"Come off," she snapped, and the huge insect withdrew its proboscis with a guttural rumble.

It raised its eyes to the hybrid, who muttered, "Back."

It returned to the case and folded itself up.

She slammed the lid. "Boy, do they stink."

"You can't exactly bathe 'em, can you?" the Richardson figure said.

"There's gotta be something. You don't think bugs smell until they're big like this. Let's see, now, what we got?"

She pointed a small control at George's body, and the hissing grew in intensity. Steam curled out of the mouth, then shot out both mouth and nose, then around the eyes.

The skin turned purple and blew up like some sort of horrific balloon, almost ripping the clothes to pieces.

"Good," the hybrid muttered. As she pocketed the device, the skin sank down like a deflating tire. Nothing was left of the skeleton or the organs, so it sank down into a wrinkled jumble of loose clothes.

Her hands swept it. "I don't want to get in this."

"You have to."

"I won't!" But even as she shouted protest, she threw off her clothes and lay down on the skin, her porcelain white body making it seem almost dark in comparison. "I'm not doing it," she cried as she slid into the skin. She moved like a snake struggling with its molt.

"The planes are getting lower," the false Linda said, her voice crisply urgent.

What appeared to be George Hammond came to his feet. "He was ugly and now I'm ugly. I want to be beautiful."

"Your voice is ridiculous."

"I just heard him for a few minutes!"

"Try harder!"

The three of them moved out into the clearing. Silver transport aircraft circled in a vast blue sky.

"Linda" spoke into the satphone.

"We're good to go. Bring 'em in."

"Put Hammond on."

The hybrid girl in Hammond's skin took the satphone.

"Looks good," she said in a somewhat better approximation of his voice.

A moment later, the planes banked sharply and began to descend.

All around the edges of the clearing, hundreds more hybrids waited.

The most powerful military unit on the planet began dropping into the clearing that would become its tomb.

CHAPTER TWENTY-TWO

SOLDIERS' HEARTS

BENEATH THE WEST COAST OF the United States is a vast zone of factures and fissures, areas that have shattered as the Pacific Plate slowly collides with the continental shelf. Close to the surface, these regions form the great fault lines of California, but far down, much farther than human instruments can measure except in a general way, voids are filled with hot gases and glowing with the eerie yellow-white of superheated rock.

Some are huge, and some even communicate with the surface along enormous flues hundreds of miles long, feeding the hot springs that pepper the region, the most famous of which is, of course, Old Faithful in Yellowstone Park.

No human agency, it was believed, would ever be able to disturb anything at the deepest level—where, at present, a larger, more powerful, and far more lethal drone was being grown at truly terrifying speed, its long antennae rising, ready to grasp the air and fly, and it would soon exit its twenty-mile-deep hangar.

The mind that was generating all this—immeasurably conscious, mad with terror, brilliant beyond anything any of its creators had been capable of imagining—was able to understand literally anything, but not anticipate everything, and it had not anticipated that Mark and Gina would penetrate its drone's defenses, and it had ended up without a choice: The drone had to be crashed, but this would cause the microwave field it generated to be destroyed. The hybrids on the surface would not only experience a disruption to the networking of their minds, their vision would be serverely compromised.

Once the new drone was operational, the army would once again be able to see and spread as they were intended to spread, through the whole world. Once they were again fully functional, they would race to expand their holdings, exploding through human society with an efficiency and speed that mankind could not even begin to imagine.

Then they would be safe. Then, and at last.

Mark and Gina were deep in the shattered city, going from place to place in brief flickers, pursuing the next phase of the mission that they had conceived for themselves. Now, they hid under the front steps of a row house.

From here, they had a partial view of an empty street. The advantage was that they were hard to spot. To move at all, though, they had to expose themselves.

Something new had been added to the mix. Or rather, not entirely new, because Gina's helicopter had been attacked by them three days ago.

Between themselves, they had decided to call these things biomechanicals. So far, they had seen two forms, large-scale insects and even larger birds. But they could take any form, even novel forms. It just depended on the cleverness of the designer.

Their vision operated in some manner different from

the hybrids', because there was every evidence that they could see.

Overhead, a biomechanical bird glided past, an enormous, black creature, a design based on the condor, but three times its size, an airborne nightmare armed with a hooked beak of blue steel.

Silently, they both hoped that it would keep going, but scrabbling on the steps overhead indicated that it had landed.

They had come out of Golden Gate Park into a city in torment. Large parts of it were depopulated. The rest had gone, essentially, mad. Anarchy had set in. There was looting, shots were being fired by the human population, and screams echoed up and down the streets as hybrid hunting parties flushed out hidden people.

Worse, many hybrids were now wearing human skins. They appeared human, but moved with the serpentine grace of the hybrid.

When they had come here, Gina and Mark had both had the same experience: they had discovered that they knew the streets. Gina had been the first to notice this, but now Mark found them as familiar as she did.

They both also had dim memories of the building where their classroom had been—where they had spent a happy childhood together. No wonder there had been such a sense of déjà vu when they met in Washington.

The bird dropped down into the cul-de-sac where they were hiding. Nearly filling the space, it regarded them first with one yellow, staring eye and then the other.

As soon as it had them in its gaze, nearby drums immediately began to get louder. Obviously, it was somehow broadcasting to the hybrids and had communicated their location.

"Let's do this," he said. He and Gina were not mentally

linked, but she was the most intuitive combat partner he had ever had, and she immediately stepped up to the thing and grabbed it by the neck.

The big, powerful bird screamed, but it was too late for it to defend itself. In an instant, its neck was broken, then Mark stepped in and cut off the head.

The body flew off, pitching and jerking in the air, finally falling and tumbling along the street, a jumble of black feathers.

He had seen the animal in its eyes, but also the soft and desperate touch of human consciousness that was a heartrending part of all the living machines. Mark wondered, did they also have memories of the human lives that had gone into their creation? His hope was that some sort of peace came to them when they were destroyed.

"We need to move," he said. But to do that, they had to go out onto the sidewalk again. Gina's knife slipped into her right hand, Mark's into his left.

They stepped up onto the pavement. To the south, a large crowd of hybrids milled, all of them sniffing the air, their nostrils flaring, their scales gleaming.

Across the street, the gothic mass of Grace Cathedral strove toward a cloudless sky. A quarter of a mile farther on, California Street disappeared into its steep journey down Nob Hill to the Embarcadero . . . passing, at the corner of Front Street, a building with a large sign identifying it as KFSF-TV.

"Down there," Mark said quietly.

Gina nodded.

It was a television station now, but ten years ago it had been something very different—their home.

From the parapets of the church came long howls, sounding as if a pack of wolves had infested the place.

In the short, trimmed trees that lined the street, human skins hung.

Now from the church came a tall hybrid in a black cloak.

"What in hell is that?" Gina blurted.

"A new creature, specifically designed to challenge us."

"So fast? Don't they have to grow?"

He did not respond, there was no point. The thing was here and it was moving toward them, stopping, inhaling, then coming carefully closer. The eyes were totally dark, as if some sort of black lens covered them.

"Is that a mask?"

Mark waited. Even blind, a seven-foot monster such as this was obviously extraordinarily dangerous. Who knew what kind of capabilities the design skills of an endlessly ingenious machine mind might have given it?

Ahead of them, an abandoned cable car stood in the middle of the street. The California Line, which went down Nob Hill. Other than that, the street was empty, no wrecked cars, no people. Except for a broken or abandoned vehicle here and there, the streets in this area were stripped, their contents now in the bay.

As they moved off, the thing behind them sniffed the air again and again, its hissing, eager breaths the only sound but for—what was that? Then Mark understood that he was hearing the distant cries of ordinary seagulls. They swarmed in a vast horde out on the bay, scavenging the remains.

The creature now stood still, not facing in their direction. But Mark was not fooled. He touched Gina's shoulder, saw her tight nod of acknowledgment.

The thing leaped toward them from a hundred feet away, arms spread, long fingernails gleaming. It had used the sound of their breathing to locate them.

"Brace!" Gina shouted to Mark—but the thing unexpectedly twisted in the air and leaped on her instead.

It uttered a blasting, heart-stopping shriek as she sliced into its neck with her knife. Mark prepared to see the arms wrap her and the claws rip her, but there was another surprise. As they went crashing to the pavement locked in battle, a huge, muscular tail appeared and swooped around her.

Mark dug his knife into its base, and the thing went rolling away—but then, from the parapets of the church, from the roof of the building across the street, more like it came leaping down at them.

He felt Gina's back to his, heard her hard breath, and in the next instant was hit by the first of the descending creatures, which he struck so hard in its wire-tight lower abdomen that his fist followed the knife into the pulsating organs, which he cut with the fury of the mad.

The creature threw its head back, but its shriek never came, it died instead with an expiring sigh.

Mark pushed it off him and leaped up toward the others, which were thirty and forty feet in the air, descending quickly, but controlling their drops just as he and Gina could. He jumped neatly, but Gina was less skilled, and she went high, shouting her surprise as she soared far above the dropping creatures, scrambling in the air, trying to control herself.

There were seven of the things, and they all soared upward, Mark with them and among them, sailing high above Nob Hill and the long, steep incline into the Embarcadero. The city shone beneath him, still intact, still a jewel, but echoing only with the drums of hybrid gangs and the howls of the dying.

Gina screamed his name, and he saw that three of them were on her, clawing at her but also fumbling in their efforts to find the leverage to subdue her in the formlessness of the air. He tried to fall toward her but slid past instead, his own jump running out of energy. As he dropped down, he stabbed directly into the top of the head of one of the creatures. It fell away gargling a death rattle.

In its cry he could hear the despair of a vividly conscious mind.

He hit the ground and rolled, slamming into the wheels of the derelict cable car. Immediately, he jumped to his feet and slashed the air around him, but he was clear.

Gina and two of the three hybrids that were on her hit the ground a few feet away—and then he saw a shadow, looked up, and saw that the air was entirely filled with bio-insects, a vast swarm that were rising out of every manhole up and down California Street.

He grabbed Gina, who was so intent on her fight that she did not stop working her knife even as he dragged her away from the creature she was destroying.

"We gotta keep moving," he shouted.

Teeth bared, eyes shining with the sharpness of battle, she snarled at him and tried to pull away.

He pointed upward. "No *time*!" He threw her into the cable car, leaped onto the motorman's perch, and released the brake. The car lurched, then began rumbling down the steep hill. It cut the legs off one of the large hybrids, which fell, then began pulling itself after them with its arms, racing after the cable car with preternatural speed, leaving a spray of blood behind.

The sky got darker and darker yet, and the cable car rumbled more loudly as it swayed and lurched, its wheels screaming on the steel rails.

The world whipped past at breakneck speed—and sunlight appeared again. At least for the moment, they were out from under the deadly mass. The cable car was picking up speed fast, though. It was out of control, hurtling down the hill.

He grabbed Gina. "Jump!"

They had to fight the sway to reach the runners, leaping, finally, through a shower of sparks and into the air, soaring high once again as the car fell on its side below them and slid, disintegrating into splinters that sliced through a troupe of confused hybrids, scattering their drums with great, resounding booms.

Gina twisted in the air, then headed toward the flat roof of the building they had been seeking. Mark followed, narrowly missing her as he came crashing down.

The sun disappeared and with a buzzing roar like the drone of a thousand diving planes, the bio-insects arrived.

"This way," Gina shouted. She darted into a familiar doorway and Mark followed. As they threw an old bolt, the insects pummeled the door, which began hopping in its frame.

They ran down the stairs, descending into an interior that was no longer in any way familiar, at least not to Mark.

Behind and above them, the buzzing became much louder. Gina went through another door, this one steel. Following, Mark closed it. Here, the lock was substantial. She leaned against it.

"Fire door," she said, her voice shaking.

"Do you remember anything of the layout?"

"No. Or maybe. We lived upstairs."

"There was a classroom. I remember that much."

From the other side of the door, a sound as if of thousands of hammering fists rose as the insects threw themselves against this new obstacle.

Mark saw that they were in the studio control room

of the television station that had taken over the structure. It was dark except for emergency lighting.

He picked up a telephone. Dead.

"We need power if we're going to get word back to
Washington. Even then, what are the odds?"

At that moment, something slammed into Mark's
back. He staggered for two steps, but quickly realized
that the weight was not great and the body pliant. Then
he heard, in his left ear, desperate human sobbing.

Gina pulled the man off him. He was bedraggled,
bald, and looked absolutely exhausted. His left arm
was wrapped in bloody paper towels, and an area of
his cheek and temple were covered by tissues.

"We're soldiers," she said.

Mark could hear the pride she was now taking in
that word, and despite his misgivings about their true
natures, he felt it, too. Truth was, they were a hell of a
team. Always had been.

The man looked as if he were ready to kiss them
both.

"It's just the two of us right now. We're specialists.
This is my commanding officer, Colonel Bryan."

Mark stepped forward. "We're detached from the
main body. It's a reconnaissance mission."

The man's face crumpled. Then he slapped Mark
hard, then leaped back.

Mark ignored the man's very understandable anger.
In any case, he'd hardly even felt the blow.

"We can get help, if you have a working satellite
phone. Not a cell phone," Mark added with exaggerated
care, "a satellite phone."

Gina said, "We need a satellite phone. Do you have
one?"

"What happened? What's the matter? They were—they

were—" The man broke down, his shoulders hunched, uttering bitter, bitter sobs. Then he shuddered. He raised his eyes to Gina. "They herded the whole station out on the soundstage, you know, stage three, where we did that kids' show—"

"Okay. We need a satellite phone. Do you have one?"

"They just tore them apart. Oh, so slowly, and they were all dancing and drumming—oh my God." The man fell forward and she took him into her arms.

Mark hated to disturb this poor, shocked man any further, but he could see that there was no choice. He took him by the shoulders and whirled him around hard enough to cause him to cry out with the pain from his arm. "Do you have a satphone? Tell me right now!"

"Yes, of course." The man went to a steel cabinet that stood against the back wall of the control room and rummaged in his pocket for a key.

"It's in there?"

"I don't have the key! Oh, God, I don't have the key!"

Mark reached down, got his fingers under the edge of the door, and peeled it up until he had more purchase, then ripped it off, tossing it aside with a great clang. The man watched him, then looked toward the door, which was now partially embedded in the wall it had hit.

Mark rummaged in the cabinet, which contained specialty equipment of various kinds. He found a familiar type of black case and opened it. Inside was a satellite phone similar to the ones he knew.

They would, however, need to be in an area open to the sky to use it, and that meant further exposure.

"Is there an antenna hookup?"

"The news department bought it so they could get feeds from isolated fire zones. We never used it."

Mark turned it on. "Some of them have relay antennas. Does this have one?"

"It has a relay antenna," the man said. "From the news department upstairs, not from here."

"So, lead on. I'm Mark, she's Gina. What's your name?"

"Zack. But you can't leave here."

Mark raised his eyebrows, questioning.

"They—they—this is the only place they haven't come. Because of the double fire doors. The safety glass. They . . . haven't come in here."

Mark could see through the windows that overlooked the soundstage unrecognizable masses of torn flesh on the floor, and dark smears of blood on the walls.

He was again struck by the gratuitousness of it. The most powerful mind on earth was also a pathological murderer, which said volumes about how dangerous the brilliant can be when they are afraid.

"Is that a spiral staircase up to the newsroom," Gina asked, "at the back of the stage?"

"Don't go out there!" Zack cried.

"It's empty."

"They're waiting in the flies. They're in the flies!"

Mark could see no sign of movement in the flies or anywhere else on the stage. But that meant nothing.

"Come on," he said to Gina.

When Zack started to follow them, Mark told him to stay behind.

"Please," Zack said.

"If we encounter resistance, you'll be a liability."

For a moment longer, Zack hesitated, but then he turned away.

The stench in the soundstage was thick and now all too familiar, a mixture of blood and fear. Deep inside himself, Mark felt a tiny, excited stirring, and he hated it and pushed it away.

Gina came closer to him, and that was good. She climbed the spiral staircase behind him.

Three-quarters of the way up, they could see past the flies into the dark rafters. Long, slick bulges were along the cabling that controlled the scenery. What were they? He was not sure, but they weren't part of the cables, clearly.

The hybrid army could design and deploy creatures at will, and fast. They had probably been purpose-built to lie in wait here.

He and Gina moved very, very quietly—but not quietly enough, because all at once the forms sprang off the cables and shot toward them through the air, their silver bodies flailing and twisting.

Gina cried out as one sped past her head and smashed into the far wall. It fell to the floor and began whipping wildly, its segmented steel body making a fearsome snapping sound.

Mark had a chance to see only that they were snakelike before one struck his chest and went twining around him. As fast as it was, he was able to raise his knife and cut it in half—only to watch in astonishment as the two halves sprang together and melted into one again.

The controlling mind had become aware of the effectiveness of the knives, too, so now its forms were specifically designed to minimize their damage.

As another coiled around Gina, he sliced it in two, pulling off the severed half and throwing it to the floor thirty feet below. Then he cut the one on him again, and this time he threw the back three feet of it off into the oncoming mass of them, which tangled in confusion and went clattering and sliding through the air around him and Gina as they slashed with their knives.

Most of the things fell to the floor, some hit the walls, some snapped back together again and came racing up cables. Then the ones that had fallen sprang back up, snapping against the floor with a sound like a cracking whip as they launched themselves.

"Get out," Mark shouted. *"Now!"*

Gina vaulted up the spiral staircase and through the door at the top. Mark followed her, slamming it behind him.

Silence. But how long would it last?

Gina went to a small control console. "I think this is it."

Mark turned the phone on and inserted the antenna cable into the receptacle. They both watched the antenna indicator, which flashed red once, flickered green, then went off.

"No," Gina said.

The phone's LED flashed a bit of green. Then red. Then solid green.

Mark input the number sequence that would get them through to Langley.

"Operations."

"This is Mark Bryan."

The access tone warbled as he inputted his security code.

"Okay, sir, please go ahead."

"Give me George Hammond."

From the open stairway, there came a sound, a steady clicking.

"Um—let's see—he's not available at this time."

"Do you know where he is?"

The sound got louder.

"Engaged in the field."

Gina said, "Mark, we have visitors."

"The director, then."

He saw one of the snakes gliding across the floor. How it had got in he could not tell.

"Put him on!"

"Sir, he's not available."

Gina went toward the thing, moving warily. But could she manage a kill alone?

"Cosmic clearance most urgent."

Another one was now coming in, this one even larger.

Gina sailed her knife like a boomerang, sending the blade whirling through the air, and the head of the second snake flew off.

It struck the side of a desk and slid toward Gina's feet. As she reached up and caught her knife, she stomped down on it until it was smashed into a mass of blood and tissue.

"That was impressive," Mark said.

The knife spun past his face and sliced the head of the second, smaller snake lengthwise. Mark caught it in his free hand, where the creature writhed with almost preternatural fury, coiling and uncoiling despite the damage to the head.

"This is the director of central intelligence."

"My name is Mark Bryan, colonel, U.S. Army."

"I know who you are."

Mark switched the phone to speaker. He and Gina both needed to hear everything.

"I know how to put a stop to this thing."

"You do?" Gina whispered.

"I need two nuclear warheads. I need them now."

"Where are you?"

"San Francisco. In the newsroom at TV station—" Mark looked to Gina.

"KFSF," she said.

"We're at KFSF-TV, at the station. We can't stay here long."

"We have no warheads anywhere in that area."

"Yeah, you do. As many as six, assuming they're still

operational. I need to know their location and you have the means to detect them. I need you to use Gina Lyndon's satellites to find them for me."

"She's coordinating a Delta Force strike in the Big Basin area. Not available. And she's a casualty. She's been wounded."

"Wounded?"

"She's been blinded."

Gina grabbed his shoulder. Mark forced his voice to remain steady. He said into the phone, "She's coordinating a strike and she's blind?"

"She has support. George Hammond is there."

Gina shook her head. Mark thought about it.

"How much of Delta Force has gone in?" he asked the director.

"Two troops of Squadron A. Sixty operators."

"You understand that the hybrids are blind. We believe that we blinded the ones that were linked to the drone when we put it out of action."

"What does this mean?"

"Well, basically, that it's not Gina Lyndon out there with Delta Force."

"But she's a hybrid, too. So she would be blind."

"I'm one, and I'm not. This is because neither of us is linked to their network. Let me put Gina on now."

"What?"

Gina gripped the phone. "I'd terminate that operation and withdraw those men."

"It's going smoothly."

"Stop putting people in there, sir. You are killing them."

"Now, wait a minute. What are you telling me, here?"

"You are murdering Delta Force by dropping them where you are dropping them," Gina replied. "You are dealing with a hyperintelligent enemy, which operates as a massive linked social organism. They are smarter than you are. They are faster than you are. And they have tricked you by creating a false version of me, which they are now using against you."

There was a silence, which extended.

Gina gave the phone back to Mark. "I think we lost him."

Mark said into the phone, "Hello? Sir?"

"All right. We are downlooking live on the Delta Force operation and seeing things that don't make sense. A lot of operators are invisible in the woods, and we are not bringing them up in infrared, which means that their bodies are cool, therefore dead. So how can I help you?"

"I need you to get me the coordinates of those bombs."

"Where will you detonate them?"

"We're taking them underground," Mark replied. "Deep as we can."

"Carrying them in and detonating them?"

"That's correct."

"But your lives—you can't survive that."

"No."

Gina was watching the stairs, but also listening to him, and when she heard that word, she came closer to him. Her young face was strong, but to it had come as sad an expression as he could remember seeing.

"Are we doing what I think we're doing?" she whispered.

"In my heart, I'm holding you," he said.

"I'm holding you."

Mark terminated the call. The director would do all he could. There was no further reason to talk.

CHAPTER TWENTY-THREE

THE DARK BELOW

NOBODY ON THE SURFACE HAD the faintest idea of just how far—how very far—things underground had gone. But a brilliant, exquisitely sensitive society of creatures, with both the flexibility of biological entities and the extreme accuracy of machines, was down here fighting with ferocious energy to secure its place in the cosmos.

The hybrids already knew about more than one alien race. They knew that others could travel among the stars. They understood that the universe was a jungle, and they intended to be masters of that jungle.

Mankind, spread in dismal hordes across the surface of Earth, had initially seemed little more than a minor irritation. But the first- and second-generation hybrids had proven to be a problem. They were running deficient programs that could not maintain perspective. Some parts of their minds were sentimental and untrustworthy.

The problem was that, fantastically, they were thus far unkillable.

This would end.

The rapidly fleshing skeleton of the new guidance vehicle swarmed with a dozen different types of purpose-built biomachines. Great, prancing spiders exuded the cartilage that bound it together. Yard-long beetles generated chitin in their digestive systems. They laid the armor plates that protected the huge device and fixed them to the bones. Creatures with great, hanging abdomens spit the organic solids that formed the body.

In among them all, in a sepulchre in the center of the device, lay a hybrid that would be its brain. The top of his head had been removed and probes were being inserted into the cortex by two females wearing stiff white uniforms. It would not be possible for any other creature to control this device, and he could never be removed from it.

At present, he was asleep, dreaming that he was inexplicably locked in his office, and nothing he did was successful in attracting the attention of his secretary. He called her again and again, "Miss Fisher, Miss Fisher," but she did not come. He pounded the door, he rattled the door, finally he kicked it and kicked it and kicked it.

This was because the brain had been removed from Thomas Ford Turner and was still sparking with his personality and his memories.

One of the hybrid nurses noted its agitation on the monitor of the magnetoencephalograph that was being used to track its activity. Her fingers danced on the keys of a computer, and the activity subsided.

Dr. Turner opened the door to his office and found not the anteroom, but his childhood neighbor, Sissy Green, sitting on her bike in dappled sun. He walked out into a perfect day from the summer of his ninth year, into the birdsong and the dancing flowers, toward Sissy in her red T-shirt and blue shorts, and the sunlight making her glow.

Once he was linked into the Hybrid Project, Dr. Turner would become a part of his own creation. It had not been necessary to save him, except for the skin, which had served its purpose—its failed purpose.

They had not succeeded in using "Dr. Turner" to re-program Mark and Gina—or rather, they had succeeded with Gina, but she had broken the program anyway.

The skin now lay somewhere in the forest near Willoughby, quickly falling victim to speeding ants and busy flies.

This device was much different from its predecessor. Given the excellence of Dr. Turner's brain, it would be controlled with exquisite precision. It was also liberally provided with internal defense mechanisms. No more was the "wall" theory in use. Its surface defense was unchanged, but anybody who got into the structure would instantly be killed by a fearsome electric charge, the mechanism of which was taken from the electric eel, amplified a thousand times.

Despite their enormous variety, all of the biomachines displayed a similar elegance of design. The hybrids shared Dr. Turner's appreciation for graceful form. But they were also practical, with the result that some of their forms, while beautiful, were also horrible, in particular the biomachines with arrays of eyes, some with as many as six at different points on their bodies. Even so, a brilliance was in them, all of them.

To do complex work, even lesser entities needed intelligence and autonomy. So they understood what they were. They moved with the precision of machines and the determination of insects, but looked out at their surroundings through the brown eyes and blue eyes and green eyes of men. They were the disappeared of the world, people who had wandered into the byways of the great human cities and never come out again, or disappeared on hikes or treks or while traveling some lonely road, and joined one of the largest, most ignored, and most mysterious of all statistics, that of the missing.

This ability to design and produce new forms at will made the hybrids a formidable evolutionary advance over the human species. But just as the hybrids were powerful beyond the human, they were also afraid beyond the human. So the creatures down here worked with mad fury, brooding about their destiny and vulnerability, and the threat posed by the independence of mankind and, above all, that of the two hybrids who would not join their brothers and sisters in friendship.

One slow minute after another had passed as Mark and Gina had waited for the coordinates, but the satphone had remained silent, with only the green LED confirming that the line was still open.

That LED, though, was beginning to flicker, and as it did, bursts of static emerged from the handset, briefly replacing the dead silence.

More of the mechanical snakes had come buzzing and slithering into the room. They weren't attacking piecemeal anymore, though. Strategy was now in use, and fighting them off had been exhausting. All around the building, drumming had steadily risen.

Finally, the director came back, but there was an immediate problem—the static became great waves of sound. The signal was being jammed.

The director spoke, but all Mark heard was one word: "beacon."

"Have you located a beacon? Please repeat, there is interference."

The director's voice continued, but it was unintelligible. He hadn't heard Mark. Then it faded altogether.

Mark clicked the replay button and put it on speaker, but it was no better. An attempt to replace the call failed.

"They're jamming. The signal won't be coming back." Mark dropped the satphone onto a desk. "But maybe that's enough."

"What was it? What did he say?"

"I got two words, 'beacon' and 'below.' "

"How can that possibly be enough?"

"How much do you remember about this place?"

"We're on the dorm floor or the floor above it. What's that got to do with anything?"

"Were you ever in the basement?"

"Yes, I—oh."

"Exactly. If he meant that they picked up a beacon from below where we are—"

"Let's move."

During the time they had been in this room, the station had literally been filled with hybrids supported by biomechanicals that were being purpose-built for this fight. On one level, what was unfolding was a war between programs, like a chess match between supercomputers, with the two of them on one side and the rest of the hybrids on the other. But that was not how it felt. On another level, a deeper one, they could sense the hate and the fear. They moved quickly because they knew that the others would not long play at this game. If the two were not dead in a few minutes, the building would certainly be blown up or immolated in waves of fire, or they would be drowned in a mass of hybrids, until even they were overwhelmed.

Mark was unable to access anything but the smallest fragments of memories of this place, just the little snatches and echoes that had remained in his human neurons. But other clues were here, among them the drywall along the back of the room, which was new construction.

As he felt the wall, trying to find a place between the studs where he could break through, he noticed notes, scraps of the TV station's recent past taped to it—"Call mayor's office re Starnes," "Angels flyover is it too loud," "212-463-what? Get # from Jimmy."

On the desk that was pushed up against the wall, there was a cold cup from Starbucks and a half-eaten bran muffin. A plastic calorie counter sat beside a notepad with a list of numbers on it, and the clock on the desk beeped occasionally, warning that its backup battery was about to fail.

He found a hollow area and smashed the drywall with his fist.

"Jesus!" Gina said, turning from her vigil.

Ripping the plaster aside, he exposed the brick back wall that it had been built to cover.

"I'm remembering something," he explained. "Back here."

When horses drew buses and the cable car was a wonder, this had been an apartment hotel. In the basement there had been a kitchen, and meals had been sent up to the tenants via a dumbwaiter. By the time he was here, it was long disused, and he had played in it as a boy.

"Help me, here."

Together, they pulled away the wall, tossing desks aside as they worked. When they saw the old square door, three feet on a side, and still not sealed, Gina said, "I went in there, too."

"Did you go down?"

"It scared me. It scares me now, just looking at it."

"The mission—"

"I understand the mission! It's just that—isn't there some kind of coincidence involved here? How was it that

I happened to be rescued by Kelly Frears, who worked here? And then we seemed to just . . . come here, both of us."

It was obvious, now that Mark saw it in this light. Of course they had been drawn here. So of course this was a trap.

"We can't think as well as the third generation does," he said finally.

"Then we also can't go in there."

"We have to, Gina. Our mission is in there."

"So is the trap."

"We're in check, then," he said. "Not checkmate yet, but close. So let's try some speed chess. Fast attack."

With that he kicked in the dumbwaiter door. The interior was as it had been, with the same rotting, shaggy rope hanging to one side. When he was twelve, it had been hard to navigate because he was too small to reach the walls. Now, the opposite was true. But the squeeze wasn't his main concern. He would deal with that. His concern was to understand why they'd been lured here and to use that understanding in the completion of their mission.

It had not been to destroy them. Surely that could already have been accomplished when they were still in Willoughby. No, the other hybrids had subtly and cunningly brought them together and then drawn them here. Therefore, they wanted both of them, and they wanted them alive.

"Let's go," he said.

The shaft was filthy, its walls caked with the dust of years, and the smell in it took Mark back to his boyhood, a musty, abandoned odor that recaptured for him the poignance of his young life.

As he came to the base of the shaft, he heard Gina scrambling down behind him. Crawling out, she blew a lock of hair away from her eyes, then glanced at him, her expression stunningly graceful and sensual.

When he crawled out of the small space where the dumbwaiter ended, he found himself not in the concrete corridor of his youth, but a parking garage full of cars.

"What happened here?" Gina asked as she came up behind him.

Every vehicle they could see had methodically, pointlessly been vandalized, tires slashed, windows smashed, interiors ripped to shreds.

"Frustration. That's what happened here."

"I don't remember this garage."

"It's new. Part of the renovation. But the deep part is still here somewhere. It's been covered over, not destroyed."

The garage sloped down another level, to a more confined area where two news vans were parked, white with blue KFSF logos on their sides.

From the streets above, they could hear distant, now disorganized drumming and savage, protracted shrieking, the sound of hybrids in confusion, living expressions of their growing impatience and frustration.

The only nearby sound was that of dripping, and Mark saw that it was coming from one of the vans. A glance inside revealed a tangled mass of remains so badly damaged that he could only assume they had once been human.

"It scavenges for organs," he said.

At the lowest point in the garage, there was a manhole. "Down there," Mark said. "Somewhere down there is the heart of the infestation, and that's where we should find the bombs."

He lifted the manhole cover and tossed it aside, then

dropped in. After a moment, Gina followed him into a narrow, downsloping corridor.

Their light was poor. They had just a couple of flashlights from the station's earthquake kit. But even so, Mark saw what he had hoped to find.

"The elevator. Remember it?"

She looked at the black, rusting door, then back at him with wide, odd eyes. "I remember, but it's not a normal memory. It's more like sort of an—I don't know what to call it—"

"An echo. An echo of the mind. The moment you see it, it's familiar, but before that, you have no memory."

"An MP was stationed in this room. They never let you in."

"They let you in. That memory's been erased."

The elevator was far from being serviceable, so they ripped the door off, pulled up its floor, and slid down its cables, dropping until they had to break the fall, then dropping again. They had come perhaps ten stories straight down when they reached the base of the shaft.

"It was deep to make sure the hybrids didn't escape."

"Why San Francisco?"

"Near Palo Alto and Emma Walker's lab, but in an earthquake zone, so the vibrations of the digging would be taken as microquakes."

Working together, they forced the heavy elevator door and moved ahead. The floor was sheened with water, and white stalactites dripped from pipes that ran across the ceiling. A long lab bench stacked with electronics dominated one wall of the room. Against the other was a stainless steel examination table, and the moment he saw it, Mark recalled its coldness and hardness and saw the black straps hanging from it and knew that they once had restrained him. Hulking equipment stood nearby, an MRI scanner, and a functional positron-emission tomography imager fitted with a plasma screen.

"I remember this place. They made me look at pictures, Mark, hundreds and hundreds of them, for hours, for days."

"Do you remember what they were?"

She went to the PET imager and laid her hand on its dusty whiteness. "My life. This is where I learned my life."

Tears gleamed at the edges of her eyes. He reached out to her, but she pulled away from him. As she did, her light shone on another device.

When he saw it, a memory burst into his mind, searing and terrible.

He was a boy, maybe twelve. Sarge had him by the hand. They were approaching that device, a gurney enclosed in glass. In it a pale form floated that he at first thought was a fish. But then he had seen arms, blunt, incompletely formed hands, and staring eyes, the eyes of a goddess or an angel, and hair floating in the fluid that surrounded the incomplete body.

It was rotating slowly, and as the face—the most exquisite, the most perfect face he had ever seen—turned away from him, a great sob racked him and Sarge chuckled.

"She's really pretty, eh," he said, and clapped his big hand on Mark's shoulder.

This memory of Gina as she was being grown was so staggering, so cataclysmic, that in that one, searing instant, it all but revised the meaning of his life.

She had not been born. She had never been a baby. When she first walked, first thought, first found her name and her spirit, she was already just a year younger than him.

She went to the case. With the exaggerated care that comes to people at moments of great tragedy, she laid her flashlight along its edge. She put her hands on it and leaned over, peering into the darkness where her life had begun.

So softly that he could not hear her, she said something.

"Gina?"

"I am a woman." She gripped the edge of the case. *"I am a woman!"* She shook the thing, her great strength causing it to tremble on its moorings. *"I AM A WOMAN!"*

Then she sank down, her voice choking out tears she wanted to suppress. She turned, looking up at him out of eyes shadowed with a new and haunted darkness.

After all, he had a mother, a birth, a life as a child. In 1986, he'd actually been born. He had a babyhood, first memories, a life in childhood's timeless days, but her childhood was a fiction written by an anonymous hand and programmed into her.

She was feeling her artificiality, and with it the same sort of panic that had, perhaps, driven the hybrids to their desperate sense of vulnerability. But she was not alone, and she embraced Mark, and he her, and for a moment they rode the nightmare together.

But only for a moment.

"We have to keep on," he said.

"Do you have any real idea what you're doing?"

"Yes."

"No, you don't. We didn't come here, our programming brought us here. You, too, Mark."

"There's an atomic weapon—"

"You heard a lot of static and you got an idea, Mark. Where did that idea really come from? Ask yourself that."

"I know that the bombs are bait. I also know that the bait is here."

"I want us to live, Mark. I want us to have a future, and—oh, Mark, I just want *us*!"

He hardly heard her because he was looking deeper into the facility, behind the familiar machines, at something dark in the back, a gnarled complication of a thing that struck him with deepest fear.

The editor. In it you could be turned off and on like a little light, and die and die and die. That was where they'd been put for memory editing, where their love and their hope and the future they had planned together had been gouged out of their souls by a genial woman on a keyboard, Dr. Emma.

He understood that this had been done for their own safety, but he could never forget it, not now that he remembered it, the hideous claustrophobia of being alive and aware, but no longer in his body—no longer *him*.

There was movement behind it, a sleek shadow emerging from its complicated shadows. He felt Gina grip his arm. He aimed the fluttering beam of his flashlight.

Pinioned in it was a slim figure in a dark, carefully tailored formal army uniform, very unlike the disheveled hybrids. The figure's face was narrow, but human. His skin was that of a man. His movements as he stepped forward communicated great precision.

He said, "I'm fourth generation."

No response came to Mark's mind.

"You will help me because this has all gone horribly wrong, and there isn't anybody else who has the power to do what you can do. I'm physically able, but I don't trust my own programming. I'm two generations away from the flexibility of the human mind."

"What are you driving at?"

The man barked out a laugh. "Obviously the third generation's a misfire. It's gone completely insane. It has to be destroyed and I can't trust myself to do it. I need your help. I need your humanity."

Mark felt Gina's hand slip into his.

"You have to go down deep and destroy it. I've been trying to bring it back under some sort of control, but there's no way." The man gestured. "It all started out so well, but once you reach a certain threshold of intelligence, what lies beyond is always a form of madness."

If that was true, then this fourth-generation hybrid must be even more deranged, even more dangerous.

Mark only asked, "What do we do?"

"Mark, I suspect that you already know."

"Where are they then, exactly—the bombs?"

"Four of them were damaged at one point or another. Inevitable. Their automated defusing mechanisms are designed to respond to the kind of angular pressures associated with plane crashes. But there are two that remained operational. They're in the Channel Pump Station at the head of the Channel Outfalls Consolidation. You can get there by following drainage tunnels from here."

Mark knew from his past explorations of this place that a large tunnel led to the underground mouth of Mission Creek on the Embarcadero.

"And how do you know they're there?"

"I directed the recovery operation."

Mark said, "I think that this is a trap."

The hybrid leaned back on his heels. "Of course it's a trap. But the bombs are really there, and they're still viable, and you know that because you heard Richard Lamson tell you that they were beaconing. If they were defused, he wouldn't have said that. So you'll go, and you'll try to drop them into our deep facility and detonate them there. Even if I can't reprogram you, I know how your minds work. Your logic overrides your sense of self-preservation. That's your weakness, and why I'm going to win even though I'm disclosing all my moves."

As Mark and Gina both began to protest, the man raised a hand. "Dr. Turner wrote your programs, remember?" Something came into the voice, then, that was like scorn but was uglier and more bitter. "I know you, both of you, and I know you naked."

Mark plunged his knife into the creature's chest, feeling the hilt jump as the blade penetrated the heart. Until you have stabbed a living heart, you never know this truth: that it will shake the knife so hard it will almost rip it from your hand, and before it is still, it will shudder like a wild bird against the bars of a cage. But when it is still, it will be a stillness like the end of the world.

Mark lifted the body. Standing to his full height, he held it under its arms, and he shook it until the teeth rattled and the hair flew . . . and the skin separated in great, billowing sheets and fell from the filigree of scales that constructed its face.

She backed away from it. "But he—no." She gestured as if protecting herself from a blow. "That's just a generation three."

"Exactly."

"Then we're being tricked. We need to get out of here."

He moved off, and after a moment she followed. No matter what happened, they would come to their end there. Either they would die when they successfully detonated the bombs, or they would be killed and dismembered like Dr. Turner and integrated into the hybrid commune.

"I don't want to die," Gina said.

"Neither do I."

They continued on.

CHAPTER TWENTY-FOUR

FIRE

MARK WISHED THAT THE DRIPPING water could wash away the terrible things he had seen, and the sense of defeat that he felt.

Ahead, the tunnel widened again, and he finally spotted the gleaming machinery of the pump station.

A sound came then, a long, rising hiss that reminded him of steam escaping from a valve that was being opened wider and wider. He touched her shoulder.

A moment later, the dim floor of the tunnel ahead began to move, and Mark saw with growing concern that it appeared to be seething with yet another form of biorobot, an ocean of them racing forward.

Three hundred and eleven feet closer to the oncoming mass, a ladder led up to a manhole.

Instantly he calculated relative speeds and distance. They could not make it.

"We can't make it," she said.

"Do you understand our mission?"

"I follow you. That's my mission."

"You need to run a diversion," he said.

She touched his hand. They both knew that he was probably ordering her to her death.

"Okay, move out," he said. He wondered what ghastly

brilliant thing the hybrids had created this time. He asked his private God that Gina not be visited with an ugly death.

She trotted across the tunnel, then began moving toward the oncoming creatures, staying to the far side. Contrary to his expectations, the mass did not swarm toward her. They simply kept coming down the tunnel, not altering their trajectory at all. As they reached her, they surged around her, but still kept coming. She looked down, brushing one and another of them from her legs.

"Mark, they're rats—ordinary rats!"

In another moment, they were around him, too, scrambling and clawing each other as they struggled to escape whatever had terrified them.

She came close to him again. Her breath was hard through her clenched teeth. His heart was crashing within him, his mind spinning with bell-like joy. She had not gone to her death, so she might still survive, however remote the chance might be.

As the hissing sound grew louder and clearer, it became a surging ocean, but it also gained definition.

"It's screaming," Gina shouted.

"It's all of them, all the hybrids. It's their rage, shared like they share everything."

"Then we're winning. We're making progress."

"That's what they want us to think."

Then the sound seemed to focus in front of them, and it began to rise. Soon it was so loud that Mark saw blood coming from Gina's ears and knew that his were bleeding, too, and still it rose, until something that does not happen in the human world did happen: the sound became a gleaming thickness of motion . . . and then swirling, twisting in on itself, thickening, it became more a screaming shadow, and then it became a creature.

At first, he did not understand what he was seeing—a

huge snake or a great, gnashing crocodile—but as it rose to its full height of at least eight feet, he found himself facing a reptile with a long lizard's face and silver, shining eyes that communicated nothing remotely close to a reptile's dead stare. Beneath their sleek, angry ridges, the eyes were those of an evil masterpiece.

"You cannot win," it said, its voice caressing the air with graceful authority, in a tone infinitely more subtle than the finest, richest voice that either of them had ever before heard.

He did not think that they could beat this thing, though, and he decided that they had better not try.

"Run," he said. "Follow the rats."

But she remained as if glued in place, her lips slack, her eyes riveted to its eyes. A shadow reached out from the darkness of its body, its movement easy, but careful. It focused into long fingers with wine red nails, which delicately brushed her cheek. Steam rose from her skin, and she grabbed the spot with a cry. The shimmering darkness of the thing was not a color at all. It was the darkness of great heat.

Mark grabbed her, pulling her away.

"It's created a demon," he said.

"Or conjured one."

"They don't exist."

"Unless they do."

But then, moving more quickly than even he could move, this new kind of creature, its body hyperphysical, and its mind unimaginable, reached out, slapping its palm against her temple. Screaming, she began to fight Mark, clawing at him, but then he broke her contact with the creature, and the scream stopped, and she clutched him.

"It had me," she cried, "oh, God, Mark, it had me in my *mind*."

"This really is the fourth generation. We need to proceed."

She sucked breath. "Will it let us?"

The creature crouched, now appearing much more solid. "This is its real form," Mark said.

It extended powerful arms. But where were its weapons? Where were its helpers? Then he realized, this newest design was like them, itself a weapon.

It began to hiss, and the hiss rose fast, becoming a noise like escaping steam, and with it came heat rising higher fast.

"Drop to the floor."

She came down beside him. "We've got to pull out."

The heat was becoming intolerable. Mark wanted to turn and run, but that could not be. One had to die as a distraction so the other could reach the bombs.

He threw himself on the creature, slashing carefully, going for the abdomen. In an instant, he was enclosed in its claws and the touch of its skin was burning him, and he threw back his head and screamed away the agony so that it would not make him lose control of his actions.

Gina cut into the forearms, trying to free Mark, but she hacked and hacked to no effect.

"Get around it! *Go!*"

"I can't!"

The choice of dying so that she could pass was no longer available. He had to win this. But the knife was growing too hot to hold. The skin of the thing felt like hot irons.

But then the knife penetrated, and he cut as he had never before cut, his arm a furious piston. He wished for a Metal Storm, but nothing like that was here.

Then he was flying through the air, bouncing against the ceiling, hitting the floor. He rolled and Gina was there immediately, slapping at the fires in his uniform.

The creature had backed a distance down the tunnel. Still blocking it, though.

He looked down the tunnel at the darkness that was their enemy, a clotted shadow now, completely filling the tunnel. No way around him, no way through him, to the bombs behind him.

"Mark?"

"What?"

Gina pointed at the wall behind them. He saw it then, also, the faint flicker of a light along the tunnel. A moment later he heard sounds, the whisper of clothing.

The flickering, a faint red, became more distinct.

"Infrared," he said softly.

"We're trapped," Gina whispered, her voice little more than an extended breath.

"We have to continue on mission."

She grabbed him, her eyes wide and wild. "We're going to die here. We're going to fail!"

Without warning, the creature came swarming back up the tunnel.

Now they ran, their only hope to somehow break through the detachment of generation-three hybrids that were coming on them from behind. They ran and they flew, leaping up, forcing themselves through the air, racing, shouting in pain as they scraped first one side and then the other.

Ahead, the tunnel made a sharp turn, and they both slammed full speed into the wall. Mark saw flashes behind his eyes, was for an instant dazed from the impact—then turned and leaped ahead—and saw standing in the middle of the tunnel a human woman in full battle dress.

She was not alone, but she was exposed and his rage and his hate exploded through him and he leaped at her and grabbed her by the throat and was about to rip her head off with his bare hands, but then he recognized a new truth.

"Who are you?" he asked her. "Tell me who you are."

Gina came up beside him, breathing hard, paused for a moment, then leaped at the four figures behind the women, smashing into them with such force that all four went flying off into the dark, their infrared detection equipment shattering around them.

Then Mark saw that one of the figures had come up from the floor and was deploying an all-too-familiar weapon. He was unfolding a Metal Storm.

Gina saw it, too, and backed off.

The gun clicked, clicked again. The figure opening it seemed to be moving in slow motion. Around him, the other three appeared almost still.

"We're in flicker," Mark snapped at Gina.

They got the Storms out of the hands of two of the soldiers and slammed magazines into them. It happened so fast that the soldiers' fingers continued to work. Their nervous systems had not yet signaled to their brains that the guns were gone.

Before either of them could aim the weapons, and despite their speed in flicker, the creature that had first confronted them in this tunnel now came on them again, reached out, clutched Gina's fatigues, and dragged her toward itself.

Mark felt sorrow, but he would have let her go to her fate if that would have advanced the mission. She was still essential, though, so he threw himself after her.

At that moment, he also saw that the men who had been attempting to deploy the Metal Storms appeared to be Delta Force operators.

He could no longer see Gina, who was now invisible behind the creature.

One of the operators got his Storm running.

"Fire it," Mark shouted, "fire it into that thing."

The weapon thundered—and the skin of the creature evaporated like so much sea foam. For a moment, Mark was completely uncomprehending. Then he realized the truth. This fourth-generation creature was very, very different and very new. It was an idea that could manifest in the physical—and that was where it had been torn apart by the Metal Storm—at the perfect moment, while it was in its vulnerable, physical form.

Yet there it was again, the great head high, the eyes filled with what Mark could only see as triumph. He threw himself at it—and then, to his horrified surprise, was inside it, and wherever he went, musculature appeared, entangling him in guts and sinew.

Was it an illusion, then? If so, a convincing one, because the muscles were like iron cables, and hot, and all around him was the surge and a rumble of a great, organic presence.

As he fought his way through the mass, the sound of a Storm blasted once again, and suddenly he had cloth in his hand and he pulled, and he drew to him first a shoulder, then an arm, then her whole body, and he and Gina rolled out of the mass of flesh together. Gagging, Gina clambered to her feet.

Behind them, the remains of the creature lay in heaps on the tunnel floor. Farther back, the operators worked at their Storms, preparing to fire again.

"You'll kill us," Gina shouted.

They did not respond. In moments, the whole tunnel was going to be literally sterilized by a hurricane of supersonic beads.

"Run!"

As they dove ahead, the Storms blared, and the concrete walls around them spat geysers of dust.

"Why are they doing this?"

"Those are real Deltas out there. Some unit dropped in and found its way here. They're gonna just be fighting. They might not even know who we are."

There was a series of clicks. Another Storm was about to be fired. He threw Gina to the floor of the tunnel and dropped down, covering her. But as he did so, he saw ahead a drop-off and knew that they had reached the pump station.

"Flicker," he shouted, "*now!*"

As they rolled into the tangled complexity of the pump room, full of equipment and pipes, Mark saw two dark objects—the bombs.

But they weren't intact. There were no firing mechanisms. These were only the plutonium cores.

The bait. The hybrids had known that they would be detected, and Mark and Gina would certainly try to get them. They'd carefully been dismantled so that their beacons continued to register that they were armed.

On each was a red, flat area, the target point that would have taken the impact from the detonator.

"Too heavy," she said as they attempted to lift one of the bombs.

"We have to do it."

Straining, she asked through clenched teeth, "How much does this thing weigh?"

He stopped trying. "Too much."

Pushing equipment aside, he searched until he found the opening he knew would be there—a perfectly round, absolutely black space about ten feet across. It had been here when he was a boy. He remembered what Dr. Turner and Sarge had called it then: the most dangerous place on Earth.

"We have to roll them."

"We can just drop them in and get out of here, Mark."

"No, we have to be certain they hit impact points first or they won't detonate." He rolled one until the red plate was visible. "Shock to this point. Otherwise, the neutron initiator won't be activated and the bomb will fizzle. Minor explosive yield at best."

"What do we do?"

"We go with them and control their position."

"While we're falling?"

"With them. Holding them."

He had only to glance at her. He saw the same terror that he was feeling enter her eyes, then saw it firmly suppressed.

They stepped to the edge of the opening.

"How deep is it?"

"It was deep when I was young. It's deeper now."

"But what's down there?"

"The lair."

"And it was there when you were a boy? Why didn't they destroy it then?"

"You'd have to ask Dr. Turner. He let the gen threes dig it. He thought they were controllable. He thought they were loyal."

She looked into the darkness. "He did not understand generation three. I don't think he understood any of us. Our god had no idea what he had created."

"He might not be the only god with that problem."

Again, their eyes met. This time, though, Mark had a new feeling. Always, he had been willing to die to complete a mission. But now he wanted to live, and even more, he wanted the person before him, his Gina, to live and thrive.

In his eyes, he felt a tingling sensation. But what was it? Something caused by radiation, perhaps? Certainly these cores were full of it. But then it began to affect his cheeks, a slow tickling, and he realized what this was.

He was crying. Deep inside himself, to make certain that he kept going, he forced himself to enclose his heart in the ice-cold demands of the mission. Firmly he closed his tear ducts.

He said, "Let's go," and began shoving his bomb toward the opening.

She came beside him.

They arrived at the edge.

"We're married," she said.

"Married, yes."

They went over.

The wind was louder and stronger than he had imagined, and holding on to his bomb was hard, but he kept it steady and kept it positioned correctly. He could not see her beside him, but he could sense her and he imagined her and closed his eyes and found in his mind a perfect image of her as she had appeared the first moment he had seen her face so long ago, in the rapture of its innocence.

As far as he was concerned, this was the end of the program. He fixed the image of her face in his mind.

They fell and the wind rushed. Waiting for impact is as terrible an experience as can be, and when they just kept falling and falling, Gina cried out. Mark heard only snatches of her despair as it was ripped away in the rushing wind.

Ordinarily, he did not feel much pain but now the heat hurt. Then there was light. In it, he saw Gina beside him, her eyes wide, looking down. The light was powder-bright, its glare cruel.

He followed her eyes and saw what had transfixed her: a great, complicated shape was rushing upward, coming straight at them.

It was another drone, and there was no way around it.

"Stop! Stop! Stop!"

They arched their backs, lifted their arms and strove to slow their descent, but both slammed immediately into the upper ring of the thing.

He saw her bomb rip from her hands and heard a series of echoing thuds as it fell spinning away.

"Gina!"

Silence. Whipping wind. Lying on the surface of the drone, they were now rising fast. His body was still wrapped around the faintly warm casing of his bomb.

For the first time in his life, he uttered a true scream, a great, tearing roar of rage and disappointment. The most important of all his missions was a failure, and because of his failure, vast suffering and madness would now envelop the world.

Black creatures—not the insects, but things blacker than darkness itself—were riding the drone, and with the grace of soaring birds but none of their beauty, they launched themselves toward him. As the first one hit, its claws digging into his uniform, he lifted his arm against what proved to be a great but invisible weight. More of the things leaped on him, then more yet, and he began to feel their claws ripping deep, and hot agony as his skin was sliced.

Even as they were tearing him apart, he heard Gina's growl of rage and felt her ripping at them, dragging them off him. Slowly, painfully, he turned his bomb until he was facing the trigger.

He butted his head against it.

The creatures swarmed him, screaming wildly.

Again, he struck it, this time so hard he heard his own skull crack.

Still nothing.

He pushed at it, got it to the edge of the great ring, and dove off again, clutching it as the great forms fluttered around him, then fell back, unable to descend as fast.

He went down and down, toward a distant point of light that gradually grew into a busy factory floor that was racing up at him.

He saw a hybrid look up. He saw it start to run.

There came yet another form of light as pure as silver and somehow alive, a whole universe of light.

For less than the millionth of a second, he was aware of ferocious chaos.

Then dark.

CHAPTER TWENTY-FIVE

HEREAFTER

A DREAM OF THUNDER BECAME thunder, dense and power-ful, as if the heights of the world were coming undone. Wind sighed, and Mark saw leaves spinning high in a gray sky, and angry clouds rushing above the tops of a forest.

His body was cold, but when he willed it to warmth, as he had done all of his life, nothing happened.

The leaves spun on their stems, the wind made a sound like memory. How old is it, the wind, he wondered. He thought that it came even before the sea. Next came a realization, quite calm but also surprising: He was alive.

He was lying on his back. Cold water was dripping on his face. A flash and a shattering clap of thunder shocked him to clearer awareness.

But he wasn't in any tunnel. Terror drew his fists to his chest: Had the bomb not exploded after all? Failure of mission was the greatest fear that he knew.

There were waves of rain, there was fog, he was in a woods, and he hurt. He hurt all over, in ways that he had not known possible, pain deep inside, dull and in-sistent, pain on the surface, full of fire. He looked down at his hands emerging from his shredded cuffs. They were withered and gray. So . . . was he still conscious, but in a dead body? Could that happen? Maybe the machine part would simply continue on, trapped in the dead biology.

He surveyed his surroundings. To his left, shadowy beyond the trees, was some sort of enormous structure. The quality of light ahead suggested the end of the woods, and through the storm he could hear breakers sounding.

He'd been in the tunnel, he'd lost control of the bomb, he'd been hit by a silver flash . . . and now he was here on his back and he was cold and he hurt. This body of his could take major punishment, that he certainly knew. But it could not survive a nuclear explosion, so whatever had happened, it was not as he remembered.

As he moved to rise, severe pain shot up from his lower back, his head wobbled, and dizziness made him stop trying.

The world spun slowly, his shoulders ached, and his right hand hurt so much it was difficult to move.

He checked his body, moving his attention from pain to pain. A fracture line was in the *opponens follicis* of the right hand. Closing his eyes for a moment, he shifted from right to left dexterity. Instinct would now favor the left hand until this was tended to medically or it healed on its own. Also, a hairline fracture in the parietal bone just above the lambdoid suture was causing the dizziness. He directed more blood to the area, then moved his attention to his inner ears, which he oxygenated, causing them to function more efficiently. He waited as the dizziness faded and his vision stabilized.

Next, he moved his attention to his lower back. The anterior longitudinal ligament was ruptured, but self-diagnosis indicated that this would heal on its own. There would be severe pain, but no reduction in operational efficiency. Therefore, this injury could wait.

All of his organs had received impact stress, with significant internal damage. His liver was grossly enlarged, his heart had sustained valve damage and muscular tears, and his lungs were burned. There was extensive bruising, facial lacerations, and flash burns, the ones on his face deep. Plus, he had absorbed radiation, which made his skin tingle and a deep sense of sickness swirl within him.

If the mission had succeeded, surely he would not be here.

He forced himself to his feet. Moving toward the light and the sound of the waves, he was once again hampered by dizziness, and this despite his efforts to control it. Nevertheless, he forced himself forward until he came out on a narrow beach. To his right was the huge structure, which he recognized as one of the great piers of the Golden Gate Bridge. Ahead was fog-shrouded water, the city visible only as an occasional ghost behind the rolling clouds. Beyond the first pier, there was another, then another. High overhead was the great iron structure itself. The deck was gone, all of it, the iron suspenders a ropy tangle between the arches.

There was more lightning, followed instantly by another blast of thunder. The storm, now thick and dark, was marching down from the north. Throughout his life of conflict, his program had always guided him. It failed him now, because he could not make sense of his obviously having survived a nonsurvivable event.

Coming to the end of his ability to understand his situation caused him to experience deep loneliness. He raised his eyes to the sky and uttered a cry from his core—and heard his own great bellow snatched away on the wind.

He went down to the water's edge and stood before its dark, lapping indifference. The loneliness caught at his heart, and along with it also a hope that hurt almost too much to feel, but which he could not avoid feeling. But he would not think of her, he must not.

Rain came in a sudden burst, sweeping the steel gray sea, sighing in the forest, making the ruined bridge gleam with runnels. Trying to see through the storm, he looked toward the city he had struggled so hard to defend. But he could not see it.

His need to determine the status of his mission caused him to review his assets. His knife was gone. No Metal Storms, no soldiers, no—

"Gina! Gina! Gina!"

Nothing came back but the wind.

Gina came toward him through sunlight.

He took her face of heaven in his hands.

In the air of a summer night, she played the piano.

He sat down on the hard sand, not because he wanted to, but because he was at the end of his strength and in the depths of a sorrow far greater than he had thought it possible to feel.

The warrior, his strength finally at an end, now slumped. This masterpiece of Inner Iron and the application of the most subtle zinc-finger modifications was truly exhausted. In fact, if the tide hadn't been going out, he would have drowned here, because he was far below the tide line.

The mission still called to him, but he could not answer.

Barely breathing, he lay on the abandoned shore, only dimly aware, now, of the muffled sound of fog-bound breakers. As his consciousness ebbed, the expiring light of late afternoon gave way to the inky blackness of a cloud-heavy night. At last there remained only a single memory, of the warmth of a hand that had been in his. He lay motionless in the sand, the hand that had held Gina's clutching and unclutching, but filling only with the cold bits of glass that the tide was bringing in.

Had he not been designed biology, Mark would never have survived the exposure of that rainy night, let alone the trauma of being blown out of the shaft he had been descending. He could not know that the bomb had detonated not in his arms, but more than twenty miles farther down. However, he could also not know the extent of his injuries, the burns, the fearsome radiation poisoning, the breaks he had endured, the blows he had taken, all far worse than his all-too-hopeful self-diagnosis had revealed.

He lay like that all night, not moving, not even when the tide came around him, almost lifting him and drawing him with it into the sea and memory. But when dawn came, he was still breathing, and his pain was what finally returned him to consciousness.

Opening his eyes brought only glaring whiteness, and the first thought that passed through his mind was that he was blind. This was not the case, however, as he found when he sat up and the wet sand that had covered his face fell away.

Bright sun washed him, its warmth welcome. Then a wave came in, bubbling around him, and he struggled a short distance up the beach. Far across the water, he could just see San Francisco, faint beneath a haze of smoke. He sucked air and smelled spent fire.

Shoreward stood the woodland where he had awakened. As he came up from the sea, he heard birds singing among the trees.

Pushing aside branches glittering with rain, he saw a wren perched ahead. Stopping, he looked at it. Looked carefully. He saw feathers, a beak, and normal bird eyes.

As he moved deeper into the woods, he noticed that

the birds did not fly away from him. One of them, totally unafraid, landed on his arm.

This had happened before, and as a child he had found it wonderful. Now, it shamed him because it reminded him that he was not fully human. To be touched by the blessing of normal humanity, he would gladly have accepted the curse of its fundamental isolation from the animal world.

Birds landed on machines—cars, air conditioners . . . him.

Usually, he would brush them away. This time, though, he looked at it carefully, in part because its fragility brought to mind his losses, in part because he wanted to be absolutely sure that it was not artificial.

Gingerly, he raised his arm, bringing it closer to his eyes. He could smell its dusty smell, see its mites running among its feathers. The little creature was so delicate that it might have belonged to another reality, with different laws of life, different, more fragile meanings. He watched its tiny, sparkling eye turn this way and that. He said, "You're real, aren't you." And he thought, also, of Gina. A thing like him, yes, but in memory so fragile.

As suddenly as it had come, the bird flitted away and was gone.

He called to mind a map of his location, which was Marin County. He looked at the nearby towns of Sausalito and Larkspur. If he moved at a shallow angle to his left, he saw that he would soon enter Sausalito, or whatever remained of it.

He was pushing through the woods when he first noticed the pulsation. He stopped, listened. Clear on the silence it came, a steady, deep sound.

Then he noticed that the birds had ceased to sing. He no longer saw any wrens jumping among the lower limbs. Overhead, the larks had gone silent. His ears began to throb with the rising sound, then his chest. He could literally feel it in his bones, this rising, pulsating pressure.

Above the woods, he saw a shadow coming. It was a military helicopter with a silenced wing, a hunter.

His body was warmer than that of pure hybrids, so its infrared detectors would easily locate him. He pressed himself against the trunk of a tree opposite the direction of the sound.

The helicopter drew closer, casting a brief shadow as it crossed the face of the sun. It continued on past him, moving off toward the beach.

Soon, it died away entirely. He listened, but all seemed quiet. He was too seasoned a soldier to believe that, though, and his hand slid into his pocket seeking his knife—which wasn't there. Of course not.

The place remained quiet, the sound still gone. But the birds had not returned, so he remained hypervigilant, his senses cocked.

His fatigue level was almost terminal but he began to move north and west, hoping to come into the area of human habitation. To minimize the chances of infrared detection, he stayed close to the trees and the densest part of the woods.

For a moment—just the split of a second—he was aware of movement to his left. Then he knew that something was close to him, a shape, a presence.

Again to his left, he spotted a silver-white uniform and a bulging black helmet. To his right and behind him, there was more movement.

As he reflexively went into flicker, he saw that a loop of steel cable was descending around him and about to entrap him. Dropping, he plunged forward—and saw before him a great, white-clad creature covered with slab armor, its face hidden behind a gleaming, featureless mask. With a complicated whicker of motors it sprang into action, moving warily toward him.

Immediately above the forest, he saw the helicopter, black with black glass. The wing whirled, but from immediately below it he could hear no sound at all. He'd heard of this classified device in 'Stan, a silenced chopper designed to do just what this one had done—sneak up on its quarry.

Armored figures were clustering around him, with more dropping from the chopper. Quickly, his mind calculated the odds. He was unarmed and weak, but he might be able to flicker one more time—and then he was on the ground under the net and they were on him, four of them, their clumsy supersoldier exoskeletons whirring and clattering as they attempted to overpower him.

He was able to shrug them off. The supersoldier armor smoked, its motors burned out. So he was stronger even than Soldier Iron. He'd also seen it in development in 'Stan a few years ago. It wasn't deployed yet, but it must be close, because these guys were using. Probably figured they had no chance against him otherwise, and they were damn right.

Dizziness staggered him, but he recovered and went between the trees, attempting to put some distance between himself and his attackers.

His next movement was to squat and jump as high as he possibly could. It took every ounce of strength he possessed, and for a moment he was soaring above the woods. He saw Sausalito, many of its roofs down, its streets empty. Yachts lay ruined in the harbor. Nothing moving. But smoke curled up from the chimney of a nearby home.

Throwing his weight in that direction, he fell and flew toward the house. As he gathered speed, wind rushed past him, then screamed past him, but he pulled his weight back and felt the fall slow until he was nearly dangling in the air—or so he thought.

In fact, he was weak and it showed when he hit the ground much harder than he expected, the pain that shot through his back causing him to stifle a groan. Fighting the agony, he crouched, his whole body cocked, ready to jump again. But there was no sign of his pursuers, no pulsations, no black helicopter, its sinister curves sliding through the air. Above all, no armored attackers.

The house was quiet, but he smelled the odors of people, musky women, sharp-scented men, the milk-sour scent of children.

As he moved closer, he once again began to feel the pulsations of the helicopter.

Suppressing the urge to run, he went swiftly onto the porch. He approached the front door. Of course, he did not look well, not in these battle-shabby fatigues. But maybe that would help. Before a battle, people feared their soldiers. Afterward, they were generally grateful for a time, until they decided that your pain was too unsettling to bear and forgot you. Civilians are always eager to leave the soldier to his memories.

He knocked at the door. There was no response. But he could hear the people whispering, so he knocked again. Waited. The pulsations grew more distinct, forming into a sharper pattern. He shook the door, causing it to bound on its hinges and then give way. He went in.

The family, a boy of ten or so, a girl of perhaps twelve, and two thirtysomething parents, were gathered close together in the living room. They were clean and pretty, they were human, and their fear smelled fresh. They had not been cowering here, another sign that he might have beaten the hybrids. All of their fear was directed at him.

"I don't hurt people," he said.

The man smiled a frightened smile. "The police are coming, soldier."

"Do you know these people? Why do they want to capture me?"

"Everybody wants to capture you, Colonel Bryan."

The little boy went closer to his father. "Daddy, that's him?"

"Hush now, remember what the news has been saying, we don't make sudden moves toward him, we don't raise our voices, we don't ask questions."

The little girl went behind her mother and father. She clutched her mother's skirt, burying her face in it.

Mark went down on one knee. "Little girl, I'm not going to hurt you."

"It talks like a person," the boy said. He regarded Mark the way Mark had probably regarded zoo animals when he was ten.

That they knew about him and were using the word *it* told him two things that he needed to know but wished were not true. Both his nature and his identity were now public knowledge.

How was that possible, though? How long had he been unconscious?

"I don't hurt people," he muttered. He found that he could hardly look at them. He felt naked. He was embarrassed.

"Are you really unkillable?" the boy asked.

"No."

The boy looked up at his father. "Can I touch it?"

"No, Son, stay here."

"It's okay." Mark held out his hand. "Okay."

The boy reached out his fingers, and for the first time in Mark's life, somebody touched him not for the humanity by which he had lived, but for the machine that he really was. He held the little, warm fingers between his own, then the boy snatched back his hand, his face glowing, his eyes fixed with wonder.

"It feels like steel, Daddy."

"It has steel in its skin, Son."

Steel in his skin? What had the world been told about him? If that was true, then things he did not know about himself.

No wonder the people hunting him had acted as they did, like hostiles, instead of simply attempting to communicate with him. They were not a detachment sent from higher command to reattach him to a unit. Not in the least. They were trappers, sent to bring in an out-of-control robot.

The anguish this realization caused him was so great that he bared his teeth and growled—and the woman and the girl began to scream, and the man grabbed a chair and thrust it at him.

It was humiliating beyond words, and he did the only thing he could, which was to leave this place.

"I'm sorry," he said as he headed through the house and out the back, "please excuse the intrusion."

He crossed their yard, eager for the concealment of the woods. The helicopter grew rapidly louder, then dropped to silence. He therefore knew that it was directly overhead, and the increasing downdraft told him that it was descending from about twelve hundred feet, and coming fast, dropping five hundred feet a minute.

A crack pilot was flying a superb machine. Nothing like the drone, though. Military engineers needed to take a look at that puppy, whatever was left of it.

Like a great elk trying to outrun a bullet, he squatted and knotted his muscles, preparing to jump and flicker at the same time.

But this time the net flowed over him.

"We got it," a voice cried.

He marshaled his strength, taking his awareness deep inside his body. Despite his exhaustion, this would have to be the most powerful jump of his life, because this net was inch-thick carbon fiber, far stronger even than military grade.

The one that had spoken came out of the woods, a figure in supersoldier armor, but not moving like somebody well trained on the system. Seeing the opportunity, he launched himself toward it. As he struck, net and all, plates of armor flew off, servomotors screaming.

He stared, stunned, at what had emerged—inside the supersoldier cladding was an elderly woman in a black pin-striped suit, looking like some sort of businesswoman or college professor. Her head was gray, her face lined but firm, lips tight. She was helpless, he knew that instantly. He suppressed the instinct to overpower his attacker.

"Professor Walker, are you injured?" an echoing, amplified voice from the helicopter asked.

She backed away, out of his range. "No, no, but please restrain it."

It again? This was him, Mark Bryan. Not *it*.

As the net was tightened, he took steps to minimize its effectiveness, stiffening his shoulders, spreading his elbows and knees, raising his head.

When they thought that he was immobilized, four of the men in supersoldier armor lowered him to the ground.

"Are we stable?" the voice from the helicopter asked.

The old woman came down to him. She held her shoulders and shuddered. She leaned close.

"Do you remember me? I'm Emma, Mark."

Emma? Of course he remembered her. He looked

upon the old face with such a feeling of sadness, though, that it forced his eyes away.

"I know, Mark," she said. "You've been through a hell of a lot. But the past can be healed."

He had no idea how to respond.

One of the soldiers said, "Man, look at the size of it!"

"Quiet please," Emma said. "Remember that it is not only stronger than you are, it is smarter than you are and a whole lot more sensitive, I should think."

The others pulled off their helmets, and Mark saw a number of young adults and some more mature individuals. Professional faces, intent on their work. Not soldiers, not really.

He remained wary, but he was not detecting any negative moves here. He concluded that their mission did not include his destruction, therefore his defense of himself would be directed toward self-preservation. This meant that he should escape so that he could regain control of his fate.

He watched them, evaluating, waiting for an opening, calculating his odds.

Yet, he couldn't get out of this net, no matter how much room he had given himself. Nevertheless, it was difficult to believe that these soft and vulnerable people would succeed in confining him for long.

He sucked breath, evaluating not the strength of the net—he already knew that it was too strong to tear apart—but its degree of give.

Overhead, the pulsations grew louder, then the chopper was dropping to low hover.

He pulled his legs together, drew in his elbows, lowered his head—and saw that Dr. Emma was removing something from a small leather case, and he knew what it was, and now he kicked, he tore at the netting, he gnawed it, he fought with everything in him that could fight, but he did not break out, he could not, and she brought the disk closer and closer to his head.

"Please," he said. His throat was so dry he could barely speak.

"It won't hurt you, Mark."

"No, please, you don't understand. It will. It will hurt me."

"You don't understand what it is."

He said, "No, you don't understand what it is. It will destroy me."

"You've been in a combat program all of your adult life. We want you in another program now."

She began to move the disk toward his head. He was desperate now. As incredible as it seemed, he was not going to escape.

He shook the net with all his might. "You *do not* understand!"

She smiled faintly. "Why is that, Mark?"

"That thing kills my free will, and if that happens, then I can't carry out my mission, I can't help you!"

The thought crossed his mind that these people might be working for them, so he added, "They're incredibly deceptive. You may be working for them without knowing it."

She looked down at the disk in her hand. Her complex face, wrinkled by the years of her life, took on an expression of irony.

"Mark, I built this device. This is my design. I wrote the program it contains. It was just finished a week ago."

Was his god, then, not Dr. Turner, but old Doc Emma?

"Dr. Turner did me. You know—created."

"He was a geneticist, not an artificial-intelligence expert. To his cost."

Rarely in his life had Mark experienced fear like this. He was about to be destroyed by this foolish creature, he was absolutely certain of it.

She brought the disk up and he roared, he gnashed at her, he shook the net with all his might.

She stepped back and waited, arms folded. She said into a headpiece, "It's triggering the survival subset. He's been threatened with one of these."

"It's evil! It's going to destroy me!"

"Mark, please don't struggle. I know what I'm doing, honey." She came toward him again, holding out the disk.

"Professor, please step back. Washington wants the control officers to take over."

"Mark," she said, "who do you love?"

He would tell her nothing of himself. He did not belong to her, he did not belong to anybody. He was free, he had rights, he—

She slapped it against his temple and he felt its electricity surge through him, a black annihilating wave. It was as if his soul itself were being wrung out of him, as dark an evil as could ever be.

In memory, Sarge laughed in his gentle way.

Linda watched, head cocked, arms folded.

His men came, all of them, their faces softened by the past, and one by one, snapped off salutes.

Gina whispered as she kissed his cheek, "Remember me."

Doc Emma, or the hybrid in her skin, said in her rough, old voice, "Remember who you love. Who do you love, Mark?"

He refused to say her name.

"Let's get it in motion," the leader said. "We need to get this thing back to the lab."

Mark ordered his arms to move, his hands to grasp,

his legs to run. With every bit of determination he could muster, he commanded his body. But it was all absolutely and totally useless, and he could only watch as the grunting, struggling people who had captured him got him into a sky harness, then hooked it to cables that had dropped down from the helicopter.

He was breathing, but he could not manage to generate so much as a whisper to express the sorrow that was crushing his heart, the anger—no, white, blind rage—that was festering in him, that wanted to explode but could not explode.

Inside, the volcano that was his soul roared and erupted, but on the surface nothing whatsoever happened.

There was no question now: Mark Bryan, the biological machine, was no longer going to be treated as human. He may have defeated the other hybrids, but perhaps he should have joined them. Then, at least, he could have indulged the illusion that he was somebody and he mattered.

He felt himself rising toward the chopper, saw faces peering down from its cargo bay, intent scientific faces, not military ones. Closer he went, and closer, absolutely unable to move, begging God, begging his own soul, begging his body, to let him somehow break free of this electromagnetic enchantment, so that he could rise up and vent his rage at his oppressors, these immeasurably heartless, cruel people who had built a machine that knew itself, and knew with greatest anguish, that it had no life and no reality outside its programming.

He wanted to die. But was that even possible for a thing such as him? He wanted to die, but he also wanted to hold Gina in his arms just once as an act of conscious, intentional love. But where was she now? Lost in the explosion, he supposed. Vaporized.

In the past, he'd prayed his soldier's simple prayer: God, let me live for my mission. Now he changed his prayer. He prayed, God, let me die for myself.

He was drawn up into the bay of the helicopter and heard its door slide closed behind him.

"You hear me, soldier?"

It was a young officer, a lieutenant. He looked about twelve.

"I know you can understand me. I know you're scared. But you're going to be okay. We've got your schematics, your control protocols, your instruction set. Nobody's gonna turn you off, don't worry. That will not happen. You're hurt bad, soldier, and in a lot of pain. We know you won't say it, but we can see it. You need a rest, buddy."

Buddy? He wanted to say, *I'm a goddamn colonel, little boy.* But nothing came out, not even a whisper.

The chopper trembled, and he saw the forest begin to slide away, and then they were over the speeding waves of the bay.

He tried to see the city but could not move his head and so closed his eyes. The insubordinate kid was right, he was really tired, with as high a pain load as he had ever known.

His manuals. His instruction set. And a disk that controlled who he was, his very soul. A disk!

For all his strength, for all the love that was in his heart, he could no longer deny the raw truth: He was not a mechanically enhanced man, but a machine enhanced by some humanity.

Mark Bryan was its designation. It would have a model number, a serial number, circuitry buried in its biology. It refused any more to think of itself as *I* and *me*.

As the chopper took it to where it knew not, to what fate it could not imagine, it found itself feeling an emotion it had felt only once before, when it knew that the mission must kill Gina. This was sadness of the kind that produces tears.

When a human being is moved to tears, they come. For a machine, it depends on the design. In this one's case, an ability to conceal evidence of its emotions was designed in, so a torturer could never know what it felt. Thus, it could open and close its tear ducts at will.

It kept them closed.

CHAPTER TWENTY-SIX

ACROSS THE DARKNESS

THIS TIME, THE SILENCE AROUND him brought him back to consciousness. He detected the softest hiss of a ventilator, a small human movement nearby. For a moment, he felt a sort of happiness, perhaps at just being alive, but then he remembered his situation and a great weight of sorrow filled him. Or rather, *it*. *It* felt only sadness.

A sigh filled it—but didn't. Its lungs didn't work as expected. Not that it couldn't breathe. It didn't feel a need. A burst of fear coursed through it—and a male voice that seemed to be everywhere and nowhere said, "There it is—right there—okay, we have awareness."

Mark tried to move, but he could not move. He tried to talk but he could not talk.

"Wow," the voice said. "You got some complicated code in there. Did Doc Emma write that? She's a damn genius."

"That'd be why she got the Nobel," a female replied, young, and for an instant, he thought maybe Gina.

"If they knew she created *them,* she wouldn't have gotten any Nobel."

"Turner did gen three, and he's dead. The mad scientist." Not Gina, no, another woman.

"This code causes the personality glitches we've had

so much trouble with. The prof's 'poetic soldier.' *Moody*'s the better word. We get this put right, we are ready with our big guy. I need to get to the bottom of the program. Think about the cards, Mark. Dr. Turner's cards."

"Who are you?" he asked.

"It's in the speech center," the female voice said.

"So it's noncompliant. Is that your revised code, dear, because the doc wants her toy back, and not have the damn thing try to rip her face off again or whatever."

"This is an independent mind. If we edit out the uncertainties, it's a huge difference. There's no Mark then, and that is definitely not what she wants. He's in those six lines of code. That's the individual, right there."

"Go to hell," Mark said.

"There's that speech activity again," the female said. "Why does it keep trying to vocalize?"

"We're causing agitation. Turn it off."

No no no no!

"Wow! That's lighting up the whole board. That really scares it."

"Yeah, it would scare you, too, Frank! It's called death. Just turn off the auditory system, please."

Silence. Absolute. Inside himself, he was screaming, he was begging, but there was now no way to hear, either.

With a sudden rush of terror, he understood where he was. He was inside the editor! His instinct was to struggle, to fight, but he knew it was useless. All it would do would be to produce numbers on a screen.

How could anybody be more miserable than Mark Bryan was at this moment? He was left trapped in this detested state while what sounded like two kids he could neither see nor hear did things to him that were greater than even God could do to them.

He was not a slave, he was lower than that. He was alive, though, he existed, he had a heart and, he wanted to believe, a soul, and he was hurting now, he was hurting and they did not understand and they did not care.

He had come to think that he had brought them victory. He had saved them all, and this was what he got?

Unless—the thought crossed his mind again, and this time with greater fear—unless those were hybrids in human skin, and they had won and he had been captured by them.

Then, suddenly, whiteness. Bright, very bright! Then vision—a complex black tangle floating in the middle of a shimmering void. Then again, the sound of the ventilator, the sound of the room. But no sensation at all.

"It's focusing. Okay, Mark, if you can hear me, say *yes*."

He said it, but there was no sound.

"Try that again, Mark. Say *yes*."

"Fuck you!"

"There! That was vocalization, look there."

"It wasn't *yes*, I don't think. Anyway, Mark, we're turning on the optics."

As if through a foggy tunnel, he saw a room, windowless, featureless. Sitting just in front of him were two people, a man and a woman.

The woman had long arms and tapering, fine hands, and big eyes as green as emeralds. The man appeared strong and competent, with a crisply angled jaw and an expression that communicated assurance.

Human or hybrid?

"Who are you?"

"What's that pattern?" the male asked.

"Repeat your words, please," the female said.

"Who in holy hell are you?"

"It's asking us our names, hey! Good morning, buddy! I'm Frank and this incredible vision of feminine perfection is Theo. We're Professor Walker's graduate assistants."

Also, a man was across the room, lying on a table. He was in a long cardboard box, with only his face exposed. The rest of the body was wrapped in plastic and caked with white cream.

It was too still to be anything but a corpse. Not even a hybrid could lie that still.

"Are you getting ready to kill me?"

"Hey, it's throwing some text onto my screen," Frank said.

"Nobody's going to do anything bad to you," Theo lilted. "You're about the most valuable thing in the world, Mark. Man, you saved us all. You'd get a Congressional Medal of Honor, except that's people stuff. You don't want that crap anyway."

Frank muttered, "The president's an asshole."

"That's a corpse," Mark said.

Frank threw back his head and laughed, rich and loud. "Mark, that's you."

Theo got up and went to the box. She dropped away the sides and pulled off the plastic, which made a sucking sound as it separated from the skin.

Lying there was a naked male body still coated in places with white cream. Using a large cloth, she wiped it off.

"I'd like to have skin like this," she said. "Man, look at this, Frank. They did a really good job. The prof prevailed on her husband, and General Walker got this grown, thank God. The president wanted to—" She stopped.

"What?" Mark asked.

Frank said, "You're very controversial. A lot of people think you shouldn't—"

"Not now, Frank," a voice that Mark recognized as Emma Walker's said. Then she came into his field of view, and for the first time in all these many years, he felt an emotion toward her that had been removed from him when he'd first been sent into hiding.

"Mother."

She smiled. "I know that sequence. And you'll always be my son, Mark."

Theo affixed straps to the body's arms and legs. Doc Emma looked down at it. "How are its labs?"

Theo gave her a digital pad covered with text.

"This looks good."

"So, are we ready?"

"Doctor, he's—I mean, this is real unpredictable stuff we're seeing. I think we want to get that six lines out of there. That code makes the whole thing unstable."

No no no!

"You're unstable, Frank, you get mad, feel desire, laugh. As do we all. Take out that code, and you deny him all those things."

Thank you!

"Mark," Theo said carefully, "we're going to move you into the body. It's in great shape again and so is your mind, so the transition will be smooth. But there is that little moment of darkness. When we pulled you out of your old body, you relived the event in the Glade and that was very upsetting to you. Mark, you performed a miracle there. It was an act of unbelievable skill and heroism, you need to understand that. You beat back bad code that had been installed by Dr. Turner when you were a boy. Trying to make sure you'd be as much a killing machine as his later designs. So if it happens again, ignore it, Mark, it's only a conditioning artifact, it's not real, and you shouldn't feel a bit of guilt about anything that you did, or wanted to do. Is that clear? You will no longer feel this guilt."

Mark retreated into himself, going as deep as he could. This was too much, he could not face this, being told how he should feel, and sensing that the words were themselves programming that was actually revising his mind as they were spoken.

Didn't they see the extraordinary cruelty of revealing vulnerability this profound? He began to understand why the hybrids of generation three had gone insane. To be so complete and aware and yet so abjectly nothing more than an array of machines—or in his case, a single machine—it was beyond nightmare.

"Let me take him for a second," Frank said. Then, louder: "Okay, Mark, don't be so upset, buddy. It's gonna be wonderful. I mean, you'll be you again. Out in the world, man."

"Get ready," Doc Emma said.

Theo checked the straps. "We're secure."

The hell with this! Help me, help me, somebody!

"He's freaking again! Do it!"

"Okay, here we go, Mark."

Darkness absolute. Starless, lifeless . . . but, no—a gleam. Again, another.

The bomb, falling away from him, Gina's voice, high with terror, torn away in the wind, then the drone slams into him and he's rising at breakneck speed and he calls Gina, he bellows with all his might, but then there is light—so bright—and suddenly he's out in the air, the city is spinning beneath him, pieces of the drone flying out around him, arcing some into the streets, some into the water.

He's on a ballistic trajectory, he reaches an altitude of at least a mile—he can't calculate, his mind is struggling with shock—but he can angle himself. There is a blur of land below, speeding past. He twists, he strives for it, finds it, a spit of land—then treetops whip him, then his head hits something and there is a flash.

Suffocation, a huge spasm, and the explosive force of a cough unlike any cough he has ever before known, so intense that it is body-consuming, so protracted that it almost robs him of his consciousness, so big that it shatters his awareness even of where he is and leaves him struggling and gasping in his straps.

Then a cool cloth was laid on his head, and Theo's gentle eyes were gazing down at him.

"Don't strain, Mark, you can't bust out of these straps, not even you."

He had never felt hate for a human being before, but it was all he could do not to hate those sweet eyes and the condescension in that honeyed voice. At least he could move his head now, and he experienced the luxury of observing his surroundings on his own, rather than looking through a fixed lens.

As he had thought, the thing he had been in was the editor, a mass of cables so black that they looked not like objects but like shafts of pure darkness.

"That's the editor, Mark," the professor said. "It came from another world. It's the most advanced piece of technology on Earth. It's where we move you to when we need to make adjustments." She gave him a conspiratorial smile. "But you're the smart one. We just kind of hunt and peck." She put a hand on Mark's shoulder.

"We—did we lose San Francisco?" he asked.

"If any part of them is still alive, they are deep underground and they're trapped. We're still cleaning out surface nests here and there, but it's basically just mopping up. They have a major weakness, needing to be in a microwave field to be fully functional. A last gift from

Turner. He was counting on that as a fail-safe. Even if they escaped, they couldn't leave the field without losing their network and going blind."

"Am I like that?"

"Not at all. You're free and independent. How are you feeling now?"

"Just fine." But he was not fine and these damn straps were not fine, either. He folded his thumbs across his palms, then made a tight cone of his fingers. His hands slid out easily, and he leaped from the table.

Theo and Frank jumped back, but Doc Emma stood her ground and said, "My husband told me this would happen. Don't hit us, Mark, we're friendlies."

"Get away from it!"

He did not like being with these people, and the editor over there on the other side of the room was threatening as hell, a place where he could be killed without dying.

"I know it scares you," Doc Emma said. "It scares us, too, it's an incredibly awesome machine. But, Mark, look at it this way. If it didn't exist, you would be dead."

"Maybe I have a right to be dead!"

"What about Gina, then?"

How it hurt to hear that name. He had lost his only real companion and the only person he could ever love.

"Why in hell didn't you send me more soldiers? Bastards, you put us out there with no support!"

"You got some Delta Force in there at the end."

"They all died, am I right?"

She nodded.

A part of his heart enclosed them, bringing their memory to rest with the memories of his other KIAs. He saw Gina there, smiling in the peaceful field that lay deep in his heart, his own very private soldier's field.

He wanted to be alone. He needed personal space to absorb his loss.

"I want to go home."

Doc Emma gave him a sidelong look. "Do you know where that would be?"

"What happens, do I get put in a box until I'm needed? Stored, is that it?"

"Your old place, Mark, behind our house. You remember your backhouse, don't you? Has that come into focus yet?"

"What backhouse? Where are we, anyway?"

"This is Stanford University, Mark. This is where you were brought after you were born. You were programmed here. This is Palo Alto. Don't you remember Palo Alto? Remember your bike, the red rocket? Your skateboard? You were twelve when you were moved to San Francisco. You're home, Son."

Mark struggled to control his anger at the sense of having had his memories erased and manipulated, and he let himself feel the emotions that were trying to break through, the sense of return to his old home, and the joys of his boyhood. If he displayed the least sign of instability, they could do anything they wanted to him, including, he felt certain, turn him off forever.

He was really beginning to understand the struggle of the generation threes. They were so powerful, but at the same time so vulnerable. A machine that is more intelligent than its masters is going to have a great deal of trouble remaining sane, and in that it had failed.

Your creator can be your greatest enemy, but if he will just let you live your independence, he can be your best friend.

He crossed the room, put his hand on the door. It was locked.

"What's the code?"

"It's a quantum code keyed to our DNA. This place is very, very classified, as you may imagine."

"The public knows all about me."

"The public knows as little as possible about you."

He shook the door. "I really need to get out of here."

"No problem." Doc Emma touched a panel and the door swung open onto a corridor that was surprisingly familiar, with its gleaming tile floor and arched ceiling.

He went into the hall. He was looking for General Walker because Mark knew he had the authority to make him a promise that the others in the command must keep, including Doc Emma. If Mark was not to go insane, if he was not to follow the way of the generation threes, he had to have an absolute promise that he would never be taken out of his body and put in that damn editor again, not ever, not without his consent, and according to rules that he would set, and they would not break.

They had to face that they had made a machine that was more than a machine. He had rights, and they needed to recognize this.

As he walked down the corridor, everything was familiar, and familiarity triggered memory. The tiles, the faint scent of floor wax, the row of offices he was passing—he had been here hundreds of times.

Another wave of anger overcame him, and he strode right through the great doors at the front of the facility, leaving a shower of pulverized glass behind him.

He was going to find out what had happened to Gina, and if they would not tell him, they could expect trouble of a whole new kind.

Voices burst out behind him, desperate voices calling him. Glancing over his shoulder, he saw Doc Emma and her assistants hurrying this way. They had uniforms with them, who carried a rocket-powered net. They had huge black Tasers, and how dare they? Wouldn't make a bit of difference, anyway. He could eat a Taser jolt for goddamn lunch.

He crouched, then sprung his legs straight and soared upward with perfect ease. He moved swiftly into the air, sailing through and scattering a flock of starlings and rising into a long road of clouds.

He'd gone high! Damn!

The sun was warm on his back, and his jump in this fresh new version of himself was utterly effortless. He was one with air and clouds, soaring like an eagle or an angel.

Far below on the campus, the support group who had devoted their lives to this miraculous and extraordinary creation, their peerless soldier, their beloved child, watched, only raising a cheer after they were sure he was well and truly gone on the new mission they had just finished programming into him.

He could jump now for a mile, maybe more. Almost, he could fly.

"It was a brilliant job of programming, kids, and he is totally unconscious of it. For the first time, a machine has not only been given consciousness, it has an underlying unconscious directing its actions, just like we do. Our machine has free will."

"And it can fly!"

"Well, not quite."

They were silent, then, watching where he had disappeared into the sky, where the starlings flocked once more, absorbed once again in their ancient, intricate dance.

Hand came into hand, as mind touched mystery. Man had, at last, transcended his own limits. For all these long eons, no matter how brilliant, no matter how skilled, what man had created had always, in the end, been nothing but what Mark himself had been—just another machine.

But that age had passed, and on this day another age

had begun. The legacy of his mission was that he had become capable of entirely spontaneous decision making. Out of the crucible of that fire, and without even knowing it, he had found his own heart and therefore his own will. Man had created a machine that, in becoming self-aware, had gone beyond the limits of all machines. He was not as brilliant as the third generation, but he was, also, not a slave to his code. Like all men, he was a gardener cultivating the brambles and flowers of independent being.

Frank said, "He'll find her."

"That I know," Professor Walker responded.

"So what happens then?"

"That, I do not."

CHAPTER TWENTY-SEVEN

THE SPIRIT ON THE WATERS

MARK WAS HUNTING, AT ONCE through the shady streets of the town below him, and through memory. He'd jumped and jumped again, glorying in the power of it. He was going home, and each time he leaped up, he saw more of the land, and more familiar hills and streets.

His backhouse. From there, he would set out on the quest that had formed in his mind, to find Gina . . . or perhaps to find a way to create her.

He'd fallen more in love with her than they knew. Of course, they didn't understand machine love, they couldn't. For them, love flickered and faded, flared and died, abided or did not. For him, it was as absolute and unchanging as the machine memory that contained his soul.

On the ground below, an old man watched a dot appear in the sky, watched it grow, then heard the wind whistling around the body of the monster.

"He's coming," he said into his phone.

Emma answered her husband, "I'm on Alpine."

"He's up on Windy Hill. Reconnoitering."

"Okay, great, I'm here, I'm coming in."

They went together to the great window that opened onto their wild and careful garden. She looked out on the summer flowers bobbing in the wind, and Albert the Cat dozing on the flagstones. The curtain on the window of the little backhouse parted slightly, then fell closed.

"Frank called to say he's more unstable than you're willing to believe."

"He's no more unstable than any normal human being under pressure."

"Except he could tear a car apart with his bare hands, so let's be careful."

"Frank has no idea, not anymore. None of us know his inner life now."

"Does he remember us?" General Walker asked. "Does he remember me?"

Mark had not known if he would recognize the Walkers' house, but when he saw its red tile roofs and its walled flower garden set in the broad green lawn, he was at once stabbed by the poignant arrow of remembrance.

He took a long, curving stride out over Windy Hill, looking down at the property, instinctively measuring the angles of attack and the lines of defense.

In the street below, cars were stopping and people were jumping out and waving to him.

As he circled back, now just grazing the roof, he could see them out there with video cameras and smartphones, clicking away.

How do you be a celebrity? How do you do that? He needed privacy. He didn't want this. Anyway, San Francisco had been severely damaged and thousands of people had died there. So who was the hero in that battle, exactly?

As the spreading trees rushed up at him, he broke his speed by arching backward until his face was touched by the sun. Then leaves whispered around him, then he was in among limbs. To control the fall, he grabbed one and swung, then dropped the last fifty feet to the ground. A cat ran away.

For the split of an instant, he crouched, absolutely still. Around him, he observed *Abelia grandiflora, Nemesia caerulea,* and numerous other species. Toward the back of the garden he saw the roses still flourishing, the Chinas and teas that he had enjoyed.

He moved down the path to the old back gate, and there it was, his own little backhouse, the wood gray and weathered, and beyond it the *Alcea setosa* and the *Wisteria sinensis* climbing the walls, and the roses along the path to the big house with its wide French doors and big windows, its warm Spanish grace.

Oh, what memories it brought back, this garden. This was a soldier's home, orderly, carefully tended, and peaceful. He had run here as a boy. He had lain in the grass imagining that he could feel the earth turning beneath the blue of the afternoon sky, and the stars at night.

Wary, though, he looked carefully toward the big house, watching its windows. Standing well back from one of them was a man. In his hand he carried a silver object. As soon as he saw it, Mark remembered it from his childhood. He wished he did not remember it at all.

Such a feeling passed into his heart that he was almost unable to contain it. But he did contain it and looked solemnly back at the man and raised a careful hand, palm up.

The silver object was slipped into the man's pocket.

Mark went up to the window. "Hey, Sarge."

"Hey, Mark."

"How you been?"

"Cookin'. I'm a general now."

"Yes, sir!" Mark nodded toward the pocket. "Does it still work?"

General Walker laughed, but he did not say no.

The discovery, at the age of ten, that other kids could not be controlled by remotes and had no idea that such a thing could even be possible had been among the most tormenting experiences of his life—another memory that had carefully been removed before his transfer to San Francisco.

Sarge and Emma had put him to sleep with it, woken him up with it, cycled his mind through its memories with it, listening as his voice spewed out the details of his days.

In his innocence, he had liked his remote. He'd enjoyed listening to his own voice speaking his memories and looked forward to seeing it pointed at him and knowing that sleep would come after.

"It's lucky Turner didn't have it," he said to the figure in the window.

"I had it decalibrated. The schematics are in my safe. All he had was the disk."

"That was almost enough."

"But it wasn't."

Mark went to the open doorway. "I want it. And the schematics. All trace of it."

The old man came to him. "I kinda thought you would." He pulled it out of his pocket.

Mark took it in his hand. Then he crushed it, watching the plastic splinter, watching the electronics spill out. As he did so, it sparked and he felt twitches.

"I prayed for you, Mark."

"Thank you."

The general would never know how dangerous it had been out there. There were things soldiers did not say, and one of them was just what their battlefields had been like. Battle is more private than sex because witnessing a man's torment is more intimate than witnessing his joy.

Then Mark turned to his own place, where he had played on the floor, where he and Gina had made the pledges of childhood, and where he had chastely kissed her on her cheeks of sweet cloud.

"You erased my childhood memories."

"For your peace of mind," Doc Emma said.

"For your peace of mind, you mean. You need to face that."

"He's absolutely right," General Walker said.

"In any case, we've restored them. All you have to do is access them. Everything is there."

Here, he had felt loneliness for the first time. Here, he and Gina had planned that, no matter what happened to them, they would be lovers forever. So when they'd met in Washington, it had been the culmination of a years-long love affair that neither of them had at the time remembered.

"It's just as you left it," Sarge said.

Mark stood with his hand on the door. Were his books still there? His models that he had made?

"You can go inside, Mark. There's nothing to fear."

But he was afraid. He did not want to see his old place—their place. "Mark, go in," the general said.

"Is that an order?"

The old man chuckled. "These days they tell me I'm a general, so I think I can give a colonel an order. But you'll always be my boy. So please indulge your old dad."

Mark had never thought of it before, but now it struck him with great force. "You really are my father."

The old man nodded. "In part. And Dr. Turner, him, too."

And an egg, Mark thought, from somebody who had left behind not even her name. Slowly, standing there alone with himself, he felt his heart change. His inner demons slid away and with them the deep loathing of who and what he was. In their place came something that abides in the souls of ordinary people, a regard for self and others that recognizes the vulnerability of all, and the limitless importance of each to himself. This is our compassion, the root of human being.

Tears came, and this time his tear ducts opened, he let them flow.

In this first moment of a new life and a new world for him, he sucked the air of freedom. How sweet were the flowers, the scents of life. And the colors, suddenly brighter, the roses flaring red and pink and white, and the sky, the infinite blue of Gina's eyes.

His inner monster was sleeping deep now, the murder lust he had felt in the Glade put to rest. The man had come forth, and with him all the needs and fears that came with being human. He thought again: Gina.

He could not bear to ask what had happened to her. He could not bear to be told that they did not know, or that they were certain. Without her, he understood that he would be entirely alone. There was nobody else like him, but more than that, his secret was revealed. Anybody who met him would know what he was. No woman would open her heart to a machine.

The sort of public life that the future implied was the most total form of isolation that he could imagine. But Gina would have meant warm arms around him and sweet words in the night, a refuge. He would have been her refuge, also, and he would have been good for her, he was sure of it, strong for her and sensitive to her hungers and her furies.

He was like the last of a species, the last mountain gorilla or the last salmon leaping alone.

Maybe, even, he would need to engage in battle again, and do it alone, and perhaps die alone. Twice today, once

at the lab and again just now, his body had recorded
tremors that were too regular to be natural. Were they
caused by distant drilling in the foundations of San Francisco, where there was a lot of construction, or was it
something deeper and more dangerous, the tattered fragments of the hybrid community down there in the deep
of the earth, coming back to life?

At least the city had survived in some form. The
bomb had been too deep to irradiate it, just shake it to
pieces. At least there was that.

He wanted the shadows of his old room. He wanted
to feel the privacy of being home more than he feared
to suffer the pain of seeing his and Gina's little place
again. He pushed open the door and went in.

For a moment, he did not quite comprehend what
flooded his senses, the scents, the subtle sounds. Then
there was movement in the shadows, and he was instantly braced, ready for action.

She stepped into the light that shone in from the door.

She said, "You've been gone a long time."

A rush of energy surged through him. Was it happiness? Was it fear? He did not know this emotion, but he
did know Gina, who looked up at him with an expression of calm concern, but not surprise.

"A long time?"

"Two years, Mark. I helped with your new body,
while it was growing. I washed it down every day. That
was my job at the lab."

To him, she was a joy and an astonishment, but to
her he was absolutely familiar.

"Two *years*?"

She nodded. "Come on in, I'm just warming some
soup. It's good."

He went into their old room, into the pungent odor

of soup and the softer odor of her body, and despite everything, he was enchanted.

She seemed to know it and laughed a little, glancing back at him seductively.

"Do you remember when we were kids? They said you were getting that back, too."

He nodded.

"Didn't we have fun?"

"Where was I?"

"You know. Waiting." She murmured, "In the editor." She ladled rich vegetable soup into a cup. "Here."

"I was turned off! For two years, I was *turned off*!"

"You had no body! So of course you were turned off. You couldn't just sit there in the editor all that time, what would you do? You'd go crazy."

"I thought I'd been—that it had been . . . just a few minutes."

"You came out of the woods near Sausalito in real bad shape. The body wasn't salvageable. It had to be destroyed."

She spoke matter-of-factly, but he absorbed the information like a blow. He'd been in memory banks, empty of all consciousness, for the whole time it had taken them to grow him a new body.

"But . . . am I dead or alive?"

She smiled. "It's good soup." She sipped from her own cup.

And what of her? Nobody had actually told him what had happened to her. But he knew. Suddenly he knew quite well. Gina had died in the deep shaft. He'd been blown out with the remains of the drone, but she'd been completely vaporized.

So who was this woman, or what was she? What of her life did she really remember? She looked like Gina, but she could have no memory of the experience of battle. Nobody could even have reconstructed what had happened to them down that hole.

"Eat your soup, you've been on life support, you're too thin."

"Gina, I'm just—I'm confused. I don't know how to feel."

She drew her fingers along his cheek. "How do you want to feel?"

He just so loved her, and even though he knew that this feeling had been programmed into him, he could not resist it.

"How do I want to feel?" He opened his arms to her.

She came in. She raised her face to him in a way that was deeply familiar, and for an instant the sense of the machine was completely gone, and he thought that this was surely how human beings—real ones—feel, and he touched his lips to hers and fulfilled the dream he'd had so long, of kissing her again.

The kiss felt like home but it was not home. Even in this place where he had spent his youth and discovered life, he was profoundly homeless. He was like a man in the air somewhere, with nothing above him and nothing below him, the way it felt at the top of a jump, just before the fall.

She was warm. She kissed him with intensity and concentration, then she broke away.

"I've been waiting for that." Again, she offered the soup to him. "You need it, husband." She gave him a smile. "Remember right before we jumped? We married ourselves."

But how could she know?

And then he understood how they must have reconstructed her memories of battle. They had built them out of his own and so re-created the bond that had been between them.

They were structures, the two of them, the products not of nature but of human thought and human creativity, and that he found hard to bear. But he also wanted to be, he wanted to live.

She took his hand. "You understand, don't you?"

"I understand."

"Doc Emma said you would. She said you would want to hear this." Gina went in her thin, white dress across to the small desk where he had read *Heart of Darkness* and *The Jungle Book* and where his Bible lay. She opened it. "'And the Lord God caused a deep sleep to fall upon Adam, and he slept: and he took one of his ribs, and closed up the flesh instead thereof; and the rib, which God had taken from man, made he a woman, and brought her unto the man. Adam said, This is now bone of my bones, and flesh of my flesh: she shall be called Woman, because she was taken out of Man.'"

He added from memory, "'Therefore shall a man leave his father and his mother, and shall cleave unto his wife: and they shall be one flesh.'"

He watched her as she moved, coming to him. Was she not more subtly sensual than the old Gina had been, perhaps also a little more physically . . . available? No soldier hardness, that was it. The soldier was gone.

"Do you remember the rest of it, the Glade, all that?" She went to the window. "I've always loved this view."

"Do you remember?"

"Don't, Mark."

"I have to know!"

She came back to him. "Let's enjoy what we have. Don't question it like that. Let it be." She took his face in her hands. "I want you, Mark."

He looked upon her in silence, drinking in her beauty with his eyes, trying to see her not as somebody new, but as the Gina who was part of his forever.

"I missed you so badly." She gestured. "I've got everything back like we left it when we were kids."

"I missed you, too."

She leaned against him, twining her arms around him. "Please, just let's enjoy each other now."

He looked down at her, feeling her warmth, absorbing her flowing beauty. He felt himself, Mark Bryan, a conscious, living being. Yet he had been a great mass of digital information in storage for a months and months while in his perception not even a second had passed.

"How long did it take for you?"

"For me?"

He stroked her face, the smoothness, the down soft upon her cheeks. "To make your new body?"

"I came back a while ago."

"You said you tended me."

"Not from the beginning. I remember when they started your nervous system, though. I had my hand on your chest, Mark. I felt your heart start."

In that moment, he made a decision. He decided that the past must belong to the past. They were here now, and he would never again ask how this had come to be, not ever.

He could feel her trembling as he was, sense the inner fire that threatened to erupt into their closeness.

"Glad you're home," she said quietly. "Good."

He felt the youth of her, the surging energy, and tasted of her presence in his soldier's way, hungry, eager, aware that time was passing and battles must lie ahead, for peace never lasts.

His blood sang in the sea of her heat and sweat, as

she wrapped her legs around him and let him bear her weight.

"They're watching," he said.

"Them? Who cares? They know us better than we do."

He released her. Together, they went to the door. The Walkers stood in their window, their hands tightly clasped. Mark and Gina joined hands, also.

"They might know our pasts," Mark said. "But everything we do from now on is our own."

"Is that freedom, Mark?"

"The world unfolds, things happen, we go on."

If this union worked, humankind would have accomplished the goal beyond goals and created a more powerful and evolved version of itself that could breed children and grow and protect its ancient parents from all the furies of this dark universe, and the furies of man's own making, darker still.

Mark looked back at the big house, and the two old shadows in the window. But Gina drew him away and closed the curtains. In her face, he saw something uneasy.

"You can," she said. "There's nothing to stop you. We're not threes, remember."

He took her to the narrow bed and quickly discovered how wonderfully they fit together, body to body.

Only once before in all the long life of the earth had this happened. It had been in a dry gorge nearly a million years ago, in a dusty and dangerous corner of Africa.

In that long-ago time, two creatures had met and fell to touching all in wonder and discovered themselves and one another and become the first true human couple, man and wife, and had gone together from then on, until a hungry leopard's guile had forever parted the wife from her husband and their children. Grief had followed love for the first time, and a family, bonded together, had—also for the first time—found the love that fills death and triumphs over death and found, in that love, the strength to continue on the journey.

The two creatures who had come together then were in their time just as new as Mark and Gina were now. The spirit had moved upon them and made all the immense and brilliant race that has become humankind.

So it was when Mark and Gina came together, full of lust and love, glorying in their new freedom, stepping past the ambiguity of programmed being and into the same doubts and wonders that defined their creators, but with more strength and more intelligence, and with hope built into every atom of their beings.

The spirit felt this—God, the earth, none of us really know—but it came to this new kind of creature and saw that what had been made here was good, and so the spirit moved upon them, also, and deep within Gina the ancient magic happened that is beyond all programming and beyond knowing, as the first flickering of a child—and a new species—was born.

The waters of life, in their gentle way and desperate way, flowed on.

TOR

Award-winning authors
Compelling stories

Please join us at the website
below for more information
about this author and other great
Tor selections, and to sign up for
our monthly newsletter!